Prais

Upon the Corner of the Moon

"Valerie Nieman's *Upon the Corner of the Moon: A Tale of the Macbeths* accomplishes the rare feat of telling a fascinating story within a scholarly reconstruction of early Scotland. Her imagining of the human element behind the historical records creates a compelling insight into individuals who are at the same time familiar and yet compellingly enigmatic. Macbeth, Gruach, and Duncan are presented with their own rivalries, ambitions, and loves. These historical figures are brought to life in Nieman's remarkable narrative where the reader will be both entertained and educated."

—Benjamin Hudson, author of *Macbeth Before Shakespeare*

"Last we saw of Lady MacBeth, she'd lost her mind and couldn't clean her bloody hands or her guilty conscience. In *Upon the Corner of the Moon*, award-winning writer Val Nieman gives us the more authentic story that Shakespeare had borrowed. In her widely researched and deeply imagined historical saga, Nieman takes us to the Kingdom of Alba as Scotland was known in the 11th century, long before tartans and bagpipes. We meet the noble Gruach who is sent north for her own protection as a new king takes the throne, as well as the boy who could grow up to be MacBeth. Nieman goes beyond Shakespeare's witches, depicting the clash of faiths in the Dark Ages. Gruach finds strength following an ancient Goddess faith that sees the healing power of women, while MacBeth is raised to the patriarchy by Christian monks. A spell-binding saga that builds in suspense toward the couple's union and toward their end in the famous play, *Upon the Corner of the Moon* will win over fans of Hilary Mantel's historical fiction."

—Dale Neal, author of *Kings of Coweetsee* and *The Woman with the Stone Knife*

"Valerie Nieman pulls back the curtain to reveal the brawling, feasting, warring world of the historical Macbeth, Malcolm, and Duncan as well as the gentler world of the trained healer who will become Macbeth's lady. Nieman's skill in poetic description soaks the senses and opens up a world I never knew, one inhabited by burial mounds and carved stones and roaring weather and spirit-gods and constant battle that leaves blood soaking the ground—this is a landscape of ancient curses, portent, and ambition. Here are laid bare the cruel games of lineage and the honor of kings, which the healing incantations of women, holy men, and poets bend toward the possibility of honor and unity among kingdoms. My eyes are opened. I can't wait for the sequel."

—Marjorie Hudson, author of *Indigo Field*

"Steeped in the myth, mystery, politics, and culture of Celtic Scotland, *Upon the Corner of the Moon* presents the world of the young Lady Macbeth and Macbeth with authenticity, a deft hand, and a poet's voice. Valerie Nieman's book is a powerful take on two fascinating and enigmatic historical figures."

—Susan Fraser King, author of *Lady Macbeth: A Novel* and *Queen Hereafter: A Novel of Margaret of Scotland*

"Nieman's grand and inventive version of the Macbeths takes an epic approach, focusing on a portion of their story before the events made famous by Shakespeare. The result is a sweeping romance rooted in the stark landscape and starker living conditions of the period, replete with historical insight and imaginative richness."

—A.J. Hartley, UNC-Charlotte Shakespeare scholar, best-selling novelist (*Macbeth: A Novel*)

"This is an entertaining, gripping, imaginative novel which brings to life successfully the brutal power struggles and tensions between old and new in the time of Macbeth. I enjoyed this book."

—Nicholas Evans, author of *The King in the North* and *Picts*

"Eleventh-century Britain comes alive in this virtuoso evocation of the time of Macbeth. Valerie Nieman adeptly achieves a narrative style that matches the time, including cadences that echo ancient oral traditions. She renders the complex melding of the myths and religions of the peoples who populated the region, and her imaginative recreation of the political strife and intrigue of the time is captivating. The story lines for Macbeth and his eventual wife, Gruach, are developed in separate arcs that come together at the end with the momentum of destiny."

—Carolyn Korsmeyer, author of *Little Follies: A Mystery at the Millennium*

"*Upon the Corner of the Moon* is a historical retelling of Macbeth that is destined to become a classic. Merging historical fact with legend, Nieman weaves a powerful tale of the man and woman who became two of the most murderous characters in Shakespeare. Lyrical and brutal, *Upon the Corner of the Moon* shows us the people who shaped the fledging nation of Scotland and how legends are formed."

—T. Frohock, author of the *Los Nefilim* series

UPON THE CORNER OF THE MOON

A Tale of the Macbeths

Book One of Alba

Valerie Nieman

Regal House Publishing

Published by
Regal House Publishing, LLC
Raleigh, NC 27605
All rights reserved

ISBN -13 (paperback): 9781646035359
ISBN -13 (epub): 9781646035366
Library of Congress Control Number: 2024935103

Cover images and design by © C. B. Royal

Regal House Publishing, LLC
https://regalhousepublishing.com

The following is a work of fiction created by the author. All names, individuals, characters, places, items, brands, events, etc. were either the product of the author or were used fictitiously. Any name, place, event, person, brand, or item, current or past, is entirely coincidental.

Printed in the United States of America

To librarians, archivists, and historians

A Map of
ALBA

ATLANTIC OCEAN

ORKNEY

CAITHNESS

SUTHER LAND

NORTH SEA

Golspie
Tarbat Ness
Rosemarkie
Am Broch
Forres · Birnie
Deer
MORAY
Lochindorb
Mouth of Ness

The Mounth
Dunottar
Brechin
ATHOLL
Dunkeld
Scoine
Kilrymont

Iona
Dunollie
DÁL RIATA
Partick
Dun Edin
LOTHIAN
Bamburgh
STRATHCLYDE
Melrose

NORTH CHANNEL

GALL-GAIDEL

Major Characters

Gruach, daughter of Boidh and Lonceta

Macbeth mac Findlaích, son of the mormaer of Moray and Doada, a daughter of Malcolm II

Malcolm II, High King of Alba

Nechtan mac Boidh, brother to Gruach

Boidh, tanist or named heir to the throne of Alba

*Alpia and Talorc, foster parents to Gruach and Nechtan, parents of Fode, Ciniod, and Derelei

Findlaích, mormaer of Moray, an independent northern kingdom

Crinán the Thane, lay abbot of Dunkeld and Lord of Atholl

Duncan, son of Crinán and Bethoc, a daughter of Malcolm II

Gillecomgan, mormaer of Moray

*Oswald, Anglish monk, tutor for Duncan and Macbeth

*Lapwing, a wandering poet-seer

Thorfinn, son of Jarl Sigurd of Orkney and Olith, a daughter of Malcolm II

*Halla, a Norse widow, and her daughters Ingigerd and Estrid

Cnut, ruler of the North Sea Empire

*Conamail, warrior and supporter of Findlaích

*Fyfa, a woman of Moray

(Those with asterisks are not historical figures.)

PROLOG

Before I was Queen of all Alba, wife to High King Macbeth, I was wife to a ruler of Moray not once but twice.

Before that, I was a student at the feet of the White Lady, learning to be a healer of the world.

Before that, I was the heedless fosterling who looked into flames for her future.

These many years I have listened for the voice of the Goddess, and at times Mary and her son and the Christian saints, and learned that promises and predictions shape the world in terrible ways.

1

GRUACH

I was standing under the porch of the guesthouse, hands inside my sleeves for warmth. I wanted my new red mantle, not this shaggy well-used thing that had been wrapped around me. My nose prickled at the strong odor of wet wool.

Servants were hurrying to load packhorses. Hooves drummed across the stone paths as the animals shied under the weight. And there was Nechtan among the men, strutting as though this sudden move had come at his whim. Why hadn't my brother been set aside, like me? I rocked from one foot to the other, couldn't decide if I wanted to join him. Finally, I crawled onto a bench, curled into a ball with my feet tucked under. But I watched. And wondered.

The bell had not yet been struck for the monks to be about their prayers, but two juniores had been roused to help. Candles and torches shone yellow in the abbot's hall and the monks' kitchen where Blathine had gone to get us food. The guesthouse door opened and my mother came out. I started to get down but then I saw who followed her—Ferchar, leader of a great people and my father's closest man. Mother turned to rest her hand on his broad wrist.

"All is ready," he said, low, but his voice carried. "Messengers have ridden on to Golspie and will arrive well before."

"Barring mischance."

"I sent three."

Light flared and faded around them as wind through the open door tossed the flames. *Why was Ferchar here?*

"So Malcolm's to be made king today at the Hill of Belief," my mother said.

"A hasty gathering, but I saw too many of the great upon departing Scoine to think that many were caught unawares by Kenneth's felling at the Plain of the Bards."

"And the king's bones are being carried to Iona?"

"Malcolm has no quarrel with him now."

"He had none legitimate before."

"Legitimacy was made in one stroke, Lonceta," he said gently, "and we must conform ourselves to the deed. As Boidh does."

"My dear honest Boidh, his brother's pledge-ring on his finger and his blade at his throat."

My father was in danger! That much I could tell, and it made me gasp. Ferchar placed his body between my mother and the noise in the dark.

"Child," he said, upon seeing me, "have you been there long?"

My mother gathered me up in her arms, wiped the tears and rain-damp from my face. "Ah, Daimhin"—Little Deer, the gentle name she called me by, rather than that ugly church-name Gruach. Mother said it low, over and over, but I was not going to be soothed. *What is happening to my father?*

"The king is dead?" I asked at last, curiosity winning out.

I saw my mother look to Ferchar, as though waiting for him to speak. "King Kenneth III is gone," she said finally.

"Who is being king then?"

"Malcolm." After a moment, she continued. "Your uncle. You remember that he gave you the hound pup at Easter-time."

"It died. Did the king get stepped on by a horse, like Runner?"

My father's man laughed, short and harsh.

"Malcolm is quite old," I said, sure of that much.

"You must call him high king, now, Ard Ri Alban," my mother said.

Blathine came hurrying from the kitchen, carrying food. I wriggled down and sat at the foot of the great stone cross. Mother seemed absorbed with Nechtan, watching as he acted so big, making a show of examining a bridle leather. Before I could finish the milk and the gritty barley bread, I was left alone again.

Juniores in drab tunics held up torches that smoked and spit in the rain. A mare urinated and workers shifted their paths around the steaming puddle. Ferchar was having something moved among the bags and bundles on one horse. His chin jutted out. Like my father, he could give orders and end confusion.

"'Tis well we weren't at Monifieth," said one man.

"Be loading boats, then."

"These horses are no less witless, all over the place," a third growled.

"They know, they know," said a man-at-arms whose damp hair, blown aside, revealed a purple birthmark.

"Like Daniel to the lions' den—Boidh goes to a king's promise or a ready grave."

"And his babes too early to fostering."

"Into Moray?" The man who disliked boats seemed doubtful.

"That would be bad to worse, with the Norse and Danes rampaging. And not south—they've scarce a bite of bread for themselves in Angle-land, much less for newcomers. North is my thought."

North. I felt the wind that pushed me toward the cold sea and strange people. I did not answer Blathine's anxious call.

"Here she is," said the birthmarked man.

Ferchar himself came to collect me. "Time to be leaving, little one."

"I'm cold. Why are we going in the night?"

The company was all mounted, except for Ferchar. Even Nechtan rode a led pony, stumpy-legged and with one white eye. I did not want to ride with the birthmarked man. I planted my feet and crossed my arms. Mother came and knelt, enfolding me in her mantle, a place of comfort and imbued with a familiar green smell.

"Warm yourself for a moment, and be still. You are going to be fostered, just as other children are."

"But I am only five winters, and some more. I am not old enough."

"But you will be with your brother, not by yourself. And you are grown very big."

We walked to the horses. One of the novices took me by the hand and I jerked away and slapped him. Just as quickly, my mother slapped my own wrist and tears came. "We are going to the Lochlannaig," I sobbed, feeling the north take hold of me with cruel hands. "We'll be taken as slaves!" I felt all eyes on me and did not care, because I was being sent into the dark and the cold and the wild lands.

My mother held me by the shoulders. "These Norse are farmers and fishers, like our own people, and not wild beasts."

I was picked up abruptly, and the juniore I'd slapped breathed unexpectedly hot breath in my ear. "You'll be kept well enough within Orkney's reach, child." Then I was set down firmly before Ferchar, and felt something sharply cold against my side where the mantle had ridden up. I think it was the pommel of his sword, but I didn't try to find out.

"Do not make me ashamed of you," Mother said sternly, but her dark eyes shone. She took my hand, then let it slip free. I blinked back tears and sat straight, aware of my importance as I was riding with a clan leader. I wiped my nose on the back of my hand and looked down proudly on my brother.

The abbot came, a monk holding up a lantern to light his way. They seemed to float in their tunics and dark cowls. A reflection flashed from the abbot's silver cross and Nechtan's mount rolled its mismatched eyes. The company was silent, even the horses hanging their heads as the blessing was made. "God hold you in his hands, God be with you," and all murmured their response.

We trotted into the seeping light of morning. Past the new round tower still being built, rising to disappear in fog and rain, because it was now truly rain, heavy and driving against our faces. Past the windowed house where monks labored over manuscripts, past wood-and-wattle cells, everything growing less distinct, it seemed, as dawn emerged through low clouds. A bird called, twice.

"When are we coming home?" I asked Nechtan.

He looked up, his round ruddy face solemn as those of the armed men around us. "When I become a man, at seventeen winters."

I tried to think what that meant for me.

We crossed the plank bridge over a ditch, the horses' hooves thudding softly, and then we went through the gap in a bank of earth.

"That's an end of holy ground," one of the men muttered.

Outside the inner vallum, we passed the low houses of Brechin's people, the grain fields, and the barns wide and dark. Then another bank, and a third, and there was nothing but close weather and open grazings and the movement of cattle and sheep. I hid my face in a fold of Ferchar's braught. I didn't care, now, that the wool scratching my cheek smelled of smoke and old blood. If my parents had abandoned me, then Ferchar would protect me from the wild Lochlannaig.

GOLSPIE, SUTHERLAND, 1007

The door flew back with a bang, as though the ceaselessly sucking northern wind had finally pulled it from its latches. Startled, I pulled the fur to my chin, but my foster-mother Alpia merely glanced up from her sewing and called, "Come in, then, come!"

Nechtan dropped something heavy inside the entry. Fode came after, struggling to shut the outer door.

"Did you not feel the gentleness of this spring breeze?" Nechtan asked his foster-brother with assumed formality. His cheeks were burnished and wet, his dark brown hair wild around his head.

"It was very soft," Fode said, struggling against the smile that broke across his face.

"Spring it may be, by sun's reckoning, but that wind has ice to it," Alpia observed, tilting her head to bite off thread close to the fabric she was working on. She wound the thread carefully on its needle and put it in its case, and then both in her sewing box. "So have you been gathering spring flowers?"

The boys looked at each other. Stifling laughs, they went out and came back, each dragging a black auk bigger than a goose.

"We went looking for eggs," Fode began.

"...even though it's early, but we found gearbhul on the shore by the little bay," Nechtan said, using the Norse word for the great sea-birds.

"And they were hardly afraid at all..."

"So we got very close and killed these with stones."

"Before the others went into the sea," Fode concluded.

"They stink," I said.

Nechtan twisted a familiar face at me, then he and Fode went to stand close by the hearth. Their clothes steamed.

Alpia folded the cloth and set it aside. She deliberated for a moment, her lips pressed together. "If the boys have brought us meat, then we must prepare it," she said, emphasizing *we*.

I pretended not to hear, pulling close the coverlet that I clung to night and day. My mother had packed it and sent it with me. It had been pieced from the furs of small, soft animals.

Alpia merely lifted it away and stood waiting. Her white hair, pulled back and braided under her scarf, make her look old, but I knew how enduring she was. She stood erect and walked as rapidly as a man. Derelei had told me, with a sort of awe, that her mother's hair had been white "as the Goddess herself" ever since she was a young woman.

"The girl will clean the fowl," I said, curling my body against the chill and reaching for the cover.

"I believe it will not hurt you to have close acquaintance with the making of our food."

I got up and shuffled behind Alpia, who caught up the birds by their webbed feet. They *did* stink, like old fish, and there was a long smear of filth down one's scaly legs. I could hardly believe they would be worth the cooking. The servant girl was making loaves when we went into the cooking area, which shared the double hearth with the main hall. Her mouth made an unhappy O when she saw the birds.

"No work for you, Murie, as I'd not care to find feathers baked in my bread," said Alpia, taking a slender sharp knife and a hatchet from the kist. "Heat water in the cauldron."

We pulled on mantles and went to the sheltered corner between the hall and the byre, to the broad stump of a storm-stranded tree. It was twice as wide across the bottom as the top, and might have been rooted there in the courtyard for the way it had sunk into the ground. Alpia deftly skinned the birds, lopped off the heads and black feet and short tails. With their long bodies and muscular necks, flesh shining with membrane, the auks looked like land creatures rather than birds. She began to draw the innards.

I tried not to pay too close attention, but my foster-mother was having none of that.

"See here," she said, as she laid the innards on one of the skins and knelt to examine them. "The lungs and the heart. And what's it been eating?" She slit the bulging crop and silvery fish slithered out. I looked toward the walls and beyond, the crashing sea, invisible in driving sleet that had hidden the world under a gray bowl.

"This is a female," she said, and I had to look. "See the little clusters? These will be eggs, when the season for young arrives." It was strangely fascinating, all the hidden parts of the creature. I looked closer. The guts of the second bird revealed no such clusters.

"The boys were not such hunters," Alpia observed. "The birds are life-mates, male and female, and will not leave one another even in death."

The household dogs had been lured by the smell of offal. One scarred hound leaped in and carried off the intestines, trailing them after as it bounded for the shelter of the byre.

Alpia picked up the hearts and livers before the dogs could steal them as well. "Take these," she said. I held out my hands. The organs had cooled and seemed already less a part of the animals. They were slippery, though, with blood and flesh-grease. Alpia wiped down the cleaned birds with a cloth, then sectioned them and put the pieces into the kettle along with the hearts. The livers were tender and would be added last.

❧

As we finished, Talorc returned home after a visit to lands that had been farmed by his man Sebbi, recently dead of a lingering cough. He grabbed Alpia around the waist, turned up her face and kissed her long and heartily. "My white-veiled bride."

"And my young warrior with his hair shining in the sun."

They laughed at the well-worn joke. Talorc was shorn like a monk, the hair gone from the front of his head to past the crown. What remained was fine, windblown, the color of sand.

I watched my foster-mother return to her work, choosing spices and roots to season the broth. I sniffed—the fishy odor dissipated as the seasonings heated. I picked up one of the little roots like those that had gone into the pot, twisted it. A pungent scent, not entirely pleasant.

"What is this?"

But Alpia did not hear. She and Talorc were discussing the character of those contending for the right to till Sebbi's ground.

"As he left no children, it is between an uncle and a cousin."

"The one who's just had a son?"

"That one, aye," said Talorc. "He has a strong arm, while the uncle has more than he can manage the tilling of now."

I tugged at the servant's flour-dusted sleeve. "What is this?"

Murie lifted her arm and pulled the sleeve from my fingers. "A root, child."

I frowned. "But what is it called?"

"For that you'd have to ask the Lady," and she nodded toward Alpia, respectfully, even as her thin mouth twisted with the strain of pulling a three-legged iron pot from among the coals. "She brings all such, down from the hills, out from the edge o' the sea."

I dropped the twisted thing back into its bowl.

My foster-parents were laughing over a tale of some drunkard's fall at a slippery ford, this dead Sebbi himself it seemed, their faces red as the man's in their story.

The firelight showed the roughness of their faces and hands, winter-scoured. They lived like plain farmers, their garments simple and this fortified hall not much greater than the longhouses where family and beasts huddled together. *Perhaps my parents did not know*, I thought.

Perhaps they believed that we would be fostered in a proper home and not this bare place.

I stepped out of the path of the sweating girl, thinking I might slip away if Alpia had completed her lesson.

"Men take twice their room, when there's work to be done," Alpia complained, smiling as she did. Talorc shrugged his weather-stained green braught higher on his shoulders, pulled his hood over his head, and went back out. "Gruach?" Alpia looked around. "There you are. Now, child, run and fill this measure with salt."

I walked between Murie and the fire, throwing her a scathing glance in payment for my having to do work the servant should be doing. A bit of fat or water underfoot and I slipped, went down hands and knees on the hearth-stones. I saw the filth of ashes on my tunic and my hands reddened by the ochre on the stones.

"I'm no slave," I protested, tossing my head at Murie. "My father will be king when my old uncle dies, and he'll know how you have used me."

Alpia crossed her arms and smiled, an infuriating smile.

I slapped at the smears of red and gray. "I'm of royal kindred. I shouldn't be here!"

"Your bloody-handed kindred is exactly why you're here," Alpia said. "Remember how you came, stolen away and pursuit riding close."

Like stolen things, yes, we had been carried away in darkness but then abandoned. I felt like a king's daughter in one of the stories, snatched away to bitter slavery in a harsh land. I added to my misery by listening to the batter of wind against the walls, and the moan of the ocean against the sandy shore. I might well be enchanted, like in the tales, under the earth with the Old Ones. But then, of course, there'd be magical light on beautiful pale faces, and wild music that made a year of a day, and incredible things to eat and drink. Here in Sutherland, claimed by the Norse king of Orkney, there was only the long darkness that filled the corners of the hall.

As the auks simmered, the men sat down where the pieces from a game of fidchell lay scattered and set up the board for a new match. Fode, whose sandy hair promised his father's tonsure, frowned in concentration, while my brother leaned forward with eagerness to meet his countering action. Certainly that was why we had been sent here, only for Nechtan's sake, to save him from that knife at the throat. He liked this rough life, this cold place where only barley could grow, and where the scattered people lived more by the raw work of fishing and hunting than by their hairy beasts and thin fields. It was making him tough, muscular, while as for me—ah!

I wished that I was less prone to sickness. In the deeps of the winter, just before the Feast of the Nativity, I had fallen sick with what was thought to be a croup but soon feared to be diphtheria. I remembered feeling tight inside my skin, and very sad. That was, perhaps, because I would miss the celebrations. My throat became swollen so that it hurt to swallow even fine wheat bread unless it was well soaked, but the fatal membrane never appeared. Alpia had nursed me with rubs and brews, but also with the press of her hands on my chest and a low, wandering song that had seemed to fill my lungs with cold, clean air.

I dreamed sometimes that my father Boidh and mother Lonceta, realizing their mistake, had me brought back from the north and sent to a proper fosterage. Perhaps to a noble family in Éireann, or among the British of Strathclyde. I had heard people talk of Northumbria, and Jorvik, and could scarcely imagine all those buildings close together and the clatter of tongues.

Ah, I might as well dream of any other enchantment!

A shiver passed through me, and I moved silently over to sit by the fire. Alpia, who had returned to her sewing, looked up as I silently tucked the fur around my legs.

"Cold there in the dark corner, was it not? Feel yourself lucky that we do not live in my grandmother's time. The weather has changed. It was once much colder than it is now; the spring now is almost as the summer was then."

"How can that be?"

"We have short lives, child." Alpia pulled a stitch tight. "We see the seasons of each year, but the earth has her long seasons that we cannot follow. Our generations are no more than her single heartbeat."

I turned that over in my mind.

My foster-mother shook out the léine she'd just mended, smoothing the patched place with her hand to make sure there were no puckers in the tunic that Nechtan was quickly outgrowing.

"Enough of this," she said. "Come, and we'll divert ourselves."

Alpia went to a kist by the wall, opened it, and brought out a carved ivory box. Inside that was a little sealskin bag. She loosed the draw-strings and poured a stream of white discs into her lap, pieces of bone or maybe walrus ivory, cut thin and smoothed. On each a picture had been incised and darkened. I recognized the symbols from the carved stones that stood all through the land.

Alpia let me turn them over, one by one.

"Had your mother ever spoken of the symbols to you?"

"No," I said. "I've seen the great stones. The Picts made them."

"That's a stranger's name," she said, which made me look up and meet my foster-mother's bright glance. "Our people were here before the Scots crossed the water from Éireann. And even before us were the Builders. These were their symbols, which they brought from a distant land and an even earlier time and passed to us."

She turned one disc over in her fingers. It had a drawing of the strange beast, all curves and a wide smiling mouth.

"This is the sea-beast," Alpia said. "It stands for dolphin and porpoise and whale and seal, all the creatures of warm blood and air that live in the water and are beloved of the Goddess. Your eyes are sea-colored—that's a mark of favor."

I waited, stifling the urge to ask, *Whose favor?*

My foster-mother turned the discs up one by one, and explained each in a low voice, as though it were something between only us. I could hear the boys shout and laugh, could hear Talorc snore where he lay stretched out by the snapping fire.

"This is the mirror and the comb. They are for the Goddess in her aspect of lover; to love another you must look first into yourself."

Another disc, snake and cauldron. "These are her aspects of far-seeing and of healing. And this," she said, tracing a mark like a broken arrow with a point at one end and curving lines at the other, "this is the action of life in the world. The Mother of Life. The plant dies into the earth and springs from it, renewed."

I took a disc that was marked with a crescent, and held it up. "Is this the moon?"

Alpia smiled. She traced the crescent with her forefinger, and then she traced the outside of the disc, smooth but not quite round, like the days before and after the full moon.

"It is the moon. And it is us," she said, touching my forehead, touching her own.

2

MACBETH

Along the Great Glen, 1009

"See there—the way turns up to the royal hall!"

The boy Macbeth, half-dozing as he was carried from one life into another, raised his head at Conamail's ringing shout.

Clouds still hung low. He lifted his shoulders and felt the rain of many days weighting his hood, the shaggy wool of his braught, the wet hem of his léine. Still, it was not cold. Rain and more rain, so that he imagined in the winter it would turn into great drifts of snow.

Now as the sun emerged in the clearing west, the waters of a small loch took fire and the slopes flared green. The path widened into a road toward the place where the king rested, passing through circles of timber-laced fortifications to the crest of the hill and a great hall with clear views through the mountain pass. He stretched gratefully in the saddle, bolstered by the bulk of the soldier, and felt the fading light on his face.

"Best hope that sun lasts or we'll be sleeping out again tonight," said Conamail as he trotted past, but the gruffness of his words was softened by the grin that gave him the epithet Ever-Smiling: it was said his face shone as brightly as the god Oghma's when he entered battle.

They arrived just at dusk, as the porter was closing the inner gate. He pushed it shut behind them and labored to set the bar across the wide slab of oak. Brindled dogs howled and lunged on their chains.

An old man twisted small by some long-ago injury came out and took the horses. Bent though he was, the slave was soon tumbling fragrant fodder into the mangers. Conamail came toward Macbeth in the dim stable, the ornate bridle of the gray stallion he'd ridden swinging from his fingers. Baetán walked with him, slowly, easing the stiffness of an old wound, and Macbeth would have hurried them if he could. The noise of feasting beckoned and his stomach answered. Not until he stood at the doors of the great hall and smelled the strong aroma of fish did Macbeth realize with a groan that this was a fast day.

Malcolm II, the High King of Alba, sat above the chattering throng. Jeweled knots worked into the front of his feasting-garment echoed the designs carved into his high seat. The space at table to his right was empty; at his left hand was his queen in pink with a deep blue headscarf that made Macbeth catch his breath, so suddenly came a memory of his mother. A tall man with a sharp face stood behind the high seat and leaned close to speak with the king. All down the long tables were men of his retinue and those drawn here by the king's presence, under-kings and mormaers, toiseachs who were leaders of clans, honored men of art, physician and lawteller, bishops, a praise-poet with his harp. An abbess and her companions clustered together in their white garments, shining even brighter than the multicolored garb of the noble wives. A well-built young monk in black sat well up the board, and beside him, a scowling boy with hair pale as a Norseman's.

"Who joins us on the heels of the day?" called the king.

"Travelers out of Moray, High King."

"And they are welcome."

Servants hurried about with platters and jugs, while the guests shifted down along the benches to make room for the newcomers.

"We thank you, High King, for the invitation to your table," Conamail said.

"Our feast is brightened by the face of the smiling warrior who holds the Valley of Heroes," Malcolm said heartily. Macbeth trudged behind the men, thinking himself small and forgotten, crunching the brown buttons of tansy where they showed among the rushes. "And especially we welcome Macbeth, our daughter's son, who comes to be made a man with us."

Macbeth lifted his head at this recognition. The king was watching him closely. He halted and made his formal greeting. "My father sends his loyalty to the Ard Ri Alban, as he sends the hope of his house," he said, reciting the memorized words.

The king's eyes were rapacious as a hawk's below the sleek plumage of his graying hair, and his lips were startlingly red. "Loyalty for loyalty is given. Come to me, boy."

Macbeth made his way to the head of the table. It seemed a long way, alone. He passed behind a black-bearded foreigner and smelled exotic spices, behind the physician and held his breath at the reek of purges. A white-breasted hound leaped suddenly from its bed near the king's feet and rolled belly up in his path, almost tripping him. Macbeth stood in the empty place at the king's hand, waiting on his attention. He looked briefly at the blond boy, also summoned forward. The sight and smell of food enticed him (fish or no) and he prayed his stomach would not grumble now.

"So I have a pair of you, the fair and the ruddy," Malcolm mused. "Duncan, welcome your foster brother."

So this was the cousin he had been told about, son of the Lord-Abbot Crinán, appraising him as he himself was being appraised. Duncan embraced Macbeth with one arm, stiff with the reserve of an older boy much aware of his dignity.

"High King," Macbeth said as Duncan moved away, "with your leave, I wish to present you with a gift from my father."

Malcolm drank off his goblet and a servant appeared quickly to fill the ornamented silver with satiny red wine. Macbeth burned with the secret knowledge that his first startled thought had been of blood when he saw the king's stained lips.

"I'd not see you color like a girl," the king rumbled, and Macbeth flushed again, then bit the inside of his cheek to quell his embarrassment. "The gift, then?"

He took the bridle from under his mantle, as he had been instructed, and gave it to the king with a little flourish.

Malcolm turned it over in his hands. The leather was black, the fittings inlaid with gold and Cairngorm stones in a pattern of woven loops that never repeated. "A nice bit of harness," he said, his voice making it seem this was a poor gift indeed. "It's become wet on your journey." He lifted it and sniffed. "And not only from rain."

Macbeth grinned then, unable to hold in the joke. "The sweat is from the fine stallion now resting in the stables."

The guests roared with laughter, following the king, first those close enough to hear the exchange and then the others. "Would it happen that I know of this horse?"

"He is the finest of my father's stud, the gray that won the Beltane races."

"A royal gift, Mac Findláich. Very good."

"The boy must be hungry after his journey," said the queen, a reminder pitched so low that Macbeth barely heard it. Malcolm inclined his head to her advice.

"Sit and eat, there by the ambassador, and amaze him with the wit of our northern youth. Duncan may go with you." Macbeth made to leave, but the king's lifted hand halted him. "But first, undo that pin."

He unfastened the circular silver pin that held his striped braught on his shoulder, and held it out in the palm of his hand.

"This is very old, Pictish work," the king said. "Did your father give it to you?" Macbeth nodded slowly. "Then I will give you a new one, as I am your father now."

The king took the brooch from his many-folded purple mantle, and put Macbeth's simple penannular pin in its place. The king's brooch, silver with gold overlays, depicted a three-headed beast with red eyes. It was larger than Macbeth's hand. He struggled to manage the point through the layers of wool, succeeding at last. Then he thanked the king and went to his seat, his ordinary mantle sweeping more grandly around him now.

"You have pleased the king," Duncan said as he joined him, glancing quickly at Macbeth's gift, then away.

"Then I have done well." Macbeth twisted a rosy piece of sea trout free from the bones and dipped it in the baking sauce of honey and herbs. There was thick butter and wheat bread as well as oatcake, cooked apples, stewed clams and cockles, whitefish with vinegar and cumin—substantial food even though a fast day.

"Our grandfather likes cleverness, but he likes good fighting more." Duncan held him with a steady gaze. "And you have a long path to tread before you can provide that."

"I am soon to have six winters," Macbeth said, as though he'd been asked. "How old are you?"

"Past halfway to a man. I have been his foster-son for nearly two years. Why have you come when you are so young?" Macbeth felt even smaller under his cousin's close questions. Duncan's hair was almost white, his eyes paler blue than the king's, and his skin fair. His own hair was rusty blond and unruly, and his gaze reflected from still pools showed his eyes as sometimes green, sometimes brown.

"My father sent me now because he must always fight—and he fights well—against the invaders."

"The king says your father's people are his wall against the North-men."

"My father is a king, too, and his people defend Moray, their own land." His angry answer had caught the attention of those seated nearby. Macbeth reached for another cake, embarrassed.

"Was your journey difficult?" Duncan asked, suddenly conciliatory.

"It rained every day."

"Here, too. The water is rough and the ways are bad."

"You are young to be sent away from your mother," said the foreign man, guttural slow Gaelic emerging from his heavy black beard.

Their bickering ceased as they stared at the ambassador.

"Permit me. Otto, emissary of the court of Henry II, king of the Germans and of the Lombards, and king of the Romans too," he said, with a little inclination of his head. "Of course, I know who you are, Duncan, and now Mac Findlaích. Two scions of the Alpins—and what of the third, I wonder, far away in the north?"

The ambassador wore a blue garment covered with a vine pattern, and over it a stiff tunic in a remarkable shade of yellow-green, brilliant with small gems at the neck and hem. Macbeth peered under the edge of the table and saw that he wore blue hose, also patterned, held close to his legs with red windings.

"It is the fashion in Rome," he said mildly, as though it were not impudent for boys to peek at his legs.

Macbeth sat up straight, avoiding Duncan's teasing glance. "I am far from home but this place is part of my family history," Macbeth said gravely, hoping to appear older.

"Indeed?"

"I am of the Cenél Loairn, the People of the Wolf, who traveled the Great Glen as they moved from Dál Riata against the Picts."

"Then you have a fine legacy," the ambassador said with somber dignity.

"How progresses that trouble with the Poles?" asked the bishop seated to the right. The ambassador turned away, saying, "We are hoping soon for a peace, but…"

Macbeth refocused his attention on the food but listened to the German as much as he could, drawn by the strange names, the titles of foreign princes, places like Schleswig and Utrecht. He wondered if all the men of those places wore such huge black beards, and if the ambassador's rich clothing meant that he was of royal blood there, as such a display of colors would indicate here.

The musicians had resumed playing. Men along the hall were singing two different tales to the same tune. A somber man came in and spoke quietly with a brown-haired woman near the head of the table, then left. Her eyes remained on him the entire time. So did the king's.

"Who are they?" Macbeth asked Duncan.

"Boidh, brother to the king. His wife is from far in the north, from Sutherland or even Caithness, which the Orkneymen claim." Macbeth thought, but did not say, that he needed no lessons in the ways of the sea-raiders, not from a son of sheltered Atholl.

Other people had watched Boidh come and go, leaving his untouched glass in the empty place immediately to the king's right where Macbeth had stood.

"Boidh is tanist, named to be king after Malcolm," Duncan added softly.

He remembered whispered conversations at home and among the men as they traveled: *The old king's bones carried across the water to Columba's holy island and his burial in the great mound of kings. Boidh had sent his children away, it was said, suddenly and by night. He was in a perilous place, so close to the high seat, always under Malcolm's calculating eye. Where were the children then? There was a son. A son and a daughter both.*

"How fared Moray when you parted from it, young Mac Findlaích?"

The hall went silent. Macbeth, startled by the king's peremptory question, still held a morsel to his lips, ready to take a bite. He saw the smiles and lifted eyebrows. Carefully, he put down the cake, stood and addressed the king.

"The sea brings evil, High King," he said, choosing his words, remembering what his father had said. "The lands between River Uisgern and the Firth were so flooded that the farmers will harvest seals, not barley."

The king smiled.

"The sea will return to its proper home," Macbeth continued, "but the Lochlannaig do not go away."

The praise-poet nodded, and the smiles became less amused and more approving. Macbeth did not say anything more.

"You are as skillful with words as your father," Malcolm said. "And as direct. The Danes have overrun Findlaích's positions at Mouth of Ness and again at Elgin, and established their wives and children on the land. They are not mere raiders after wealth such as we have seen before. They seek sword-land for their families—and that they shall not have, neither in Moray nor in Alba!" Great fighters cheered, Conamail loudest among them, and there was the rattle of metal on metal, the thump of fists on tables. "Your father will have our aid, once our armies are gathered."

"In Moray, there beyond the Mounth," came an insinuating voice, "it's never certain if the King of the North holds his ground against the men of the sea—or the Albanaig at his back."

Macbeth flushed. He looked for a long time at the sharp-featured man who'd said that, the one standing behind the king.

"We'll soon move to Moray, grandson—son, now—and drive out the Danes as the Norwegians were expelled and the Orkneymen sent to their ships a hundred years ago."

3

MACBETH

Dunnichen, 1010

The air was harsh with the outcry of herons disturbed from their rookeries. At night, pale flames flickered above the surface of the still loch, said by some to be the souls of long-ago Northumbrian invaders who had been lured to their deaths in the marsh. The king waited as levies came in from all quarters of the wind, of men and of supplies, of monkish prayers and horses, each small company joining like fish to a school as an army prepared to support beleaguered Moray.

Macbeth and Duncan had companions, foster-sons of men who had been summoned to the king. Some boys were much older, almost men. They practiced apart, casual with weapons as deadly as their fathers'.

The younger boys had only a small corner of the field. Even that little space was encroached upon by men and horses, harness and stacked weapons, tents, barrels of ale, salt fish, sacks of grain. They had set aside their hurling sticks and the biggest of them cut a target deep into the trampled soil, where they practiced driving small spears into the circle. Every good blow drew shouts, and challenges. The boys felt like proven warriors amid the noise and stink of the encampment.

Macbeth's blows were aimed for Duncan to see, and he admired every clean thrust his cousin made at the target. He longed desperately to be older, bigger, his arms as long as his cousin's, showing muscle.

A tall boy, Kenelm, who came from the disputed borders of Bernicia, stepped forward and drove his spear into the circle.

Macbeth waited, imagining that they faced a boar, even one of the great boars of the scéalta that were recited in the long evenings, magical red beasts with bristles golden as the sun, or black ones that came from the Underworld. The circle was the boar's heart.

"Look," whispered Kenelm. "The king."

The boys went on with their practice, trying to appear as though nothing had changed though everything had changed with the appearance of Malcolm outside the wall.

All morning the king had conducted the business of Alba, planning the war with his council, sending his word by messengers' mouths and scribes' letters to Findlaích. Now he warmed himself in the intermittent sun, already prepared for battle, his plain war-going tunic belted up to his knees, a sword at his side. He came out to study his army and the fickle weather, and sometimes his attention fell on the play of future warriors.

Macbeth moved forward. *I alone of the throng would face the beast that carries doom on its tusks. I am the king's chosen champion. My weapon is ash-wood cut from a sacred grove and tipped with one of the leaf-blades of the Old People, too heavy for an ordinary man to lift.*

He drove it into the enchanted heart of the beast.

The wooden point struck a buried stone and the spear clattered away, while the force of his thrust sent him sprawling across the target.

"A mighty blow," snickered Duncan.

Macbeth brushed dirt from his knees and the heels of his hands, where streaks of blood showed. "Aye," he muttered, hiding his face.

The laughter faded quickly. The boys redrew the circle, erasing the scar his fall had made. Duncan stepped forward, hefted a practice spear. He glanced toward the king. Then he drove his gath hard into the ground, the point gouging deep, opening the boar's heart.

ॐ

Meigle, 1010

On an earlier day, Macbeth had found a target more suited to his talents.

The young monk wore a Roman tonsure and the black garb of southern monasteries. He had been named Oswald after his godfather in the normal fashion "but perhaps it would have been more apt had my name been chosen in honor of the archbishop, because I was intended for the church from my christening-day," he said to Macbeth, without a hint of bitterness.

"Our tutor is unlucky enough to be the fourth son of a Mercian lord," Duncan explained as he went to the door of the hall and, rousting a hound from the stoop, stood looking out across the open ground toward the church. His shadow reached across the floor almost to the table. "In their lands it is not worth of arm but first-birth that carries leadership."

"I thought you looked like a fighting man," Macbeth said.

"Indeed!" The monk laughed and scrubbed a wide hand across the pale sprouting of his odd tonsure. "If you were a later son in Anglia, you would be a scholar in a monastery school, and many of the lads beside you, younger sons who had been devoted to the church by their families, would not ever go home to take up the sword and the governance of lands."

"Then you had to become a monk?"

"I took the vows freely."

"Why?"

Oswald carefully closed the gilded book, which Macbeth recognized as one of the Gospels, and folded his hands upon it. His eyes, cool and steady, reminded him uncomfortably of a captured Danish huscarl who had been brought before his father.

"You ask a great many questions."

Macbeth, expecting discipline, did not turn away.

"That's good. You will learn, then." The monk glanced toward Duncan, then back.

"I already know my letters," Macbeth said, flushed with this unexpected success. Duncan, still leaning on the doorpost, made a rude noise.

Brother Oswald smiled blandly down at his smooth hands and the Gospel.

"I know very little about you, Mac Findlaích, though I have come to know much about your noble cousin, having tutored him for more than a year."

"My father is the King of the North, which is Moray and Buchan as far as the River Dee, also Ross and Cromarty, rich with grain lands and pastures, even if parts of it are mountainous and wild." He heard the slow scrape of Duncan's feet as he came to the table, felt the vibration as he dropped heavily onto the other end of the bench. "My father says that those who rule should know more than fighting. He would even write letters with his own hand to abbots and bishops."

Oswald opened an iron-bound box that sat on the table. He took out several books and set them in a row, his hands lingering on each of them. "This is my treasure. The Gospel of St. Matthew. St. Augustine. The historian Eusebius. A Latin grammar and colloquy." That book he opened, and, turning it around, pushed across to Macbeth. "From the top of the page."

Using a flat stick to keep his place in the close book-hand, Macbeth haltingly spoke off the Latin, sounding the letters slowly, words unfamiliar except when he came to the name of Jesus the son of God.

"Very good." Turning to Duncan where he idled at the end of the bench, he asked, "Mac Crínáin, which are the Latin letters not found in the Gaelic?"

Duncan's well-formed mouth, sullen as usual, rounded up, then he frowned. "V," he said, "and..."

Oswald waited.

"Ahh," he groaned in frustration. "What does it matter? A monkish king is no king at all."

The monk's long face darkened. Macbeth looked at the set of his shoulders and thought again that he would have made a good fighter.

"The king demands that I teach you," he said, his voice controlled. "Teaching I can provide, but the learning rests with you."

The monk stood and began to pace the length of the table. His black robe moved heavily around his legs but he did not shorten his stride.

"If you would be a powerful king, or ruler of any people, Duncan, Macbeth, then you should follow the example of Charlemagne, most perfect of kings. Maker of laws, founder of schools and churches. A monkish king? Most Christian of kings, and most powerful thereby. Charles who could bend thick iron in his hands..."

Macbeth listened, fascinated, though he saw in Duncan's settled slackness that he was not hearing this lesson for the first time. Oswald broke off, though obviously he could have continued. He returned to the table and sat down beside Macbeth. With his guidance, he began to piece together sonorous Latin words.

"You are making spells," Duncan said abruptly.

"Perhaps it would not sound so if you could read better yourself," the monk said. "Letters carry messages, indeed, but do not hold the power of spell-making as those pagan wanderers claim, clinging to the error of the past."

"My father welcomes the filid, who are wise. Had you poets in your household, cousin?" asked Duncan.

"My father welcomes history tellers and musicians, but he bars the poet-seers."

"A wise father indeed," Oswald cried. "These filid bring error wherever they are allowed, pagan ways, superstition wrapped in verse."

"Are we not Christian enough at Dunkeld Abbey? But we honor the poet-seers too."

Duncan took the knife from his belt and drew a line in the blackened table-top, then cut thin strokes along it, slanting or straight, some neatly divided by the line. "My name." He turned the knife in his hand and offered the haft to Macbeth, his brows raised in challenge. "These are the letters of our own people—ogham—runes with power. So was I taught."

Oswald, who had remained silent through this, reached over and took the knife and tossed it clattering into his iron-bound box. "You have a destructive temper, Mac Crínáin, and shall not have it back—no, no matter who has given it to you—until you have made penance for your disruption. And for your willingness to pagan superstition. Now, as to power..." He tapped his books. "Power indeed in the words—the Word of God foremost, and in the writings of the saints and the church fathers. If you would have poets, then let them sing not of vain things such as cattle-raids and bloodshed, but of Christ."

He stood and began to pace, again, as he talked.

"Juvencus, whose work opens all the absurdities of the pagan religions and replaces them with the great truths of the Gospels. Paulinus of Nola. Arator—his *De Actibus Apostolorum* is subtle argument for heaven." Macbeth could not help a careful smile, hidden behind his hand, as he recognized the monk's fondness for oration—and Duncan's growing impatience.

"Oh, to have many books!" Oswald touched those on the table, rapidly, his fingers running over their edges. "All those books that were burned by the Danes and Norse! I could wish for a great library, many volumes."

His long jaw tightened and he closed his eyes, made the *signum salutis*.

"Forgive, oh Lord, the acquisitiveness of my nature. Remind me that books are for your greater glory, not mine." He opened his eyes but sat entirely still, as though the prayer continued. When he stirred, however, Duncan was not quick enough to settle his mocking grin.

"St. Patrick was set upon by evil forces," Brother Oswald said, stressing *evil*. The orator was not gone, but changed. "He was threatened by druids with their bloody spells, and those who believe they can predict the future. He overcame their arts when they lay in wait to assassinate him."

That drew Duncan's attention.

The monk leaned down, looked closely at them. "This is the story that I learned in my boyhood, from missionaries of Éireann. Patrick and his followers were walking along a road singing the praises of Our Lord. His enemies were concealed in ambush. But when the saint came within the deep place where the enemy waited, then he spoke this prayer and he and his men were cloaked by the power of God. The murderers' eyes were filmed and they saw only the passing of a herd of deer."

Brother Oswald stood straight and clasped his hands behind his back. His voice lifted as he recited, the words somewhat oddly accented:

"Fri tinchetla saíbfháthe
fri dubtechtu gentliuchtae
fri saíbrechtu heretechdae
fri himchellacht nidlachtae
fri brichtu ban agus gobann agus druad."

The monk's gray eyes had glittered as though he'd confronted the armies of Hell itself. "And so the saint put to fight the pagans with their charms."

అ

LOCHINDORB, MORAY, 1010

The forest known as Edinkillie was dense with oak and beech and pine. It pressed around the loch, darkening its waters. The shadows of the trees reached almost to the island stronghold, Lochindorb. The noise from the hall beat back against those shadows, reaching much farther than the light of torch and lamp. It went over the wall that enclosed the island, washed across the water, silenced the lynx, mixed with the distant howls of wolves. It swallowed the silence of Macbeth where he sat on the mossy stones.

The king had brought up the army at Findlaích's urgent call and together they had met the Danes and defeated them. The Albanaig army then left the ravaged area around Murthlac, crossing the Spey to reach the fortification at Lochindorb—built on a man-made island, it was the nearest safehold large enough for the entertainment of the host and secure from treachery of Danish sword-bands who might have only seemed to row their ships away. Findlaích and his men had remained behind, taking a position close to the coast.

A laughing roar came from one of the many knots of men around a fire. The great were feasting inside the hall, celebrating their victory, while the rest of the army ate and drank outside, each company of men keeping to its own fire, each singing the songs of the clans and lands that had answered the call to arms. The voices and instruments clashed and brayed into a fair imitation of battle.

Macbeth looked for the ship-star of the north. He turned, tucked his feet up under his legs and looked toward the North Sea coast of Moray. A fish leaped, not far from shore, and the ripples spread, catching the light of a crescent moon. He thought about fish swimming in dark water. Grit of sand against rock, slow footsteps—Macbeth stared across the loch, ignoring this latest of the drunken men who'd come to the wall to piss or howl against the forest.

"Are you the watch for these revels, Mac Findlaích?"

"This is the land of my people," he said, twisting around to look at Brother Oswald. "I should watch over it."

Oswald climbed onto the wall, little hampered by his long garment. He sat down and folded his hands in his lap. His face and hands appeared disembodied against the darkness.

"Why didn't the king help us drive out the Danes, as he said he would?"

"That is for Malcolm to say," the monk said. "But the army was much damaged by the enemy."

"But we won the battle," Macbeth argued, still angry that, while the combined armies had forced the sword-bands to leave in their boats, both kings had agreed that the Danish families already settled in Moray might remain if they swore to support the King of the North and the Ri Alban, keeping lands they'd gained through blood.

"Victory only extends so far. Your father could tell you this. Better to make a useful peace than to pursue and perhaps lose all."

"What about the farms the invaders stole? The burned churches? What about those who were killed?" He swallowed against the rage that came close to tears. "When I am a man, I will take better care of my people."

Oswald laid a cautionary hand on his arm. "These matters are beyond you. A man cannot always achieve what he wishes. And a boy need not keep the walls for an army."

Macbeth frowned into the darkness. He wished he was far from this island. He had killed his first bird here, with a stone, and felt such a pang at its bloodied eye that he did not try again for a little space. He wanted to talk with his father about the Danes, stand beside him and watch that same moon shine on the ocean.

"Is there another reason why you are here?"

The loneliness swelled up in him, then, filling his chest and his throat until maybe even a small sound escaped.

"It's no weakness to long for your family and your home," the monk said.

"When you are old, do you still feel sad?"

Oswald laughed softly. "Old—as I am? Yes. My father and mother both died while I was studying in France. I have not seen my brothers in many years, though we were once close as four fingers."

Interested, Macbeth asked, "What are their names?"

"Werferth and Liulf, and the eldest, Athelstan—also not a well-loved name in Alba. But what of your people? Your brothers and sisters?"

"I know there were others, two. They died before I was born. And then my mother died. I have no one but cousins like Duncan, who is also my foster-brother."

"Your mother was kin to Malcolm, was she not?"

"Her mother was his first wife. She died giving birth."

"So then you, and Duncan, and Thorfinn in the north—all grandsons, each differently descended." Oswald started to say something, then stopped. They sat in silence for a time, until Oswald shifted on the wall and sniffed deeply. "I can smell the deer roasting, can't you?" Eddies of wind brought smoke and wonderful smells. "Shall we join the feast?"

Macbeth jumped down from the wall. His feet, gone asleep from sitting so long, stung at the impact. Oswald bunched the hem of his black garment in his fist and leaped down, then settled his cowl properly before they entered the hall.

No one noticed them come in. Everything was noise and confusion. The king wore a shirt of fine scale-mail, gilded; a Dane's nasaled helmet hung from the tall finial of his seat. Other warriors too displayed their trophies, helmets or gold or war-gear, though they were some days from the battlefield. Weapons were stacked everywhere, as though another attack were imminent, and at least one long-simmering feud had broken into a knife fight that had required the services of the physician. A joke brought a roar of laughter and the banging of fists on the board. The hearth-fire flared as someone tossed a piece of fat into the flames.

And the smells! Macbeth was so hungry, after denying his need, that now he was almost nauseated—roasted deer and boar, ale and berry-wines, seared oil, honey in the comb, hares cooked under the ashes and wildfowl seethed in broth, bread, wild greens, over all the heavy scent of herbs and wild onion. It was a hunter's feast, game providing what the activity of the king's purveyor could not. The army's stores, those the Danes had not looted in a daring raid, were nearly gone, and this part of Moray was as wild as Duncan would have the whole.

Oswald scanned the room. Macbeth followed where he looked, saw him find Duncan in the company of some older boys, note and dismiss him. They found a place at table, greasy from earlier occupants. As food was set before them, the monk made a brief thanksgiving. He pulled a strip of meat from the slice of boar-haunch. It was lean and tough. Macbeth followed his tutor's lead and ate silently.

He was tallying the warriors he knew had been at the fight, though he and Duncan and an Anglish hostage had been safely, and dully, stashed with the purveyor at a monastery far from the battle. He went around the room once more—no Conamail. A swelling emptiness took all the savor from his food.

"Praise to the warriors of Skir-na-Luach!" someone cried, and others joined.

"And those of Coil-dur, who fought with St. Ewan at their side!"

Another cheer.

The king's fool went to the glittering heap of Danish treasure that held a place of honor at the center of the hall. His true name was forgotten, and he was known only as Wry-face for the terrible burn in childhood that had puckered one side of his face into a permanent grimace. Wry-face picked up a massive helmet, deeply dented on one side, and put it on backward. Then he gripped a thrusting-spear close to its lugs and brandished the butt at the heroes.

A man kicked the spear from the fool's hand (the point nicking his fingers as it flew) then picked him up and held him upside down with one broad arm encircling his knees. The helmet dropped away.

"Easier to take this helmet the second time," he growled, and let Wry-face fall. The fool, shaking blood from his hand, went back to the head of the table and the comparative safety of the king's pleasure.

Macbeth touched the monk's elbow. "Where is Conamail?"

"I do not see him."

He turned to the toiseach seated beside him and asked, and he asked another. The word came back—Conamail was unhurt, and had remained with Findlaích. Macbeth sighed with relief, knowing that his father had the aid of his strongest fighter.

The bishop of Birnie, who sat among the other members of the king's council, stood and lifted his hands until, with whispers and nudges and occasional friendly blows, the hall was made quiet.

"The victory has been given us," he began, and was greeted by cheers. The bishop, whom Macbeth slightly remembered from an Easter feast, acknowledged them. Stiff sprigs of gray hair poked out from under his cap, so that he looked a bit foolish despite his blue robe and crook and ornate cross of Christ. "We should offer all praise to the Father-God who arms the righteous for battle, and glory to the Prince of Peace who has restored His rule over this torn land."

There were many calls, including a couple of Latin responses from clergy.

"Thanks be to the Lord God for the safety of our brother bishop Béan, who fled Murthlac before the heathens but who shall return to a greater church indeed!" And the cry went up, of joy and triumph, echoed by those outside the hall. "The king has provided that prayers be given at this day in perpetuity, at the altar of Birnie, for the souls of our dead."

"Perhaps we should drink their souls into the hereafter as the Danes do!" called out a tall man who looked half a Dane himself.

The bishop did not frown at the soldier, but looked indulgently at him, then signed the benediction on the company and sat down, taking up his own drink as though following the man's advice.

Now the praise-poet Aengus rose and went to the treasure, standing in front of it with his arms crossed and his head thrown back.

"A new night comes in, and comes in triumph!" he called, his trained voice pealing loud across the space.

"Hear how our king, descended of strong Fergus,
returned from defeat, of defeat made victory,
and forced the swilling Danes to down their own blood
who had drunk down Alba's finest yield.

This but one year's turning, harvest to harvest,
from when the white grain bowed before
invaders' tread until the rightful reaper came.
Strong as the boar that one spear-thrust
cannot kill, Malcolm once wounded of the Danes
then healed the stronger, till bursting like the sun
from winter's thickets he felled all before him.

Hear how our king advanced through the narrow ways
of Achindun, proud-armed like the stag,
and how his wisdom ordered stones set in the river,
holding back its flow until released with morning
upon the enemy! Divided by the Dullan Water,
Enecus' men did not lose heart but came forward,
came down boldly, boldly marching
from their strong place to prevent rightful
kings from their own—false hope!
For I saw three cranes fly across the hill
where the Danes were camped, three cranes sent
to steal all valor from their bones.

Hear now the clashing of our swords and shields!
Hear the brazen shout of foreigners' trumpets!
It seemed then the crowned mountains must come down:
Better it was for the Danes that they had so done,
better to face cold stone than eager steel!
The battle joined beside St. Molocus' church,
where Dullan's banks the green lands divide,
in the land's heart near to the Fiddich water,
where brave Findlaích assembled the men of the North
and fell upon the Danes like the Mounth itself.

Hear now how Alba's guard came bravely forward,
their footsteps paced by drums, lit by hero's light
shining from the forehead of the king, and all cold fear
melted from them by the sunlike heat of his anger.
At first shock brave men fell—women of the isles
will mourn Kenneth, and the lord of the Greenlands

and proud Graeme of Strathearn were lost there.
They have gone into Spiral Castle.
They have gone to live at the back of the North Wind
where all songs ever are in harmony together.

Hear then how the battle bent evilly against us!
The Danes were fierce, and their iron loosed
much hot blood, but with it was not quenched.
Some lesser men lost heart to see new-fallen
the finest warriors of the host, heroes forced back,
but Malcolm came like a salmon against their tide,
and the great men around him, making a wedge against them.
As they passed the church, there Malcolm made his perch,
iron-beaked and sharp-taloned as the eagle
on western heights, and he stopped the outward flow
as though the moon had reversed in the sky
and the sea swallowed back its rushing tide.
"Hear me, Molocus," he cried.
"Your chapel I will enlarge by three lengths
of this good spear, if victory fall to me!"

Hear then how dismay fell upon the Danes, disarrayed
in wild pursuit, and the Ard Ri Alban himself slew
their vaunted chief, the battle-winner Enecus
became battle-loser there,
and then the whole host of the Danes turned
before the king's great wrath.
Balvenie's hill would not allow their rally
but shook beneath them, and the invaders
howled like tailed dogs, and fled, and many died,
leaving the field strewn with swords and hewn armor
and much Alban gold that the Danes had looted
and in their doomed pride dared wear before us!

See, then, the end of all invaders: a cairn
of four corners holds them naked in the earth,
of wealth despoiled, of pride and life denied.
But the king in his greatness ordered Enecus

buried as the Danes do, with shield and spear,
and a great egg of stone rests above his heart.
See, then, that the battle be remembered
and the weaponed valor of Alba's sons
Both north and south!
An obelisk will be raised at the church-side
to the height of a tall man, and skillfully there
sculptors will cut the whole tale
of early defeat and Malcolm's lasting victory!"

The praise-poet bowed deeply to the king, and all cheered his artistry. Macbeth battered the table, a little noise amidst the men's racket. He shouted in Oswald's ear, "Wasn't it just like the battle itself?"

Oswald continued to smile politely. "It was well-done, if pagan," he said, leaning close so Macbeth could hear.

"But he called on the saint."

"Yes, indeed—one saint amongst a horde of demons. But I will not say it was not artfully created, for all that."

Malcolm beckoned his poet, who stood waiting for that invitation, to the head of the table. He rewarded him with a heavy silver chain, then passed him the gold-chased drinking horn that had been a Danish chief's, and from which the king had himself just drunk. The seanchaidh lifted it to the king, drank, and would have handed it back except that Malcolm pressed it into his breast and waved him away.

Boidh, seated to his right, stood and called loudly, "Well sung, Aengus!"

The poet inclined his head.

"I thank you for recalling the battle to our ears—and hope that our wounds do not bleed afresh!" The tanist, red-faced, leaned against the table. "But in your praising, you have forgotten esteemed guests at our feast."

The poet's lips compressed, whitened.

Boidh walked around the table, his strides made overly cautious by drink. He passed the treasure-heap, and threw back the lid of a plain wooden kist sitting against the wall.

"Honor is due our guests," he said, reaching inside and pulling out two heads by their braided hair. The muscles of his arm showed as he hefted them higher.

"I have slighted you, Jarl Throand, forgive me." Boidh put his left hand into the chest and lifted a third head.

Their eyes remained open, no one having closed them, and they appeared startled at their introduction to the feast. A whiff of preserving cedar-oil spread through the room.

"Praise or not, you have the best portion, my fine jarls," Boidh said, lifting the heads so that he addressed them directly. "Three niches are to be built into the new church-wall for your homes. Enecus will have his stone, but you...the prayers of the Church will wash you every day... perhaps wash you even into Heaven."

4

LAPWING

Raven. Top of the birch tree shakes and sways at his lifting-away. Birch tree, beginning tree, first of the letters used by the wise.

Another raven rises, flaps, glides flat-winged. A pair of ravens.

What does this mean for Lapwing? Is this sign complete?

"Cru-u-u-uuk," I cry. What message from the Morríghan, from the one-in-three, to her servant Lapwing?

No reply. They fly to some battle, perhaps, to slake her thirst.

Keep feet to the path. Narrow and winding, finding the way of the land around stone and grove, brook and fen. Path of deer and men alike, and my path now, to Dunkeld and its warm places. Old men have brittle bones. Night air snaps them like last season's reeds. Bright day brings black frost.

Loose clouds not gathered in their armies drift like masterless men, shadows running after. Up the slopes of the blue hills and down the other side, to the Mounth that divides river from river and Alba in twain.

Third raven!

It speeds after the others, then veers away, toward the monks' house.

The battle-goddess herself flies, perhaps, unity in three. Riddle closed and all complete. What does she command? Birch and raven. The beginning of change, by violence.

Wait. Wait.

"Cruu-u-ukk. Cruuk. Cru-u-uuuuk-k." Louder than the babble of wind in trees, the cries of little birds, insects.

Perhaps I should not go there. Monks pray where once red blood poured. Perhaps I should. Did ravens fly for me alone, or for my eyes to interpret for another?

Turn round and ask the land. There the river broad and silver in the sun. There the rock. Silver flows in the rock like water, if you can find it where it springs. There the moorlands burning down to winter ash of gray and brown.

Cloud shadow. Woad-blue cloth pulled across the hills. Unveiling. Revealing. Land's green breast that suckles men. Sun strikes water and light comes to me breaking and flashing through the trees. Squinting against, I discern the lines of the letters that say "Aye."

I salute the land that answers.

There are patterns in the world, paths. From a high place I see their winding. Feet feel when they stray onto hummocky grass, my bull-foot thumping off path, on path. Lapwing sees a world that most do not, blind to truth as some men are to the color red. What then do they see when blade strikes to blood?

There lies Dunkeld tucked inside the vallum, a mole's-work on the land, little walls around the brown buildings and tower. They try to climb into the sky, these monks, into a Heaven that is no-place. What man wants to die into nothing? The knob of the former pilgrim's staff is warm and round in my hand. Hah! A plea to that sheep-Jesus once was carved there, but I whittled down to new wood. Narrow cuts of my invocation run round it now, above and below the center line, ogham invoking protection of the God Who Sings.

Too long in the south. Too long.

The gods are strange and distant in Northumbria, their names uncouth. The high moors, though, I sing the high moors full of the loneliness of the holy. Echo of the brimming sacredness of Lochar Moss. Up the Roman road rattling with carts, scar on the land straight as the slash of an unturned blade. That was a people of order but scant of spirit.

The strangeness of the gods drew me to Melrose Abbey under the hills. I blame Loki, Dane-brought. He plays with signs like a wandering juggler. Black monks! Crows of another significance, rooks gossiping together. Their malice meant shackles at Bamburgh. The galls are brown, yet, on my wrists. I sang them satire until the keepers withered and the king's officer vomited blood, and the abbey's finest copyist was struck with palsy and marred his making.

Dare to touch a man of art! Dare to chain one of the filid! Hah! Their sheep-church no sanctuary then.

Careful, here. The stream's course shifted, the land marshy. Soft earth, firm earth. Staff, be pilgrim here. I took it from the first pilgrim I met on the road between Bamburgh and Berwick. He wore a lead badge of Santiago on his shoulder. It crumpled at my words, metal soft as his faith, for he called on only four saints before he pledged himself back to Lugh the Long-Handed.

Path down and up, up and down. A mound covered by trees. I know it is no burial place but a fort from old wars, mounded turves backing on a jut of rock. Blood spilled here. Trees grow straight with such nourishment, a shadow-shifting grove, a nemed gleaming with holiness.

Rustle and sway. Thick pig-stink. A boar comes from among the ash-trees and young oaks. Yellow tusks. Red eyes. Trots across my path back into the trees. A royal welcome!

Brother Sacristan, summoned to the gate, says, "God be with you" but frowns the blessing upon me. I run my fingers over the knob of my staff, chanting my own prayer round and round. The last time my wanderings brought me here, there was no colored glass in the narrow windows of the church.

"The hour is past and tables cleared. There is beer and bread in the kitchen, if you do not wish to make a sacrifice of your hunger until vespers."

I do not wish. Brother Sacristan is fat. Monks call the barnacle goose a fish so to eat flesh on fasting-days.

My twisted leg pains me after walking. The gods impose and demand, demand and impose.

In the guest-house is a Wessex merchant sitting on his merks of silver and a canon of Jorvik, puffed out like a dark rock dove, who tells me, "I am traveling to Kinnedar, but have stopped here that I may celebrate the feast of St. Etheldreda, twice-virgin abbess."

Great faith in virginity have these priests, but hardly a one but is mistressed as well as wived.

"Then let us sing her praises and those of women less holy!" The merchant rattles his purse of pennies significantly. "Unbind your harp, my friend!"

Strings, muffled by worn leather, at a touch whisper counsel.

"This clàrsach came father to son, and not for the singing of bawdy songs. Do you of Southampton not know that strings may be tuned to other purposes?"

The merchant jumps at my divine knowledge, and the canon fingers his cross. Lapwing has no use for them. Twelve years repeating words into truth, until I was filled like a bladder for the rest of my days. I know the colors of gems, the properties of the days, all language of trees and of numbers. I am filled with the sun that nourishes and blasts.

I sing the future, crop-crammed with the hazels of wisdom. I bring blemish and sickness on those who err. Truth a shout in my head, all things shout together like boys released from chores.

A novice brings a chunk of coarse bread, a slab of cheese, and thin beer. The bowl is light to the hand. My tongue tastes the wood. Lingering sweetness. Birch. A knowing man would have brought Lapwing one made of willow, sacred to poets. But birch has spoken once today and now again, beginning and beginning.

This pallet has no more than the usual vermin. Sleep will come.

A dream of eating pork in a dark house is broken by the sound of a hunting party. Horses whicker and whuffle at their bloody burdens. Dogs. Laughter.

I am angry, because time was not given me to learn if this was a dream of the Sow of Death or mere memory of the boar on the path, simple hunger or a prediction of royal favor. And who breathed unseen in that dark, no gleam of star or ember to show a form?

Turn my face to the wall and seek the broken thread. Lost again to tramp and jingle of a heavy man entering the guesthouse.

"It's said we host a poet here." His voice is a thunder, a summoning. I turn from the wall and its solace. "You are the one?"

"I am called Lapwing." Conceal, conceal, as the lapwing does his shallow nest. Mislead, mislead, as the lapwing does, fluttering and crying until the nest is forgotten and the hunter seeks only the bird. Only the discerning see through plaintive guises.

"I am Crinán, protector of this house, also called the Thane."

He takes the Anglish word in a Gaelic land. I know of him, lord of the blood, Lord of Atholl, holding Dunkeld by inheritance and protecting it by sword and prayer. A man like the cliffs of the Rhinns, broad face, high brow. Heavy in the stomach but strong. Hair faded from a young man's gold. Retainers crowd the door behind him.

"Brother Kevin told me that one who bore a harp had stopped with us."

Bile burns my mouth. No foreigner this, but a fool, to seek songs and flattering histories at his meal.

"I am correct in thinking you one of the filid, and not mere tale-singer?"

"You are a man of perception." Under the fleshy face ride the bones of a man, a fighter, a strategist. This lay abbot does not guise himself as a cleric for his soul's safety or body's ease.

Test his mettle, warrior sword against granite.

I stand, and my heel does not touch the ground.

Hah! See the fear crawl swiftly across his face and disappear many-legged into the crannies of his mind.

"The sacristan said you wore a cloven foot, but I discounted that, for he sees signs and wonders everywhere."

"Brother Kevin is wiser than he appears, then, to allow wonder."

Crinán purses his lips. "My bishop, were he here, would have you fed and gone, but he's off to aid the High King's angling after Lothian land."

"You mistake the source of my crippling. This is no cloven hoof of your devil's making, but the bull's-foot of the god."

The Lord-Abbot pulls a gorse prickle from his hair. Stands in cooling sweat and darkening of blood. Now he raises a hand and motions all away—monks, men, gawking merchant. Our canon of Dane-held Jorvik gone already, no doubt kneeling and mumbling.

"I will sing you the tale of myself, Thane Crinán, if you will listen."

Open the leather bag that holds the harp, secret of music, as my mouth is a bag catching the secret of language.

Left hand, treble hand, high singing notes. Pluck a life from thirty strings, each the year of an Age, and Lapwing numbers an Age and half another.

"Jacob lay beside the stream
at the ford of Jabbok.
No women to see, no servants to look,
Alone and holy, Jacob lay.

Jacob wrestled long with God
beside the stream at Jabbok.
Until the crowing of the cock,
against God's arm, he wrestled.

Jacob was strong and did not fail
at water-speaking Jabbok.

God for God was not mistook
by Jacob when he was strong.

Jacob demanded a blessing then
beside the stream at Jabbok.
God touched the hollow of his thigh,
sinew pulled, and foot of bullock
gave he for blessing to Jacob.

Jacob asked of God a name
at the ford of Jabbok.
Would not release his mighty hold,
though light showed on the hillock,
till name for name was given.

Morning shone on Jacob,
at water-speaking Jabbok.
He passed before the face of God
limping and lame across the rock,
after the sun blessed Jacob."

"I have not your facility for riddling concealment, or for interpreting
it."

"No, nor would have without many years of learning and more of
living."

Crinán laughs. "I've lived a bit myself, Lapwing. You are good company in slack time. Bring cloak and clàrsach out of this place and stay in
my hall. You may instruct me better in this matter of bull-footed men."

The boar brought rightful place. How will ravens' word be fulfilled?

5

GRUACH

SUTHERLAND, 1011

Derelei sat placidly in front of her home-fire, hands crossed on a swelling stomach that settled her in this place more assuredly than her marriage vows.

"This is to be steeped, as you well know, for the nausea." Alpia pressed the little bag into her daughter's hand.

"I've been spared the sickness," she said.

"Ah, you are lucky! I could not break a fast for more than a moon, when I carried you." Alpia brought out a stoppered vial from another pocket and explained at some length its use for when the pains came, should the labor arrive and Alpia not be present. All this was not very interesting, although I thought for a little space about the pains. I remembered a woman screaming in another room, someplace.

I felt something strange, here. I looked around the hall, a little smaller than Talorc's, but found nothing unfamiliar. There was a shelf on one wall with its ware of pewter and wood, a pair of smallish kists along the other. Table and benches, their wood still young and light. A few embroidered panels that swayed with the drafts.

Then I realized that what was missing was the sound of the surf.

Derelei's husband held land that closed around a long arm of the sea, reaching far inland to receive, near the house, the stream coming down from Loch Sin. The water was brackish—I'd tasted its splash as we crossed on the boat that a holy man oared as a work of God—but the ocean grew sullen in its confinement and only rose and fell slowly with the distant tide. It was like paying attention to your heartbeat, and then forgetting and being panicked to find it gone.

The men had gone to hunt. It made for even more silence, without the dogs quarrelling and scratching in the strewings. And the men, of course, taking their particular noises with them. When we sang, there was only the crossing of our own voices.

Alpia had brought large bags of carded wool, spindles, and whorls. The visit to her daughter was not a time for idleness. Una, the mother of Derelei's husband, had her own spinning ready to hand. Her eyes were covered with the blue film of sky-sickness, but her gnarled old fingers could twist a thread finer even than Alpia's.

My spinning was still uneven, but I was gaining skill. The women could spin without pause, winding out carded rolls of fleece into span after span of close-twisted thread, the thread extending like the stories until it seemed that one was the other. I rolled the spindle on my thigh, easier for small hands, but the women twirled theirs from their hands. Their wooden spindles, dark with age and handling, were as long as the space from elbow to fingers, with the notched ends worn from the passage of fiber. Stone whorls rested at their middles for balance.

I liked to spin wool, less so linen. Unlike sewing, with its close work and needle-pricks, it was calming. My skin was softened by the clean fleece. On the matter of spinning and weaving and all such, I knew, my mother would have agreed with Alpia. Even the wife of a High King must know the making of thread and cloth and their decoration, if only to direct others. It was a never-ending task. The people must have their rough garb, the men-at-arms their leather-armored jackets, landholders their long-sleeved saffron léinte, and the great their finery of imported brocades, cloth-of-Bruges, and silks.

I glanced at my new traveling braught, spread out to dry. The shabby thing I had worn north had been passed to a child of Talorc's people, and Alpia had made me this new one. The thread had been spun from the fleeces of island sheep and colored a handsome blue with woad grown in the fields of the Danelaw. It was almost as fine as Flemish cloth, if plain except for the crimson fringes at its ends. The next one, Alpia had said as she draped it around my shoulders, would be from my own hands.

Derelei began to sing, a sad throbbing song. Her voice was high and sweet. The other women joined in—Alpia sang smooth and deep, like water flowing under, while old Una's voice was surprisingly firm. Under and over the melody ran the whisper of the spindles, whirling, and the shadow-play of repeated motion, the drawing-out of the thread, and then the spindle dropped to make it strong and tight, then the winding of the new thread.

The song went on and on. Lovers met, were parted, travelled gray seas and brown paths until they were reunited. I joined on the chorus.

"Ah, singing and spinning, both thirsty work!" Una said at the end.

"Indeed." Alpia set her spindle aside. "How is your brewing, daughter?"

Derelei made a proud face. Her chin lifted and her long nostrils flared. "You must say when you have tasted my new ale."

"'Tis fine, a fine brewing." Una licked her dry old lips.

They paused while Alpia, hushing her daughter to sit, fetched the cups. Derelei made a skein of her finished work. Una hummed a sad melody. A log broke and the fire sighed. I played with the clay whorl on my spindle, taking it off and turning it around on my finger.

Alpia's whorl was of stone, flat and dark and soft with much handling. The flickering light showed it smooth gray, then revealed a swirl of fine lines. There did not seem to be any beginning or end.

"What is this?" I held it up to Alpia as she set down brimming cups.

"Symbols of the One, child. As on the stones."

The women shared smiles among themselves.

"She is the mother of the Christ," I said assuredly, expecting to catch them in their secrets.

Alpia laughed, long and rich. "Indeed, she is!"

"Mary of the Sea is ever mother of the Divine Child, and Jesus the Perfected One, greatest of them all. But the Mother is older than Christ's church. She has as many names as the grains of sand on the beach."

"The priests talk of none but Mary."

"Mary Mother has many names, even among the priests," Derelei put in. "Is she not called Queen of Heaven, Holy Virgin?"

"You are one to listen long into the night, so I know that you have heard the great stories sung," added Alpia. "Think now of Lugh the Long-handed. Did he not come again as Cuchulain when Dechtire swallowed the fly? And Dylan the Fish Child of Arianrhod returned again as Llew Llaw. Even the tales of Arthur, much muddled in the telling, send him over water to the Isle of Apples and rebirth."

I nodded. "All are great heroes, who died and lived again."

"That's because men tell them," Derelei said shortly.

"Men have forgotten," Alpia said. "Like boys who are lured by noise and destruction, they have chosen to believe in the divinity of the hero and forgotten whence his divinity came."

"A borrowed garment, only," Una agreed.

I turned the whorl in my hand. I was confused as a knot of threads. Maybe I had misunderstood the stories all along. Or maybe there was another set of stories.

"The Goddess, pure and uncreated, creates the Son of Life out of her body, and he grows and dies and is reborn," Alpia explained. "In this world all things born are imperfect, and must come to death before they are united in wholeness of Flesh and Spirit."

"But you said she was Mary."

Alpia shook her head, and a lock of her white hair came free. She tucked it behind her ear.

"Mary is one form, one aspect, child. She is the mother of the world, and is due the highest honor. But men have forgotten that She is also lover of the world, and She who buries it in herself. Until we all, by the example of her great Son, are reborn in wholeness."

"But where is she? Mary is painted in the churches." I saw the exchange of glances, the gestures that might be no more than spinning of thread or tipping back of a cup but seemed to mean more.

"Now is your time to be young. You hear, but do not yet understand," Alpia said. "Soon you will move to womanhood, which is action, and finally to wisdom. Like the Goddess who is eternal, coming to no end, not to die and rise again, but to change and to be. Women share in that eternity of the womb."

Alpia held out her hand for the spindle-whorl and I gave it to her. My foster-mother weighed the stone on her palm, then closed her hand over it, rubbing her fingertips across its smoothness.

"This was my mother's," she said at last. "Mongfinn's goods are mine as she received them from her mother—the ivory casket and the bone discs were my grandmother's and back, back. You see, our people who were lately called Picts reckoned all inheritance from the woman, from the womb."

Something tumbled into place in my thoughts, like a stone dislodged and rattling down until it came to a ray of light, and with that, shone differently. "My mother's belt. The silver clasp! She told me it would be mine, as it had been her mother's, and that it was a sign of another inheritance."

Alpia smiled. "Listening and looking bring all knowledge. Lonceta's lineage through her mother, your lineage, is more ancient than her father's, and equally royal. Your brother bears a name from the king-lists—Nechtan."

"But so do yours!" I burst out in sudden realization. "They have names of kings."

Derelei smiled, hands crossed on her stomach. "Fode and Ciniod are worthy of kingship," she said. "But were they Kings of the North, even of all Alba, in the old reckoning it would not be their sons, but mine, who would gain the right of kingship."

I stared at the mound of her stomach where it seemed so much of women's secrets were hidden. But nothing more was said. The women picked up their spindles, and after a time Una began a new song. Things were different, here in Sutherland. I scarcely noticed how the thread came quickly and smoothly from between my thumb and fingers.

When Nechtan came in, shouting with his success on the hunt, I rose, greeted him and brought him ale without being asked. He looked at me strangely, aware that something had changed.

When you are king, I thought, *then perhaps my child will be the next king of Alba*. I smiled with the secrets of women.

☙

GOLSPIE, SUTHERLAND, 1011

The last of them could be seen coming along the strip of beige sand north of the little community at Golspie.

"There she is," I said.

Alpia raised her head, but her gaze seemed unfocused. "Where?"

"There, just coming round the point."

"Yes, I see her now." Alpia stood, and we her students rose after, because our teacher was often quick to begin her instruction; that instruction itself was nimble and unpredictable. But today Alpia only stood and waited, as though sorrow had caught fetters around her feet. I was the youngest of her students. Next came the two daughters of the Norse widow, Ingigerd and Estrid. The oldest girl, trudging along the beach from her father Sythak's house at the confluence of two streams, was Finnchaem.

There was no hurry. This was the time of long daylight, when the day-hours stretched and winter was forgotten. The moon showed its lopsided disc above the sea, while the sun had angled behind the furrowed mountains, leaving its red glow on the sky. The land between was soft, diffuse—the sand rosy, the grassy slope brilliantly green and rippling in the breeze, the mountains wrapped in purple.

Finnchaem arrived, puffing a little with her walk because she had a tendency to fat. She nudged her way into the circle between the sisters.

We all looked to Alpia. "This is a gathering in remembrance," she said. "There is sadness now, for Derelei who did not survive the dangerous passage into motherhood. But there is hope for new life in a perfected world when the One has birthed all to newness."

Her voice strengthened as she spoke, and her eyes cleared. "Derelei learned at my feet as I did at my mother's. If your line is not cut short— if it is not fouled and tangled—if Christ's church recalls that it once embraced us as sisters, before it drove us out with blows—then perhaps you also shall teach your daughters."

Alpia held up her hand: Remember. "What are the Three Virtues?"

"Song, Meditation, and Memory," we chorused.

"What are their places?"

"Song is the Waxing Moon, a white bowl filling with heart's delight. Meditation is the Full Moon, round and complete, shining in, shining out. Memory is the Waning Moon, recalling all before the dark drains all."

I recalled the chant perfectly, but heard Estrid stumble. The girl was big-boned and inattentive. I couldn't help but think of her as a heifer content with her cud.

"The White Lady has three Aspects. Even those who have forgotten her names remember as the moon crosses the sky that we have birth and life and death, and she controls all. But there is another secret, that Three is closed in Five and encloses Five. Listen, now, closely."

This was new. Alpia stepped away from us, to where she had laid an oblong of worn-thin cloth. I had been curious about what was hidden inside but hadn't dared open the folds. Now I lifted on my toes and leaned as far as I could to see past my foster-mother's hip, to see the cloth opened. Branches. No beautiful or precious thing. Just branches, some of them green but others wilted. I went back on my heels.

"The moon reminds us of the Three Aspects of the One," Alpia said, lifted hand and raised voice warning there would be new things to remember. "The trees recall the Five Aspects."

She held up the twigs, one at a time. Juniper. Spiny gorse. Heather. Aspen. Dark yew.

Alpia presented the juniper twig to me. "The juniper is the birth-tree, green of origin. The juniper is the tree of hope, that the sun grows again after the longest night. The juniper is the tree of purification and new life, as the Child is born and the World rejoices."

She moved to Ingigerd, who was thin-boned and dark.

"The gorse-bush is the swelling-tree, green of growth. The gorse-bush is the tree of increase, when the sun warms the soil. The gorse-bush is the tree of fire, devoured by it to make it grow the more."

She handed heather to Estrid, next oldest. "Heather is the tree of passion, green of maturity. The heather-bush is the tree of love and loss, when couples meet among the hills."

Finnchaem held out her hand, solemnly watching Alpia's face. The shaking leaves of aspen trembled in her clutch. "The aspen-tree is the tree of paradox, green of decline. The aspen-tree is the tree of combat, when stags battle in the rut. The aspen-tree is the turning-leaved tree of hope fading and renewed, the autumn that leads downward toward new birth."

Alpia stood with the slender branch of yew in her hand. She raised it but did not sing her verse. She hummed a slow melody and began to dance a moonwise circle. She touched me on the head as she moved by, and I followed, and then the others did too. Alpia touched me again, and I sang my verse. Each of us sang the stations of the year until finally Alpia sang, and her voice trembled at first before settling and strengthening.

"The yew-tree is the arrow-tree of fate, green of death. The yew-tree is the enduring tree of winter wisdom, the tree of divination, cold as winter snows. The yew-tree is shadow-sister to the juniper, as all must go down to death and all rise toward the great Light of Being."

Then we danced together, opening our mouths to voice the song without the words. The light was a mingling of sun and moon, and our shadows were soft. Alpia swayed stiffly like the yew-tree in an icy wind. We followed her example, lifting our arms in the way of our trees, sway-ing deeply or nervously or merely quivering with the wind on prickly branches stripped by fire. Alpia took my hand and pulled me from the circle, and lifted my hand in hers, palms sweaty, yew joined to juniper. "New hope!" she shouted, and her face shone with the promise. "Death into Birth! Death into Birth! The circle is One!"

We shouted after her and ended by falling onto the soft whispering grass, giddy with the song and the circling and Alpia's renewed joy.

She taught us other Five-things to remember. The senses. The elements of earth, air, fire, water, and spirit. The flowers of the small white rose that grows on dunes, and harebells in the forest. How apples preserve the memory of Five in their hidden cores.

"All things knit together," she explained, locking her work-worn fingers, "as the roots of trees intertwine and reach deeply. The World is a circle, and the circle is One, though you will see people trying to divide it into pieces they can claim."

We sang a memory-song together and then parted, Finnchaem to walk round the point to her home, the Norse girls accompanying her until they turned off to their mother's house in Golspie village. I walked silently, not having to trot in order to keep up with Alpia, as I usually did. Alpia walked with her hands clasped behind her back, looking down at her feet as though gathering herbs. And, in fact, she did stop at several places and snap off green plants and young fruits. She layered them in the cloth, the twigs it had enfolded left behind, scattered among the limpet-shells and sea-wrack, emptied of purpose.

The moon was higher and its light paler in a sky the sun had at last relinquished, but its light had been captured in the clouds and they glowed like lanterns. The sea, which deepened gradually green to blue in the day, darkened to blue-black tipped with the white froth of breaking waves. Wind curled around us and lifted our hair, the hems of our garments, like the half-foolish, half-frightening spirits that the Norse girls said were everywhere in the land.

I looked over the ocean and imagined that I could see a dragon-prowed ship riding there. I shuddered with an old fear of the raiding Lochlannaig—a different people entirely, I was sure, from the widow and her daughters.

"Mother?"

"Yes."

"Are you ever afraid?"

"Of course." Her laughter was reassuring. "Is there any particular thing that I should fear?"

After a moment, the questions surged forward again.

"Do you think Derelei was afraid?"

"I hope that she wasn't. The baby came too early, and violently." Her voice was hollow as the sea.

"But did she—know?"

"That she would die? Do any of us? Even when the blood pours from a man's wound, I think he hopes that it will be staunched by some miracle and he will live. We might be frightened of the pain that comes before death, but if we have learned well and walked peacefully in the world, we shouldn't fear the passage."

I heard seaweed pop and felt shells pressed into the sand from my step. I saw the empty cups of urchins, dropped by gulls to smash their spiny shells so they could be devoured. I moved closer to the water, to the cold edge of the waves, and away from the destruction of the tide-line. The water washed and washed against the sand. It seemed it might take it away entirely but didn't. The water moved, the sand moved, sometimes even the stones when a great storm rose off the North Sea, but all remained.

It was different, this death. Closer. The other deaths—the king my grandfather, my father's men in battle, the fishermen lost at sea, or farmers crushed by their oxen—those were distant. I thought about Derelei's stillborn son, now laid beside her, still flesh of her still flesh.

This rebirth Alpia sang of was something I did not understand, knowing it was like the stories but not the same. Like what the priests said but not the same. Death was the gate to—something. The priests said that death was the gateway to heaven, but beautiful as that might be, people clung to life and did not want to go there. Watching Derelei, I had a dim sense of my own future, of marriage and childbirth, but when it ended in blackness then I gave up trying to see any more.

The things Alpia had taught seemed so wonderful and strange. Difficult, too, though Alpia said it was enough to hear and remember. Understanding would come later.

6

GRUACH

I stepped from log to log, laid to pave the sandy mire in the narrow lanes between the houses. A rock dove fluttered across the space, roof to roof; where it landed, its feet dislodged a bit of dung-smeared thatch onto my shoulder.

Everywhere the Norse built close together. Maybe it was a way for the men to forget the empty sea, the summers spent in viking. Or was the sea how they forgot the gray wind-battered longhouses, the smell of people and animals close together?

Some of the oldest houses were familiar as Talorc's hall, sway-backed with age, built of rock and timber long since grayed and streaked with weather. This had been a holy place when our people had ruled from Birsay to the Rock of Dun Breatann, and the Scots had not yet crossed over the sea to seize land and call it Dál Riata. So Alpia had told me. But the people had turned away from the cold north in the bitter years. The great king's hall at Birsay was taken by the Norse. Ancient hillforts stood abandoned, while round brochs bonded by lost knowledge and unbroken by siege guarded an empty shore.

The Lochlannaig had taken Orkney and then Caithness, a land of moors but also forests to be cut for timber and floated down the rivers. Then they filtered into this land they renamed Sutherland, because it lay south on their eagle-flight down from Norway. They came to Golspie and planted themselves among the scattered Albanaig. Their houses had low walls supporting steep-pitched roofs, to bear the snows of Norway. Timbers that capped each end crossed at the peak, extending into carved heads of bull, dragon, wolf. As houses were repaired, one began to look like another. There was Norse carving on the new timbers of that old one, while this thatching went to the Alban pattern. Things blended. Houses, people. Golspie had been claimed for more than a hundred years by the Jarl of Orkney—partly because he was strong, partly because there was not enough value in this land to make the High King wish to wrest it back.

I shifted the bundle under my arm and stepped wide over a rut wallowed by the hooves of pigs and horses. The settlement was quiet, the men to sea, most of the women and children with their flocks on the grazings.

Halla's house was among the largest. Her husband had been a blacksmith, a craft honored even more highly among the Norse than among our people. I stopped for a moment to look at the intricate panel over the door, the sign of the hammer, with knotted and snarling creatures made more violent by the cracking of weathered wood. Then I called out and entered, two steps down to the beaten earth floor thinly strewn with sweet grasses. I almost lost my balance, blinded by the sudden darkness after bright sun.

"You have brought it! And so early in the day. You have deer's legs. Daimhin is a proper name for you, indeed."

I stumbled at the sound of the endearment my mother had given me and that Alpia occasionally used, though I flinched at hearing it from my severe foster-mother. My mother lived in that name, calling for me, laughing as I ran in the open meadow, but the sun of my childhood had been put out and everything was dim. I felt for the wall with my hand and stood blinking until my eyes adjusted. Light came from partially shuttered windows, and the fire, and from small flames at the tips of soapstone lamps hanging from knotted cords. A thick smell filled the house, of smoke and food, old urine, wool, burned tallow.

Halla was kneeling in front of her loom, warping it for a new weaving. Her rear end was broad as a cow's, while her nimble hands moved among the threads like a harper at his strings.

"You must forgive me, but this is a task not to be set aside." When she laughed, she sounded exactly like her daughter Estrid, hearty and untroubled.

I sat down on one of the benches that lined the walls. The long hearth in the center of the room gave off a gentle heat from a fire almost banked; Halla sweated at her task. Threads hung between the broadaxe-smoothed timbers of the loom, each held taut by a water-rounded soapstone pebble, pierced. They clacked together as she made the half-knots to hold the warp threads apart and in place.

"I have plenty of saddening here," Halla said, talking into her work, "but was wanting to make a bright yarn and Alpia spoke of having light alumen if I wished."

"Saddening?"

"She would call it mordant. Fixes the color in the wool. Iron and copper bring down the color. Make it sad. Saddening. Now I have this bundle of weld to use, and it would be a pity to dull that yellow when the alumen will make it pure and bright." I thought it would be wonderful to wear a color bright as the sun on wide fields, instead of the dull shade we used. With borders worked in green and purple embroidery. There was a momentary pang as I wondered what colors were popular among the women at the court of Malcolm, whether sleeves were deep or narrow. I loved all things bright, butterflies and the blossoms they visited, and in winter the great bannering of red and green lights in the north sky.

My thoughts (as though disciplined by Alpia's tongue-lash) returned to more immediate matters. How much of the dyestuff would be needed? Weld, I recalled, was a dried plant and not a root, so likely less strong. This yellow cloth was meant for one of the daughters; they were of marrying age both, Estrid even being somewhat old.

"When Farulf lived, I had any colors I might desire, for the asking. His work brought good pay in metal or byzants or pennies or goods. Once he was paid weight for weight in rubia, not the type of Gwynedd but the true red-root madder out of the south of France. The red was…"

My attention wandered. The Norsewoman could talk about spinning and weaving and dyeing until your ears refused the drumming. Spinning and weaving were all very fine, but dyeing was nasty, stenchy work I did not intend to practice. Even if Alpia said I must. Well, perhaps then. I had never yet won a contest of wills with my foster-mother.

"Farulf, he liked bright colors. It was from his youth. Hand me that skein."

I looked around until I saw the thick hank just beyond the weaver's reach. I gave it to Halla, who kept talking as if there had been no interruption.

"…then we might have lived in the south but did not. If Farulf has gone into Hel's country as he believed, there is no brightness for him, but I will say there is the Christian heaven, or the Western Island, or Arianrhod's castle in the sky, or the Sun of Souls—many worlds besides the lower one."

"Was he buried in the churchyard," I asked, puzzled at what I knew of Farulf, "to go to the Christ-heaven?"

Halla turned herself around and sat back on her heels. "Are the gods concerned with what span of ground the body holds? If Jesus Risen wants my Farulf, he will find him where he is, among the ship-mounds."

I waited. Halla always talked, but usually her simple chatter went nowhere as interesting as this.

"Farulf, now, did not go into ground like a merchant, with wealth to rot around him. We burned him in the old way and all went to the flames." Halla put a hand down to help herself up, but she rocked against the base of the loom, setting all the weights to clacking softly, stone gossips. "We gave him metal-things he made himself and most valued. A bronze belt buckle at his waist, a fine dagger in its scabbard, good iron adzes at his feet. There was warm sunstone from the Amber Coast, of all gems the one he loved best. We sacrificed a bull and set its head before the house. Also in his pyre were two spotted dogs, and he had a cross of Christ."

Surprised, I glanced at the empty seat and the hammer suspended in place of honor behind it, half obscured by the drooping strings of last year's dried apples. I had always wanted to ask, was the hammer the dead man's, or Thor's?

Halla clucked as she untangled threads, shook her gray head.

"Oh, he went in viking as a youth," she said at last, and I shivered at the word. "In the Varangian Sea, through the territories of Rus. He was Christian when he shouldered an axe in the emperor's guard in the great city—twice Christian, but Thor would not mind."

"Twice?"

"He was prime-signed and put on the white garment two times." Halla laughed, showing dark gaps where teeth had been. "He said some would convert many times over to gain new cloth for their backs rather than a doubtful heaven for their souls. For that, the water-baptism was needed."

Halla's broad face became thoughtful. The net of wrinkles cast by laughter softened. "He said it seemed very possible, this heaven, when a man was at Constantinople and saw the emperor's throne raised on high and the great churches and all the light, candles as many as the stars. But returning north Farulf found the forests remained dark. He took up Thor's hammer again and I was pleased, for we were to marry.

Understand that I have no quarrel with Jesus Risen, who is, after all, much like Balder and like the son of your White Lady, but priests bring no luck. Not that luck was with us, even in Norway."

She waved her hand as though to shoo the bad luck away. "Enough sad talk. Come, I have something for you to see with Alpia's eyes." We went into the byre. There was light, here, through the open door and windows, buttery light on the clean stalls and the empty stone hayrick base. The Norse widow kept only some goats and sheep (now grazing in the upland in her daughters' charge) and ran pigs in the forest.

Something—more than one thing—whimpered piercingly from the far stall.

Halla beckoned me forward.

I saw animals squirming in an old garment on a bedding of straw. A gray cat, not a wildcat of the forest but something softer, tamer, and two striped kittens that cried as they nuzzled after milk.

"Only the two survived, both females," Halla said. "The cat came to me already bearing a belly, but where she came from is a question, for there are no such cats among us."

I knelt and reached out cautiously.

"She'll not bite. I've handled the kits myself."

I stroked the nearest one's pointed ears. It mewled, showing a pink mouth and slender tongue, and then rolled and stretched, unsheathing delicate claws. Its belly was spotted.

"So soft," I marveled. "I've never touched a cat before, or even seen one except from far away, and those were wildcats."

The kittens made a throaty, throbbing sound, like the voice of the sea heard inland.

"Pretty creatures but not biddable as dogs." Halla bent and picked up the kittens. "Look how their tails are ringed."

Still on my knees, I tilted my head to see.

Halla held the kittens close to her face, one on each side. The kittens became quite still. They raised their tiny paws and touched her cheeks. She smiled, but not in her broad way. An inward smile like—yes, that of the painted Mary in the church.

Light fell strongly on her from the facing window, warm yellow.

Then it changed.

The light dimmed and flared, pure white, a light clear as though stars had gathered into a new sun. Halla was no longer a garrulous widow, but someone remote and white and silent. And young—her once-faded eyes were sharp but innocent. The kittens laid their paws reverently against her face and no longer cried out.

The numinous glow flickered, as though rainclouds passed quickly over, then sun and more clouds bringing life to the earth.

And then gone. Familiar Halla joggled the kittens like babies until they mewled and twisted and had to be set down.

I knew I was wide-eyed; I looked away until I could control my face. It was some trick of the light, surely, after the cavelike darkness of the house. When I looked back at Halla, I saw nothing but a simple old Norsewoman, lonely for company. I wondered if I had seen something not meant for me at all—had seen with Alpia's eyes indeed.

"So what do you think of my kits? Do you think your mother would want one?"

Halla waited on my answer.

I could only nod.

"Good." She walked out of the byre; I trotted after her. "When the kits are off the suck then you may take one. They are a fine thing to have about the house, for killing mice and other vermin."

The woman in the byre, that could not have been Halla.

I was still trembling with the strangeness of that moment as we re-entered the dark closure of the longhouse. Halla gave me milk from a stone jar and a flatbread to munch, meaning that she expected me to stay and talk. Listen, actually. I settled back on the bench, and drank and ate while Halla worked.

"After Farulf returned north, we married and then we left. Left good timber houses, and streets well paved with logs, and thralls enough even if they were Finns and stupid as mud."

"Why did you leave?"

"Our people were not pleased with Jarl Haakon, nor he with us. And too, there were many families and many children. You must plow sea when there is not an alen's length," and she held out her arm and chopped across it between elbow and shoulder, "of land worth turning. We might have gone to Hedeby, or Holmgard, and been rich. Or to Dublin, or west over ocean to the new lands. But we had to stay with his cousin Bjorn, like or no, because of the Following Woman."

I tried to swallow the dry mouthful so that I could ask what that meant, but it wasn't necessary.

"She had been his father's guardian, following him over land and over water. A giant-woman with a grim iron helm, and her hair where it flowed out beneath was white on one side, golden on the other. Farulf inherited her from his father. She told his future and said he must stay with Bjorn until Bjorn went under earth on a far shore."

Halla inclined her head toward the place where the ship mounds were.

"We stopped at Sumburgh, but the Following Woman said we should not stay. Bjorn at first would not listen. She appeared to him, and with her great spear killed a bear—his namesake, you see—tipped it up like a mead horn and drank its blood. Our ships put out at the next day's tide for Orkney. There it seemed, for a time, that we might stay. We lingered at the Isle of Priests for three seasons. Our cattle were heavy and the calves went by twos behind every cow, and the fleeces lay thick on the sheep."

I recalled what I had been told of Orkney, its rich grazing lands, and the Building People who had left behind the ancient holiness of the Ring and the Marker stones. Soon I would see them myself.

"A curse came over Farulf at that place, that he should not be touched by light of moon while lying in his own bed. He shuttered the windows of our house and made the door small and narrow, and even the smoke hole in the roof he cunningly fitted with an iron cap so that the moon might not look upon him." So that was the reason for the strange thing on the roof. It let out some of the smoke, but more of it puddled under the thatch than was normal. No wonder the widow's house was such a close, rank den.

"I told him that since the Following Woman did not protect him from this curse, then her power over him was gone." Halla clucked and shook her head. "But Bjorn insisted we must go, and go we did. I called it mere wanderlust, that he wanted to fly over water again."

"And then you came here?"

"We came to this place, and not a day after we dropped sail and beached our knarr on this shore, Bjorn lay down and died. That was the end of the wandering, for Farulf at least. But Grani at my breast had suckled the sea air. He followed the swan's path but did not return. Nor did Angantyr."

"You had two sons?"

"Three. One died when he was just walking. We lost also twin daughters at birth. But two fine, grown sons. Vaud daudr i grikkium," she murmured. "He died among the Greeks. I had that carved into a stone for Grani and set up beside the beach where we landed. For his brother, the same. In a storm the stones went into the sea, perhaps to the Following Woman. Much good may they do her in place of a Farulfsson to watch and ward."

There was little bitterness in Halla's words. The loss of her sons was something fated, as much as Farulf's death, as much as her eventual own. I looked around the dim space, thought of it filled with children, Farulf in his seat and the fire flaring out of the hearth and coloring the plain pillars with orange light. Now there was this frugal darkness.

"Why didn't you return to Norway?" I asked softly. "To your people?"

"What waited for me there?" she answered gruffly. "Here I have a house of my own, you see, and friends of long standing."

"But you have no man here."

Halla laughed then, deep and long. She rocked back on her heavy haunches and laughed.

"If I had wanted a man, I might have taken Farulf's apprentice Egill into my bed. He would have had me, old or not, for the wealth of Farulf's smithy. But why should I let a youth, scanty-bearded, tell me what to cook and how to do all the rest of my days?"

Halla laid her shuttles out, considering each one as a man might consider the heft and edge of his blades.

"Farulf used to stand and call across the valleys, to hear the dwarf-voices mimic him. It was a hollow sound, their returning call from out of the earth. When young Egill Haraldsson asked if we might marry, I went to the ship-mounds and I shouted into the earth, but Farulf did not answer nor any other. And so I did as I wished, and gave Egill the tools. Shears and tongs, files and chisels, hammers and planishing hammers. All, all that wealth."

I had passed the forge, nearly at the opposite end of the muddy path. The former apprentice, himself gone gray at the temples, had been stoking up a pit to make charcoal when I went by.

"Sometimes I go to watch him," Halla admitted. "I miss the smoke and the sparks flying from red iron. Watching his shoulders, and his strong arms, sometimes I can believe that it is Farulf come back to work at his own anvil."

I stirred on the bench, restless. I understood less and less of this woman, who had loved a man but did not need one, who had been wealthy but took poverty like a nun—who was not bound to anyone or anything. She had followed her man's vagaries all up and down the sea, but after him had not been willing to follow anyone. *That is how I will be,* I decided. *I will belong to no one but myself; I will be strong as Halla. Or Alpia. Even if it means being poor.* My thoughts lingered on that. I would not be poor, of course.

I stood and shook out my mantle. "I must go, or Alpia will be troubled." My foster-mother had laughed less and frowned more since the death of her daughter.

"Tell her you allowed a foolish old woman to remember, and she will not be angry with you," Halla said, but her smile was hardly foolish.

I yawned. I felt tired as if I had worked all morning, and I still had my lore-verses to tell over.

"And the kits…"

There was a sudden shriek outside the door, pounding footsteps.

"Mother!" Ingigerd darted into the house. "Estrid made me carry more than my share, and she so much bigger!" Estrid followed, smiling at the tale. She carried a skin filled to tautness and a large cheese. Her younger sister carried only a cheese, swinging the cloth bag in which it had drained, dried, and cured.

"We have had such milkings," Estrid sighed. "The grass is good, and the does and ewes are making almost more milk than we can manage."

"I can manage," Ingigerd boasted. "I have no trouble with cheese-making." Then she poked her sister in the ribs, and we heard that shriek again.

I was reluctant, now, to go, when her girls were there, laughing and teasing. I was warmed by the company of these women, who liked to talk of simple things, when at home I was surrounded by men and closely disciplined by Alpia's flashing intelligence. I shrugged my shoulders, moved irresolutely toward the door.

"Stay," Estrid said.

"Yes, you must stay. We have news," added Ingigerd.

That made me stop.

"A wanderer came yesterday…"

"…and be sure we watched the flocks closely then," said the younger sister, her thin dark face suspicious.

"He took nothing but a sup of fresh milk and did not ask even for that," Estrid corrected, folding her arms across her matronly breasts. "But he said he had news out of the Anglish lands, that an archbishop had been martyred this spring, by the Danes."

"He would not give them money for ransom, and so they pelted him to death with cattle-heads and leg bones."

"And one called Thorkell the Tall, he tried to save the priest but could not."

"Thorkell," said Halla in a musing voice. "He is of the strong-hold at Jomsberg and no priest's-man."

"You know him?"

"Only what all know, that he is a great warrior and much loved of Svein Forkbeard. He fosters his son Cnut."

"Was it a good thing he did, trying to save an innocent?" I asked.

"A foolish thing."

"The wanderer said that the Anglish and the Danes will fight now, and that the Anglish will win." Ingigerd frowned as she told this.

"It is not the first foolishness of drunken men, or even sober ones," said Halla, sitting down heavily on one of the benches. "Perhaps these Danes remembered St. Brice's Day ten years gone, when Aethelred—a fool beneath a crown—ordered the murder of all Danes. Few of the Angles listened, for these were their neighbors and wives, but at Oxford many Danes were burned alive inside the church where they sought God's refuge."

"Oh," I breathed, feeling flames licking my own skin. The sisters shuddered in unison.

"Men's affairs are full of violence, always, and the worse because they boast to control their own fate," Halla said. She stirred the fire with a length of twisted iron and stared into the glowing coals brought up out of the ash. "The weaving-women sit at the loom of events, and their warp is made of warrior's entrails," she said, slowly. "Their shuttles are arrows pointed and barbed, and their weaving is black and red and flashed with fire as the shuttle goes back and forth, back and forth. They sing the names of the brave they have selected to die in battle."

The house was silent, dark and smoky. The oil lamps flickered in some small breeze.

"Twelve battle-women ride horses of thunder and shake their gray spears, slashing the sky until blood falls like rain. They feed the Wolf

who is never sated. Their names are Battle and Staff-carrier, Brandish-
er, Spear-goddess and High-towering, War Fetter that binds a doomed
man's limbs so that he may be struck down."

I was chilled and enthralled, and saw that the sisters were no less so.
These goddesses that Halla chanted were not Alpia's solemn Goddess,
who had been honored with blood in ancient times and distant sun-
drenched lands, but whose followers had established a purified rite in
the north. These battle-women were wild as wind on sea.

"Tell us about the cloud of ravens," Estrid urged. "Tell us about the
ravens you saw when you were a girl."

Her daughter's voice seemed to call Halla back from a far place. She
set down the iron poker, which she had held tightly during her chant.

"Enough of blood," she said firmly. "To talk of it merely invites the
letting of it."

"Was this made by Farulf?" I asked, touching the worked iron, hoping to turn the widow back to happier memories.

Halla bit her lip and nodded.

"He had iron-luck. And perhaps woman-luck, that I cannot say. He
was never so good with weapons as with implements, axes and billhooks. Farulf had fine light hair, like Estrid's—she will remember, how
vain he was of his hair, and how I used to comb it." Her voice was filled
with affection and some puzzlement. "I would use a bone comb set
with red stones that he gave me. My hair was never half so beautiful.
The comb was carved with ram's heads, their eyes red-glowing and the
tips of their curling horns. I gave it back to him for the next life, ashes
with ashes."

I felt grieved that I had not known Farulf.

"I hope that we marry men as good and as handsome and as strong,"
said Ingigerd.

"I know a way to see them," I said timidly.

"You do?" the sisters chorused.

I looked to Halla. The widow smiled indulgently. "Go ahead, go
ahead."

I blushed, now that I had brought this about. "The servant taught
me this. It is nothing holy as Alpia's work." I was half frightened at
this poor little ritual and doubted that I would ever have the courage to
handle the withes and waters of true knowledge. "But we need meadowsweet—perhaps there is none here."

"We can get some at the damp place in the meadow," said Ingigerd, half doubtful, half urgent.

"Oh, surely 'tis good enough to use the dried." Halla fumbled among bundled herbs, dusty and scattered on their shelf (what Alpia would think!) and lifted out some half-bare sprigs tied with a thread. It was meadowsweet—that could be seen from the square stem and the small white flowers that had mostly shattered and dropped.

"Then I need some of your hair," I said, gaining confidence.

I pulled out strands of my own light-brown hair and tied them around one twig. I did the same with the sisters', dark and blond, and returned a charm to each.

"Meadowsweet was given scent by Pretty Aine, who lights each summer the fruitful fires," I said slowly, not sure if this was exactly what Murie had said that night when Alpia was out under the moon and not there to scoff.

I held up my own charm, because Alpia always raised the elements of her worship, and then tossed it on the coals.

"The face of the man who'll marry me, marry me, marry me—come to the fire, that I might see."

The sisters did the same.

The charms caught and burned, a scent acrid and fragrant at once. I stared into the small flames that flickered out of the embers and disappeared as quickly. There was nothing to be seen but coals, and licking flames, and the widow's face on the other side of the hearth. How long must I continue this? I felt the color rise in my cheeks at the failure of my boast.

There was a brief sizzle as the heat claimed the last bit of my hair, trailing untidy from the knot. I started to turn away.

The air abruptly thickened above the hearth. It roiled like river-water when the tide rushes against its flow. A man's face appeared. He seemed to be searching, looking out of the fire, looking for someone. His eyes were sad and deep as a child's, yet marked with age or grief, and full of a hunger that was not of the flesh. I leaned forward. Flames licked around his face, sparked red in his hair that hung wet and uncombed. He was dressed in mail and a padded tunic and dark braught, plain gear, but the double-linked silver chain that signified a mormaer's rank draped heavily on his shoulders. The flames rose, came in front of the face like a curtain. When they fell, he was gone.

I leaned on my hand. My heart pounded. I was filled with expectation and shaken by a feeling of doom.

Fire brought him, fire took him away.

"I saw a man with a great red beard," Ingigerd announced. "He was a jarl's son, with a fine ship."

"Mine was a merchant," Estrid said, and her sister pulled a face. "He was very rich, so rich that there were different servants for every day of the week."

"Did you see someone?"

I began to answer, but could not put the vision into words. "No," I said. "Nothing but the fire."

The girls looked at me curiously, then at the hearth. The coals remained subdued as before. They had seen nothing, I knew then. Nothing at all.

❧

SUTHERLAND, 1011

A man came breathless and sweating to the door. "The White Lady" was all he would say, or needed to. Alpia was afield, gathering, but I was home, laying out herbs to dry.

"What is the matter?"

"My brother has the gravel, which pains him by spells, but now it has seized him and he lies on the ground and cannot stand. He was working on the stone church and the priest is with him now."

I went and found Alpia, who said, "Brew horsetail and dandelion," and sent me off with a wave of her hand, *Go, go ahead.* I ran, mentally sorting through the medicinals—*horsetail, gathered from the boggy places, dried, stored on the high shelf farthest left.*

When we left the hall, we carried the tea, an infusion of wild garlic, and a bottle of hot oil heavily wrapped. We found the stonecutter crumpled by his carving, helpless and moaning, the priest kneeling beside him. Holy water marked his knotted forehead and a crucifix was clutched in his dusty hand. The priest, having given what comfort he could, gave way to Alpia without a word, taking himself out of the hot sun and back into the gloom of the slumping wooden chapel soon to be replaced.

I had accompanied Alpia on visits to colicky children and mothers whose milk would not come, domestic visits, but this was a grown man who curled around his pain. Alpia spoke low in his ear and the man allowed her to pull down his trews.

"You must look for swelling, discoloration, or fever in the flesh, to see if it is stone in the bladder or some other cause." Alpia put two fingers against his groin, just above his manhood. The stonecutter wept like a child. "The oil, quickly. On the cloth." I spilled hot oil into the cloth, and Alpia pressed it to the man's body. He sighed, eased by the warmth.

Alpia got him to sit up and gave him the garlic infusion, followed by the tea.

"The stones passed before," he said faintly.

"They will pass this time as well." Alpia held her hand to me. "Help me, now."

My thoughts ran like mice from a stook of grain. I had never been allowed to participate in a healing. But Alpia lifted away the cloth and pressed her hand directly against the man's body, then placed my hand on hers. She began to chant, and I recognized a lore-song I had been required to learn.

> "Water flow, water run, water take its course.
> Down from the hilltops to the sea,
> down through the body's land,
> passing freely, passing freely on.
> Remove all impediment,
> break the dams, roll the stones,
> unblock the natural ways,
> water flow, water run, water take its course."

I chanted with her, tentatively at first, then more strongly. I felt Alpia's hand grow warm against mine, felt my own fill with heat like a rock in the sun. Was it only our heartbeats that pulsed in our palms? Where did this heat come from? We chanted and the heat grew, spread, and I could see the man's face begin to unclench. A final burst of heat, almost too much to bear, and Alpia released and sat back. I turned over my palm, not sure what I expected to see there.

The man rolled to his knees, got up, though he was still hunched over, and then I heard urine splashing with stops and starts and many groans.

"You have been sweating at your work, without enough water,"

Alpia said. The man nodded. "You have had gravel in the past, your brother tells me. So your body is making these stones, and when you do not give it enough water, the flesh dries up and the stones are clenched in the tubes."

Perhaps it made no more sense to him than the priest's prayers.

Alpia turned to me. "What should he do to avoid the stones returning?"

I tamped down my scurrying thoughts. "Drink much water. And drink barley water as well. When you feel the gravel building, use rainwater to brew horsetail and dandelion." Was there more? I glanced at Alpia and saw a tight smile of approval.

The man seemed suddenly to realize he was naked before his clanlord's wife and fosterling, and he pulled his clothing together. "There was blood," he said.

"I would think so. You have passed the stone. If your urine does not run clear by the next sun, then let your brother come again. We will return if you need us, but you will not need."

Need us, I repeated in my thoughts. *Need us, not need me.* I felt that the warmth of the healing had passed into me as well, dislodging some barrier in my heart. I looked at Alpia with admiration. No longer the whining complaints of the little child who first came to her, or the fear of a student who is lagging at her lessons. *I am worthy of Alpia's teaching. Someday I can be the White Lady.*

ॐ

SUTHERLAND, 1012

It was pleasant riding along the shore, on this warm day when there was wind enough to keep off most of the biting flies and midges, but not so much to lift up loose sand into a stinging cloud. The sky had cleared, though a line of darkness on the western horizon threatened more rain.

"The people will be watching that storm, gauging the harvest to be fine or evilly wet," said Talorc, indicating the cloud bank.

Alpia nodded. "The weather sets its pattern now."

My hands lay easy on the reins. The horses seemed to follow their own paths, which braided across and into other ones trodden in wetter times or in winter.

Already there were signs of the hamlet ahead, hidden past the point. A three-bench boat plied across the glittering estuary. The track underfoot widened steadily. Where we splashed through a marshy stream, stumps fingered from the stout trunks of willows where withes had repeatedly been harvested. Now and again came the scent of smoke.

Bees made their roads on the sky, absolutely straight between flowers and hive. "Worthy birds," I had heard a preacher call them, though from Alpia I knew their true nature, near to flies and wasps.

This had been a golden summer and promised a peaceful fall. There was no war for which Talorc was liable to be summoned, nor Ciniod, now a man grown. Travelers brought word that the ever-wavering Aethelred had decided to flee, leaving his land and people to Svein Forkbeard, but that meant no trouble for Sigurd of Orkney. For Malcolm, the Danish king's accession might bring opportunity. Talorc said the the Ard Ri Alban was waiting. Perhaps next year he would harry the borders of a disordered English realm. Then the men of Alba would be called to bring horses and spears, their sons and swords, and men from the farms and boatmen from the coast. They would be rewarded for blood with silver, with cattle and horses from Northumbrian farms or house goods from Durham halls. And should Malcolm instead turn his attention north? Loyalties were difficult things, in distant places. Talorc bowed to Birsay, not Scoine. He had no love for the Ard Ri Alban; still, he was bonded by friendship to Moray that was Alba's ally, and by blood to many in both realms, including Boidh my father.

In absence of war, the fine eastern weather was spent in hunting and gaming and music-making as we made the regular circuit of Talorc's lands, accepting the hospitality of his holders in their homes. A portion of all the land's produce was his. In return, Talorc heard disputes, set boundaries, confirmed heirs, dispensed justice on thieves and housebreakers, honored his supporters with gifts—lengths of fine cloth, silver and bronze bracelets, a duck-hawk for Sythak, a gold-ornamented dagger for Ulf who held the Whitewolf lands. (These were quite simple compared with the gifts our father had given and received, or so Nechtan recalled for me.) Talorc's household was small, fitting the thinly populated nature of this region. There were few servants, and scarcely need even for sharp-eyed Gestgurcich, rechtaire over his hall and people when Talorc traveled or was called to war.

Talorc and Alpia rode side by side, on the roan horses they favored, birthed at a single foaling. Talorc watched (without seeming to do so) the woods and dark stream-beds where ring ouzels whistled. At his right,

Alpia sat very erect, white hair shining at the edges of her scarf, mantle folded back, her comb-bag hanging at her belt. Her eyes were bright, noting each flowering bush and weathered rock. The sorrow which had lain across her for so long after Derelei's death had lifted. It seemed that no shadow had ever darkened her thoughts except at infrequent times there came a haziness in her eyes and a distance in her voice. Nechtan rode a small black horse with a white blaze while I had my short-legged sorrel pony. Fode had mounted Dubh, a once-unmanageable colt that had been gelded. It was heavy through the neck and powerful; he prided himself in ruling it. Two of Talorc's men, veteran campaigners, rode strong horses like those that hauled our bedding, clothing, hunting-gear and gifts—as well as the necessary luxuries of spices for cookery, and oils and scents for grooming. Murie was among the servants, flushed with the excitement of seeing young men.

Fode cried out and slapped at his neck where a flesh-fly had bitten. His horse whickered and tended down toward the water, avoiding the pests. Nechtan turned his mount to stay beside his brother.

Ciniod was no longer with us. He carried payment to a weapon smith at Thingvollr, then would ride back around by the Black Isle (visiting with a holder who was a friend to Talorc) and to Rosemarkie, delivering a message to the bishop there. "I am my father's best messenger," Ciniod had declared, laughing. He pretended to mutter over a simple message, counting letters on the joints of his fingers like the poets of old, turning it inside out.

Yesterday morning, we had ridden close together and spoken in low voices. Sleep was still on us then and tucked into the shadows of the trees. We sang songs as the light gained, until at last a song of parting. Ciniod smiled with the joy of venturing out. His teeth were even and white, his form slender, and his lips as red as if he tinted them. Sometimes I thought he was the most handsome man in the world (for all his early-thinning hair) but he was after all my brother. Then he sang the final verse again, loudly, and urging his horse to a gallop, was gone. We were subdued by his parting. Finally, Nechtan had plunged his horse into one of the shore-running flocks of birds to make them lift in a great wave. It had made us all laugh to see the birds rise, a plainting storm, to settle ahead and be flushed again and again.

"There have been fish-traps here as long as there have been people on this land," Alpia said. I reined my attention round. It was my foster-mother's teaching voice, conversational but somehow commanding. "Salmon and finnock come into this river in great numbers. They can be caught with nets set up in the mouth or cast from boats, or taken with lines and hooks. Higher in the river, wicker baskets are set in the channels. Spears are used at shallows. The places are marked." A cormorant broke the uneasy surface of the bay, then dived and disappeared.

I wondered if symbol-stones marked the fishing places. We had passed a slab at evening, set up near a cairn encircled by stones deep-sunk and mossy. Symbols of mirror and comb, sea beast, crescent, were incised in simple lines—honors to the Goddess, and a record of the woman whose family-land this had been. A series of ogham letters had been roughly cut along one side. Alpia said, with down-turned mouth, that they had been made later, by wandering poets out of Dál Riata. A strange wisdom, or stranger foolishness, I could not decide, that like our teachers, the Building People, we would not commit sacred matters to secular letters. So generation by generation our history had been passed voice to voice, and in the tangles of migration and war had been twisted, compressed, disputed, lost with this death, with that accident. Even within our own lands we had become known as Picts, that Roman epithet, and had struggled with the Scots pushing east from Dál Riata. Those who would not be quelled by blade or marriage-bond had moved further east and then further north. Our language was unheard but for the words that lingered in the names of places and people. This late-coming tribe had covered us like snow, sifting steadily, obscuring all. As we had, long ago, overwhelmed the ancient race of Builders.

"Salmon come up the river at all times, in greater or lesser numbers. The larger fish come later, stay lower, closer to the sea," Alpia said.

I nodded, heeled my sorrel forward to stay even with Alpia, who had outdistanced the men and showed no sign of dropping back.

"The salmon is the fish most honored of the Lady." Now I knew why we had drawn apart. "It communicates between sea and land, swimming far into the heads of the streams, exhausting itself in this effort to spawn, then falling back to the sea carrying the land's word in its flesh."

That was all. Alpia reined in, and soon the rest closed around us. She spoke for a little while more about herring and their arrival in the bays. We rode past the remains of an earthwork that had commanded the estuary, its mounded walls now tree-grown and collapsed on one side. The hamlet was barely hidden by the swell of the land, but a cloud of gulls could be seen, wheeling to mark the place. Their harsh cries echoed.

"I'll be glad of a halt," Alpia said, so low that only I could hear. Her erect stance was an effort of will. Her shoulders sagged, just a little, and her hands clenched the reins.

"Are you ill?"

Alpia did not make any sign, yes or no.

I brought my horse close alongside, and prepared to steady Alpia in the saddle if needed. Alpia smiled at my concern, a brief tight smile, and shook her head. I moved away, though not too far. Next summer we were to go to Orkney. There I would learn the rest of the mysteries. There I would "come up to the light."

What if Alpia were to become sick? What if she should die?

I savored that, a bitter berry on my tongue, until I could not stand the taste. Once I had longed to return to the lands beyond the Mounth, pined for my mother and father and a gentler way of life. Now I wavered between desire and fear.

The cluster of houses at this place tilted down to the shore as though sliding season by season into the bay. They were made of cut turf and wood and wattle, thatched with reeds rather than straw or heather, and on a shelf of rock above the tide-line was an empty cot for the boat that was out on the bay, its crew working with a net. The shore was littered with barbed spears, lead weights, cordage, baskets. Behind the houses were the fields, small and crooked, bending around rocks and areas of poor soil, but the grain on them was thick.

The entire people seemed to be on the beach. Wooden frames ran haphazardly, leaning this way and that with their burden of drying salmon. Barrels stood empty and full, as well as panniers of salt from Talorc's saltworks. Children ran around with long poles to drive away dogs and the black plundering birds.

A heavy-bearded fisherman came running.

"This is not Lutrin," Fode said.

Before he could respond, the man was standing at their stirrups, red with exertion.

"Welcome," he panted. "We are near end of the fishing."

"Lutrin—where is he?" Talorc sternly echoed his son. "I do not know you."

"Lutrin died on St. Peter's Day. He broke his arm and a poison in the blood took him. I am called Cairpre of the Long Valley. I married Lutrin's daughter."

Talorc nodded with memory. "He paid the marriage fee in sealskins. Yes."

"Dunegal is in the boat. I greet you in his place. He is the headman chosen among us, if you will."

Talorc swung down, followed by the boys, then me. I caught Nechtan's eye and he came over to offer a steady shoulder for Alpia to grasp.

Murie and the men laid out tanned hides, blankets and pillows, but did not stretch the tents used in unpeopled places. There was time enough by sundown to reach the usual stop at a snug house beside falling water.

Alpia lay down and quickly dozed, her scarf pulled across her eyes. Too restless to sit, I walked and saw an answering restlessness among the people. They shouted, ran when walking would serve. The rough sealskin shoes they wore—pampooties, the Norse called them—made broad scuffling tracks in the sand. I myself had worn them, laced front and back, hair outside. As long as they remained wet they were soft and wearable. They were good on wet rocks and did not damage the hide hulls of currachs. Such caution was not needed in the sturdy boats at Golspie, built in the Norse manner with riveted strakes.

A pile of stones, a huge cairn—no, a hermit's beehive cell—could be seen at the edge of the woods. I went to see what sort of man lived in that darkness, but his grave-like room was empty, abandoned. When I came back to the center of the village, Talorc was talking with Cairpre about the loss of a quarter-davach of cropland to the stream's new channel. He looked out frequently to the bay, as if to gauge how long it would take the boat to arrive. It came slowly, three men laboring at the oars while two managed the net; the boat heeled over against a great weight of fish.

I sat beside the sleeping Alpia. Murie had disappeared, but a girl brought me a cup of elder wine, which was a fine change from ale. The girl was well built and had good skin. Sometimes people inland had skin diseases or swollen throats, but places along the northeastern shore (especially in Moray) were reputed to be healthful. I sipped the wine and watched a pair of sea eagles floating overhead, each a dark cross of wings and body, a white wedge of tail outlined against a clear sky. Their beaks were heavy, knife-sharp. Watching them soar on the ocean breeze, effortless, their wings like sails, I thought them the Lochlannaig of the air. One rose above the other, towering on the ocean breeze, higher, higher, higher. It paused.

And fell.

I wanted someone to see, to witness. Alpia, but she was curled asleep. No one nearby. All were on the shore, encouraging the men in the boat. The sea eagle plummeted, talons out. I felt my heart pound, my breath quicken. It dived as though intending to kill the other. At the last second the other bird turned on its back and they locked talons. The great birds cartwheeled, turning over and over, falling toward me on useless wings. I threw an arm across my face, sure that I would be struck, but the birds separated just above the ground. Their pinions flared as they recovered and flapped heavily to regain soaring height. A shiver of joy and pain ran through me, until I closed my eyes against it and felt my body taut with the pleasure of this secret. Intolerable, wonderful.

I put my hand on my mother's wrist, felt the pulse beating deep and sure. Alpia did not wake. The long ride and unbroken sun had made her faint, nothing more than that. I stood, pleasantly languid with the aftereffect of the eagles' plunge but still restless, and wandered down to the beach where all had gathered except for Talorc and Cairpre, still deep in discussion. The people cheered their men as the boat came on. The net sagged with the mass of fish, but the men with red faces and taut mouths showed no willingness to release even one of this catch.

All around me, chatter about the fishing and the end of fishing, the likelihood of a dry grain harvest. Most of all, they talked about the fire-feast of Lugh Nasadh and the horse races and contests held then.

"There is a fine horse from Rowanhill that will take all around."

"Last year's horse is swinneyed, the loss."

"The Rowanhill horse will win the races."

"Who will take the wrestling? Eimin has broken an arm."

"He'll not cheat, then."

Rough laughter, and side-eyed jokes about marriages of a year and a day "if they might last so long as that."

"Come up there, come up, or the salmon will escape!" The urgency broke into their chatter and sent them down to the edge of the water.

"D'you see the size of the fish!"

"It's the like of Our Lord's netting," a boy said fervently, with a glance toward the empty cell.

I was amazed at the beauty and terror of the great salmon. Tails thrashed and jaws with strong teeth closed on air. Silver bodies spotted black quivered against the knotted net. Farther out in the bay, seals twisted and dived, while the black backs of killer whales arced in groups as they harried the migrating fish.

"Such a run," a woman whispered, as though fearing to make them vanish. "Never have I seen such a run of summer salmon."

The whooping became more urgent. I looked up to see that the boat had veered from its regular beaching place, pulled by current or weight, and had grounded on a muddy bar just off shore. As it tipped, the net slackened and the fish, sensing their freedom, began to leap.

"The net!"

One man vaulted over the side, staggering as he set his weight to keep the fish in the net.

Old men with ragged beards and weather-darkened arms, strong women with their braids flying, crowded forward to snatch at lines and the thick top edge of the net, slipping and falling in the soft footing. A great fish thrust itself against the others, up and out, slithering toward the bay. A woman dived after it, caught its tail, was shaken loose like a small dog.

A cord snapped, another, angry sounds like a wasp rushing past.

"Take in the gap!"

I saw a salmon work into the hole, thrusting its hooked jaw back and forth. A cord frayed; knots slipped. I splashed into the water and grasped the net with the others, shoving the fish back with my shoulder. Someone moved in beside me. Nechtan. I staggered with a wave that pushed the whole mass toward land. My shoes were gone, sucked deep into the miry sand.

We dragged the damaged net onto the beach, but pebbles caught and held us back. Then Fode was there. Holding the net, holding each other, we made a final lunge over the tide-mark and into the low place on the other side.

Salmon poured out. Flopping silver, smelling of the deep sea and its secrets. I felt one slide across my legs and cried out at the strength of it, the cold sleek clench of muscle. What joy, to go on the water and bring beautiful fish out of it!

Nechtan helped me up, and we embraced, laughing, covered with slime and blood and sand.

"A maiden of the sea," one of the villagers said.

Suddenly self-conscious, I stepped behind my brother. I ran my hands down soaked clothing that clung to my skin. My hair lay flat against my skull and my scarf was gone, my throat bare. Blood oozed from a tooth-raked place on my arm.

"The young lady, to go into the water for our fish," the first man marveled—a grizzled, stout man from the boat, Dunegal from the way he made quick orders assigning the women to run for their knives and the men to break the spines of the gasping salmon before they could thrash their way back to the sea. I felt my face go red at his attention, and at my blush he turned away, as though mistaken in his meaning.

I felt a blanket draped over my shoulders. Alpia. I pulled it around me, feeling the salt and slime drying on my skin.

"I wanted to help," I said to her, very low.

Dunegal nodded—he had heard—and Alpia whispered in my ear, "That's the mark of true nobility, to forget yourself in love for your people." Those words left me more confused than ever. I had not loved the people but had been drawn by the power of the salmon.

Dunegal turned to the call of another of the boatmen, who had picked out a beautiful fat fish, and together they carried the salmon to where Talorc stood.

"A tithe of your share," Dunegal said. "For this evening's meal at the Riverstep hall."

"I thank you," Talorc said, and ceremoniously touched the salmon, still quivering with its last reflexes. The men took it away to wrap it in wet seaweed and lapping cloth.

Dunegal was looking over my shoulder at something. "Have you been parted from a member of your company?" he asked.

I thought perhaps Cinoid had returned, but a lone stranger approached along our track, on an exhausted horse that he urged to a stiff trot. The fisher-folk moved back, and Talorc settled his hand casually closer to his sword. Without a word, Cairpre was at his side, and Fode and Nechtan fell into place a step behind.

"He is no local man," said Alpia, and I agreed without being able to say why. There was something odd about the cut of his garments, something troubled in his face.

"I seek Talorc of Golspie," he called out, pulling up at the defensive appearance of the group. A jacket armored with leather showed beneath the weather-stained folds of his checked braught.

"Who asks for me?"

The messenger swung down, stumbling as his foot hit the ground. He was as worn as his mount, mud-splattered, uncombed, and a definite stink of sheep-fells came from his clothing. The people were silent at this apparition.

"I bring a message from Ferchar, who was the right hand of Boidh, to Talorc his kinsman."

"Was?" Talorc challenged.

The messenger paused, closed his eyes as though to gather up some string of words. "Boidh is dead, and peace be on his soul."

I saw Alpia glance at me, prepared for some outcry, but I said nothing. Could say nothing. Cold had taken me, frozen my body.

"How did my father die?" challenged Nechtan, fire to my ice.

Talorc motioned quiet, but the messenger looked at him as though for the first time.

"You would be Nechtan mac Boidh." His tone was level but his eyes said all. The tanist's son, of royal lineage, wet and scale-smeared and filthy as any child born of the soil.

"I am." Nechtan's angry pride made the messenger look down.

"Boidh was killed during an argument, some private disagreement that ended with knives pulled."

"The man?" My brother's voice was hard as a seasoned warrior's, though tears went steadily down his red cheeks.

"He comes of a small people close to Strathclyde, Ennae by name. Boidh's party fell on him and would have taken his life, but the Ard Ri Alban raised his hand and ordered him executed, for the fight occurred at his board. The man was dragged to the nearest water and roused to confess, but could no longer speak. He was drowned, a summary execution. Both men were declared forfeit, for the insult to the king."

"Forfeit?" Talorc frowned. "What had Boidh's people to say of this?"

The messenger made a strange, abortive motion with his hand. "There are mutterings all around, though they are quiet mutterings. The lawgiver said at first that cro must be paid by Ennae's folk but soon found his memory of the law was in error. A brave one or two of Ennae's party protested the king's action, for he had Ennae's head displayed as a traitor. His wife and children have disappeared, some say sold to a Flemish trader, into slavery, while others claim they have been spirited away to Angle-land with silver to quiet their wailing. Malcolm claims the attack was against his own person and gives no ground."

"Where did this happen, and when?" Talorc asked almost absently. He seemed to be concentrating on something else.

"King's Seat near Dunkeld. Nearly a moon, as of this nightfall."

"Why so long! Why did you delay!" Nechtan shouted. "You might have come and gone back again in that long a time!"

"I have come as fast as a lone messenger not bearing Malcolm's mark nor given his horses might come," he said quietly. "The weather has been foul to the south. Streams were swollen too high to ford. I lost a good horse in this journey and came across water to Portmahomack in a boat bearing lamb-hides to the monks. This horse I borrowed on your name, Talorc, or would have been walking yet."

With that, he handed the reins of his lathered animal to Talorc's man, and stood as though awaiting judgment.

"I do not fault you," Talorc said. "I am sure you met with obstacles more than you've said." The man's eyes narrowed but he said nothing.

"What of Lonceta?" Alpia's voice was startling in its softness.

"It is said that she wrapped herself in her husband's slashed garments," he said slowly, "and that she had herself walled into a cell at St. Brigid's foundation at Abernethy."

"She took anchorite's vows willingly?" Alpia asked, outrage in her voice.

The messenger, uneasy, said nothing. Alpia nodded understanding.

A long silence in which every wave crashed too loudly on the shore, and the seal-barks and gull-cries were harsh.

"And Boidh's children?" asked Talorc. "What of Nechtan and Gruach?"

"His titles and lands—you understand, Talorc, what Malcolm has done. All forfeit. As to his children, there were no instructions."

No instructions. The ice that held me together shattered, and I drew in a long shuddering breath. Alpia put an arm around me and I shrank away.

Talorc said something—what? His words were meaningless. He gripped me firmly by the shoulders and his touch made me keen like one of the wild spirits of the mountains.

"This is not seemly," he growled. His hands were angry against my skin.

I wrestled free of him and ran. Wet linen slapped at my legs, tangled, pulled. I ran away from the widening of the water, the cool silver spread of the river-mouth and beyond, the blue endless line of the ocean. I ran until the houses were behind me, the stink and sounds of people.

The land rose, a green slope to tree shade. I climbed heavily, leaning my hands on my thighs as I paused for breath. I crossed the overgrown wall of the old fortification and sat down on a pile of stones under a tree.

I caught my breath. My vision cleared.

Now I was ashamed of fleeing Talorc—ashamed for fleeing his man's touch. His anger had not been directed at me. Nor was my fear of him. I stared at the gleaming water, the sun flaring off the swells. Perhaps the tears would come. Tears that would wash grief into my soul in place of the lingering night-terror that gnawed there.

The dream had come at the last full moon.

In my dream, which had felt like waking, I rose from my bed. All the others breathed deeply, asleep on their beds soft with fern. I treaded lightly and they did not wake.

I went to the door and sat on the stone stoop, under the calm light. There was no sound in the world. I touched two fingers to my sex and held them up to the moon. A mark showed on them, more black than red. I rejoiced at my new phase and smiled up at the moon in its fullness.

When I looked down, I saw a dark pool spreading between my feet.

The little mark had become a flood. My legs were dyed red, and my feet. I heard the sea pounding on the shore, louder and louder. A storm. A drumbeat. The pool rippled and began to flow around me, up the stone step, into the hall.

I followed. The room was dark but I could see everything—Alpia and Talorc, wrapped in each other's arms. Nechtan and Fode and Ciniod, their heads close together where they could whisper secrets and challenges. Murie curled alone, dreaming of men, and Talorc's retinue spread about. A visitor had been granted a space close to the fire.

The visitor lay on his back, with arms flung wide, and no blanket to cover his nakedness. Blood crawled through the dry rushes, rustling like wind. It crawled to the visitor. As I came closer, I saw that he had been wounded in many places—head and arms, a deep thrust into his chest.

The blood found its way into every wound, but he did not heal and did not wake. Suddenly I knew that the blood had first come from his wounds, and gone into me. I had woken, drenched in sweat.

I held my arms close around myself and rocked back and forth. A stone shifted with a grinding noise. I hadn't told Alpia about my dream. It was too frightening, too shameful. It had troubled me for days. A dream of foretelling and I had not acted. My father's death was linked to my womb.

"Sister." Nechtan stood beside me. He must have climbed the back side of the knoll. He did not touch me, did not try to hold me, but waited nervously like a hunter prepared for cornered prey to spring.

"I won't run."

He sat down and for a long time he said nothing. Then he bent forward to touch something on the ground, and I looked too. Blood on the grass... My breath caught in my throat.

"Your feet," he said, and stroked the side of my bare foot near a gash from a shell or sharp stone.

I looked at him, felt a blossoming awareness of pain. "What damage have you done yourself," he scolded, sliding down and lifting my bruised feet into his lap. "Run off like a silly babe, no shoes on your feet." He picked out a thorn, then took the hem of my garment and pressed it against the worst places.

"I didn't feel it."

Nechtan dabbed at the cuts. He could be quite gentle at such work. I had seen him once, binding up Fode's arm when their rough play ended in a real wound.

"Do you remember what our father looked like?" I asked, pushing back the night-fear.

"Not well."

I thought of the man I had seen long ago in the charm-fire. That had not been him, I was certain. There had been a feeling of a more distant future in that vision.

"Black hair, but fair skin. And blue eyes, I think, like yours," he said, looking up. "I have nothing of him about me."

"Why do you say that?" He shrugged and stared out toward the sea. "I cannot remember him at all. Not his voice, not his face." If I could only remember his face and know that the wounded visitor in my dreams had not been him. "I do remember his hands. They were very long. He used to play a game, of hiding his thumb." I glanced at Nechtan for confirmation. He remembered much more than I did. He nodded. Yes, that was how he had been. Boidh had played silly games with his children.

I tried to recall something else about him. I could not. My father had been always about men's business, fighting or attending the king. Even my mother's image, to which I had clung so tightly in that barren first year, seemed faint now, like a recollection of someone else's mother. I grasped at warm insubstantialities of voice and hair and scent. Dark eyes, brown hair darker than mine. It might be anyone's mother, soothing and patient. Daimhin. My mother had called me Daimhin, because from the time I could walk, I had run, darting around the house, the fields. The word fled into the forest.

"Talorc and Alpia are our only parents," Nechtan said. "Truly. We are without land or kin, thanks to a knife blade and Malcolm's dignity."

"Is that why we were sent away to fosterage, so that we might acquire an extra father and mother?" I had not meant to sound so bitter.

"I think that is part of it, yes."

The usual order of things, of course, was to send a child to a family of higher rank. Our fosterage here was exile, I thought, setting us a bit beyond Malcolm's reach. For how long? What had our parents intended? Surely not that we live forever in Sutherland, forgotten, unaware of the greater world except through traveler's reports and the occasional letter written out by a monk that Talorc read to me.

Alpia's words seemed a mockery now. Nobility. Royal blood, twice royal, blood of Dál Riata and of our people. Royal nothingness. Worse, endangered by that thin thread tied to the long ago.

"This was where the well was," Nechtan said. I looked at him, trying to catch his meaning. "These stones. When a stronghold is taken, and you cannot or will not hold it, then you destroy it. And you throw carcasses and trash and rock in the well so that it may not be reused." He kicked one of the mossy stones and it rolled unevenly, twice, and stopped. The underside was dull black from fire.

Talorc would have taught him that. His good-natured but insistent teachings became very serious, like my own instruction by Alpia. What I learned was how to keep the world intact, maintained in its course and in its proper seasons. What Nechtan learned was how to shatter its peace.

My brother was almost a man now. He had grown rapidly since last summer, and his muscles were hard. His face, no longer fat, was high-colored still under a thick mat of brown hair. Boidh's son, I thought, fatherless, and longed to put my arm around him. But the innocent joy of the fishing was gone forever, and I could scarcely bear the touch of his thigh against mine. I saw him lying in his blood, on a pavement of stones. I keened again.

"I thought you had ended that," he said crisply. I shook my head.

"What? Tell me."

I couldn't speak of that brief vision. As real as the face in the fire, as the naked visitor with his wounds.

"We must be leaving," he said. "There are decisions to be made."

I caught his arm as he started to rise. "Listen," I whispered, finding my voice. "I dreamed of blood—of a wounded man in our own hall, and his blood running." There was no mockery in his eyes. I said the rest very fast, how I thought it had been our father, and an omen, and that I should have done something.

"There have been omens from the day Malcolm seized the throne," he said calmly. "Omens enough for all to see, and our father was not blind."

Fear and foreboding. Wet darkness at Brechin. "He goes like Daniel into the lions' den." But God had stopped up the lions' mouths, and Daniel had survived.

"Malcolm grows old. He fears what is to be taken from him, by violence or by age."

Daniel to the lions. Daniel escaped.

"But that is no matter. You had this dream when? You could not have saved him, unless Alpia has taught you some woman's magic to go back in time, or fly from here to Scoine like a swan before the north wind."

No such magic.

Nechtan gave me his hand and I stood, painfully aware of my wounded feet as my weight came down and opened the gashes. "I can carry you across the worst places," he said, "or I can bring your pony."

His brows arched in concern as I took a couple of steps.

"I can walk. It was my own foolishness."

A year ago, he would have answered with a quick teasing remark. Days ago, I would have baited him for his concern.

I leaned on his arm. The paths were full of mud and stones, and so we walked in grassy places and across patches of moss. I hopped across driven sand. He never walked too fast or failed to support me when needed without being asked. This awareness, this easy gentility, must have marked our father. Almost I could remember it. I built a picture in my mind of Father and Mother, but it was a flat thing, like figures of ancient kings and queens worked into a tapestry. There was no life. Only Nechtan was real. I recalled that I once had envied him and could not imagine why.

As we came back into the village, I saw where a salmon rolled in the shallows. It was not silver and sleek, like those we had helped bring to shore, but emaciated. It lay on its side, mouth open, gills moving raggedly. Spent. The current moved it, sliding and wallowing, down to the ocean. The salmon seemed to fight the current, fanning its tail and moving toward the center of the stream, then went limp and let the water wash it back to the sea to die.

"Where are we to go?"

Nechtan followed my line of sight, watched the salmon borne away.

"We can stay here—for a while," he said. "We'll just go on as before."

I felt immensely older than twelve winters. But I had not yet walked in the Ring.

"If our mother also is gone out of the world…"

Nechtan nodded at that.

"Then who directs our lives?"

"It would be Talorc and Alpia, who have fostered us, if we were fortunate. But it will be Malcolm," he said, in a plain hard voice. "Our uncle will remember a use for us soon enough and send for us to come home."

7

MACBETH

Scoine, 1013

"You have misread the tense," Oswald chided.

Macbeth closed his eyes and pictured the verb appearing in each of its garments. He repeated the passage, correctly, and the monk closed up the book and put it back into the box.

Macbeth sat attentive, but his feet danced under the table. It was difficult to shut out the sounds of drums, harp, and flute, the songs and laughter from the great hall, here in the antechamber. The lessons took so long. Other tutors were content to recite the learning they had learned by rote, and let their students repeat until the words were carved into memory. But Oswald taught as though Macbeth were a scholar at Cluny or the new-built monastery he spoke of at Jumièges, demanding that he grope among foreign words for meaning.

Ultán, a man of the Fyne valley, leaped up with a shout. He had won again at dicing. Unmoved by the wild shadows thrown by the gamblers and dancers, Oswald took out another book. It bound together all sorts of texts and histories and poems, a book for a traveller to read and pass the time.

"We shall read again from Seneca."

More Latin. Macbeth thought of his native language as silver, a smooth and malleable tongue. Latin, however, was an old and burnished bronze; in the mouth, it tasted of green tarnish and worn metal. Once Oswald had told him some Greek. That had not been metal at all, but sharp and glittering like glass.

The gamblers were all on their feet now. Ultán held the bones firmly in his hand and would not give them up to the others who complained of his luck. An old scar showed livid where a sword had sliced his cheekbone before lopping off the tip of his ear.

Noise swelled. Women laughed. Men sang across the tune of the musicians. Two of the younger boys wrestled on the floor. The dicers argued. Ultán threw the dice into the space they had cleared on the flagstones. The loudest of his opponents scooped them up and peered closely at their sides before tossing them aside with a curse.

"Seneca was a suicide, and so damned, but was nevertheless a wise man and recognized the nature of leadership. Here," and Oswald turned the pages, "where he writes of Cato. This Cato did not slay wild beasts or fabulous creatures, but he struggled heroically nonetheless, against the desire for power and the hydra-headed monster of ambition."

Macbeth wished there were pictures of the monster. He glanced up at Oswald.

"Hydra?"

"That was a serpent of nine heads, slain by Hercules."

Oswald returned to the text, touching the place with the carved ivory marker that preserved the pages from dirt and grease.

Macbeth read the Latin, then, haltingly, translated the passage. "Wickedness is not stronger than virtue; therefore the man of...wisdom...cannot be injured." Oswald nodded, and Macbeth was warmed by his approval. "Only the bad try to hurt the good. Good men are at peace among themselves. Bad ones do evil...do evil equally...to the good and to each other."

"Good and evil are simple things for bookmen," Malcolm said from behind them. Wet clumps of snow clung to his shoulders. Oswald and Macbeth stood to greet the king.

"People are not cattle, to be driven by the rod here and there," Malcolm said, shaking off the snow before sitting down and resting his elbows on the table. Sleeves fell back from his wrists, revealing their corded strength. Heavy bracelets of gold and silver seemed armor rather than ornament. "The strong leader, if he honestly weighs the results of his actions, will find they cause evil as often as good. What seems to be a bad choice may eventually bring about good."

"Then how are we to know what to do?" Macbeth asked.

Malcolm looked intently at him and Macbeth did not look away.

"For the slave, it is to obey. For the farmer, to sow and reap. For the churchman, to pray. For the warrior, to fight. The king, however, must seek the course that will enlarge his realm and enrich his people."

"But an evil action often may bring wealth."

"Hah! You have been making him a brehon, Oswald, to parse laws," the king said. "Read him the words of kings instead."

"There is the edict of the highest king, that we are not to repay evil with evil but seek to do good to one another always," he answered quietly.

Malcolm's thick white brows drew down, as though he searched his memory for the saying.

"Well enough, well enough," he murmured. He glanced away, caught sight of Duncan where he slumped on a bench against the wall. "It does not appear that your learning has clung too readily to Mac Crínáin."

Duncan, hearing his name, looked up from honing the edge of a favorite dagger. He slipped blade in sheath, stone in its slot, and came over.

"Have you become a philosopher as well, my boy?" The king gazed on him with indulgent eyes.

"I would preserve Brother Oswald's precious books by not too much turning of their pages," he said. "The law teller will provide me what law I need, and as for my soul, will not the monks for their bread see after that?"

Malcolm laughed at his insolence. "Duncan the warrior indeed!"

Macbeth did not look at his brother, for fear that envy would show in his glance. He did not think he was any less brave than Duncan, but the king admired the older boy's recklessness. He was as rash as one of the heroes of legend.

"Finish this, and let the boy come among men," Malcolm told Oswald. "He fades like a plucked flower."

The king went off to his high seat. Macbeth watched him go and touched the brooch at his shoulder, tracing the three heads of the magical beast, and wondered how he had gone amiss with his foster-father.

Duncan looked down on them, like a rider at those who walked.

"I have a question for you, Brother Oswald." The monk's long face showed only willingness.

"I have heard that you Anglish obey the counsels of your women."

"We value wisdom where it is found, at times among women."

"No doubt it was women's counsels that persuaded Aethelred to abandon his armies." Duncan licked his lips, waiting for Oswald to respond but receiving only his quiet attention. "Beware such advice, my gentle brother, whether from woman or monk, or find yourself similarly disgraced." He sauntered away to rejoin his coterie of young men. Macbeth felt their rude eyes. Duncan, basking in the king's favor, became more arrogant each night. A burst of laughter from the group pierced his heart.

"You know why the king so favors your cousin?"

He nodded. Malcolm had lost a young son, one with hair as blond as Duncan's.

"Do not be ashamed of learning," Oswald said softly. "It will not betray you." He touched ivory to page, and Macbeth could only smile bitterly. More dead words.

"'The more noble a man is by birth, by reputation, or by inheritance, the more valiantly he should bear himself,' the monk read, 'remembering always that the tallest man is to be found in the vanguard of battle.' Here, read on."

Unwillingly, Macbeth found the place and began. "'As for insults, slurs, disgrace, and other blemishes, he should bear them as he would the cries of the enemy, or darts or stones flung from a distance.'"

Oswald finished the passage from Seneca.

"'Even though you are hard pressed and violently attacked by the foe, still it is base to give way; hold the position which has been assigned by nature—that of being a man.'" His voice rose at the end. Laughter followed from Duncan's friends.

"We will not take your prayers, battle-monk, but will demand your sword to aid us," one jeered.

"I ask pardon if I have disturbed you," Oswald said, his voice so quiet that it could not be accused of menace. "Perhaps you find my translation is in error?"

Duncan stared at the monk, began to speak, then turned his back as if he had not heard the exchange. After a moment, he and his group swaggered to the upper end of the hall and the warmth of the fire.

"It is a pity that Alba was never made part of Rome," Oswald mused.

"We were the only people to reject the Roman yoke!" Macbeth felt his blood rise.

"Do not take offense!" Oswald held up his hands, pax. "I mean only that Roman rule brought many benefits."

"Slavery. And armies to keep the slaves unfree."

"You have not seen enough of the world to know better. You have seen only the works of invasion, the walls and forts. In France and even close as Jorvik, the heritage of Rome is temples and amphitheaters and baths—beautiful, but only a symbol for the greatness of Rome that is found in its laws and literature. Ancient truths brought out of Greece and renewed in the Church."

"This is a free land. We are a free people," Macbeth argued.

"Indeed. The Romans ruled Britain for 409 years, so Nennius tells us, but could not conquer Alba. Claudius sailed to Orkney and brought war even so far north, but still the Picts and the northern Britons would not be quelled, and so Severus built his wall from sea to sea."

Oswald was admitting he was right!

"The ancient rights have been maintained," the monk continued, unaware that he had already ceded the argument, "and ancient ways. But think what might have been, had Agricola's successful attacks ended in colonization."

Oswald began to enumerate the virtues of Roman rule. "Merely look at how the throne is juggled here," he said, his warrior eyes fired by the bloodless battle of ideas. "To nephew or brother or cousin, rather than to son. Such a tangle, when it might descend regularly, without dispute."

"What if the son is weak and foolish?" Macbeth almost invoked Aethelred's name once more, but thought better of it. "Why should the under-kings and men of the blood not say who is the most fit leader?"

"If it were truly the best man chosen, then I would allow some value, but it is not always so."

"Men should choose their king," he said again.

"Macbeth mac Findláich, this is no ideal world," Oswald said sternly. "Stability is more valuable to a kingdom than the debatable merit of one man over another. It is a lingering taint of the Picts, who were strong indeed to hold off the Romans…"

Macbeth inclined his head to acknowledge the rightness of that statement.

"…but whose realm faded because of a flaw of succession. If the Picts chose a king from among the many sons of the royal women, did not that make the succession ever in question? Bede, blessed be his memory, tells us it was done only when there was a doubt, but he erred for in Bernicia it is recalled when a Pictish queen took Eanfrith as husband, it was not he but their son who ruled."

"That was long ago."

"Not so long ago as the Romans, and their ways endure."

Macbeth considered that. "We do not choose a king at random as you claim," he said, pulling together the threads of old conversation.

"Rule remains within the derbfine, the brothers and sons and uncles and nephews. A tanist is named and stands ready should the king die, always chosen from the alternate king line. So, there is—there is not tyranny." He finished less decisively than he had begun, because Duncan had returned.

But Oswald, hot with the hunting-down of truth, did not seem to notice him listening. "But see how uncertain things are now! Boidh is dead, and no tanist yet named in his place. And Malcolm grows old. What chaos there would be if he died!"

Duncan leaned on the table. He looked smug.

"Do not worry about the security of the kingdom, Brother Oswald, but pray for the continued health of the king who keeps your belly filled. Though the meat did not seem to be to your liking at the day's meal."

"I keep my Rule as best I may while serving here at the will of my abbot. When the king releases me, I will return with lightened heart to the peace of my house." He folded his hands on the table. They did not tremble, show white knuckles or red blotches of anger—hands often revealing what the face managed to deny. His fingers lay gently as those of a child. Macbeth wondered, again, how this man born to the sword could accept abuse and not forget his vows. *As for insults, he should bear them as he would the cries of the enemy and their darts.* It would seem Oswald gained as much strength from the Romans as from the Nazarene.

Duncan turned away from the monk. "The king wishes you beside him, cousin."

Macbeth stood and bent his head in acknowledgment of the gift of learning. Oswald put his outspread hand on Macbeth's head and whispered a benediction before the two boys ran to the meal.

The king from his high seat overlooked his royal hall, now considerably quieted with the departure of the over-lucky Ultán. The musicians had paused, and Wry-face, as desperate in his magpie labor as ever, was telling bawdy riddles and acting out the answers. His thin loins thrust spastically. Macbeth and Duncan took their places beside Olith, daughter of Malcolm and wife to Sigurd of Orkney, who had been sent here with her son while Sigurd was at war. Retaliation was feared through the familiar sea-roads between Éireann and Orkney. She looked much like the memories he had of his own mother, but perhaps all mothers in some way looked the same. And Thorfinn Sigurdsson was a boy quiet and watchful, with black hair and an intense gaze. He seemed to speak only Norse, or perhaps chose not to converse.

Two clan leaders attended the king, from the borders of Marr in Findlaích's territory and from Strathearn, but neither sat at the king's hand. To his right sat the favorite, Gillecomgan. His face was ravenous as that of the wolves carved into the hall's supporting pillars, thanks to prominent cheekbones and a pointed chin, but his voice was unexpectedly soft and high, the sound of wind through a reed. It was Gillecomgan who had made the remark about the men of Moray on the night Macbeth had arrived in court. He had kept that face and voice in memory, not realizing at the time that the man was his own cousin, son of Findlaích's estranged younger brother.

Macbeth saw greed carved into his face, the avid dark gaze that with his pointed chin had earned him the nickname of The Stoat. It was a good name for him, though not breathed in his presence. He smelled like a dog-stoat, rank with sweat, and he was as rapacious. It had become known that he had played both sides in the dispute that had ended Boidh's life—pouring lies first into Ennae's ears and then among Boidh's party. A few dark whispers said it was true enough, but that he acted on the king's wishes, removing two uncomfortable men in a single moment. Macbeth tried not listen to such rumors.

"And so what was out came in, and what went in, came out again," Wry-face cackled.

Malcolm laughed, and Wry-face made an elaborate bow, his face contorted into what passed for a smile. All the time, Macbeth could see the glittering control in the king's glance. Malcolm was dressed with special magnificence this night. His scroll-bordered mantle was purple and fastened on the shoulder with a sun-rayed brooch. He wore a garment of the Anglish fashion, close-fitted on the body and then full below a belt woven of many colors. It was adorned around the neck and down the front with gold embroidery on panels of green, set with gems. The bindings on his hose were brilliant red with a line of gilt, the thin leather bands crossing and recrossing his calves from soft shoes.

He beckoned them closer. "Duncan, Macbeth—what do you think of our visitors?"

Emissaries of the Norse-Irish who controlled the land beyond the River Nith sat drinking in their own group. Their clothing was not outlandish, nor their appearance. Some wore short trimmed beards, others were clean-shaven. Their hair was long or trimmed back. It was the way they clustered together and watched the room that marked them as foreigners.

"What do you think they want of me?" the king asked. He was not in good temper.

"An alliance," Duncan said promptly.

He nodded.

"For war," Macbeth offered.

"Perhaps. Or perhaps they want to make a marriage-bond," the king said. "One of their tall girls to wed one of my foster sons, perhaps?"

Duncan grinned uneasily. His younger brother Maldred—only a year separated them—had recently married the daughter of Uhtred, earl of Northumbria.

"Consider this an addition to Oswald's lesson," Malcolm said. "Now, then—if these men have been sent to ask alliance, how should I answer them?" Macbeth began to speak, but caught himself as he saw the king continued. "We are surrounded by a net of Norse jarldoms. They draw close around us, from the islands north, from the west coast and beyond, to Éireann. The Forkbeard grasps beyond the Danelaw to take all that the Anglish have lost—at least until one of the Aethelings proves better steel than his sire."

He looked to Duncan, who nodded gravely.

"We might give these foreign Gaels our favor and improve our position with the Norse, but that would put fear into the King of Strathclyde," Malcolm said. "Owen bends the knee to us but we know he treats secretly with Jorvik and Dublin."

"And he is important in war," Macbeth said.

"All the book-time hasn't taken your sense. Indeed, we rely on Owen for men and horses, and a western route to Angle-land when that should be needed."

It had been some years since the king had tested Northumbria's defenses. That same Earl Uhtred had turned him back in 1006 without St. Cuthbert's relics that he sought. The warriors spoke often of another venture to gain the riches of Carlisle.

"Your father admires the Northumbrians greatly, to give his son one of their names," the king said to Duncan, not caring to hide his displeasure. "Now he's fitted him with an Anglish wife. Maldred should pray that she has not inherited her father's temperament."

Duncan's eyes widened at the rebuke.

"It is no matter. Crinán's affections will not shorten the distance between Dunkeld and Durham," Malcolm added.

He called for wine. Macbeth smelled a vinegary tang and saw that it had been diluted even more than usual. War had left Alban barley heaped in the storehouses; even the king had to do with less of the continent's luxuries. Malcolm turned in his seat and offered the goblet to the fosterlings in turn. Duncan drank eagerly, Macbeth politely, as he had not developed a taste for the drink that soured in its casks.

"I shall hear the embassy. What do you think I will do? Let's see what moves in your heads besides the wine."

"You will let them go away holding hope like an empty sack, but will never fill it," Macbeth said.

Malcolm raised an eyebrow. "A politic answer. We may not ignore offered friendship, yet the foreign Gaels are of lesser importance than their neighbors."

"We could satisfy them," Duncan said boldly. "Then, if Strathclyde balks, we could conquer Owen's little kingdom and, turning east, take back the greenlands. The Norse-Irish will bargain for their very lives, then."

"A warrior of your blood," Gillecomgan cried, his eyes moving rapidly from king to grandson, seeking the approval of each.

Malcolm laughed and clapped Duncan on the shoulders. "The spear's point is persuasive, my son! Always persuasive."

His smile shifted away. "But remember, too, that power can be used by being restrained. Give hope to a suppliant, or give him something in place of that which he desires, binding him to you but not the reverse."

The king set down his goblet and looked across the room.

"A marriage alliance is always useful, creating a loyalty nearly as close as blood," he reflected. "Perhaps we could induce Strathearn to provide a daughter."

Macbeth saw how the lines were thrown out, fine as spider's silk but strong. To satisfy the emissaries. To punish a man who felt himself of more importance than the king deemed appropriate. To threaten Owen, to put fear into Uhtred. The king might be a master of such delicate work, but webs touched him as well.

Macbeth watched and learned.

8

LAPWING

FALLS OF BRAN, 1014

Crinán comes walking, indeed like the Jesus, on water.

He is too great a man to nimble over earth-mound and rock-hedge between the fields, stealing dry path from the flood. Straight on through the river unbound across the land, his feet parting wide water.

The Thane is troubled. Signs any man of perception might note and that is the better part of art. His shoulders are slumped. He speaks to himself, muttering over the thing he will ask of me.

He has learned to ask of me.

The gods leave their subtle marks for the wise. He wears a dark gray mantle. The color of iron and not of water. The color of battles to come. "Lapwing," he calls.

"Lapwing waits like a duck amidst the flood."

"I sought you in the guest-house."

"You were meant to find me here, naked under sky and free of prying man, to say what you will say."

He does not like where Lapwing stands, god-bent in the midst of deeper water, but will not shout across. He picks up his hems—his tunic long and embellished like a king's—to come to my shriveled presence.

"Why do you think I wish no listeners?" He puffs; the man carries too many stone around his middle.

"Monk's ears are deep."

"Yes. And their mouths wide." He picks his feet up dainty as a mare, sets the water turning, puts them back. Crinán needs the illusion of solid ground. "No word comes, and I must know."

"War and rumor of war."

Crinán tries to hide his startlement, but I see his eyes and the soul-pit at center grows. I hear much.

"You know, then, what I ask."

"Farseeing."

"There comes no word!" He ignores the water and begins to pace, splashing and slopping. I count the steps, four before he turns, five back. The number of wisdom.

"The Forkbeard has died. Northumbria took him early as king, when others had not, and now will it suffer? Will a Sveinsson rule? Will Aethelred return? Prayers have been offered unceasingly in the choir but there comes no word, no sign."

Their god is too far away. They should keep gods in the earth and not in the sky if they wish answers.

"You do not ask all."

The Thane rumbles and groans. "I fear for my son. Earl Uhtred makes hasty choices. The consequences may be long for Maldred."

Wait for direction. Touch the knob of my staff, run fingers wise to seek the letters, but all is jumbled.

The bell sounds at the narrow church. It is the hour they call Terce. Mark time from the middle of the night rather than from the go-ing-down of the sun. Monk stomachs grumble as they chant, thinking of the single winter meal to come.

Patterns? None offered. No birds fly. No shadows speak in their slanting. Ripples run out from my staff as I stir the water. It laps with a thin voice. Aye, the imbas.

"I may perform the imbas forosnai."

Crinán wrinkles his forehead. "That is blood-sacrifice. I cannot allow it. The bishop will note."

I walk away. Deeper water chills my balls, shrivels my manhood. "Do not tell the bishop."

He is pulled and tugged, tugged and pulled. Scot by blood, Angle by spirit. A man who holds and a man who seeks.

"Patrick forbade all rites with offerings."

"He did indeed."

Something stirs in the great man. "Yet when St. Becc foretold the death of a prince and the future of the kingdom, then Columba himself called it marvelous prophecy."

"God-sent prophecy."

"But that was in a dream, and no blood." Decision in his voice.

"I cannot promise to dream such as great Becc dreamed. But in the imbas forosnai I will use no blood of pig or dog to speed the vision but will ask merely upon my thumb."

Crinán wavers. "Agreed."

There has been too much of water in my dreams. Water runs, water stays. Lapwing does not know if he is river or tarn. When I am at Dunkeld then I go. Tay and Isla babble and churn, leading me away. When I am gone then I am urgent to go back. Gods pull me between them. Not the same ones who pull Crinán.

I made sacrifice to Lugh the Skilled, to Donn in his gloom, and also that Horned One who holds the life of creatures. I walked to the falls named for Bran, and there was overcome by a vision of a speaking head. I lay down among the alders and was hedged around by them, purple branches a net to hold this great Fish.

But Bran of the Britons is a dead god, overcome by another and beheaded, and his cauldron of resurrection did not bring him back. The alder is his tree. The alder brings fire to free the earth from water.

Gods rise and fall.

I have walked down Tay through the green valleys, through the holiness of the land, until the water tastes salt. Old holiness, dead gods, all through this land of Atholl, of Fotla, and I know all its names before. It is hollow as a bee-tree with lost things. It echoes the war-cries of my people tramping to Forteviot and there spilled bright noble blood, mastering the ones who worshipped the female, driving them to the deadly embrace of the Norse.

I knock on the door of the land and hear the emptiness beyond. Empty with the past and the future. Something hums like bees in this place, great happenings to come. Too much water in my dreams.

Among the alders, I dreamed of a holy spring hedged with alders. Like a woman I gathered bark to make red dye, its flowers to make green, twigs to make brown. The dyes ran down my naked flesh and dyed me treewise. My own lopped head was then cast into that spring, singing prophecy.

Now I return to Bran's falls. The bishop's conscience will not be stung, here. The water comes between us. Much power in the sound of water.

Crinán has set one to aid me and to watch me. The juniore is simple but corrupt. This night he watches the gods come into me. The night before he sang psalms. His mouth is perfectly slack. I see he has made a hut of branches to shelter his shorn head. Weak flesh.

New night comes in. The bright star on the horizon, constant and inconstant. Then one high up and I say its name. When ship-star shows at north then I go behind the waterfall.

Wet rock. Cradle of rock where water once ran, hollowed and smooth.

Why do these Christians so fear blood when they eat the body of their god and drink his blood? The Lamb of God, and his blood flowed.

I ask upon my thumb. Put hand to mouth and bite hard in the soft place where the letter M resides when we men of art speak hand to hand, each place a letter in a silent message. M, sacred to vine and bramble, black fruits bleeding wine. My tooth a tooth of knowledge as was Finn's. Let out blood and the gods scent it. Hot as wine in the mouth, warming stomach and head.

Come hidden knowledge.

Come visions of what happens far from here.

Come secret light.

Lapwing smears his heart's-blood on the rock and sings the gods over it.

I chant on my finger-ends, I chant the letters of truth where they live on my hands, on the bones, on the joints where knowledge is concealed. The tenderness of M!

Oghma Sun-Face, who brought letters to us on golden chains, lead them now to tell me truth.

I lie in the rock's embrace and wrap myself like a chick in its shell. Before I cover my face I see the watcher watching. Now in the dark Lapwing puts his two hands to his face, flat incantation of all knowledge against his cheeks so that none leaks away.

Silence fill me first.

Silence fill me.

Then knowledge drive silence out.

Old night falls bearded and frosted; the young sun rises.

Comes the bray of battle. A place called Clontarf in Éireann's land, where the Norse are driven back to the sea. The Raven Banner falls and Sigurd with it. His babe devours a man's portion. Malcolm grants what is not his to give. He thinks to gain a distant land through Thorfinn's soft fingers and a hireling army.

The sun rises, yellow-haired and mighty. Aethelred gathers men, a great mass of men. When he turns to look on his army, it dissolves into smoke. Svein will take his geld and then his kingdom. His sons to divide the north like a piece of meat, by point and blade.

There is among the Danes a warrior called Thorkell who has two faces. One is Anglish, one Dane. He puts them off and on. Sometimes he wears both and looks behind, before.

Old greatness falls, a tree in the forest, and sun shines in the gap, a young tree rises golden.

The blond king sits in his high seat. One stands beside the young man and guides him.

Oh! My dream aches. My dream is the taut cord at back of leg, full of destiny. Knowledge may be sought where it hides, weasel-winding in the burrows, or it may be remembered. Memory goes back and forth through all the bodies worn before and yet to come.

I am doomed with the acts of the men I have been.

Ah, the pain of sieving these many-selves through the veil of what is not permitted to man without the sufferance of gods! Sun rises and the old frost smokes away, the land is green and welcomes the sun.

Wait, wrapped in blackness.

The vision comes clear.

The old king dies. A young king, a blond king, takes his place. But there is a mirror! A second aged king, a second blond youth, and the one who guides him is Lapwing. Lapwing grayer. It is for the future, then. He stands beside the young king and moves his hand upon the pieces of a board-game. The one played against cannot be seen. He sits with his back to the fire and is dark, outlined by ruddy light.

Frost king falls, a blond king rises.

Lapwing guides the hand of the young king.

"I did think he was dead, Lord-Abbot." The juniore's voice cringes like shoulders under the lash. "He cried out but there has been no movement since."

"You did not disturb him?"

"No, my lord, as you ordered."

I unroll myself from cloak and dream, both dark now, and see the two of them through the scrim of water. The watcher under his hood is a wavering spirit before Crinán's anger.

"If he was disturbed, while you were running foolish from his outcries…"

I emerge from the cave, and Crinán stares. Hungry as a fasting monk. The watcher gallops toward Dunkeld's safety.

"Frost-king fails; sun rises."

Lapwing is still in the grip of the other world. The words come clotted.

"Frost-king fails, and sun rises."

Crinán waits.

"The frost-king goes into the earth, a blond king rises."

The gods tell the poem into my hands.

"Old night is long, and long rules.
White the earth, old brows, old bones.
Dawn comes, and comes quickly.
Frost fades, into earth, always-taking earth.
The old dies, the young lives.
A blond king comes into his own."

"A new king. But who? Where?" The Thane is impatient of prophecy. "What visions came to you?"

"I saw visions of many places and many things, but one was true. An old king is tottering and will fall like a tree rotten at the heart. The one who will take his place is young and blond as the sun."

Crinán folds his arms on his chest. Does he think he has fully paid for revelation? I must tutor him like the dullest child.

"The blond king. Who can that be but Cnut Sveinsson? Aethelred is a tree that appears solid but which will fall easily to the axe, and this Cnut is blond as the sun and young but strong with his father's strength."

"That is what it means?"

"That is what it means."

I am stiff with cold of two worlds, but inside, fire burns.

The gods have granted a vision wearing two faces. One to show Crinán, for now, events to unfold of great moment. And one vision for Lapwing to hold close, to conceal, while Malcolm yet rules and Crinán becomes desperate for his son.

9

MACBETH

Above Loch Earn, 1014

Now they could hear only one of the dogs, and its cry fading, fading. That voice, strident even in distance, ended abruptly. Duncan cocked his head against the whipping wind, as though trying to entice the cry back around, over the scoured hills and returning to them.

"That was the Bamburgh Hound. He is the slowest of them all," Macbeth offered.

Duncan gave him a dismissive look. "It wouldn't matter if it were swift Alipes. They're gone, gone in every direction."

So were the other members of the hunting party. Cathal said he thought a wolf had split the pack and sent it crying cross-trails. Somehow the men, too, had gone this way and that, chasing a favorite dog until only one man had remained with them. And now Cathal also was gone, his horse slipping at a stony ford and falling, flailing, the icy water carrying both away.

They had followed along the stream as far as they dared, until there was no footing for the horses on either side and the hills rose too steeply to be mounted. They saw no sign of man or horse.

"The Sidhe," Duncan proclaimed, "have lured off the dogs and the men. Now they have summoned the storm."

Macbeth's sure-footed pony sidled and worked the bit in its mouth as they turned around. He flexed his fingers and grasped the reins more surely. It was gloomy enough in this narrow cut, where the stream foamed and lashed at the black stone, but the weather had turned abruptly and now heavy clouds running in from the southwest had darkened the sky almost to night. He did not wish to add the possibility of phantoms.

"I am not frightened of them," Duncan said loudly. "Perhaps we shall see their women in this wild place. It is usually the women who appear. A battle-hag washing bloody garments, or a beautiful maiden in white and gold who weaves a charmed belt while she walks." Duncan's chin lifted and he sat his horse, if it might be possible in the battering weather, with stiff dignity.

Macbeth leaned his head away from a thorny bush growing out of the hillside. He didn't believe in the Aes Sidhe, not in the way his cousin did. The great mounds, glittering with a pavement of white stones, and the wide circles of upright stones were daunting to see, but he believed, as his father once told him, that these were the works of a long-vanished race of giants. Or, as Oswald said, ancient mute creatures who had been gathered back into the sea when Jesus came.

The wind shrieked until the pitch struck some answering chord in the hollow places and made them thrum.

They reached the ford and the track that showed empty across the folds of the hills. No one was there. Their horses turned tails to the freezing gale, unbidden, and hung their heads.

"We'll go back ourselves," Duncan said confidently. "The horses will pick out the way."

The light was greenish, the color of corruption. It leaked from the edges of the low black clouds. Lightning forked.

Macbeth was blinded, stunned, by the nearness of the strike. He felt his hair stand up and his backbone prickled. As the horses screamed fear and danced in place, he held the reins securely but gently, tightened his knees, and concentrated on not falling. A wind-stunted tree smoked and sparked where the stroke had cracked it from fork to root.

"Down from this ridge," came Duncan's cry, muffled by the ringing in his ears.

"Hear me holy Mary and St. John," Macbeth whispered, "and Jesus and God the Father. Protect us in this wild place." He tried to remember which saint's day this was, to ask for special aid. Martin's day was past, and Britius his fellow of Tours. He added a plea to Martin, who had been a soldier first and would remember dangerous nights.

He rode after Duncan, along an uncertain track that for now trended just below the ridge line. They were within a spear's-throw of the driving clouds. Lightning came again and again, harrying them. He repeated his invocation. It was not a round and proper prayer such as Oswald would make, but he did not have the attention to frame it properly.

The wind dropped. Before he could be thankful for the lull, the wind slammed back from a new quarter, toothed with hail.

Macbeth tucked his face deep into the shelter of his hood. He watched the hailstones bouncing off Duncan's hunched shoulders, felt them striking his own. The horses flinched, and steam rose off their backs and came in blowing clouds from their nostrils. Duncan turned in his saddle to look at him. Blond hair whipped across his face, pale as foam, and he looked like one of the Fair Folk himself, his face suffused with a wild glee, his eyes afire like the bluestones of Boath.

The horses stumbled from a walk to a jarring trot, then dropped back. The path—a deer's way—led across a high moor, dropping into the cuts of small streams dark with tannin, skirting small tarns and pools. In these high pastures sheep and cattle grazed in summer, but they were now in the lowlands and all was deserted.

The ground whitened. Hail came in rattling drifts, bouncing from the horse's heads. At length, the stones became smaller until they were no larger than coarse sand, mixed with stinging rain. Macbeth opened and closed his hands, one at a time, to chase the numbness. His face was stiff. The almost invisible path twisted downward into a scrubland of dwarf pines and blaeberry and heather. Surely they would soon cross the main track.

This storm tore at the land. Soil flowed from gullied hills; streams foamed into waterfalls. Naked trees bent away from the wind.

If only the party had not split. Macbeth listened to the wind howl and thought he heard the howling of wolves as well. The track wound on. Nothing appeared familiar.

Duncan's horse reared, pawing the air. A dark blur thundered from beneath its feet and came straight at Macbeth. His horse threw up its head and danced backward. The bird veered away and disappeared into the stunted trees.

When he had settled his own mount, he saw Duncan's bay on the ground.

"My brother!"

He leaped down and threw the reins over a bush.

The horse rolled, tried to get up and fell back, its eyes panicked. One leg was broken. Bone showed, gleaming in the strange light. The saddle was twisted around and the cantle crushed.

"Duncan!"

He was not under the horse. His spear had landed to the right, but Macbeth found his cousin to the left, crumpled, his head resting against a lichened boulder. Duncan's face was slack as death when he rolled him onto his back, but the pulse was strong in his throat and he breathed. A bruise was beginning to swell on the angle of his jaw.

"Ah, ah. My brother, what am I to do?" he said, squatting on his heels. He tried to lift Duncan but could not. He already carried Crinán's frame, and Macbeth was acutely aware of his own slightness. Each night he prayed that he would grow to be at least as tall as his father, who was no large man.

A rock ledge overhung the path, a little way back. Perhaps he could drag him onto that ledge, and then steady his pony beneath it and roll him into the saddle.

Macbeth thought for a moment, but no other idea came, so he led his mount over and fastened the reins as well as he could around the rocks. Then he went back for Duncan. He took him under the shoulders and began to tug him up the slope.

Duncan's head tipped back after one hard bump, and his eyes opened. "I am not dead."

Macbeth stumbled back. "I know. I was going to put you on the horse."

Duncan sat up, rubbing his jaw and his shoulder. He looked to where his mount groaned and struggled at each retreating crash of thunder.

"Not that one, I hope."

Macbeth slid down beside him, laughing with relief. "No, not that one."

"What happened?"

"A bird flushed. A grouse, I think."

"Ah—that." Duncan wiped the rain from his face. "I saw something leap up. But how were you going to lift me, little one?"

Macbeth burned at the casual taunt. He indicated his horse where it was tied, and the overhanging ledge.

"You might have killed me in the attempt. But I thank you." Duncan got to his feet, cautiously. He went to his struggling horse and slit its throat. Blood fountained from the artery, then sagged, streamed, ebbed.

"An offering, now they've run us to earth," Duncan said, and laughed harshly. "Perhaps the Sidhe will offer us some of their magical ale for our pains. The mound must be close by, where we might be taken to dance and dally for a thousand years and think it but a night."

Duncan pushed himself clumsily up and into the pony's saddle. Macbeth went up behind and they moved heavily down the track. Wind rattled in their cloaks and the cold rain intensified and began to freeze. When the black oblong of a doorway showed in the hillside beside the path, Macbeth was willing to face wildcat or rarely seen bear, or even the ancient people, whether Beautiful Ones or giants.

"Let's shelter," he cried into Duncan's ear, and was surprised that he agreed.

But the doorway opened, after all, into a mere shieling that the people used while tending herds, a little cave widened into a chamber with stones laid up to wall in the front. Nothing magical about it, and little of comfort.

Lightning flashed. Macbeth could make out the lines of a rough hearth and a stone shelf with something on it. He reached and found a lamp, with a bit of rendered fat in the bottom, and a flint. He struck sparks to the rush-wick until it caught. The lamp gave a guttering light that showed how mean the place was.

"It smells of dung," Duncan sneered, obviously disappointed. His face was even paler than before. He stripped water and ice from his garments. "Whatever has broken our party and harassed us with storm has not destroyed us," he boasted. "I'll bring a priest here to poison their spring against them with holy water. I'll have a bishop, even—the king will agree."

Macbeth said nothing. He admired his foster-brother for his size and his strength, his skill with weapons, but as he grew older, he could see Duncan's faults as well. He was superstitious, wearing amulets and crosses indiscriminately, believing the Other World might be threatened, placated, or bribed. And Duncan could be malicious, the more as he became older and stronger. He no longer acted thoughtlessly, followed by an apology, but with considered cruelty. He was sensitive about his lineage, stronger on his mother's side than his father's.

Duncan finished his boasts and sat back against the wall of packed dirt faced with stones.

"You should not sleep," Macbeth warned.

Duncan opened his eyes. "Why not?"

"Sometimes when a man has been struck on the head, he will seem to recover, but then in sleeping will slide into death."

"Truly?"

Macbeth nodded. Conamail had taught him that. If Duncan listened to men's talk—other than recitations of their own bravery—he would learn a great deal about wounds and their treatment. Fighters were often better at healing than the physicians, carrying dried boneset and yarrow with them into battle, while others relied on finding wound-herb on the field. Honey was valued not for eating but for wound-packing.

Duncan kept his eyes open, but was as silent as though asleep. They listened to the storm beat against the shelter. Rain fountained from the overhang and puddled and ran.

Eventually, the storm blew itself out. A slant of weak moonlight showed at the door. Going out, they found the quarter moon shining in a band of clear sky between the end of the last storm and a second building over the water. Lightning showed red inside the clouds like blood under the skin.

"Let's go."

"We should stay through till light," Macbeth argued. "The moon is only a sliver and there is another storm to come. The paths will be dangerous."

"Caution, caution. You'll make a creeping warrior, cousin, and never a winner of glory."

Duncan mounted unsteadily and announced, "I am going. You may cower in the dung here if you wish. I'll have food and a fire."

He pulled Macbeth's small mount around in a tight prancing curve. Its eyes rolled white at the harder hand. Macbeth sighed and took his foster-brother's hand up.

It was a stumbling nightmare passage. The track was slick with rain and ice. The pony's hooves pocked in the slush, and it slid and shied and trembled. The moon was quickly overrun by new clouds. Macbeth remembered, as the dim light faded, that they had left the oil-lamp to burn itself out. There would be no welcome light for the next wayfarer forced to shelter. As they dropped lower, they came into driving fog. Mist rose off the warmer land and water, but as it lifted was caught by the wind and pulled apart.

Finally, they crossed a wider path, lower down than they had expected.

The second storm began. Rain, some wind, a little lightning—nothing like the savagery of the first storm.

They were quite close to the hunting lodge when they were met by men with hissing torches.

"Here they are!"

"Who?"

"How many?"

"Both the king's fosterlings, God be praised," the nearest man answered, and he meant every word.

Macbeth was lifted onto a led horse. He realized as the man's hands closed around him that he was shaking.

"Cold," he said. "Only cold."

"You're near frozen," the man agreed. Macbeth was drowsily relieved that the rescuer did not think he was frightened.

"Two search parties were out in the hills, and we could not bear the king's anger and left as well," the fervent man said. "What happened?"

Macbeth raised his head. Duncan stared at him, commanding silence.

"We were separated, man from man, until I was left with the child..."

10

GRUACH

ORKNEY, 1014

I opened my eyes and closed them again. There was no light. Had I slept from the midpoint of the year until the long night of midwinter?

Island on the water like a midsummer sun, riding low and green.

I was hugely tall, a giant-woman who straddled the roiling water between Caithness and the islands.

I flew over the water like a kittiwake.

I was small, but immensely heavy, iron-stone searing from the sky. I fell. Fell over cliffs delirious with sea-birds, into hissing darkness.

The ground was cool under my body. I lay face down, naked. On stone. Not sea-rock, slippery with kelp and moss. Flat stone swept clean of mud or dirt, cool and dry. A hearth. A threshing floor. A tomb.

I sat up quickly. Darkness enclosed me. My buttocks rasped on lingering sand.

The dead were supposed to wake to light.

The moor stretched wide with broken hills, as though the wind had finally beaten the land into submission. Great emptiness. At the end of the land, cliffs were vertical, cut off. Yellow-brown, brown-red, gray-brown, deeply gashed and cloven, the cliffs were overhung by trailing plants that drank the salt-spray. Gannets and fulmars nested there, and snake-necked cormorants on pillars washed by sea. Their droppings dyed the rocks white. They swirled, wings black and white and gray, screaming.

I flew with the sea-birds across the heaving strait.

I saw all the islands of Orkney, strewn across a hazy sea, green and brown, rising higher to the west and kneeling to the east until they gave themselves to the sea.

Everywhere, light. Clouds passing, forming, still bright after the sun took its short summer passage below the horizon. A sky without stars, a sky white as the sun that folded itself in that fleece.

I was back in the lightless place. I sniffed, smelled rock, old enclosed earth. Bones? I stood up, carefully, found that there was a ceiling. Stone, again, not far above my head. I shuffled forward, hands outstretched, until I touched a wall and followed it with my fingers lightly brushing the stones. Though there was nothing to see, I kept my eyes open. Sometimes a flare of light would come, like a falling star, a carried candle.

The sea was rough and gray, spray flying. We entered the water gap. The island to the right was outlined by a sandy beach.

The boat was rowed by three men. They were silent, shoulders rounded to the task. The oars lifted, slid back into the waves. Waypoints were marked by round towers, there on the headland the men called Hoxa, and there, there. Thick-walled and silent, though smoke rose from houses nearby. Stone pens for the sheep, stone, only stone. The hills were marked with standing stones, circles of stone gone knee-deep in sand, mounds where other tombs or towers or stones had stood.

I tasted bitterness softened by honey.

Alpia had given me that drink.

I remembered Alpia now, and that Alpia was in the boat. Alpia and I and three men laboring at the oars.

Fertile Orkney, kindly veiled by summer fog and warmed by the long summer sun that fled in winter, leaving the sky to the red and green lights, the dancing warriors some called them, while others said they were the fires that encircle the ocean. Low hills green with grass, cattle and sheep grazing. Boats drawn up at every shore.

We passed between the islands into a watery plain, a great circle of sea with islands large and small all around.

Boats shot out from among the islets the Norse called holms. Swift straked boats with high prows, oars flashing.

Alpia greeted them in their own tongue. The men brought their boats all around. Light reflected from shield-boss and spear as the boats lifted on slow swells.

Who comes into the land of the Sigurdssons?

I and my daughters, Alpia replied, to walk among the stones. As Sigurd permitted, and all his fathers before, now Einar eldest and Brusi and Sumarlidi and Thorfinn give passage to the White Lady.

I wondered, Who was this woman revealed in white, with a crescent of gold at her throat?

And what is this boat beside ours? Three rowing men, three women.

"Estrid? Finnchaem? Ingigerd!" I called, remembering the other girls who had come, like me, to be initiated among the ancient stones. "Are you here?" The stones drank my voice.

I was alone, alone as in a tomb. Perhaps I had died of the bittersweet drink Alpia gave us. Dark. No Sun of Souls. No sweet land. Cold in the stone box, life ended. Derelei in her kist, the baby tucked in the crook of her arm. But if I were dead, my skin wouldn't prickle with cold as it did now. I felt the hairs standing up on my arms.

"Ingigerd? Estrid? Finnchaem?"

I began to trace my captivity, fingertips brushing the gaps of unmortared joints. The blocks were huge. Who could have lifted them into place?

My hand slid off stone into air. An opening. I feathered the span of it with my hands. A door. I stepped carefully over a lintel I could not see.

A promontory between sea-lochs, and on it the Ring, and overlooking the water and the Ring were the rough uprights of two Markerstones.

The air smelled equally of sea and land. The Ring's sixty stones seemed to float.

Alpia leaped ashore, urgent. Hours yet till Midsummer, but she had been impatient of delays—two days while the tidal currents and cross-grained storms held us on the other side of the strait. Surf boomed in the skerries. Time enough allowed, time till Midsummer, but Alpia had not rested tranquilly. She had paced the wrack-strewn beach where we waited.

I sniffed the air inside this room. Damp and lifeless as that in the chamber where I had waked.

The Ring was set between waters. There were openings to the northwest and southeast. Another group of stones stood southwest, in the direction of the Midsummer sun.

We entered from the southeast, through a wide ditch cut down to rock. The Ringstones, irregular, their tops cut at a slant, were set upright around the inner edge of the ditch.

The sky was wide above. Wind hissed through the tough grasses, moaned through the heather. It was caught by the stones like breath in a flute. It was the beginning of the world, when divinity walked, when there was only the sea and stones and speaking grass. I heard cattle lowing, a familiar sound in that bleak place, and was comforted.

The room had no doorway other than the one I'd come in by. I crept back to the first chamber, and turning left made my way around the wall, touching the dark. It did not seem to be a grave. It did not seem at all familiar. It coiled in the dark like a serpent. A spiral. Spiral Castle was the home of death, Spiral Castle that spun inward and out, revolving around the cold heart of the northern sky.

I moaned as my courage coiled inward and died.

But as the spiral coiled in, it reversed and coiled out, eternal.

Alpia had danced the dance of the Aspects, familiar as the dance of the trees, but this time she went first to each of the mounds heaped outside the Ring and knelt, before returning to the center, then out to the next, drawing a web across the heather-carpeted Ring with her solitary footsteps.

Alpia, who had been impatient on the way north and urgent on the beach, now was solemn and unstirred. She was the White Lady, her mantle thrown off like last winter's leaves. She went unveiled as a maiden, her hair loose and glistening white as her gown, a crescent of beaten gold at her throat.

Her hands cradled the waxing moon. "Accept life, grow and learn, and take passion in the moment."

Her hands rounded the full. "Be productive, and in your fullness be the support and strength of the world and its place of peace, its sacred lap. Fill yourself to be poured out."

Her hands cupped the waning moon. "Be silent in wisdom, give voice in counsel, the flesh drawn thinner and thinner to darkness and the return."

I saw moons dance across the sky, boating through the noctilucent clouds. Their movements were aligned with the barrows around the ring, dancers moving, dancers waiting.

Alpia danced a spiral out and one back in. At the center she was a pillar of white. "In the dark time come dreams, the truth hidden in the cauldron of time. The darkness is the Mother of Life remaking herself, and the world, as the tomb encloses the body and yields the spirit to new life."

Then the tiny cauldron on a tripod, and a dipper of horn. I had been last of the four to drink. Honey laced with bitterness. I traced the irregular moon of the dipper, rolling back and forth where it had fallen.

Slowly I resumed my circuit of the first chamber. More rooms, all self-contained. I realized it was a wheelhouse. The central chamber, the rooms divided by stone. I traced the whole in my mind, my prison one of the ancient Builder dwellings, though in darkness it seemed huge, wide as the circuit of the stars.

My mind cleared. I recalled the ritual, now, climax of my years with Alpia. All the days in which I had learned what a woman needs to keep the world aright, crop charms and herbs of healing, ways to bind wounds and promote births, the gifts of brewing and extracting, the invocations and the petitions, weather-wisdom, earth-sense.

I watched as Alpia broke the stem of grain and laid it sorrowfully in the earth, and watched as it sprouted and bore grain, a summer's worth of growing.

The grain hastens, but I do not. I am not a woman, yet.

The comb and the mirror, in which the young Goddess regarded herself and eternity. The cauldron of knowledge, the bowl of revelation. I remembered it all. I stood straight. A slight eddy of air came against my back. I turned to it, breathed deeply. The smell of fresh earth.

I walked, keeping the air against my face. My hands touched nothing, but my feet found a sill and I fell forward, into soft earth. A hole smaller than a badger's sett admitted the sweet air.

I scraped away the dirt, widened the hole, wriggled into it and followed it upward.

The soil became damp and slick. For a moment I could not go forward, my shoulders trapped and my feet unable to push. I spasmed on my belly like a worm. The soil was in my mouth, ears, nose. I coughed and hawked, spat and felt it dribble on my chin.

The black dark eased. The tunnel's soft wet clay was now gritty with intermixed sand. I made a last effort, thrust myself out of the earth, and was stunned by light.

"Life out of Death," Alpia intoned.

I sputtered the response, "Life is one, life is whole."

Alpia crouched behind a single, slender flame, cupped by her hands. She was naked and frightening in her woman's nakedness. Then she laughed, deep rolling laughs. Ocean roaring against shore. Powerful joy.

"Welcome the Spirit born of Earth, coming out of darkness and confusion into light!" she cried.

I stood. The candlelight, at first so piercing to my night eyes, was eclipsed by the midnight radiance of the north. Alpia gave me the candle, the movement releasing an intoxicating hot scent of beeswax and honey. I reached for it, saw my red hand, and almost dropped it.

My arms were bloody, my body as well. I touched the wetness and carried it to my nose—it did not smell of blood, but of earth. I looked back at the tunnel from which I had emerged. So small! A smear of red earth showed where I had wriggled free. I had been birthed out of red clay. I rubbed my arm, but the redness seemed to have dyed my skin.

Alpia laughed again, and the sound drove out my fear. She stood naked in her skin, under the great sky like a rich blue cloak.

Another light showed in Alpia's hands. This was not a candle, but a single stalk of barley; clear flames rose from the tip of each spikelet but did not consume the grain. In her other hand, she held up a reaping sickle.

"Come, daughters, and be made new!"

She turned and walked toward the sound of the sea. I followed. There came Finnchaem, Estrid, Ingigerd. Each was naked and stained red. Each clutched a candle, as I did, walking like stunned creatures toward the sound of water.

We were in a strange place, close to the open sea—no longer at the Ring above its enclosed waters, nor in sight of it. The hills were not mounds but sand dunes, anchored by grass and sea-thrift that waved in the wind. Alpia halted at the edge of the tide-line. She pushed the barley-stalk (still dancing with light) into the sand, and laid the gleaming sickle in front of it. We did as she did, following her silent action, setting our candles in the hissing dunes.

Alpia walked into the waves.

The sea was bitterly cold. I clasped my arms around my chest, but Alpia eased them down and began to wash the red earth from my skin with the soothing sounds of a mother to a baby. I was ashamed of my childlike body, even more so as it came white from under the layer of soil. My breasts were barely beginning to swell, while those of the other girls (Alpia now washing Finnchaem) were round and fertile. They had thick hair between their legs.

Alpia herself, while strong, was thinning with age. Her breasts hung empty; her stomach showed the slackness of several births.

When we were clean, we came out of the sea, on fire from the freezing cold water. Alpia dried each of us, kneeling like a slave to rub the water from our legs. Then she brought out new léinte of white and long mantles finely woven of black wool.

Alpia took up the grain-flame and the sickle and began to sing.

"She is the tilled soil that births plenty.
She is the water that brings growth.
She is the moon that tugs tides in sea and flesh.
She is tree of the forest and herb of field.
She is fish in ocean and in free stream.
She is bird of air.
She is the insects that feast on carrion death.
She is our mother's belly that shaped us
of sea-water and veins of copper.
She is the breast that nourished us with milk like rain.
She is the mind that yields truth like honey.

The world in all its forms, She is.
We are born of her and love her and die to her, and are reborn."

Alpia paused.

"She is lawgiver, peacemaker, protector of the people.
She governs light, renews the seasons, fixes the elements.
She grasps the thread of fate and untangles knotted courses.
She is the Green One, opener of the womb.
She is the Queen of Heaven.
She is the Silent Rest, lady of the dark time.
In Her grace she shows us the aspects of our lives in Her:
To be born new, to grow, to be full with life,
To decline, to enter the pregnant darkness."

Alpia lifted the burning head of grain, to the northeast, the southwest, the northwest, the southeast. She tossed the stalk high and it turned over and over, sparkling, and fell extinguished.

"We are Her image.
We tend the soil and it grants us food.
In the sea Her image is the porpoise, the sea-beast that suckles.
Its body makes crescents of devotion on the water.
It is a friend.
It herds the silvery fishes, the crop of the sea,
sprouted like grain to nourish Her own."

Now I recalled the sea-voyage clearly, and that halfway across the strait, a sea-beast broke the surface and swam beside the boat. Alpia had hailed it as sister. The men had been silent.

"…the Mother of Life.
She gives birth to light, wraps herself in it, and swallows it.
Mary-of-the-Sea births a Son in the day out of time.
In the depths of winter, She labors to give the world a bright Savior.
The grain is His sign, rising out of Her body.
In the warm days she takes His freely sacrificed body back into Her own.
From the sowing of spring He rises renewed.
In full summer He yields holy sustenance,
the bread of His body, for the renewal of all.
He dies and is reborn, the Sun of Life.

She is deathless as the returning Moon.
This is the great secret that Ninias confessed, and Columba,
finding us sisters of the Word:
Philip the Apostle knew Christ was virgin-born of two virgins.
That He was of the spirit and of the earth,
joining two that had been sundered.
He shows that there is an end to death, and all rise
again to light and life.
We confess the Mother of All Living,
and the Son of Salvation from fear."

Alpia danced again, a new dance in slow steps inward, in light steps outward. The spiral of resurrection, drawn on wet sand.

Other women appeared, spiralling back toward the center with her, making a great wheel turning on a center. First came two women with the heavy steps of those who have worked hard for too many years, but their eyes were sharp. Women of the islands.

Then appeared tall women, broad-faced, wearing crescents of gold around their necks and armlets of copper. They danced naked. Their bodies were tattooed with the symbols found on the symbol-stones. And who were those that danced after, with long faces chalked white and eyes marked out with ochre? Their hands were blunt from building with stone.

And dancing last of all, in and out, bending the wheel around to the start—ancient women, short and bent, wearing rough animal skins. They were at once young and immensely old.

The wheel returned, and on each return the strange women fell away, until only two middle-aged women, plain women of Orkney, danced beside Alpia. They reached out and pulled us into the dance. I stepped high, bent low, whirled. My body hummed with strength. I smelled the sharpness of sweat, my own, the others. We danced until Alpia led us out of the center of the wheel, to lie panting for breath on the grassy dunes and watch the sky smolder.

The evening after Midsummer, as the sun rode on the sea, Alpia prophesied the past.

"This knowledge we carry in our hearts and recall in the sacred symbols that we do not profane with worldly workings."

Alpia sat with her back against one of the Ringstones as though it were the familiar wall of her own house. The scarf that modestly covered her hair at other times was draped around her neck. The White Lady—had she truly been Alpia, or some other?—was gone. I, the Norse girls, and Finnchaem sat in a semicircle facing her and facing out of the circle toward the first sea loch. We still wore initiates' white, though it had already been soiled with grass and sand, and Estrid had a blotch of crushed berries on her sleeve.

"The Tale of Winnowings is to be told and heard and told again. You will, in your time, recite it to your daughters."

Estrid blushed. She was to marry Rognvald the Strong at the next moon.

"Hear the Tale told!" Alpia intoned.

"The first people had no name and no story. They were in this place from the beginning of time and came, perhaps, from the stones themselves, for they were small and tough and silent. They did not grow grain.

"The second people came from the south, from a place of blue water where the sun rests in the winter. They sailed into the north, bearing their religion with them, a devotion of blood and sacrifice. For them the sickle of prosperity reaped death, and the Son born in the dark of winter was at Midsummer sacrificed on the altar of the year. Some came to shore in Britain, and many in Éireann, and some in the western isles. But on the long voyage a few were deeply tested by the Mother of the Sea, through storm and wind. They were rescued by her sea-beasts—the porpoise, the whale, and the seal—and guided to these northern islands.

"The woman who led them was given a new prophecy here. She said that the sacrifice of blood was forever ended among them, and that the Mother and her Son of Light were to be made sacrifices of the land and devotions of the spirit. There would be no sanctuaries but the open sky, and no rites but the Names of the Lady and the signs of her Aspects. The people were to devote their minds to peace. Her final prophecy warned that there would be Winnowings—a first sifting and then a second. From the many, few would survive, and these grow again into great nations. And then she died. Her name is not now recalled.

"These were the Builders. Everything they built was of stone, and not only here in the treeless isles. Under the guidance of the White Lady, they erected villages of stone, tombs for the dead, and places of worship were open to the air.

"This was a great work of peace, to express the harmonies of the world in the Aspects, the monthly passion of the moon, the turning of the stars in the Great Wheel of 100 months, till sun and moon moved in harmony once more. But, in honoring the cycle of time, they began to think they might control it. They became wise."

Alpia made a familiar half-smile at that, one I had often seen when I had boasted of some accomplishment.

"They built the first circles of stone. The one by Stenness," and she nodded across the center of the ring to the smaller group which stood southwest, "was made then. Others have been destroyed. The Tale recalls that the sand came to the cities built of stone. People who had been wealthy with sheep and cattle, who had carved intricate spheres and worked in metal, found their works buried under sand. Their homes were deeply buried after magicians' daring brought about the sandblow.

"That was the first sifting. It was soon followed by another, as a tide of new people swelled into the north, into the land of rivers, and washed against every place of the Builders."

I saw them in her mind, the women with the broad faces, the many ornaments of copper and gold.

"These were a people of blood, not of peace, and they did not honor the woman as the Builders had. But the prophetess had said there would be rebuilding after destruction, and so there was. The invaders learned to revere the fruitfulness of the Mother more than the bloody skills of their war-gods. They called this land Alba, the White, for the women's dress and the men who chalked their faces pale as the moon when they stood to defend their people.

"This united people built the Ring." Alpia looked around the circle, her eyes sweeping hawklike from stone to stone. "They were great again. For a time."

"The second pair of Winnowings arrived with the great cold. Places that had yielded grain no longer did. Summer pastures were brief, winters long. The people of the north suffered greatly. As their numbers were reduced, they were struck by a new invasion, the People of the Horse, bearing harsh weapons.

"They turned from the labors of peace to ones of war. Despite their defensive works and great valor, they were conquered, but again the legacy of the Builders turned the conquest into new strength. The invaders adopted the wisdom of inheritance through the woman. They adopted the ancient symbols and carried them on their bodies and carved them on stones."

From here, the Tale was familiar. I had heard it told (with different emphasis) in the households of the Lochlannaig and in the songs of men. How new tribes arrived on each coast. How the Belgae thrust into Kent, driving out the British, forcing them into the north.

"This was the time when many towers were built," Alpia said, "the brochs raised in the isles, along the northern coast. Refuge from the raiders became the abodes of sea-lords, soon pirates. And all were built by a forgotten art, a re-found skill of the Builders.

"The Stonebinders went two by two, a man to order the raising, a woman to bind the stone. Far into the south and the west they travelled, · the fame of their work going before them. Their work stands as strongly as the Rings and symbol-stones, but it should have been a warning that this skill came late, and it was a skill of war and not of peace."

I saw Finnchaem shift and caught her eye. Was she thinking the same thing? How would we ever learn all of this, without a rhyme or song? Maybe she was thinking that she needn't learn this. But who would be the teacher, the White Lady, after Alpia? I recalled the plain hard glances of the Orkney women. The Norse girls would not take up such a responsibility, and anyway, they confused the Lady with their people's many gods and goddesses, with Frigg or Freya. Finnchaem was too slender a reed, Derelei dead.

Myself? Nechtan did not think we would stay here much longer. There was so much to be learned, and I had only thirteen winters. I prayed for quiet years at Golspie but could not see myself sitting at Alpia's feet. I could not see myself anywhere.

Alpia told of the arrival of the Christians, and the early times when the faiths had entwined and found support in each other's prophecies, the eternal Mother and the Son of Light who goes into darkness to rise again and open the path for others.

"It was a time of renewal. Great symbol-stones were raised with the marks of both faiths. Our fleet ranged far south to trade, and less happily, to raid. The kings were great and our people wealthy, when more than one hundred of our swift ships might be lost in a single year off the northern headlands and the greater body remain.

"A new Winnowing had begun, in the midst of happiness, so gently that it was not recognized. It was seduction, not attack."

We leaned forward, and Alpia looked solemn.

"This was the winnowing-basket of learning. Of those who came across the sea from Éireann, and led us into breaking the holy Name and using letters for no greater purpose than to mark the boundaries of a piece of land, or to recall a king's deeds. Of the monks with their foreign writings. And as this learning seduced our wise women and men, our whole people was being lost. The men of Éireann, latecomers who had destroyed the elder people of that island and then in fear of fallen greatness titled them the Sidhe of the mounds, crossed the narrow water to make a new kingdom, Dál Riata, in the west.

"These Scotti came violently into the land, but soon respected our warriors, and were awed by our ancient truth. They called our queens the Ladies of Alba, the White, and then, because they were handsome and easy of converse and generous, our queens took them as consorts. That too was the unmaking of our people."

I recognized the twin heritage I bore and winced to think that I had been so innocent when I came north.

"Among the Dál Riatans, before the coming of the monks, the Lady had been hostage, enslaved, her Aspects divided so that she might be weak—forced to mother the bloody young gods, or cast out as the carrion-crow of battle. Even the early joy with which our people found acceptance with those of the Christian faith was tainted and fouled by suspicion of the woman.

"Even as we were pressed from the west, the Norse and the Danes came against us from across the cold sea. In great battles with the Lochlannaig, our warriors died almost without number, and kings died, and the one land of Fortriu was split into the Kingdom of the North centered at Inverness of Moray, and Kingdom of the South in Atholl.

"The Scots streamed across to their new Dál Riata and throughout the land. Kingship was claimed by the sons of the consorts of Alban queens, and there was war and war. Some claim that the flower of our people was killed by Scots treachery at Forteviot, but that is a small part of a greater loss."

Finnchaem lifted her head.

"We were lost in a relentless rising of a tide, not in a storm, like a child who plays on a rock while the sea comes in. So, we are winnowed surely, the last of the White Lady's people here in the north, and we slide into the Norse and are swallowed."

"But we will be strong again!" I cried.

Alpia shook her head. "We are few. This winnowing may have been too close."

"But it cannot end! There was no prophecy of ending!"

"The world does not end but is remade. We do not end, but we are being reforged, I think, and old metal loses the shape it once had."

Ingigerd said slowly, "My mother has said that all falls to sadness and darkness and decay, and that at Ragnarok the world will end in fire and blood as even the gods are lost." As though her words had brought on that last battle, there was sudden darkness.

And silence.

I groped about me, wondering if I had been thrust back into the buried wheelhouse. Perhaps all this had been a dream and I was just now waking.

"Ingigerd?" I called. "Estrid, Finnchaem? Mother!" I was alone. I stood, felt about, struck stone. But underfoot was grass, and no ceiling overhead. I was still in the Ring.

I turned away from the Ringstones, walking toward the center. A flare of light blinded me.

"Who is there?" I complained, trying to shield my eyes from the brilliance.

A great voice came into my mind, a voice like wind or sea but shaped to the plaint of the plover—*techat, techat, techat*—and then the bird's cry became the wail of an abandoned child. Then silence, and the voice spoke.

"You will marry in fire. You will bear in it and lose in it, before being burned free of the world."

"Mother?" I whispered, knowing it was not, feeling panic stiffen my hands.

"You have asked."

Inside I cried, *But I have not asked!* And knew it was a lie, saw myself tossing a charm into a bed of embers, saw myself chasing after the meaning of dreams. I knelt, before the light consumed me.

"Bride to one," came the voice again. "Strength to another. At the end, mourning."

The light disappeared, though at first I could not tell, my eyes aching with its aftereffects.

I stood, waiting, but there was nothing but wind and sea.

"Mother!" I called. "Lady!" My voice sounded as if it came out of the ground, the cry of a spirit trapped under earth. The sky lightened slowly, from starless black to midsummer night blue.

I saw a light, moving, and started to follow and then stopped. Perhaps I was not meant to follow.

But this was only a torch. I could see that as the world returned. I ran to where the torch was planted beside a pair of boats, men waiting at the oars. There were the other girls, and Alpia, shielding her eyes as through she too had been blinded, looking toward the Ring.

11

GRUACH

GOLSPIE, SUTHERLAND, 1015

As it happened, we were granted only a year.

I sat on the little stool and looked out the window. The wind against my face was chill, denying summer though it carried aromas of growing grass and pungent tide-edge. Women moved along Golspie's shore with baskets, gathering seaweed at low water.

Only a year. And a little more. Midsummer Night (St. John's Eve, I thought, that is how they will mark it, how I must learn to mark it) was some few evenings past.

In the yard between the buildings, the people sent by the king to collect his due seemed a greater number than they were because of the noise, like bramblings and chaffinches wheeling to light on a shorn field, chattering, rising, settling again. The wind caught the rich fabrics of their garments as one then another turned to look at the hall and its closed door. *They think we are odd folk. We wish our partings to be private.*

A bishop sat round-shouldered in a cart, beside him, the abbess of a daughter house of Brigid's foundation. She wore her graying hair dressed long and ringleted under a silk scarf the color of violets. Two men said to be of Boidh's kindred, but some degrees distant, were with the party. Nechtan did not remember them. There was a nervous young monk to assist the bishop, men at arms, and many servants. The noise washed through the windows, subsided like the light itself. In here it was cool and dark.

My brother knelt before Talorc, Alpia at his right. Nechtan was dressed in his best clothes; a new braught was open over the hilt of a fine new sword. At each indrawn breath, a sliver of bright steel glinted at the lip of the bronze-bound scabbard. I knew where my brother wore an old dagger, its darkened blade and worn haft more precious to him than this gift-sword from the king, because it had been Talorc's, and his father's before.

Talorc held his outstretched hands and spoke in a low voice, steady and familiar, but without the sudden uptilt of good humor that often marked him. Why did my brother seem so large, kneeling there, and our parents so shrunken? Even the hall appeared to have closed in, but in a different way than at first. I could remember that fretful child who once saw this only as harsh exile. Now I recognized the modest comfort in this place—but it seemed so small, too small. The kists, the blackened rafters bending beneath their age, the open cupboard with plain pottery bowls and plates and two heavy soft silver goblets. A fitful hearth fire sent its light around their curves and bosses, but had few other glittery things on which to play. There was more precious metal on the shoulders of the traveling party, out there, than in all this place.

"You will lack for nothing, when I come to my proper place," I heard Nechtan say. He was nearly seventeen, of an age to go home as a man grown. Restless to do, to go. The few forays made against intruders had only whetted his need. When the men had come with Malcolm's summons, Nechtan had breathed deeply with a release from long tension.

"Malcolm, second of that name, Ard Ri Alban, summons and welcomes his brother's children to return to the land of their birth."

The messenger had had more to say, about the party coming after, and the king's high regard for Talorc and Alpia who had fostered them, and for Jarl Thorfinn—though that last was a polite fiction. Thorfinn was still a boy, though he'd men and the wherewithal to keep them. Sigurd lay dead after Clontarf, and with Malcolm's help his son Thorfinn was ruler in Caithness—a move to draw the northern lands away from the other Sigurdssons, according to Talorc. "Orkney's fate is not Malcolm's to decree. Thorfinn soon enough will look to the powerful Jarls of Lade for support," he said.

Nechtan and I had talked through two nights before the escort arrived. Wicks had blackened, curled, and fallen under their flames. Alpia and Talorc said little or sat in their own silence when it was impossible to speak. We decided again what had been decided long ago: to return to Alba and gain our lives, if perhaps to lose them.

"Our father took the risk, of all or nothing," Nechtan reminded. "He might have fled and lived."

"To be friendless, landless, poor, and bitter," I had added.

Nechtan stood. After bowing to our foster parents, he turned quickly away and went to stand beside the window that did not have a view of the travelers. He looked fixedly at a scrubby tree outside the wall.

"Daimhin?"

I rose and went to them, my knees finding the hollows pressed by Nechtan's obedience.

I placed my hands in Alpia's to receive her counsel about the dangers of Malcolm's court, the illusions of friendship, the urgency of young men, the snares of untruth.

"Find an older woman of good repute and good sense," she said. "Let her be your mother." I felt a sharp pang, to be bereft of two mothers, to have to seek another. "Take your fears and your concerns to her, but only after she has proven herself trustworthy. As you will be in the company of Christian people, honor the fasts and feasts of the Church of the Son of Light, but remember the Lady in all things. You will recall what else I have taught you."

I bent my head, thinking that I could not possibly forget. Especially I thought of the deeper skills of healing and peace I had learned in the past year—and those lessons cut short.

"I go, but what do I leave unlearned?"

"You have learned enough," Alpia said, but her eyes were troubled. "It is less the learning than the remembering."

I smoothed my hands across my thighs, looked away from Alpia's haggard face.

"You must discipline yourself. I will not be there, and you are of an age to set your own path and not deviate."

My foster-mother let go of my hands, leaned over, and felt along the side of her seat. She brought out a little basket of plaited reed and willow, the round cover held down by a silver clasp.

I took the basket and was surprised by the soft interior slither of bone discs in a sealskin bag. "Oh," I said, realizing that she was sending these away with me. I did not want to seem so childish but began to cry anyway, tears coming heavy without sobs, wetting my cheeks and sliding down my throat.

"These are not mine," I protested, remembering poor Derelei and her pride in the pregnancy that killed her.

"You are my daughter."

The basket tilted in my grip and I felt a different weight shift. I opened it to find the bag of discs that she used to keep in an ivory box, but also her worn spindle whorl with its incised symbols, a flat bottle of green glass that I knew contained an extract to bring sleep and gentle dreams, and one small bone, like a finger-bone, lying loose on the gray sealskin.

I looked up.

"Hidden inside the flipper of the porpoise is a hand," Alpia said softly, and Talorc seemed not to hear. "A sign of our kinship."

Alpia closed the lid and pushed the clasp into place. "Keep this as your own. There are few women in the south who will share your knowledge. You will know them—do not profane your truth among others, but serve discreetly all that you can, and teach when you find young women ready for the gift."

I took the basket and stood. We embraced, parents and fosterlings. I heard Nechtan whisper that he wished that Fode were here and Ciniod.

Our belongings already had been loaded, two bags and a metal-strapped box. We had not amassed wealth here in the north that might be packed and carried in cured leather. I opened the bag containing my most personal items, combs and scents, and tucked the basket inside.

I smelled the impatience of men and beasts. Though it was full day, in the green of summer, I could not help but remember the hastening-off from Brechin. I heard it had been burned by the Northmen some years ago. The porch where I had sheltered from cold-falling rain was no longer there, the bench consumed. I remembered the abbot lifting his hand, the juniore who had whispered so angrily as he lifted up a peevish child.

I pinned a mantle of checkered blue at my shoulder, close nap of wool that I myself had spun and woven as Alpia said. I mounted the cart behind the abbess and settled my garments neatly. I wore linen dyed the bright yellow of weld, trimmed in green, with a green scarf that showed my brown hair—I knew why the youngest of the kinsmen looked at me from under lowered eyelids. The clothing was a show, like the composure of my face, like Nechtan's confident smile.

As we moved out between the buildings, Alpia cupped her uplifted hand in a private blessing, placing me under the protection of the Lady of the Waxing Moon. I sketched the response. The others would think it no more than a wave.

One of the men began to sing.

I leaned my head forward, eyes blurring with tears. I stared at my hands, traced old scars with the affection of memory—this burn from the night we roasted Fode's deer, that mark from a fall while following Alpia across rounded cobbles near a broch. I considered the crescent moons at the base of my nails that indicated health or sickness. Were they were tinged with pending summer-chill? Alpia would have laughed and said that I was a creature of easy imagination.

We had not gone far from Golspie, the cart jolting along the track, when the abbess spoke to me.

"You were close with your foster-mother. You are fortunate, as I was not," she said. The abbess was yet a handsome woman, her fine features sagging toward jowlishness; her pale skin and fading hair were set off by the dark subtlety of her scarf. Her appraising eyes were deep with knowledge.

"Yes, Abbatissima."

At that, the abbess laughed.

"So formal, for the High King's niece," she said lightly. "I am not in major vows, dear Gruach, but hold my cell by kinship back to holy Brigid."

I nodded silently; this was how these things were done. The color in the abbess' cheeks, I realized, was from skillfully applied ruam and not sun.

The abbess laid a slender hand on my arm. "Dear Gruach," she said. That rusty name again, a church name by which all would know me, all but my brother and the people of this little, already distant place. "You may call me Cipia, dear child," said the abbess, but I did not return my other name. I was only Gruach now.

12

MACBETH

LOCH OF THE CRANNÓGS, 1016

"Young Edmund leads the army himself, all but king."

"He has a name of iron."

"Cnut will temper him, then," came a voice broad with native Norse.

Macbeth rode just behind the king. He was enclosed in his own silence, while the warriors argued, the men of art held learned dispute, and the women chattered with their own concerns.

The warriors would have included Duncan in their talk, were he present. He had been allowed to accompany a small band meant to persuade a holder to part with some wealth, as he had made borderlands a reason to claim two masters and render no taxes. Macbeth had watched him ride out with sword and shield, as big as many of the men though in truth he was not old enough to claim that dignity, and he was certainly not looking at his foster-brother who had to stay within the gates.

"I tell you that Cnut will surely win. The army chose him, no matter where Svein's mantle fell."

"He fled Lindsey speedily enough, at Aethelred's return."

"And left maimed hostages to warn against his return. He will not be turned back to Daneland this time."

With calculation harsh as any made by his Viking forefathers, Cnut had cut off the hands and noses of captive Lindsey-men. "He might merely have killed them, but graves make briefer memories," Malcolm had said gruffly.

"Edmund will fight."

"It is his mother's blood showing, not his father's."

"Queen Emma is Norman. Strong steel there."

The debate turned to appreciation of women, and Macbeth followed its twists and turns with a budding interest he tried not to make apparent.

The path followed a great stretch of water. It was much like the familiar long arm of Ness, except that its tranquil surface was dotted with crannógs, island-lumps of timber and stone and mud, ancient refuges in time of bitter war. Most of them were overgrown, the bridges to them broken. Otters made safe dens in their banks and nesting birds filled the trees with song.

This water was not always so calm. The marks of last fall's great floods showed on the banks of loch and stream. Gray banners of leaves clung in the trees. There were drifts of sand and rock and mudflats where new plants sprouted vivid green. Floods raged through the rivers and scoured the shores of lochs. They were cleansing, in a violent way.

A foul smell clung to his skin and clothing and made him wish that a flood—a small, controlled flood—had washed through the hall where they had been so long confined. Sudden weather had shut in the king's party at a modest place, scarcely suited to be a night's stopping-over for such a crowd. There was not enough food or drink. Not enough water for washing. The hall was quickly verminous, the jakes overflowed and the area inside the outer walls stank of excrement and urine.

"I have heard that Thorkell fights beside Cnut."

"It's true."

"The Sveinssons must indeed think him a brother, to allow him at their sides after three years with the Anglish."

Macbeth listened closely, but the conversation turned again, in the directionless way of idle talk. It did not move neatly back and forth, like a ball thrown hand to hand.

(What is a word? The mind's expositor. What forms a word? The tongue. What is the tongue? It whips the air. Oswald said that the son of Charlemagne had so interrogated his tutor, numberless questions posed and neatly answered.)

Thorkell's name had caught his attention, however. He thought often about the warrior who among tall men was called the Tall. One year he ravaged cities, the next, he tried to save clerics. He was Cnut's fosterer, then Aethelred's savior, then returned to Cnut. Some said he had become Christian. Some said that he was the conscience of Cnut. Macbeth worried that over like a bit of gristle.

The loch curved into a bay, the trail bending beside. The horses, restive in the morning, had settled to plodding. At the king's side, the bishop of Dunkeld nodded in his saddle, but his hands remained firmly on the jeweled reliquary he carried.

The Brecbennach was itself beautiful, covered with silver and glancing gems, secured by a braided chain. What it carried was of much more
value, for inside were some of St. Columba's mortal remains. Macbeth
wished that he might carry the reliquary, even from the bishop to the
church or chapel when they halted for the night, but it was not allowed.
He had touched it once. The metal was warm as living flesh. Warm with
sanctity and power. It was more precious to the king than any wealth,
his father's long Frankish sword, or his most impregnable fortification.
The Brecbennach was victory. The king could defeat any foe when it
was carried into battle with him. So long as his cause was just.

Did God Himself look to the justness of battles or was that left to
the saint whose name was invoked? Columba was said to be vengeful
against those who displeased him, snappish as the Fox that was a name
he also bore. Perhaps that was why Malcolm had been so badly beaten
at Durham. Or perhaps St. Cuthbert had been even stronger, his bones
content in their rich king-given garment, not wishing to be rousted out
to Alba.

The bishop snored once and woke.

At the end of the loch, where the river flowed in, a tongue of land
ended in a beach. Pale sand could be seen now through the trees, and
above it, the walls of the fortification. It was a strong place, a center
of Dál Riata's ancient kings. Macbeth looked forward to swimming in
the cold loch, bathing in hot water, having his matted hair combed out
and fragrant oil soothed across his midge-bitten skin. They had left
the pestilent hall as soon as the storm eased and light came in the east,
men and slaves moving as though whipped to haste, all the company
in disarray. When the wind came from the bishop's direction it carried
a bitter reek of the unwashed. The Church did not believe in tending
the flesh. Oswald (who had ridden ahead with the king's purveyor) was
cleaner than most, a lingering trait of his noble birth.

The path swung away from a marshy place, circling a knob of rock
and tracking farther out to ford a stream before closing back to the
reedy loch-edge. A ruined crannóg stood offshore. On the mound
crouched a lone figure.

"Who is that man?" Macbeth asked.

"That hermit's roosted on the crannóg for some years," answered
Eamon, a native of these lands.

Macbeth had passed here once before and seen this crannóg little different from the others, except for its worsening state of disrepair, but he had never seen the holy man. As they approached, the man stood and came to the edge of his island. He wore only a ragged bit of a garment, once saffron yellow, hanging ungirdled from thin shoulders to thinner hams. He was wild-bearded and long-haired, overgrown as the island itself.

He raised his arms. A benediction? A curse? Such hermits were often mad, and remorseless as the very saints. But there was an aura of peace about this man, a lapping tranquility of glinting water and ancient rock. Macbeth eased his horse off the path and stopped.

The holy man lifted his arms again.

Macbeth dismounted. He let the company move on, the packhorses and slow carts last under their creaking burdens.

"If you mean to relieve yourself, best not in sight of the hermit," remarked a man guarding the rear, "lest he curse your water to be held within your body."

Eamon and two others made their way back, while the king waited ahead.

"Why this, Mac Findlaích? The king's mood is not one to tempt."

"I would like to talk with the holy man."

They laughed and crowded their horses close around him. "Come on, boy, we're close to decent food and drink for the first time in half a moon." Macbeth saw the irritation on their faces.

"The boy has some great sin to pray off," cried Eamon. The bishop nodded, as though in agreement.

"I am called to speak with this hermit," Macbeth said, his words loud for the king and the bishop, not the men who chaffed him. He could feel Malcolm's eyes on him, assessing him, weighing his action. He stood calmly, ready to obey whatever the king ordered.

"Let him go out, if he wishes—and if the holy fool will have him," Malcolm said, with a glance toward the tattered man. "A boy's curiosity. But, Eamon, and you, Mac Domnall, wait on him."

"He might lose his way on this beaten track, indeed," Eamon whispered.

Macbeth's face burned as he walked away from them. He could have ridden on alone, the fortification visible from here. Perhaps the king feared for his safety with this hermit. It might not be wise to intrude on his chosen isolation. But he didn't dare change his mind now. He stepped to the water's edge and called to the man, asking if he might speak with him.

There was no connecting bridge, lost in a flood or broken away by the holy man to ensure his solitude. The hermit disappeared around the back of the crannóg. The two warriors laughed behind him. He had frightened the holy man into hiding.

A log floated free of the island. Not a log, but an ancient canoe hollowed from a tree-trunk. The holy man sat in it and paddled toward the shore. He nudged it into a depression in the bank and Macbeth climbed in, felt the sodden weight and age of the boat as the man pushed off from shore and drove it slowly back to the crannóg. The canoe fit into a slot in the timber structure of the island, so that they left it without wetting. Macbeth followed the silent man, who walked bare-footed through a midden of freshwater clam shells, turtle shells, and fish bones near the water's edge.

The holy man crouched. "Water feeds me," he said, the words bursting out. His hands moved restlessly, like one of the filid counting out his words. "Live from the living water. Fish and herbs to cool the raging blood." He looked up from his hands. His eyes, sunken as they were, glowed with anguish. Macbeth had expected holiness, not pain.

"How do you live?"

The holy man tilted his head toward what had been a conical structure of wood and withy, but was now slumped and overgrown with weeds on the sodden thatch. Some untrimmed sticks had been thrust into the walls to hold them up, and rushes bound loosely onto the roof. Macbeth stared at the ragged den, cold and cheerless. There was no sign of fire or smell of smoke. He must eat the fish and water-creatures raw. Did this make a man closer to God—or to the animals?

"Why?" The man clutched his shoulder. "Why?"

"I felt a call. I saw you. I wondered why you are here."

The man relaxed his grip, surprisingly strong for a praying man reduced to bone and tendon.

"You are a seeker. I am no seeker. God hunted me."

He went into his den on hands and knees and backed out, holding a string of jet beads in his hand.

"I was riding spear in hand. Blood hot to let another's, when I was struck down." His voice, rusty from disuse, gradually became clear. "The saints built an abbey by this loch." He pulled the beads violently through his fingers, smooth from working in the water. "The abbey now fallen. I was struck down and lay dead. When I was restored, my enemy was gone. I do not remember him now. I found these beads laid in a ring around my horse. It would not move until I gathered them. I tied my weapons to the saddle, my silver ornaments, garments, all but this cover for my nakedness, and drove the horse away."

His voice had drifted lower and lower, as though running out, until Macbeth leaned close to hear.

"I had great pride in my hair, and I pulled it out to twist a cord and thread the holy beads. I tell my prayers ceaselessly."

The quieter he spoke, the more his face shone with harsh holiness.

"I was deep in the flesh, and labor to pare this husk from my soul. Sight of the face of God has been promised me."

He stared at the man's emaciated arms. He had thought the hermit lived in peace, while all the time he was at war for his soul. Across the water, the men, bored with their wait, were competing at stone-skipping.

"You are close to God."

"I am far from God."

He thought of Cnut and Thorkell. "Tell me, can one man serve as another's conscience? Can someone be the conscience for a king?"

"We bend under the burden of our own souls. They are eternal and our flesh is short. Some who seem to walk lightly have killed their souls."

"But what if a man is a great man, a leader of men?" he persisted.

The hermit looked across the water and then turned to Macbeth. His eyes were angry. "Those who ride with a king should know that he must secure his conscience in his heart, as in a reliquary, and look to it often, as he does the saint's bones. If he does not, then he will be the ruin of his people."

The holy man stood and draped the beads around his weathered neck. "Seeker. What have you found?"

Macbeth was unable to say.

"Should you build a hut, so that we can blend our prayers?"

"I am not intended to be—so."

"By whose word?"

"I am of royal blood," he began, and realized that had little to do with it. "I believe—myself—that I am meant to act in the world." He was surprised at the sudden assurance he felt, though what the action might eventually be, he could not say.

"Then you have found something."

Macbeth followed him to the canoe. The hermit's face was blank now, passionless, and he did not acknowledge the fighting men gleaming with leather and steel as he pushed the boat onto the shore. He turned back to his island without a parting word or blessing.

Macbeth started to take the reins of his horse, but Eamon pulled them away.

"Does a holy man ride?" he asked in mock wonderment.

"And, look, he has neglected his tonsure," Mac Domnall added.

"Indeed! He has been so long away from his brother monks."

Eamon pulled his dagger, the edges well-whetted during the long days weather-bound. "We will shave him, then." He started toward Macbeth. There was too much intention in his eyes for mere play.

Macbeth jumped back, away from both men, and pulled out his own short blade.

"The monk bares a fang." They laughed and started forward, leaning toward him with their arms out and fingers spread to tangle in his hair and pull him down. Their teeth gleamed like hounds' teeth.

"Do not," he said.

"Do not, oh, do not!"

Though he was trembling inside, the dagger was steady in his hand. He readied himself to spring, or run, observing the horses where they stood.

They faced each other for a long moment.

Eamon stood straight and puffed out a little breath. "Enough." There was new respect in his eyes, and Macbeth was surprised to see it. Was it because he had acted as a man, or mindfulness of the king? Eamon nudged his companion. "I'd rather be resting my backside there ahead." He slipped his knife back in its sheath and mounted. Mac Domnall followed.

"Will you ride with us, Monk?" Eamon asked.

Duncan's teasing echoed in his thoughts. He grated out, "I am no monk."

"Macbeth the Monk we call you, and you are to us."

13

GRUACH

The young man Tómméne, limber as a young willow and nearly as tall, leaped up on a bench, sending it groaning on its stout legs. He put out his arms, balanced, then lifted his hands like a priest.

"We took cattle from fair green fields, and no man dared oppose us!" he cried.

Other young men cheered his impromptu song, stamped their feet.

"White cattle heavy in the hindquarters and brown cows, these we took, all that we desired. Also we took heavy silver, bright pennies wearing king's heads, fine dirhams out of Rus-land."

One of his companions ululated a battle-cry. It blended with the general din of musicians and singers and talkers, all in the smoky overheated air.

Tómméne leaned with the drink, like a tree in a gale, but righted himself. "Cattle ran before our spears as captives. They were light-heeled as girls pursued by brave men."

Laughter, and the young men glanced at the young women. Many glances were turned my way. I flushed, looked down, tried to appear as though I was examining some stain upon my sleeve. The uproar died down and the measures of a dance could be heard. "Now comes a tune that these bellowing bulls will not drown," I said to my new friend Samthann, but not too low, "so we shall show them light heels." She smiled (though she was plain, and few eyes followed her) and we moved through the knots of men to an open space.

I whirled, the stirred air rising up my sleeves and cooling my feverish skin. The hall was not the largest, and many travelled with the king while others had returned from the border raids. The air was thick with torch smoke and beeswax, the aroma of burning wood, and the scent of bodies, some washed and scented, some still reeking of cattle or blood. Samthann stepped lightly, lifting her heels and kicking out. Plain she might be, and only from a small place in the foothills, but she could dance.

We stepped past the young men, who boasted of their deeds and demonstrated how they'd struck skillful blows, while all the time they watched and hoped to be watched. Sometimes it was wearisome, to hear them expand the snatching of a few cows into a great battle. But it was never tedious to look upon young men, bright and quivering with valor, their blood up. Their bodies were taut with heroism each new evening, and each night the ale had its effect. The young men sagged, slept, snored. Became boys, their cheeks rounding red with a day's exertion.

Samthann led the dance through the hall, closer to the thudding beat of drums, closer to the singing strings. I tried to match her footing but often could not—these southern dances were quick and giddy. I limped for a few measures after turning my ankle on something lost among the rushes.

The melody ended, and I dropped breathless onto a cast-aside mantle.

"Enough," I panted, as Samthann sat beside me.

"Dancing makes a woman beautiful," Samthann said.

"It makes you red," I answered, "and sweaty in too many clothes." I pushed damp strands of hair off my face, licked the salt from my lips.

"Perhaps we should dance naked." The Ochil girl tossed her head. An unfortunate gesture, with her long face and horsey teeth.

I gasped, remembering how I had danced naked, wondering how she came to say that. Perhaps it was my silence that made Samthann rise. She would find us something to drink, she said, and disappeared into the crowd.

Even more difficult to learn than southern footings were the dances of speaking and silence, praise and barb. Battles fought by women, their words no less edged than men's blades. Battles for position, and, yes, survival, in Malcolm's court. There he sat, high on the elaborate seat between pillars carved with wolves and twining large-eyed serpents, High King Malcolm II. He scowled at everyone and no one, while men and women fawned around him—particularly that narrow-faced Gillecomgan, always at the king's side—and his praise-poet recited ancient tales and past victories.

The old king would smile at times to hear his fighting men shout or sing of battle. Most of the time he looked troubled or angry. I'd overheard one man say that the king could not get the smell of other men's wealth out of his nose, and that after failing to take half-fortified Durham with the aid of Strathclyde, he'd lick his wounds and plan another expedition south, perhaps to Bernicia. He lifted his head, saw that I was looking at him. I turned away, chilled by his wintry regard.

I ran my hands down the front of my overtunic, rich red and cut in the Byzantine fashion, stiffened with embroidery and jewels on the neck and front and thigh-length hem. The familiar léine beneath, sufficient for Golspie, was pale blue, like my narrow veil. My slippers were red leather from Galicia.

Cipia had from the first seen to my new clothing, clucking over the plain sturdiness of northern garments. Noblewomen now dressed after the fashion of the German Empress Cunigunda and the great Empress of the East, she said, and to dress like a farm girl following the herds would not make me friends among the women or admirers among the men.

"And your ornament is important, dear Gruach," she'd reminded that afternoon, as day faded and we had prepared for the evening meal. Cipia considered a string of ornate glass beads, then draped a necklace of amber around my neck and pinned a circle of gold at the center of my breast. Both were gifts from the king, who had provided every stitch of clothing, even the shoes on my feet, as I no longer had family or lands to support me.

"You should wear only bronze or gold, to make your hair more golden," Cipia said. "Silver draws you pale."

I remembered Halla in her dim house and her tales of lost wealth. I touched the beaded gold and recalled what Alpia once told me, that near all the silver was melted down from Roman loot, and that most of the gold had been dug out of barrows in Éireann or Alba, ornaments of the dead worn again or melted to make new vanities. Ailech had seldom worn jewelry, and that always silver, holy to the Goddess. But I liked the glow of gold, and despite myself was proud of the price I wore. I loved the touch of silk and colors bright as a field of flowers, filling my soul after the gray shades of the north. While I missed Alpia, this was where I should be.

The court had traveled easily along the Tay, following the old road that came to the Roman bridge where the River Amon entered the Tay. This Bellathor was less a fort than a palace, though the site had been

been a fortress even before the Romans made a troop-station of it, naming it Bertha. Now it offered comfort in the shadow of the mountains. As we combed and dressed our hair and touched our faces with color, Cipia had spoken of some great occurrence she expected after the meal. Perhaps that excitement, too, attached itself to the heavy gold. I had never felt so attractive as I did then.

During the dinner, wine spun my head as ale did not. The abbess chattered and lifted her slim hands in the air like doves. She ate only sparingly but drank meddyglyn, a Cymric concoction of mead, spices, and medicinal herbs. "For heart's ease," she said, tipping the goblet for me to taste. I wondered why her heart should ache. The abbess was beautiful, and powerful, though she was old. Like all the court she looked toward Malcolm in hope of finding favor, the way certain flowers turned their faces always toward the sun.

Cipia smiled encouragingly at me over the rim of the goblet, like a mother urging me to take the medicine. She drank another swallow of meddyglyn, closed her eyes as though her head was whirling. When I looked again, the abbess drained the glass, her mouth drawn down at the corners as though she might cry.

"Here." I was startled to find Samthann pressing a bowl of something into my hand. "You looked halfway to sleep," she said, sitting down with her drink.

"A memory," I said. "Or too much wine."

I sniffed—mulsum—and set it aside. The blend of too-sweet mead and Frankish wine going to vinegar was more than I could stomach.

"Plain water would be good," I said mournfully.

Samthann sniffed. "If you want the sickness, then. The water is always tainted. It breeds worms and flies."

I ended by drinking the mulsum because I was thirsty. Samthann laughed, and the sight of her lips pulled back over those horsey teeth sent me into helpless laughter.

When the drums said to dance again, we danced.

I swayed, so that my long sleeves swayed. I whirled, and the silk-bound hem of my tunic lifted and flared. The world did not go forward nor back but crabwise scuttled. I was a woman now, yet younger, younger, as though I had been for a time an old woman bent over my devotions and was, by art, shifted back to my true age. I felt the blood pound in my temples. The faces of the hall were bright blurs, like the time I had fainted in church and the images had spun above my head, Mary and the angel, his hand upraised. Daniel between lions. Jesus enthroned in Heaven, with his right hand drawing up a chain of the righteous, while from his left the damned spilled down to the claws of Hell.

Now these faces were seemingly caught in a tapestry's weave. Two old women gossiping, glancing out of the netted corners of their eyes. A fork-bearded layman from a monastic house. Beside him, a tight-lipped monk of the Culdees, who found no joy in sweet life but only in silence and poor food. A brehon argued a point of secular law into a heedless ear. The law-giver was white-haired, and he tilted his face just so, impassioned with argument.

He looked then like Alpia.

I stumbled. I had promised not to forget her disciplines, and I had—but not willingly. It was only that many of the observances were rigorous, even dangerous when so many churchmen looked on. Muttering clerics did not love Mary-of-the-Sea, but only the Son and the Father. I could not easily slip away now in the night time or go walking alone in the woods to a solitary clearing. That was not appropriate for the king's ward.

In the first light, I would say the Names and make a ceremony to recall the Aspects.

A falcon, loosed by some prankster, arrowed past my ear toward the fire. The young warriors whooped after it.

I had not imagined how it would be, this life! The very colors of it were different. When I remembered Golspie it seemed that all was gray, black, brown, as though wrapped in mist, and even the greens faded to the dull green of dying foliage, the rusty green of weed at the tide-line. The land had magicked the people and made them dun as winter fields. Everything here was bright and soft, like the silks carried through the Rus-lands and across the cold sea, or bright and hard, jewels frozen in gold settings, and steel that everywhere showed its edge. Had it been this way when we were children? I could not remember. Nechtan said it had been so, but I had seen him stunned as well by the color and noise.

I was thankful for the abbess (though I had learned to call her Cipia), who had guided me in the ways of the court and taught me games and pastimes to ease the boredom of endless riding about and waiting on the whims of men in this bare fortress and that noble hall. She taught me which women to beware, because of their constant intrigues. She taught me how to artfully listen as a warrior maundered of some battle.

I had gone once with Cipia to her foundation, a cell of eight consecrated virgins living in plank houses beside a small lochan. They had servant families to tend their household, and across the fields, a monastery where they went to Mass and sang psalms from the left-hand side. It was no ascetic life, scarcely even the little death of "white martyrdom" when beloved things are abandoned.

The abbess did not spend a great deal of time at her house. She travelled with the court and had gone in pilgrimage to Kildare, where a college of virgins tended a sacred flame in honor of Brigid, and to Patrick's house, and to many holy places in Northumbria. Cipia knew of holy Lonceta at Abernethy and had seen her stone cell, but none spoke with her through the barred window through which food temporal and spiritual was passed. "She took a vow of silence," she explained, "but I have myself heard an unworldly voice from her cell at night, reciting strange prayers to the Queen of Heaven. The abbot says she has been visited by a bright angel who speaks the tongue of Eden."

I knew those prayers. I had asked, often, but not yet been permitted to visit.

The abbess had become my third mother, as Alpia had said. It was to her I had confided a few days ago the arrival of my bleeding, my coming-of-age so long delayed that I had thought myself cursed.

Now Cipia smiled sleepily at me from the table, where the brew was easing her sad heart.

Why sad? The night was full of song.

I turned to dance again and collided with a youth, one of the king's grandsons and fosterlings. It was the young one out of Moray, his hair a rusty shade, so quiet and bookish that they called him the Monk. He stammered an apology and ducked away. The other fosterling, now a young man, was far more likely. Tall and broad-shouldered, with hair as pale as any of the Lochlannaig, and soon to be the king of Strathclyde, or so it was rumored.

The last whirl of the music lifted me up and set me down on a bench outside in the coolness. I put my hand to my chest and felt my heart pounding. I rested my head against the wall and breathed deeply, feeling the drink begin to ebb. I smelled the grain ripening on the farms and a strong fecund scent of bog and water-edge. The blue night air was sweet with summer berries.

Samthann found me there. I sighed, thinking the Ochil girl must find some other partner. But Samthann sat down beside me, not leaning back but nervously upright, on the edge of the bench as though prepared to leap up at any moment.

"The air is sweet," she said, echoing my thought.

"It is."

"Such a night," Samthann breathed, her voice taut with expectation. "It would be fine to have a young man, on such a night."

I thought of the warriors already reeling from drink, but handsome, yes, even when they slept and snored. Maybe more so then.

"You were fostered in the north."

"Yes, in a place you've never heard of."

"That is a place of legend, for us here," Samthann said. Her eyes shone as she looked out across the land. "It is said that the women of the north are very wise."

I felt a swell of longing. "My foster-mother knew as much as any of the king's council. More. She knew true history, and…"

I caught myself, realizing that this girl was barely met and no one to confide in.

"History," Samthann said impatiently and turned to face me. "All men can do is talk of battle and death, how King Domnall died here and King Constantin was killed at this very place not very long ago at all. We're alive and all they can talk about is who's dead and dust. We are alive now! Tell me—I know there are flowers to bring healing or sleep. Or love."

I bit my lip on laughter. *An aphrodisiac.*

"Mugthigern," Samthann sighed. "You have seen him. The curly-headed one who was behind Tómméne when he sang."

An undistinguished-looking young man, thick of neck. I had thought at the time that he looked slow-witted as the stolen cattle.

"Did she teach you about this?" Samthann pressed. "Can you give me a mixture to sprinkle on his bed or to put in his drink?"

I shifted on the bench, embarrassed by the girl's urgency and by this tangled understanding of the women who maintained lore and wisdom from ancient times. I had sensed a kind of caution or interest before, from both women and men, but never such a request!

"Please! I will die for him!" Samthann caught my hands and pressed them in her damp grip.

"I do not know any such potion, to bring love where it is not," I said. Samthann's long face lengthened. "I do not think there is any such thing."

She slumped against the wall. "I hoped, perhaps— But it is nothing."

I knew of plants that could raise desire, but they were set apart by Alpia's stern warnings that they were not to be casually employed. This miserable girl! Perhaps Cipia, with her powerful connections, could speak with Mugthigern's people.

"Gruach!"

I cocked my head, not sure if I had heard my name called.

"Gruach, niece of the king!"

I stood and went into the light fanning from the door.

A servant was searching through the room. He saw me and threaded through the curious crowd.

"The rechtaire has asked for you, on the king's word," he breathed.

When I came to the rechtaire, he stood frowning with his arms crossed. "There you are," he said, as though to a simple child who had wandered away. I laid my hand on his arm and was escorted through the whispering crowd, toward the glaring light of many candles and Malcolm in his high seat surrounded by his supporters.

The king smiled, with fatherly pride it seemed, and my heart swelled in my chest, driving out cold fear.

I straightened my back and carried my head high. I was conscious of how my blue silk veil shimmered on my hair, of the drape of expensive garments. Here among the high-born, I was as regal as any, inheritor of both the kings of Dál Riata and the queens of the north.

"My child!" Malcolm said loudly, extending his hand. I offered my obedience. "But you are a woman indeed," he said, quite low.

I lifted my face. The king smiled indulgently, but now I saw that his blue eyes were cold as the hand that gripped mine. Pride and expectation and fear swirled in my stomach. I searched through the crowd for Nechtan and found him, far back near the wall, standing stiffly with his hands clenched.

The Ard Ri Alban indicated that I should stand at his left hand. "This my niece, Gruach, daughter of Boidh mac Kenneth and Lonceta of the kindred of Urguist, being both fatherless and motherless…" His voice boomed through the hall, the voice of a king directing men in battle. "…is as a daughter to me. Of age to be married…"

I remembered the image of the man whose eyes had searched from the fire. My thoughts settled on Duncan, but that was not the face I had seen. A chill passed across me, chased by heat.

The king lifted my right hand. I watched him place it in that of Gillecomgan.

"No!" I shouted and snatched my hand from the favorite's damp grasp. He had an evil name among the women.

Gillecomgan flushed and his lips went white. His narrow face was stretched on its bones.

"I cannot marry him!"

I saw ripples of surprise, horror, amusement pass through the crowd. There must be a kind face somewhere, a friend. The faces looked like depictions of sin, that one Envy, another Greed, a third Cruelty.

"What is this?"

The king's harsh question brought me around like a clap of thunder. Gillecomgan's anger paled beside the king's blood rage. Malcolm reached for my hand—still hanging, as though forgotten—and his fingers closed hard upon it as on the throat of an enemy. I felt the blood hammer in my wrist.

"I believed..." I whispered. "I believe my mother must give her word."

"Your mother is an addled nun," Malcolm growled.

No, I thought, *my mother is the White Lady.*

"I am both king and father, and you will go where I command and marry as I deem fit. I have been assured that you are finally come of age to bear children." His cold eyes fixed me with a basilisk's stare. I felt as though my clothes had been cut from my body and I stood naked before the court. Displayed like a captive from some defeated enemy, a slave—indeed, I was, captive and friendless. Except for one who was equally bereft.

"Nechtan," I whispered, lifting my gaze past the stares of the crowd to find him struggling forward, his hand curled as though already around a weapon. His face was set and pale.

"Nechtan," the king repeated, very low, as though he had meant only his own ears to hear and his mind consider that name. I glanced toward Malcolm and saw that he was watching my brother.

My own fear drained away, a shallow thing compared to the real terror I now knew. For Nechtan, who was two ways worthy to be king.

Into the lions' den.

If he meant to challenge the king, to demand his say in my marriage—old blood called him, our grandfather's and father's blood
spilled—then I would lose him too.

"If noble Gillecomgan will have me, then I will be his wife," I said,
quickly, before the words ate themselves, before Gillecomgan's brutal
glare took all my courage. My voice came high and trembling. "I beg the
king's mercy, and his, on my youth. This came as too much a surprise."

"You are but female, and weak, it is no wonder," the king said, nodding, suddenly as beneficent as a priest over his blessings. Then, loudly,
"My niece shall marry Gillecomgan, feared in battle, wise in counsel, of
the great people of Cenél Loairn. It shall be at Kilrymont, when we rest
there to celebrate the feast of St. Luke."

I found Nechtan had made his way quite close to the high seat. He
stood motionless and silenced by my acquiescence.

Does he know why I do this?

Does it matter? Surely if I had not agreed, I would have found myself prisoned by silence and stone like our mother.

I heard the shouts of men and women, and the harper jangling some
melody, but it was all quite distant. Nechtan and I might have been
alone on a green bank, and he comforting me in my fear. He raised his
open hand, as though in farewell, then turned and pushed his way back
through the crowd toward the door.

Malcolm patted my bruised hand and spoke of gifts. I could not look
at him, kin and enemy, uncle and murderer, but his voice was gentle as
though it had never crashed like a sea against me.

I will be married in the month when leaves flame and ivy blooms, I thought.
People will say, bad omens for marriage.

"Marry in fire, bear in fire, lose in fire." So the Goddess had promised. Or threatened, truly, because there was no comfort in those words.
Where was the fire now? And where was the young mormaer with the
sorrowful eyes, shown to me and no dream, truly shown? *Promised.*

"I wish you many children and easy bearing," Cipia said, as she took
my arm and pulled me into a circle of chattering women. "The amber
beads are lucky, are they not?"

"As gold is said to be good for sore eyes, I'll find that useful too," I
said huskily.

"Why, child, don't be afraid. I was myself married, until he died in battle and I went to God's bed." The abbess smiled and smiled. "A good match, dear Gruach, that lifts the king's disfavor from your house."

"It was your doing that brought this on me!"

Cipia moved back. Her chin trembled and her eyes were vague.

"I trusted you! How long have you spied on me for Malcolm?"

"Gruach, I have not! I was asked if you were grown and of course...I thought you would..."

I whirled away from Cipia, brushed off the good wishes of women and their congratulatory hands.

"I envy you," said Samthann quietly. She stood between me and the door, and the clean night air, the darkness where Nechtan waited. Angry words boiled inside me, but when I looked at the girl's plain, honest face, they were quelled.

"Do not." And then I was past Samthann, and outside.

I had thought Nechtan would wait for me, but he was not there. I walked twice around the inner enclosure and asked the porter if anyone had gone out the gate. He pulled his head back between his shoulders and told me no.

I sat at the lip of the well, which did stink of sickness. I found a loose stone and tossed it into the shaft, heard it plunk into the water. The women had not followed me into the darkness they so feared. I could not bear the sight of them, their faces eager or sorrowful, young and old, all versions of the Goddess who should protect me in this land where men ruled all.

"Where is your power?" I asked the darkness. "How can you let me be given to such a man?"

I felt the cold breath of the well against my arm. I could lean into its mouth, be swallowed. Into the earth to rise again, but that promise might be as empty as the others.

"Marry in fire, bear in it, lose in it..."

If there was truth in the words, and there was, there must be, then perhaps there was hope in the second prophecy.

"Must I marry Gillecomgan?" I asked. "Bride to one, strength to another? What does it mean?" I did not dwell on the last words of that triad—mourning, mourning.

A bat or night-flying bird swooped close. The peregrine, maybe, unhooded and released from its perch in a jest but too accustomed to captivity to fly away.

"Why have you abandoned me? Do you live only in the north?"

No answer.

There was never any to be given. It was an illusion, had always been an illusion, made real by my own belief.

I let the black rage have me. I was alone. I burned like a red ember inside a dark shell, no longer a child but a woman grown facing a woman's woes.

14

LAPWING

Dunkeld Abbey, 1018

Crinán's son rests at Dunkeld as he travels on to Partick. I have watched him at meals and at prayer (to which he is indifferent) and I am drawn to him. A sun in its rising, first light dawning on Strathclyde's realm. A blond king to rule, and Lapwing to be his ruler.

Young supplants old, the young tree sprouts from the stump, the young horse lifts its hooves and the young stag its antlers against their sires.

(Tell me, spirit of the water, how long? The pebble I toss into speaking water makes rings that slide to ripples and take these marks away unread. It is a woman who lives in this stream, like all, fickle.)

The Year divides itself in two, and turnabout each twin destroys the other, Winter Born is oak-bound, iron-bled at the height of summer, and it is Tanist Summer takes his life to live it, until he lose it again to the reborn King at the hinge of the Year.

Lapwing has seen. Lapwing feels sun's pride and sun's defeat.

Frost king falls, sun arises.

Count their lives on my finger-ends.

Cnut's sun swells over Anglish lands, and the prophecy fulfilled as I spoke it. But the unspoken vision yet to come, blond Duncan, this young king, Lapwing at his shoulder.

Malcolm remains hale, despite his years. A king will not fail of age before ninety winters, and his reign suffer no plague or disturbance, if he keeps the requirements of his geis. Lapwing does not know what burdens the gods have required of Malcolm, who keeps a praise-poet but no fili at his side, and a physician to make his ills and heal them. Comes not a windstorm, he could reign for more years yet than Lapwing may have.

But Duncan, ah, he is to be great. The gods have made their wishes plain.

(Tell me, overflying lark, how long? The lark does not speak. Tell me, water, how long? She swallows pebble and runs away, laughing.)

"You've gone back to boyhood, to be flinging stones into water," says Crinán, at my back.

I throw another, for his watching, and he laughs.

He does not laugh when I rise and stare him down. He watches finger-flicker and fears satire.

"Boys may be wise, if they know that water is soft as a woman's thighs but strong as them as well. Boys are wise to know that pebbles are strong if thrown and strong if held in the hand."

I give him a flat disc and he turns it in his hands. "A stone can hit its mark and kill. A stone in the hand?" He skates it across the water and it skips, once, twice, on the lower pool before sinking.

Two hands, two eyes, two ears, two legs. Man is a twin divided against himself.

I feed his hunger. "Thrown, mere pebbles. Stones in the hand may be powerful beyond that."

Crinán's brow comes down. "Like the greenstones of the western shores that carry prayers to Columba and the fulfillment of wishes?"

"So small petitions are answered. But perhaps even here is concealed that stone by which your saint healed the Pictish king and magicked away his people."

"Is it? How would one know?" The furrows dig deeper on his brow. "Do you search for it here?"

"I know the eagle-stone that women use to bring on birth. I know the snake-stone sloughed as serpents twine to choose a new king, which ensures success before princes. I know the toad stone burrowed from its flesh by ants that prevents all poison. But your saint's stone I do not know."

"It would be a great power, if it could be found."

"Ask it of your bishop, then, for it is a Christian thing and Lapwing no follower of that shepherd."

"That I will."

Crinán walks away, his shoulders tight with this new desire he has found.

Lapwing asks the water, Does the stone exist? The water laughs.

15

GRUACH

The red mare in the next stall whickered and set her ears forward, now that the man was gone.

Ah, sister. I felt a kinship with horses as I hadn't since I was a little child and had cried out at their spurred and bloodied sides. Whipped and pricked, their tender mouths broken by the bit, perhaps impaled by spears or cut by swords, ridden to lameness—and if they kicked at mistreatment, then more whipping. Or maybe a merciful death.

I shifted my feet, seeking a higher place. One foot slipped in the stable muck, and I was hanging then by my bound hands, my shoulders wrenched by my swinging weight. Thank the Eternal Lady and her Son that the bridle leathers lashed around my throat were not likewise tied to the rafters. I levered myself up on my toes. The bindings eased.

The mare thrust her whiskery face closer. I looked into the mare's eyes, saw only a liquid gleam and animal curiosity. The White Lady did not show herself in such guise, though wild tribes of Gaul still worshipped Epona, the great Mare-Mother. And the people of Gwyndd had their curious tale of the goddess Rhiannon.

I breathed through my nose. The bit he had forced into my mouth still tasted of horse saliva and my own blood, mildewed grain and manure from where it had dragged the ground. My teeth ached, perhaps broken, and my tongue had swelled. He had wrapped the reins tightly around my neck and ears.

"You have no tongue for questioning, now?" Gillecomgan had mocked. "If ever you speak so boldly again, you will find yourself properly whipped." I did not doubt him.

It was the fourth day we had lingered at a hunting lodge, and still planned were visits to Forres and other halls on the way to Dunottar and then south along the coast road. The Ri Alban seemed reluctant to leave behind the fertile Laich of Moray. Findlaích its ruler was graceful and smiling as if this lengthy hospitality were no burden, no burden at all. He had greeted his half-grown son Macbeth with bright eyes, if also the formality of the father who was now a stranger to the child he has fostered off.

That morning, many of the king's party had gone hunting on the wasteland, but Gillecomgan hung at the king's heel like a half-weaned pup. I had been sitting beneath one of the windows where the sun slanted onto my handwork. This familiar northern light, climbing toward full summer, seemed to bless my fine stitches, while swallows burbled from their mud cups under the eaves.

Close by the hearth were Malcolm and Gillecomgan and a buck-toothed, balding Orkneyman who was here to plead the cause of Einar and Brusi against Thorfinn's latest claims. The doors were open, the shutters all fastened back; nevertheless, a fire crackled loudly in the hearth. The king felt his age and so his hangers-on sweated.

I flattened the seam between my two hands, palms pressing warmth into the silk.

Weak-eyed Budadh, who had charge of our travelling household, came hedging and cramping his way through the western door. He stood just outside the circle of men, pale lips working over his say, until Gillecomgan saw him and motioned him closer. "I must tell you, you have suffered a loss," he said.

"What of?" Gillecomgan asked, as he leaned down to pull burrs from his hose.

"One of your pair of garnet cups?" Budadh's voice rose at the end.

I looked up. The cups were ornate Kentish work, silver, set with large garnets. *He could better bear the loss of a friend, if he had one worthy of the name, than such wealth*, I thought.

"Lost?" Gillecomgan sat straight. He had that unpleasant look of disbelief, his upper lip pulled back from his teeth and his thin eyebrows arched. "How could they be lost?"

"Not both. One is missing."

"Stolen?" Malcolm put in.

Budadh wilted under their twin stares. "I accuse no one, but stolen, probably stolen."

"As it has happened here, then Findlaích will make up its price," the king said.

"Indeed he will." Gillecomgan smiled, as though it were already forgotten. Then he stood and walked a few steps away and then back, Budadh trailing him and looking concerned. "But I would rather catch the thief," he added.

"Then leave the other cup where it is," I said. "The thief, thinking himself undetected, will surely return for it."

I knew even before the silence that I should not have spoken. Knew before Gillecomgan's shadow swept across me. I smoothed the work in my hands and looked up. The hearth fire behind him seemed to catch and run up his side, his arm.

"Marry in fire," I heard, as I often did. I'd heard that whisper as we made our vows before the glow of candles on the altar. On our wedding night he had gone to the fire, his naked body limned by red light. He brought a burning twig and pressed it carefully to my right breast as though a token of love. The flame went out as the twig seared my skin. Smell of hot ash, singed flesh, and the close, rank scent of Gillecomgan himself.

"I have marked you," he said, after returning with a second flaming stick to finish branding me with two slanting lines that were the initial of his name. "You are mine by king's gift and will remember that every morning when you dress."

I had not shouted nor cried, so well had Alpia's discipline held, and that had angered him. He had taken me then like a bull covering a heifer in the field, with might and force, rutting into me, biting my breasts and arms and neck, leaving me smeared with blood. That had finally seemed to satisfy him. I had learned time and again that his rage might be damped, or covered as with gray ash, but was always ready to flare.

A nerve leaped in the back of his hand as he stood before me now. I prepared myself for a slap, the small correction that would be followed by others, later.

Instead, he took me by the wrist and pulled me to my feet. Cloth and needle dropped to the floor and I lifted my foot not to step on my work as he moved me toward the door. I saw him glance once toward Malcolm, who said nothing.

Do you fear my uncle? Do you know how much I fear him?

Gillecomgan hurried me along. We passed the maw of the well and I felt relief. His grip relaxed a bit and I tried to slip away from him, hoping he would not pursue in the open yard where all could see. His fingers, hardened to the sword, clenched deeply enough to send me off my feet. Gillecomgan dragged me up and I twisted in his grasp. The bright, cloudless sky of the northeast dizzied me. I looked out across the hills, the shining river. Where the mountains rose above the river was Craig Phadrig, the ruins of Brude's fortress. A fire lit there would be seen on Dun Sgrebin's hilltop, and from there leap to Dun Jardel and to Tor-dun and on and on, spreading the alarm through the ancient kingdom of my mother's people. I wanted to set a torch to the watchfire, raise an army of white-faced warriors out of their tombs to destroy Gillecomgan. I wanted Alpia to come, clothed in the radiance of the White Lady and speaking with her ocean voice. I wanted, only wanted, an interval of peace in the modest hall at Golspie, where Alpia advised Talorc on many matters.

Gillecomgan turned as we passed the church and headed for the stables, close to the gate opening to fields protected by a rampart. He half-threw me into a dark byre where sick animals were housed.

"Boidh's spawn," he hissed. "If he ever claimed you. Shameless as a Frankish whore."

He thrust me into a stall, beside a lame mare that roused and slammed her haunch nervously against the wall; he blocked my way with his out-spread feet while he looked around, above—reached for a coil of rope.

I dove for the gap between his legs, but he caught me and came down hard across me. The wind whooshed from my lungs.

"You wish to raise your voice before men." Gillecomgan puffed as he struggled to hold me and manage the rope. "I'll cut off your breasts and nose and turn you out."

I stiffened to fight and he backhanded me across the jaw, my head snapping against the stone. Dizzy and faint, I nonetheless shrank from the hairy rope as it brushed my throat, and I could not suppress the crawling of my skin. Gillecomgan laughed. I opened my eyes and saw a loop of rope swinging. But the loop did not go around my neck, as I expected.

He bound my wrists, pulling the loop savagely tight and then tossing the end of the rope over a beam to yank me to my feet. For a moment he put his weight against the rope and lifted me well off the ground; I felt the bones crack in my shoulders. Then he let me down, until my toes could touch, and tied off the rope out of reach of my teeth.

Fire, fire, I thought, as the rope seared my wrists.

Gillecomgan went out of the stall and I resigned myself to wait out his anger. I heard him pushing things about, and his returning footsteps.

He draped a worn bridle, the injured mare's most likely, over my head. "You'll learn your master," he crooned, secure in his unchallenged power, "as an animal does. You are mine, my property. I asked for you, and the king gave you to me and with you the promise of more. Soon to be much more." He forced the bit against my teeth, pressing with his spread fingers against the hinge of my jaw until my mouth relaxed and he thrust the pitted metal far to the back. My lips were stretched to cracking. Then he pulled the leather through its buckles, slowly, lovingly, tightly, and lashed the reins around my throat to hold it in place.

"Stupid Gruach," he whispered. "More stupid than an animal. Nothing restrains you, not sense, not shame, not words. Only force."

His eyes were bright with interest, with unusual desire, and I tried to turn away. He stroked my cheek, running his fingers from the bridle leather onto my skin and back onto leather. Then he bit my stretched lower lip and I felt blood run. He casually pushed me off my feet so that I skidded and swung.

Gillecomgan stood watching me scramble for purchase. He lifted his léine and freed his erection. Again, harder, he kicked my feet from under me and watched me struggle and groan (just once) at the agony in my shoulders. He pulled at his penis and when his climax was upon him, sprayed semen across the front of my garment.

"I will not waste my seed in your useless body." Then he'd turned and left.

I stood on tiptoe for a little while, easing the rope, until my legs trembled. My wrists burned and shoulders shouted. I passed the time by silently reciting old rhymes and lore songs, half forgotten. The Five Aspects, the trees, the signs, the names, the times for cutting and healing and sowing. I did not invoke the Lady's action; I expected no intervention in my daily pain. "Marry in fire, bear in it, lose in it."

"Song is the Waxing Moon, a white bowl filled with heart's delight," I hummed. "Meditation is the Full Moon, round and complete, shining in and shining out. Memory is the Waning Moon." I tried to swallow and gagged. At least it kept my attention from the alternate agonies of legs and arms.

It was difficult to tell how late in the day it was. The sun moved so slowly at this time of year.

Flies buzzed around my wrists where blood oozed from raw scrapes, tasted the stain of semen, and walked upon my eyes. I blinked. They settled on my cheek and crept back to the corners of my eyes, and maddeningly across my bloody lips and onto my swollen tongue. I listened to rats rustling in the straw, heard the mare's lips whuffle for fragments of hay and her stomach churn.

Now the crunch of footsteps set me shuddering.

I made no sound, like an animal that cannot run. I feared it was Gillecomgan returning, burned with shame to think it might be Nechtan come seeking me.

Bare feet, light pressing. I twisted in my bonds to see Seaxburh, my servant, coming slowly along the dim passage. Holes in the roof let in bright reeds of sun that glowed on her colorless skin and coppery hair.

The girl paused. "Lady?" she whispered. "Do you live?"

She came closer, and I tilted my head back.

"I've been sent by him," she said. "Time for the meal approaches and he wishes you to be there."

Of course. He must flaunt his possession, my flesh carrying kinglines like a reliquary for Gillecomgan's hopes. More valuable than the metal and furs that he draped upon his body. It might damage his position to have his wife, the king's niece, absent from the banquet.

Seaxburh climbed precariously onto the angle of a support beam and leaned out to work at the tight-drawn knot. I flexed weary legs once again to ease pressure on the rope. I glanced up to see how quickly the girl worked, met her bright assessing eyes, and looked away.

Daughter of captivity, Seaxburh was the child of a Northumbrian woman taken on a raid. She was Gillecomgan's slave but had been assigned to my retinue, a girl of no more than twelve whose pallet he visited most nights. I could not avoid hearing, and sometimes was ordered to watch, as he took the slender girl as brutally as he did me. He seldom coupled with me any longer, though often enough to deride me each time for failing to give him a son.

I had never liked the girl. She was thin, red-haired, her skin an unhealthy white like that of a shoot pulled from the soil. Her eyelashes were invisible except in direct light, when they flared golden around her blue eyes. Her beauty was in the fragility of her skin, veins beating beneath. I had seen my husband thrust his weight against that birdlike pelvis, his hands pressing down on her delicate wrists, could imagine how he longed to hear the snap of bone and the outcry.

"Take care, now," the girl said.

Suddenly, the rope was loose, falling heavy and rough across my shoulders. Despite the warning, my trembling legs gave out and I fell flat in the muck.

Seaxburh hopped down and unlashed the bridle from my head. I could not meet her eyes. She helped me to my feet, supporting me until I could walk across the open glare in my filth and blood to the shelter of a bathing room where soap and oils had been laid out with jewelry and fresh clothing. A fire-blackened copper steamed beside a wooden tub of well water. I stripped myself of the garment smeared with dung and straw and semen, rank with the sweat of my torment. The girl poured hot water into the cool and stirred it dreamily.

I stepped into the tub and Seaxburh began to wash me.

I would have thought my body perfect, once, but now I merely wondered where the illness lay. My breasts were high and rosy, my hips properly full and legs straight and strong. A faint line of down extended from my navel to where it shaded to a mat of light brown hair. The water caught in it and shone. No birthmarks anywhere on my body, no wounds except for the slick scars on my breast. Spotless as the Christian lamb of sacrifice, properly a queen.

My mouth twitched at the thought.

I felt a light touch on my shoulder. Seaxburh murmured something and began to wash my back, tentative as though I might turn and strike her to ease my own humiliation. Water runnelled between my buttocks. She ran her fingers down my spine and there was an air of control in the force of her hand. I studied the pattern of rope-burns on my wrists. I would not let this concubine and spy for my husband know that I was shamed at the touch of a slave.

Seaxburh washed my hair, carefully working the dried blood from where my head had struck the stone. She dried my body and my hair, poured a clear oil into her palms and began to rub it into my skin. It was something new, with the sharp green scent of herbs from fabled Greece. My mind became warm and sleepy. I closed my eyes, allowed the girl to lift my arms, rub my sore muscles, anoint my breasts.

"You have such a flat stomach," the girl said, smoothing the oil in a circle.

It was like icy water thrown. My belly was flat with the lack of a child, despite Gillecomgan's brutal thrusts, despite my own secret, shameful wish. I opened my eyes and shoved Seaxburh away. The girl stood fast against my anger, her open hands gleaming and her tunic, a worn-out thing of mine, spotted with water and oil.

I cursed her silently. I cursed her for the taunt in that statement, for her childish arrogance, for her foreign face and her bloodless skin. I visioned Seaxburh's tiny sacs of waiting eggs like the auk's, burst and scattered, Seaxburh's stomach remaining the shallow dish it now was, until it went slack with age and hopelessness.

The oil in Seaxburh's hands raised a thin blue flame.

The girl did not speak. Her eyes were wide and depthless. Flame danced in her palms; more flame appeared above her coppery hair.

I locked my knees against the trembling that warned of collapse.

"To curse is to reveal weakness," said the slave, though it was not her voice but that of the Queen of Heaven, Lady of Green Fields, Opener of the Womb. "You have been given power to heal and to preserve. It is not your season to use a withering power. Be warned."

The flames disappeared. The crescent of a waxing moon balanced on her left hand. "Time of growth," she said, and the moon swelled, "of fruition and nurture," and it rounded, "of waning when wisdom arrives," and the moon was carved down to the thinnest of crescents. "Do not seek to advance your time, daughter. Be content and wait. Untimely use of power will blast your life beyond repair."

The crescent became intensely bright, too bright to see. I shielded my face with my arm.

The light was gone, and the room seemed dark and hollow. Seaxburh waited.

I dropped the fresh tunic she had brought, the delicate color of sea-thrift flowers, deliberately onto the wet flagstones. The girl stooped and picked it up, rolled it into a ball to be taken with the other things and washed.

"Do you wish the green one instead?"

I nodded and the girl went out, carrying her damp bundle.

I was shamed again, this time by my intemperance. I concentrated on combing my hair, year by year fading from the bright shade of girlhood. The smell of stable clung to me still; I was sure I could scent it at each stroke of the comb. And there was some other aroma, of spilled power, of cold distance.

The slave returned with the new leíne and an overtunic with sleeves that extended over the wrists. They hid the marks well enough. Seax-burh dressed my hair, braiding and coiling it. I felt a cold chill when those hands, so recently filled with divinity, brushed the nape of my neck.

We settled the heavy, jeweled garment on my shoulders, added nearly all the pins and chains that had been laid out. I clasped wide silver bracelets over the rope-burns. Let the men see nothing but gleaming metal and lapis and the set mask of my face. I dabbed oil on my broken lips, then reddened them with ruam to conceal the bruises. I also put it on my cheeks where the bridle leather had rubbed, and outlined my eyes with the greasy black cosmetic carried all the way from far Egypt. Finally, I concealed my swollen head under a scarlet turban such as the Empress of the East wore. Or so said the merchant as he'd displayed his wares.

I felt like one of the ancient standing stones as I entered the hall, animated but cold around the secrets of its heart. Gillecomgan glanced at me and his face was drawn with tension. I went to him and stood until he took my offered hand and seated me beside him. Then, assured of my compliance, he turned back to his low-pitched, urgent conversation with a short, dark man who seemed to be from the lands around the Solway, and I clasped my hands in my lap. After a moment, Gillecomgan stood and, with his arm around the southern man's shoulders, went to urge their suit before Malcolm. He was politicking far afield, and I wondered if his ambitions were only for Moray.

No one came to sit beside me. I lifted my wrists slightly away from the silver bands, felt air bite against the rope burns.

Life at Malcolm's court was what I had hoped, in my girlish excitement, and it was also all that I had feared. There was no violence from the king but there was no relaxation of his hold. I and my brother were like the hostages he kept of subject kings. If Malcolm knew how Gillecomgan abused me, he did not make a kinsman's objection nor invoke Adomnan's law protecting innocents. My husband sat beside him, his hand familiarly on the king's arm, closer than a brother. And Nechtan—there he stood, among Findlaích's men—had learned how short the rein was that he wore, having been snubbed back on several occasions. He would not confront Gillecomgan.

My husband was feared. Even in the violent dance of blood feud, he was more ruthless than the rest, and more cunning. His hatred might be long held until it flashed, as when he surprised old Diarmuit by the wall at Heth, knifed him through the lung and left him to bubble out his life in repayment for the years-before death of Gillecomgan's nephew.

When I had been a girl and a dreamer, I had imagined that this adult life would be one of freedom. The lowest slave out with the pigs in the forest was more free, for at least he could curl in the straw and rest until morning. I feared spouse and kin alike, harried even in my sleep by thoughts of them.

I watched my brother. A sturdy warrior among warriors, he looked at ease among Findlaích's men. He had taken to wearing subdued clothing as they did, carrying himself in the same upright manner.

I thought he should not be seen so familiar with Findlaích's supporters.

Nechtan was my only joy and my greatest sorrow. He was graceful in his constraints, as our father had been, but grace was a veil, not armor. He had told me that here in Moray, beyond the rough flanks of the Mounth, the people had kept their independence, remembering the power of the Pictish kingdom. "They know how Malcolm shed blood to gain power and keep it. They would support some other of rightful lineage."

"Do not think it," I had urged. "There is no hope in that. Our hope is to wait for Malcolm's death."

"But Conamail, the smiling one, tells me—"

"Be friends with all, cultivate many but trust few. When Malcolm dies, the alternate kingline must rule. The election will fall to Findlaích or to you, and our fears will be past."

I heard myself saying that again and wished that my brother would be even more circumspect than he was. Nechtan at that moment broke away from the Moray men, as though he had heard my warning, and joined a roistering crew of young fighters.

Throughout the great room, people were divided into groups and knots. They mixed like oil and water. Elaborate jewelry and silks and bright gold marked Malcolm's train, like laughter and dalliance made visible, while the people of the north were watchful, dignified. They wore plain braughts, striped or solid, and their garments were not overly ornamented. For the most part, they eschewed the silks carried by the ships of the Lochlannaig in favor of their own wool and linen. Their ornaments were ancient, simple and painfully familiar to my eyes, silver penannular pins and crescents, some older than the first tide coming out of Éireann. Their weapons, however, were bright and sharp with constant use against sea-raiders.

It was Gillecomgan, though a son of the north, who set the tone for the king's court. He wore the most elegant clothing, with as many colors as tradition allowed an under-king and none to deny him, and fur even in high summer, his vanity winning over sense. He had an animal smell of his own, and new perfumes applied over old ones, and damp silk and fur.

Dog stoat, I thought sourly, watching him smile and lean his head toward Malcolm. *A lithe killer. Loyal as a stoat, and trustworthy as one.*

And most of the rest inclined their heads to Gillecomgan.

The rechtaire announced the arrival of the meal, and people began to drift toward the long tables. Bowls of stewed fruit and platters of meat were set out and stacked-works of bread, while servants moved along the tables with pitchers of drink. Gillecomgan looked to me and I rose to join him where he sat at the king's right hand.

Poor Budadh came with the one cup, polished to perfection, its metal and garnets shining. He handed it to Gillecomgan.

"Take it away," Malcolm said. "I do not want to look on evidence of a thief. Here, my friend."

He pushed his own goblet, fine glass enclosed in a web of gold, in front of his favorite. Gillecomgan murmured his appreciation, lifted it in both hands to be admired, then drank.

Budadh reached for the Kentish cup, but Gillecomgan stopped him.

"Let it be my wife's," he said.

He picked it up, sipped from one side, then gave it to me as he'd shared the cup at our wedding feast, his eyes gloating as I acknowledged him and drank. The wine burned my broken mouth. He smiled sardonically as I set the cup back on the table, and a sudden tremor of my hand made it rock and spill a spot of wine.

Gillecomgan chose meat, slicing it free with his knife that bit deeply into the board, presenting tidbits to me on the trembling point as one lover does to the other. I held a piece of plain bread in my hand and nibbled at it whenever he prepared to offer me a dainty.

Findlaích acted as though unaware of what had happened in his stables, as if he did not scent the manure-smell of my humiliation. He was busy conversing with Malcolm and with a delegate from the Wends.

Finally, he introduced the bishop of the House of Deer and asked him to recite a poem he had written in honor of the Virgin. The man stood and fumbled through an explanation of what he had written, the how and why.

Malcolm's extended tour in Moray, presented as a way to renew the alliance between the High King and the King of the North, served to remind Findlaích of his pledge, and perhaps reduce him by impoverishing him, but this visit was punishment as well for Malcolm. Findlaích was devoutly Christian, a scholar as well as war-leader, who read books and kept company with clergy. His halls were cramped into fortifications built and rebuilt against invaders; all eyes turned toward the sea. They were dull refuges compared with palaces in the gentler reaches of Alba.

The bishop completed his explanations and began, at last, his poem. I listened with interest at first, for it was a devotion to the Lady herself, but soon became lost in learned wordplay and Biblical allusions. Others were less polite—or at least had a table companion to share their boredom. Some men began to argue a battle. Two young women gossiped about a third. The cleric labored on, his cheeks mottled with fright or the effort of memory. Only Findlaích appeared to listen. He was chestnut-haired and so compactly built that he appeared even smaller than he was. A widower who had taken no new wife, he had just the one son, the king's fosterling, an unbearded youth who seemed to be always tagging after Duncan. Something attracted me to this somber man, a sense of restrained power. He wore the ancient double-linked chain of the mormaer of Moray, a title he held as well as king. As befitted a war-leader, he was ever alert, poised as though ready at any moment for attack.

There was something aloof about him, as there was with Nechtan. They were wolves among the snarling dogs.

Finally the bishop finished, wiping his sweating brow and bowing to the oblivious guests.

"Excellently done," said Gillecomgan. "Your poetry took us to such a high place that we are left gasping for the nourishment of air."

The bishop smiled uncertainly.

Gillecomgan continued, his words mingling poison with praise. The bishop nodded and nodded; the mottling returned to his cheeks.

Tiring of such a meek target, Gillecomgan turned on the host himself. "Shepherd of the Sea," he said, playing on another meaning behind the lesser of his titles. "Oh, great Lord of Water, how is it that your subject intrudes so boldly on your lands?"

"No man commands the waters, as my nephew knows," Findlaích answered, with a hint of a smile.

"Even the King of the North?" Gillecomgan leaned his elbows on the table and thrust his chin toward Findlaích. "King beyond the Mounth? Is he lord of half the land, or is it that he is half a king? A whole man to rule half a kingdom—or is half a man enough?"

Gillecomgan's teeth showed in an unpleasant grimace. All within earshot had fallen silent. They waited for Findlaích to challenge the insult not only against him as host but as leader of their shared kindred, but he sat quite still, his reaction to the baiting visible only in the tight control that kept his face emotionless. The king watched him very closely.

Findlaích lifted his shoulders and the heavy chain rolled a muted chorus as it settled. "King of the North, like mormaer, is an ancient title that speaks less loudly now than it did in the days when Fortriu's realm extended both north and south. I am the Ard Ri Alban's friend and sworn ally, a wall against the terror that comes from the sea. And if this wall is not as high as some," Findlaích said, standing and glaring at Gillecomgan, "then perhaps it is better anchored in that Stone which fools reject but all wise men claim."

Malcolm looked again to Gillecomgan.

16

MACBETH

Kilrymont, 1019

The ancient monastery of Kilrymont was at first sight a smaller place than desire made it, there on the peninsula once called the Boar's Head, caught like a pebble between the working jaws of the gray sea and the gray sky promising more snow. Clouds appeared to touch the square tower as they were driven by the sea-wind.

Macbeth heard Oswald chant a psalm of praise, each word taken on the gale. Otherwise, the little company was silent, intent on the end of the journey. They passed the cross marking the outer boundary of the monastery. Oswald signed the same. It was the morning of Christ's birth. They were late arriving—a tribe of horses scattered out on the snow-streaked grazing showed how many were celebrating the feast with the king.

They rode among the buildings just as the bell was struck for Mass. Monks surrounded them, moving with unhurried haste to the church. Their fresh garments shone white as the robes of the blessed in heaven. Each monk touched the great cross in the courtyard, the *signum salutare* to ward off the constant presence of the enemy.

Some of the *familia* took the horses away, and Macbeth and Oswald followed the monks to the new church of St. Regulus.

They pushed through the courtyard throng of layfolk. The king's retinue, along with the abbot and dignitaries of the monastery, occupied the middle of the oratory, with the brethren to right and left. A penitent, unwashed, his hair snarled with dirt and straw, lay flat on the stone floor with hands outstretched toward the altar. His bare back showed lash-marks self-inflicted for his sin.

The church breathed light and heat, candles lavishly spent in praise of the Incarnation, the heat of so many bodies. There shone Malcolm's white hair and beard. There, Macbeth saw his brother's broad shoulders and golden head, king beside king.

It had been many months since he had seen Duncan.

As the festal service rolled forward, familiar, and the chill of the morning went out of him, Macbeth found it difficult to stay awake. He occupied himself in reciting psalms in his thoughts, until he began to nod, then in numbering the ornaments of the church. Crucifixes, candelabra, reliquaries. Gold and silver and jewels, all freshly polished for the great Feast. The frontal of the altar shone. The relics of St. Andrew the Apostle, carried from Patras to Constantinople and then to these shores by St. Regulus, rested in their casket. He imagined the bones softly glowing in response to the praise elevated all around. The bishop's vestments were embroidered with bright colors and golden thread by the exceptional skill of Anglish women. Candle flames fell and lifted in the swell of air as the monks bowed after each psalm. A seething shore, flame-washed.

Macbeth jerked his attention back to the litany. The voices of the oblati, boys given to the church, were light but sure among the deeper voices of the monks. At least one of them, he judged, was of an age with him. Next year, or perhaps the next after that, the youth would confirm his vows and devote his life to God, as he would devote his own to leading men. Only monks were assured of heaven. They moved toward it every day in the extinguishment of their bodies, like candles burning down the dross wax until they expired in pure light. Macbeth longed for the light of heaven but felt dark and weighted by the world, its blood and possessions.

Wine and water mingled in the chalice. The prayers lifted on incense, sweet. The offering of gifts. The remembrance of the dead, each brother who had died in sanctity since St. Kenneth founded this holy place. The consecration. In a great sigh of longing, they went to their knees and prostrated themselves before the renewed miracle.

The weight of his journey was lifted from him by the Presence. The sense of foreboding that had ridden with him fell away like the fetters of that warrior celebrated by sainted Bede, who was released from his bonds each day at the hour of the Mass, as a result of his brother's devotions.

"Missa acta est. In pace."

With an orderly shouldering, each man finding his proper distance from the king like wolves around their leader, they made their way out of the smoky church.

Still savoring the sacrifice, Macbeth greeted Duncan warmly.

With a brief, angry glance, Duncan pulled his arm from Macbeth's grasp and turned away, sweeping the folds of his mantle close around him.

Macbeth stood for a moment, watching his cousin stalk away. He had thickened, his arms and chest become more massive in the months since they had parted. Malcolm's influence had him installed as king of Strathclyde on the death of Owen the Bald—now Duncan was securing his new realm, an uneasy place, British rather than Scot, a byway between the Norse-Irish and Northumbria. Malcolm was pleased to grasp it through his fosterling's hands.

Macbeth went after Duncan and caught him by the arm again. Duncan glared down at him with eyes that were more and more like their grandfather's.

"Have I angered you, brother?"

Duncan moved forward, his strides deliberately long.

Macbeth would not let him go, though he had to half run to keep up.

"Duncan, I will give you no peace until you tell me why you are angry."

They stopped by the yard where the holy dead lay. "You give me little enough," he said, snapping out the words, a knot of muscle white on his jaw.

"I have not spoken with you since we parted at Moncrieffe and you continued to your father's house. I can scarcely have disturbed you, short of magic."

Duncan laughed. "Magic perhaps. You prideful little men of Moray cause trouble at a distance, stirring a pond to raise a tempest on the sea." Macbeth warmed at the insult, felt the blood pound in his wrists. His father was lately out of favor with the king, yes, but he had not expected that to come between him and his foster-brother.

"The gesture of a moment comes after a month of thought, with you. How was I to receive your gift then?" Duncan leaned on the fence that divided holy earth from daily traffic.

The jeweled belt could not have offended. It was the book, then.

Macbeth came to the fence, which groaned under Duncan's weight, and rested his hands lightly on the top. He stared at a stone that marked some dead saint, worn by the touch of faithful hands, and spoke as if to the dead.

"I am honored by my brother's greatness equally as if the honor had come to me. Because of that, I sent you two things of value. One was my most treasured possession."

"Meant as a reminder of my shortcomings?"

"It was not."

He snorted.

"That book was copied in Rome, bound by Moors with their finest art. The drawings and gildings were added by a Bangor monk. It would be a treasure to a letterless man, much less to a king who knows Latin well enough, and who has others to read it out when he is tired."

"I have read the book," Duncan admitted. "Parts of it. This Suetonius, he was a merchant of gossip."

"Warnings, rather."

"And you believe I need them?"

"We each of us need warnings, and wardings, on this earth." Macbeth pulled a stick from the fence, broke it and dropped it into the frozen mud at his feet. "I must ask, did the messenger not tell you my words to accompany the gifts?"

"Your man had died of a chill and entrusted the gifts to another."

"The misunderstanding came there, my brother." Macbeth held out his right hand. Reluctantly, Duncan gripped it and smiled a tween-season smile, his eyes cold as snow that lingers on Ben Nevis even as his mouth offered sunshine. Then he pulled away as though in a hurry to join the crowd.

Macbeth did not follow him. He waited by the graveyard until the ones who watched from the corners of their eyes lost interest, and then he went into the abbot's hall.

The place was as crowded as the church, plainer in itself and brighter in the people who gathered at table. The silks and brocades and furs were set off against the garments of juniores and monastery servants who circulated with bread and meat and drink. Like the monks, they themselves would not eat until the sun was well down the December sky, but the king's presence demanded full hospitality. The cellarer stood at the door from the kitchen, observing that each dish was properly made. His lifted hand sent a dish of stewed apples back as underdone and liable to cause distress.

Macbeth found Donnemor of the Uisgern Valley, his father's close friend. Donnemor was graying now and had recently lost two fingers of his left hand. "If it had been swordside," he joked, "then I would be no more than a mouth at my son's table."

Oswald joined them soon after. He wore that severe look that came upon him when they visited any holy place, partly, Macbeth thought, out of longing and partly from guilt. He had been away from his cell for these many years, at Malcolm's demand and the prior's acquiescence, and his way of life had by time and company slacked from the Rule. Recently, he had begun to observe brief but harsh regimens of fasting and mortification. When they ate, Oswald took only a little small beer. He had changed his black garment for another, of rougher rather than finer cloth, and had renewed his Roman tonsure. He looked younger with the dome of his skull nicked and shorn.

Donnemor celebrated heartily, unhampered by vows, pulling a chunk of roasted deer from the bone with the crablike pincers of his thumb and third finger. "The monks say that wild meat causes no bodily lust," he said, between bites. "But I say, they've never speared a stag in rut."

In honor of Christ's birth, Malcolm dispensed gifts to those who had assembled. Many of the gifts, Macbeth knew, were tribute that had flowed out of Bernicia and the green lands after Earl Eadulf's loss at Carham ceded the borderlands, at last, to victorious Malcolm. Bracelets, earcuffs, necklaces, brooches, both newly made and robbed out of grave mounds. Hawks and hounds and horses. Folds of Flemish cloth. Weapons. Silver that stood for the weight of cattle or heaping bolls of grain. Malcolm smiled on each person honored by his generosity. Duncan, seated at his right hand, and Gillecomgan at his left, smiled as well. They were an oddly matched pair, yet stood in perfect synchrony when Malcolm got to his feet.

"Welcome to our guests, our kinsmen, and our friends, the long familiar and those new-come among us. Drink deep of the cauldron of hospitality which is never emptied!"

The crowd roared. Men beat their hands on the greasy tables.

"We celebrate the birth of Our Lord, the Sun in mid-winter rising for our salvation. The good brothers of Kilrymont reflect that great Light and warm us all." Malcolm made a gracious sign to the abbot and the bishop and his brother bishops, and they lifted their hands to bless him. "It is a proper day, as we celebrate the King of Kings, to take care for the management of earthly kingdoms."

The hall grew suddenly quiet.

"I grow old, as all may see." Malcolm touched his white hair, the long beard curled and flourishing that marked him as no longer a fighting man.

"But strong," one cried out.

"An arm to strike down all enemies," came an answer, and then a chorus.

The king smiled, waiting.

"Old, and no earthly power can stay the time appointed. Kings die but the people continue, and they must be well-led, with a mighty arm to take up the sword from a failing one. So, on this day of Christ's birth, in the nineteenth year after the millenium, with the advice of the men of the blood and men of wisdom and men of holiness, I name the tanist, the one who stands ready. He is Duncan mac Crínáin, son of the Lord-Abbot, son of my daughter, blood of my blood, continuing the strong line of Alpin."

The shouting swelled again, and the clatter, but as the men moved forward to pledge themselves to the king's tanist there was soft conversation among them. Macbeth heard the private words.

"Who among the men of the blood did he consult?"

"The smallest of groups," another said.

"...only himself, perhaps."

"Who will deny him?"

Macbeth allowed himself to be pulled forward by the crowd. He saw where Nechtan mac Boidh stood, the young warrior who was enforced to idleness, always under the king's eye. He leaned against the wall as though trying, but failing, to pass unnoticed.

"The king has abandoned the line of Dubh."

"It should by rights be Findlaích."

"I say Nechtan, also of the line of Dubh."

"...and royal blood as well through the mother."

"Malcolm remakes our leadership."

"...why he fears the north."

"Findlaích would unite Alba and Moray as one, Pict and Scot."

"We are not Angles," said a man of Boidh's wife's kindred, his voice rising, "nor are we Franks. If the proper succession is discarded, our practice of choosing the best from one kingline and alternately the other, then soon we will be kinged by an infant, his blood carrying more weight than his ability."

A friend clamped a hand on his arm and drew him back.

"It should have fallen to your father who is King of the North," Donnemor whispered against Macbeth's ear. "Or to Nechtan."

The whispers died as each man approached the high seat, and at the king's right-hand Duncan sat to receive their pledges. He gleamed, as though power were oil on his body. He might have seemed the actual king to a stranger there, and Malcolm his aged counselor. Behind them both, Gillecomgan smiled, his lips pulled back over his teeth with the effort. He extolled king and tanist, his words an ornate weaving, but raw envy gleamed through.

Macbeth stood before his brother.

"After the Ard Ri Alban, you have my first loyalty. I give you my right arm and my left," he said, holding Duncan's triumphant gaze, requiring him to accept his words. "I pledge you first blood spilled and my last blood emptied on the field of battle."

"Little monk," Duncan said negligently, "little monk. You shall whisper right conduct to me when I am king in Alba, and keep me from error."

"You shall have what you wish." Macbeth placed his hand under Duncan's. He remembered, from a long time ago, his brother's outburst, *A monkish king is no king at all,* and put away any thought other than returning to his father's side and his own lands when he reached his majority.

Macbeth stood aside for the next man.

He saw Nechtan approaching the high seat, his face composed as a body's for the tomb.

17

GRUACH

Adrochta's child sucked noisily. She lifted him from her teat and resettled him at the other, rotating her shoulder to ease a cramp. He fretted and coughed, and with his little fists battered at her breast. "A warrior indeed," she boasted, and tucked him close. Her rich milk spurted from the corner of his mouth and trickled down her veined and swollen flesh.

I compelled myself to look away. My glance moved restlessly across the half-dozen women and their young children who had fled the ranting in the nearby hall to find peace here in the monk's guesthouse, a sad place with a stained and leaking roof, dusty beams and uneven wattle and thin pallets. The place had suffered the invasions of Vikings and Angles alike and been only partly rebuilt. Finally I went to stare out the door into the courtyard where the sun burned.

This summer was no different from the one before, or the one before that. When the roads firmed, men's winter restlessness broke out into raiding and later, major campaigns long in the works. Lately a small army under Gillecomgan had been dispatched to Moray. The women waited, whether at home or, if their men were of the king's remaining retinue, following his peregrinations. Sometimes their boredom became as angry as the men's, but they had no edges but their tongues. They bickered and gossiped about everything. Everything except their fears for their men, lest they call down a fatal wound.

I guarded my tongue more closely than ever but did not guard my thoughts. The sharp relief of Gillecomgan's absences had faded like the bruises he left upon my body when he chose to assert his rights upon it, like an old wound become a place of numbness. At first, I had pictured him slashed and dead, lifeless tallow slack inside his shell of adornment. It did not matter—he was charmed and in battle suffered no wound. I never crossed the line from imagining to acting, heeding the White

Lady's warning. If I could not call down vengeance upon him, then I tried not to think of him at all.

A boy toddled past, chubby legs bowed and arms flailing for balance. I remembered his birth, and how wailing Catnea had bled until she was altogether changed, sunken, silent, near death. My offer of help was rejected with suspicion. Given the *viaticum*, she had rallied and lived. She regained her strength, slowly, and clutched the baby as though he were her savior and not her near-destroyer. He made another unbalanced rush, then stopped. His face twisted in puzzlement and he began to cry. I moved to pick him up. "Have you stepped on a thorn?"

He looked at me and backed away, face taut and wet.

"Dubh?" his mother called.

He turned and ran screaming to her.

I smiled ruefully. "I think he has found a thorn among the rushes."

Catnea scooped him up and rocked him, soothing his tears. She examined his foot, spitting on her fingers and scrubbing away the dirt, but found no thorn. She looked at me with narrowed eyes. *Look, then,* I thought, and stared back. *I could remind you that your son bears an unfortunate name.*

Catnea turned away. I bent over the sewing that lay in my lap and wished I had been left behind, unmarked, unheeded, in some forgotten corner. I made precise stitches while feeling the women's stares lick across my shoulders. Some of the women were unkind but not all. I knew they wondered at my continued lack of a child, especially as Gillecomgan had bred many on the bodies of slaves. I could hear their questions as though they had spoken aloud. *Does she unman her husband? Does she by unholy art prevent a child? She was fostered, recall, in the north where ancient ways are remembered.* I trusted none of them. Not after Cipia's betrayal.

I had learned to yield like a willow in a gale on those infrequent nights when Gillecomgan enforced his due. When he could wring no more response from me through pain, he made fewer and fewer demands on my body. (My body, as though it were entirely separate from my self. My body, sad beast that suffered burns and bruises, the sting of blows.) He had gained a prize from the Ard Ri Alban, and he would maintain his rights. He was balked, however, in the expectation of a son. My hand spread across the barren plain of my stomach. Sometimes I dreamed of a baby and what should be happiness, until the child's face came clear and it was Gillecomgan's.

Seaxburh had remained his favorite long enough to bear a fox-faced daughter. He now had a Norse slave with hair pale as ice, skin with the blue tinge of carefully skimmed milk, and a wall-eyed terror of him that the girl could not hide. That fear only made her more attractive, and he tormented her almost nightly, twisting her limbs, slapping and striking her, biting her nipples until they ran blood, then mounting her from the back like an animal.

The conversation circled around me. Catnea, bold now in the success of her child, complained about Macha who had left two days before to join her husband. The unlucky man had fallen against his own spear before the army had even crossed into Moray, opening his side between two ribs. He had gone home where he would die or perhaps recover.

"Her babe whined each night through," Catnea said. "Her milk is bad."

"It was born in May and will wither."

"I believe it is under a spell," Eimear confirmed, eager as always.

"Mere colic," sniffed her cousin, and I smiled gently at her wisdom. "She has eaten something strong-flavored, wild garlic perhaps, that has flowed from her blood into her breast-milk."

They argued then about the herbs that could taint milk, and holy charms and superstitions. I focused more closely on my handwork, trying not to smile at their ignorance, wishing I could offer my knowledge without having it spurned. Aniseed would ease the colic, if Macha would chew it or drink a tea brewed of it. And rose hips eaten raw would strengthen her for nursing. Or she might use that plant the Saxons called betonywood that they planted all about their churchyards. That too was good. In summer, its flowers showed like flecks of blood on the hedges and a tale of violence went with those blossoms.

"She'll suckle that babe for three years as she did the last one, lest she be made heavy again!"

They shrieked and laughed at that, and Eimear choked on the urgent words that came along with her harsh laughter.

I felt myself grow cold, like a pillar that once was cut with symbols but now was worn away to brooding silence. I folded the silk band and replaced it and the fine embroidery needle (a gift from the king, one of five steel needles brought all the way from Persia, sharp as his eyes on Nechtan and myself) in the covered basket Alpia had given me. I left the guesthouse, my back stiff—the fresh round of laughter was aimed at me, I had little doubt. I wandered past the pool, where the monks washed their hands to make them acceptable for the Christ, and watched insects dip and pock its surface. The appearance of my own face, rippled by their testing of the water, bothered me; my blue-green eyes (what favor there?) wavered and did not look steadily back.

There was a path to the river, but I avoided it. In the rigs left fallow between fine strips of barley, long grasses heavy with last night's dew wet my legs—I had belted up my léine, set aside the gilded shoes of dependence, and walked bold and barefoot.

As I approached the water, an otter slipped from the bank. Minnows sprayed from its path, then returned, the school flashing in a still back-water. The path turned and I followed it. The monks and the people of their familia came here to gather willow; heavy trunks sprouted withes where they had been pollarded for generations. Smaller paths slanted down the banks to the places where fish baskets were set. I went down and squatted beside the water, holding my garment up from the mud. At a low angle, the sun no long glared and I could see fish twisting inside the wicker, water that was their freedom rushing past them while they battered the openwork prison. But the river provided no more consolation than the pool of the monastery.

Restless, I left the waterside path and struck back across the mead-ows. Buttercups and daisies turned their faces up among the grass. Harebells nodded in the breeze, asleep in their own deep blue like the summer night, and as always, the droppings of hares were among them. I knelt and stroked the bells, their repeated curves precise as goldsmith's art. Were they behind the season? I looked up at the path of the sun in the sky and at the shadows the trees cast. I would hardly know what season it was, were it not for the priests' reckoning. All this riding about, north to south and west to east; the king's land was broad and now ex-tended far south toward Hadrian's Wall. When winter had whitened the northern peaks, it was still apple-time at Lothian, and when grain had already dried in the east it remained green and liable to ruin in the west.

I broke a stem of grass and tasted the sweet juice. At Golspie, I could have given the very day when harebells would blossom in the sheltered curve by the stream. I felt a sudden pang, a sickness for home like that I had suffered the first months after Malcolm's summons.

I sat down in the field and the tasseled grasses rose above my head. A black-bibbed finch flew over and did not veer from its course.

Close to the earth, I saw the wondrous braid of life—mosses and creeping catspaw, thistles and mints. Each in its proper place and proper time. I was sharply reminded of Alpia and the girls with whom I'd chanted the world in its order. The memory of summer songs crowded forward, and my throat tightened with the high invoking note. The White Lady did not answer me any longer, among these harsh men and these priests of men. It was enough to find a trickle of peace in the down of a leaf, the slight fragrance that sprang from a plucked blossom. I closed my eyes and listened to the birds sing, to the stream washing its stones, to the crow of a cock sweetened by distance and the brushing wind.

A startled plover circled overhead. "Techat, techat, techat," it cried, but it did not settle.

I heard the plodding hoofbeats of a horse, half hidden in the river's talk. The horse approached slowly, heavily—some worn-out beast. I sat close among the tall grasses and hoped not to be seen. But the sound came clearer, closer, along with a murmur like monks in their church at night. A tangle of voices, high and low. I stood up, covered my head, shook down my garment and brushed off the leaves.

The horse was ridden double. Two men of fighting age. Behind them trailed farmers drawn away from their fields, women with babes in their brown arms, three children, and a brindled dog that nipped at the horse's hooves and danced away. The horse didn't kick. It was too heavily burdened by the men who, oddly, showed no weapons. I shaded my eyes, wondering why one did not walk and ease the animal.

As they approached, I saw that the one who rode before was a sturdy warrior of middle years, the lines bracketing his mouth those of a man who has laughed more than he has frowned. His eyes were darkly shadowed. Closer still, and I could see that he had no eyes. In their place was a crusted ruin of blood. The man up behind him, who rested his head on the blinded man's shoulder, had no hands. He clung to his companion with stumps wrapped in blackened cloth.

"The path turns sunwise ahead," cried one of the women.

"Take care for our grain, in pity," called a farmer, but none dared to take the reins and be tainted by this curse.

The men did not answer. I watched them pass, and their poor retinue. When they had slowly turned on the path toward the king's hall, I ran through the meadow and arrived before them.

They came through the gate and dismounted near the chapel. The blinded man, first down, supported his companion, and then rested his hand on his shoulder to be guided. They were kind and close as lovers. I slipped past them, my hems dark with dew, and found my place among the women who had hurried there. The mutilated men waited, just inside the entrance to the great hall, where the sun shone around them and showed them as mere silhouettes to those in the darkness inside.

Malcolm remained in the same foul temper that had driven out us women. He sat by the fire, with his fosterling close at hand. He was angry for the lack of wine, as raids by Norse and Dubliners had halted the trade from France and Spain. He dared not break God's seal that protected the sacramental wine.

Macbeth sat at a little table close to the king's feet, writing the letters his grandfather required but would not give to "a wretched, soft mouthing, womanish monk," as he had shouted that morning. There were few other men nearby. Many of the king's warband were with Gillecomgan on his punishment raid into Moray. Their women and young children, the men of art, and the elderly made up the court. And of course, Nechtan, like a haltered bull, brooding in Malcolm's close grip. The hall was silent except for Malcolm's demands, and the scratching of the quill as his grandson translated them to vellum. A final burst, and Malcolm closed his eyes and sat back as though wearied. Macbeth stood from his scribe's labor, gathering up his tools.

The visitors had been announced—"Two men already nameless among the dead"—but the king made no sign.

Finally, Malcolm sat forward and looked to where the men waited.

"Come and speak."

The handless man walked toward the high seat, his companion keeping step with him until he halted and the blinded man stepped two paces closer.

"I know your voice, Malcolm, kin-killer, as you know my face or the wreckage of it."

I saw Macbeth start forward, his mouth open to cry out, then sink back as Malcolm lifted a commanding hand.

"We have come from the last battle," the blinded man said, his voice harsh as though it too had been maimed in some way. "We are the messengers of Gillecomgan angbaidh."

The epithet was whispered around the hall, like a faint echo, Gillecomgan angbaidh, angbaidh. Gillecomgan the wicked, the ruthless. *Yes, indeed, yes, he was.*

"He has killed Findlaích, his kinsman, the son of Ruiadri, of the ancient line of Loairn and of the Peace King." His voice rang out with the harshness of steel grinding against steel. I saw the quills and ink slip from Macbeth's grasp and clatter onto the stone where Malcolm's feet rested. "He has killed Findlaích, who was a free giver of gifts, an honored man, a lover of God and His son Jesus Christ. Findlaích mac Ruaidri, ruler of Moray, of Ross and Cromarty, defender of Sutherland, king and mormaer, king beyond the Mounth, King of the North."

The king's neck stiffened at the ancient titles, ones that extended back to when King Brude ruled from fortresses at the Mouth of Ness and the new-come Dál Riatans feared those Pictish armies.

"I call him true king, rightful to hold the throne of all Alba."

Malcolm's hands were tight on the carved arms of his seat; I saw the clawed fleshnessness of them.

"I use those titles that he would not take himself because lying enemies have made his fealty and blood freely shed for both Moray and Alba into a threat, Gillecomgan first among them. I, Conamail, give my slaughtered lord these names of honor, as I give names of execration to his murderer."

I looked for Nechtan. He was staring at the ruin of Conamail, toiseach of a prosperous people in the Valley of Heroes, now a broken helper to shattered dreams. The blinded man paused, for strength, for recollection.

"Gillecomgan and his brother have killed the best of warriors and a king indeed, but a loyal ally who used his strength unsparingly to shield the northern lands from wild seafarers. Gillecomgan angbaidh let out his noble blood because Findlaích would not bend to him, a creeping favorite. He died with the double-linked chain on his shoulders. We come from the ancient stronghold on the promontory between the forest and the water, where the King of the North stood last. For each of his true men who was blinded, there was one with no hands. Most have flung themselves from cliffs or gone into the depths of Ness, their swords and all weapons being taken from them, but we to save our sons have held our useless lives this long, to bear witness before you."

Malcolm did not answer. Perhaps he was listening to the whispers that ran around the hall. I heard them halt on either side of me, for none would complain to the butcher's wife that the raid on Moray had been intended as a warning only, a punishment in cattle and wealth because it was rumored that Findlaích grew proud.

But I knew differently. Gillecomgan had come to me in the dim morning before he rode out. He had spread my thighs with the flat of his sword, laughing as he did, and told me to remember its cold steel should I fail to breed him a son. One to hold the northern kingdom he went to seize with Malcolm's blessing.

∾

MACBETH, ST. VIGEAN'S, 1020

The sight of Conamail and Lorcan told him before words were spoken: the one who held the Valley of Heroes would have stood to the last beside his father. Now Macbeth moved forward, pushing past the king's hand again upraised.

Conamail turned toward the sound of footsteps. Macbeth took his hand and held it between his own.

"Who is this?"

"Findlaích's son."

Red welling came from the corners of raw empty sockets, where fluids and crusted blood made a horror. "I cannot smile any longer, but believe that I cry for joy at finding you."

Macbeth put his arms around his old friend and protector. He kissed him and touched the battle marks he wore, the gashed hands, bruised face, blackened blood. "Dear Conamail, how did my father die?"

There was no answer for a time. Macbeth thought he saw Findlaích in his plain war-gear, stained with the blood of Norseman and Dane and Northumbrian, and now some of Gillecomgan's men as well. Perhaps he had fallen near that veined rock at the corner of the north wall, perhaps near the water gate.

"Findlaích died fighting his nephew, sword against sword."

"Then he should not have died."

"Your father has grown older," Conamail reminded, "and Gillecomgan has great skill at battle if no virtue. And Findlaích had already fought long against many lesser men."

"I ask, you whom my father chose to escort me to fosterage," he began, tears coming, and he swallowed then started again. "Why were you not beside him? I ask because I must."

Conamail threw his head back and stood as though his dead eyes might make out something far away. The sweat of fever showed on his forehead and a sweet reek of flesh-rot came from his suppurating face.

"A part of us were drawn off in a strong feint at the outer wall. We did not know there were so many men against us. Too many. We had feared there might be a raid, but this was an army, Gillecomgan's men with foreigners among them. When we fought clear at the wall, we found those hirelings had come in at our backs. We fought until our blades dulled and spears broke and still came more. We cut our way to where Findlaích stood, too late."

Macbeth searched within himself and found his grief, round and contained, a stone in his belly like the ballast of a ship. A burning and doomed ship. He thought it insufficient, that he was an unfaithful son to be so calm.

"As your father was a father to me, you have been as my son," Conamail said, low. "Findlaích's son, my friend, will you honor me with a blade having Moray in it? I would die easily then."

Now Macbeth's eyes burned and he could almost wish they were gone, so that he would not have had to see this good man beg for the end of his life.

"Our lives are God's," he whispered huskily. "His for the taking as for the giving. You can still seek the face of God."

Conamail grimaced; tears mixed with blood runnelled into the familiar creases of his face. "You smell of ink and softness and of a God kept close in books. You have not learned the Lord of Hosts and God of Battles yet. I will think of you with my last thought, as surely your father did, and take that with me to gods I know."

He found Lorcan's shoulder and they made their way out of the hall. None followed.

Macbeth turned heavily, the rock in his stomach holding him down. He looked at the man in the high seat, the foster-father he had learned to love but who did not greatly love him. All he wanted to ask was why, yet he could not.

"I ask the king, what about my father's people—my people? Who will protect them?"

Malcolm's bright gaze, little dimmed by the years that had made his hair pure white, did not waver.

"Moray is a barrier against the Danes and Norse but could also be a blade poised at the back of our kingdom," he said, loudly, for all to hear. "After proper consideration, and with the consent of the kindred, Malcolm called Cerr, son of Máel Brigte, will become King of the North. His younger brother Gillecomgan, my trusted adviser, will support him as mormaer and rule over the eastern portion," he said. All the time, his cold eyes had not left Macbeth's face. And Macbeth in turn tried not to show the anger that stormed up.

The hall was silent.

"The men of Cenél Loairn are not to make the choice, naming their leader?" Macbeth did not give voice to his own rights over family lands that were now under the overlordship of the murdering brothers.

"Gillecomgan struck harder than he should have," Malcolm said, his voice dropping to a private tone. "But he is a strong hand in war. It would not be wise to deny him this title, or Cerr the kingship due him by his birth and his age. The men of your kindred have agreed."

Macbeth weighed that, a king's duties against a man's. He would never accept butcher Gillecomgan walking the pine-shadowed shore at Lochindorb.

"My father did no wrong. He has supported you in battle and welcomed you in his halls with an open hand and open heart."

"The men of the blood affirmed he was ambitious and plotting against us," Malcolm said. "Do you think I casually apportion a land that was ancient when our people came here from Éireann?"

"I would not give my assent."

"Grandson, and son to me in my age, you are still some years from taking your place as a leader," he said wearily, seeming to lean back into his chair, seeming to be an old man. "Is it not enough to be for a while at the right hand of the Ard Ri Alban?"

Macbeth thought of Duncan, a king already, and of the child Thorfinn moved into leadership by Malcolm, like a playing-piece with others' hands upon him. He saw Nechtan, futilely closing and unclosing his fists, and could not look away. He saw what he might become and refused. He looked down at his own hands, stained with ink.

I will become the man my father's death demands, he vowed, *beginning at this moment.*

Malcolm started to rise and go, his retinue immediately rousing, but then he paused.

"The full value and weight of cro will be given to you, understand, as is the custom and law. That will settle this matter. You will accept it, and there will be no revenge."

❧

Gruach, St. Vigean's, 1020

I saw the youth step aside as Malcolm walked past him, unafraid of any impulsive act. He had that much confidence in his hold over Findlaích's son or that much unbending steel in his soul.

As Macbeth's haunted eyes followed the king, and the room broke into tumult, I felt the cold touch of prophecy. I had not recognized him until loss aged him, in that short space turning the youth into a man. The boy with the hair between gold and red who had accompanied the Ard Ri Alban. The slight youth who had remained steadfast as his older foster-brother gathered all the sun to himself. Now that grief had scarred his face and darkened his eyes, I recognized him—the vision had been of someone older yet, but this was the man who had regarded me so thoughtfully from the fire.

I stared, caught in confusion and despair, unable to stop myself. Findlaích's son scowled back. He wheeled and walked quickly to the other end of the hall, his stride breaking like an untrained colt's between the awkwardness of youth and the decision of a man.

"Bride to one, strength to another, at the end mourning."

The White Lady's warning had come to seem as empty as the vision in the fire, an illusion, a child's imagining, nothing.

It will not happen, I told myself. *It cannot happen. He is still a youth. It will not be.*

18

MACBETH

Fharfair, 1021

As he pulled the javelin from the target, Macbeth's fingers slid across an unevenness in the shaft. He looked along it, then held it lengthwise against the light and rotated it slowly in his hands. At one place, the smoothed wood lifted gently, like an ancient grave-mound all but washed back into the earth, circling where a small branch had emerged from the tree. How many ash trees had been cut to make these throwing spears? He tested their individual heft, the bias of wood and forged iron. How many trees had been cut and measured, smoothed, then tossed on the fire as unsuitable for killing men? To grow straight was a matter of chance—that light would come there and water, that no rock would press nor tree fall across the green sapling and forever mark its growth. He turned and ran lightly toward the target, the spear held high, then twisted and released with the weight of his body. It traveled cleanly and struck hard.

Macbeth put his foot against the base of the target and pulled the spear free. It would come more readily from a man's chest, and blood would follow. Blood of Danes and Albanaig, alike in color and hot scent, the same from a stranger—or a cousin. Alike in the way it slid along the metal and clung to the shaft.

His shadow skewed around as he turned. It was long in the evening sun, rippling across the bare ground where boys played the game of war as he himself once had. A man's shadow that he had been chasing all his life, his legs lengthening from childhood until he could claim it. Once he had imagined himself as Roland, as Charlemagne himself, Alexander, a Roman hero or a Greek. His tutor had shown him those figures like the flat shapes carved on the sarcophagi of Pictish kings as images of what a man should be. They were handsome shapes but empty. Now he wanted only plain things. To be the son of Findlaích, on Moray soil and among his people. The political power he needed was not to be gathered as easily as the muscle he was gaining in shoulders and thighs. He threw again and again, feeling each release deep into his back. The spear traveled true each time.

With hot shame, he recalled childhood failures, the slowness with which his body had learned the skills of a fighter. Oswald had been at his side to urge him to book-learning, the king well satisfied with his passivity. He had struggled to emulate Duncan, unequal at every turn, each contest ending in failure.

Until the last.

In the winter before his brother left to claim Strathclyde of the Britons as his kingdom, the court had been stormbound at Glamis. The wet wind brought heavy snow, which fell and froze in the night and then was covered by more snow. The dark ribbon of River Isla bending south was hidden by the driving snow, until it whitened and froze. When the storm broke with a warm breeze, they remained caught within the walls, trapped by melting snow and floods. He and Duncan were together at all times, and at all times bickered.

"Little monk," Duncan would say, "find in your prayer-book a prayer to dry the paths."

Twice he challenged him for this mockery, and twice Duncan turned away as a man will from a child who shakes his threatless toy and screams.

One early morning when the light was slant and silver on the beaten ground within the walls, Duncan was passing him on his way to the jakes when he called out to him, "Little monk, little monk, get to your kneeling," and his companion had laughed.

Macbeth turned sharply, and in three steps he reached his brother and caught him by the throat. "I am no monk."

Duncan pulled free, but there were deep red marks where Macbeth's fingers had pressed.

"As you are my brother, tell me that you will not call me that any longer."

Duncan's fleshy face twisted. "A man does not plead for recognition."

And Macbeth took a spear and threw it with all his strength at the weather-stained planks of the gate. The point drove deep between them. Old oak groaned and closed around the metal and Duncan could not pull it free, not even with the help of his companion. Finally, enraged, he had chopped the shaft off, leaving the point embedded like some enemy's mocking reminder.

"A fortunate throw," Duncan had said, tossing the splintered ash to one side, breathing hard with effort. In his eyes deep resentment had showed, not respect, resentment that was no longer disguised as competition.

And I tried to assuage that fearful anger with gifts, Macbeth thought. *A double error to have sent the book. Trying to show respect, I offended even more deeply. Blind as a bent old scribe to the layered shadow-play of the world.*

"What is it you watch?" Nechtan's voice called him back to the present moment.

He shook himself, was surprised at how the light had gone out of the land. Nechtan was coming toward him from the gate that would soon be barred.

"I saw you standing for a long time, your spear drooping to the ground," Nechtan said. "You were looking across the valley and I thought surely there was some army approaching."

"There is nothing," Macbeth said, dismissing memories. He stretched and felt his muscles tight and hard from his daily practice.

"Then you haven't been enchanted into a tree with the shape of a man?"

"Perhaps you think to topple me?"

Nechtan bent as though to remove a stone from his shoe, but Macbeth saw how his shoulder was squared and slipped aside as his friend threw his body forward. Nechtan landed hard, rolled, reaching for Macbeth's leg, catching it and bringing him down. Pain knifed from his knee driven against a stone; no matter.

Like wrestling a bear, he thought, twisting forward rather than back to break a powerful grip. *He is as big as Duncan himself.*

Nechtan grunted as he tried to exert his weight. His moves were slow; he was heavy with uselessness.

Macbeth knew that agility was both his defense and his best means of attack. A dramatic growth spurt had finally raised him to an adequate height, but he did not have, would never have, the bulk and power of his opponent. He hooked his leg through Nechtan's and levered him backward. Balance shifted. He pressed his advantage. Nechtan tried to grapple him close but the slope of the land and the angle of his body let Macbeth thrust his opponent over. Nechtan went down and he rolled with him, hot with the fight now, ignoring the strength of those arms covered with a pelt of curling brown hair.

"Huh!" Nechtan made a plunging move, too far. Macbeth half-rose, came down with one knee on his opponent's arm, caught the other hand with his own.

Nechtan's face was red and swollen. Macbeth forced his free arm down, pinned it to the rocky ground. His opponent arched his back and he felt himself lifted but did not let go. He breathed in the aroma of sweat, torn earth, blood. The muscles of his shoulders trembled and in the heat of the fight he all but reached for the short blade that would finish a downed enemy.

Nechtan stared up at him and suddenly went limp.

Macbeth leaped back, panting with excitement and exertion. He offered Nechtan his hand.

"You have become a dangerous friend," Nechtan said, pulling his belt around and settling his tunic back into place.

"I imagined—some other battle."

"Then God help that enemy," Nechtan said, "but I think God will be on your side, if the opponent is the stinking weasel I imagine."

Macbeth said nothing.

"You're bleeding," Nechtan offered, and he looked down to see a dark bloom at his knee. The flesh had been opened in a three-cornered cut.

"A sharp stone," he remembered, now feeling the wound.

They walked together to the gate, arms across each other's shoulders, where the porter leaned against the heavy post and smiled at the entertainment of their wrestling match. They drank cool stone-tasting water, one then the other, from the hide bucket lifted from the well. A rock dove flew down and strutted back and forth, its bright eye on them, casting the ground for spilled grain.

Friends. He could count his friends on one hand, Macbeth reflected. Oswald, of course, but he was a counselor and no warrior. Some of his father's men who had been absent from the disastrous battle and kept their lives only by taking their skills to new leaders, north or south or over the seas. And Nechtan who, by the similarity of their positions, had become a natural ally. Few wished to be closely linked with Boidh's son, or Findlaích's. Most of his kinsmen were likewise Gillecomgan's, and either fell in with him or were neutered by fear of him.

Retribution against Gillecomgan and his brother had settled deep in Macbeth's belly, where it was harbored and hidden, revenge to be taken in the way of the Hebrews. Eye for eye. Life for life and death for death. He was coming to know the God of Battles and Lord of Hosts, as Conamail had said, hearing with a new ear the martial cadences of the Old Testament. He waited, not forgetting, but waiting on God's good time, unlike Nechtan, who seemed to have swallowed down his rage and extinguished it after his sister sacrificed herself in that marriage. Not even a raving fool would speak, nor Macbeth hear, of revenge on the Ri Alban as author of this bloody chaos.

"Look there." Nechtan nodded toward the south wall, where Oswald sat and rested his back against the sun-warmed stones.

"He eases his eyes on the mountains."

"What does he write, all the day long?"

"A life of St. Ceadda. A Mercian, one of four brothers. They are all saints, he says, although I do not know if Rome agrees."

Nechtan glanced at him, his eyes appraising. "Do you study with him yet?"

"I have studied enough." *Perhaps too long.*

"Then why does he not return to his monastery?"

"Friendship," Macbeth said immediately, but knew that was not the reason, or not all of it. "And I think he would not find the Rule agreeable, now that he has been so long in the world."

"I think Malcolm believes that he keeps you patient."

"My patience is my own," Macbeth said heatedly.

"Patience is something you can grow used to, without realizing—like a monk too long in the world."

"When the time is come, I will act."

They sat in silence. The air chilled and fog began to spread across the low ground. There was laughter from the hall. "I am hungry," Nechtan said abruptly. Macbeth grasped his friend's arm for a moment, then let him go.

"I will be along." He watched as Nechtan crossed the open space, a slow shape in the growing darkness, until he came to the doorway and was for a moment outlined then plunged into the light. *A branch falls across this life or that,* Macbeth thought again, *uprooting, bending, breaking. God tends a forest of souls, and must care more for those that twist and strive than the few he allows to grow straight.* His own life had been knotted, first around his mother's passing, so distant that it was no more than the whisper of a falling leaf, then the inescapable granite of his father's death.

He went to Oswald and found him snoring, with his poorly tonsured head tilted back against the stones. The Anglian's face was worn and gray in the twilight. His broad shoulders were rounded from too long at scholar's labor. His swollen left hand lay cradled in his right; it was crippled by the harsh penance Oswald inflicted on himself, the rod held in his right hand punishing the left for the world that both held too closely.

"Oswald," he said gently. "Oswald."

The monk came awake slowly, not like a warrior. A thread glistened at the corner of his mouth. *An orphan like myself*, came a sudden thought.

"What do you need?" Oswald asked, sitting forward.

"Nothing."

"Sit here until the moon is up," he said, nodding toward the east where the sky was pale. "I will tell you how Ceadda built his monastery at Barrow, and you will let me know if it should be written down in that way."

He sat beside him, hunger sharp now but ignored, and listened as Oswald recited a holy life.

19

LAPWING

Dunkeld Abbey, 1021

In this chamber, stones gleam where bowls once waited on shelves for the brethren. Not one is holy. Not one is the pebble that Colm of the Church held, removed from the circles of the wise, we who know thrice fifty names for everything, the powerful stone by which he stole a nation for his shepherd god.

Those who believe themselves thinkers are caught in past or future. Crinán leaps between. Grasps toward the future for his son, with other hand seeks back for strength. Lapwing knows his secret. Lapwing knows the belly that is not filled. Like a naked boy Crinán gathers stones, carries them home to Dunkeld, delighting in their roundness in his hands and promise of power. He seeks one among multitudes, sees holiness in all, does not recognize their name or nature.

Lapwing knows both. The litany of stones comes:

"Deer stone leaps on the threshold of thirteen.
Goldstone follows, young sun rides in January sky.
Beryl sea-green, wind on water, mother's eyes.
Garnet shows a crimson egg, sun mist-seen.
Bloodstone glows, blown coal hissing, hawk cries.
Lapis from a navigator's sky, flower in bud.
Flesh-stone follows, holy flesh and bone arise.
Yellow crystals of blue hills; sword-mouths speak them red.
Agate rippled, a sky at sunset, a salmon swimming.
Winestone has power to stop the breath of wine.
Serpentine in mottled adder-skin entwines.
Jasper follows, of glass-green waves roaring.
Malachite, swelling breast of the earth,
Suckles the new Son, amber, fire-hearth."

Ha! Lapwing has seen Crinán and his bishop like two fires fanning each other. They confer, holding speckled rocks tumbled by river and sea where the Moray Firth joins the great northern ocean, turning over pink and green pebbles from the shores of Iona. Mutter Christian prayers to wake a truestone!

The saint's pebble rests in a pond in Circinn. That I know among the things I know. It rolled from Brude's hand in Asreth battle, down the green to blue and through blue to a hidden darkness. But Lapwing lets Crinán cast wide and far. I have told him how things find their own path, choose pocket or flooding stream. My path is a bird arrowing north in spring. I draw Crinán after.

The hall in slow afternoon waits for its master, and he comes. Crinán and Duncan, like and like, call one call both.

Duncan counts every hide of his kingdom's wealth as if it were his own body. He is proud, a king's pride that is armor. He tells himself in his heart that the distance he keeps from Lapwing is no longer a boy's fear but a king's majesty.

"Lapwing, honored among poets," Crinán says, and folds his arms on his wide chest to show that he can confront the gods that strive in me. "My son has come from Malcolm's side, and tells me the old king weakens."

"His hands do not perfectly obey him. I have seen," Lapwing tells them.

They glance from one to another—the binding of father to son, and both to me.

"Malcolm grows old. I ask you, poet, tell my son of your vision that has underlain all my labors on his behalf."

The clàrsach is silent, song-emptied. It is a sleeping child until I strike the strings.

Treble notes carry Lapwing to the cave of the future, where I sing what I have seen. "This hand hatched with letters and signs, this hand called the gods."

Again, I stroke the clàrsach. "In the thickets of my fingers, in the holy of secrets I found them."

I hold up my hand. "See where the blood beats. In the rite of imbas forosnai I let my own blood spring. The water-carved rock of the world accepted my gift, knew me and my question. Lapwing covered his face against the world and chanted the future on finger-ends. In the darkness by the rush of water the other world rises to be seen."

Duncan's hand gropes at his chest. He touches a crucifix, and then he holds a stone of Manannan.

"The gods came like a storm. They came upon me where my hands lay flat upon each side of my face. They brought visions of battle and of great men. Battle in far distance and far time. Then like clouds before the sun, all these things were blown aside.

"I saw a forest where man never walked, a forest of oaks planted by the gods. And there was a great tree, wide-spreading, and under it no light came and no seedling sprouted. But the gods spoke and a gale came, roaring, and the great oak shuddered. It groaned and cried out, and then it fell. The eyes of the gods sent into that place a great light, and a young oak quickly grew, its leaves golden."

My hand finds the strings and fills the spaces in the oracular chant.

"Old night is long, and long rules.
White the earth, old brows, old bones.
Dawn comes, and comes quickly.
Frost fades, into earth, always-taking earth.
Old dies—young thrives.
A blond king comes into his own."

Crinán waits. "I had asked one question," he says at last, "and he gave me one answer. But when I asked again then he revealed his vision had been doubled."

Duncan's feet make a noise. He is impatient, thinks all is decided at the moment a sword enters flesh, and not before the blade was ever bared, ever tempered, the steel folded and hammered, the iron bled from stone. I must make it plain for him. "The vision of the young tree, when it came, came blurred. I petitioned the gods again and was answered. The tree split in two, and its blond head divided. Two blond kings stood, twins of the sun's power. One already has been fulfilled."

"Cnut," adds Crinán, lest Duncan fail to understand. "The fair-haired Sveinsson is king of lands on both sides of the cold sea and will gain yet more. Another blond king rises like a sapling in the forest, you my son, to rule the land of Alba."

I see them flayed by hope, their hearts naked to me. Crinán's pride is all in the son who has grown taller than he, and greater. For him he will make any sacrifice. But Duncan hopes for no one but himself.

"So Malcolm will soon die," Duncan says.

"The vision is not time-bound."

"It cannot be long."

Duncan, considering my vision, paces the width of the hall. He pauses in front of the cupboard and stares at the stones. These stones have nothing to tell him.

"Whether sooner or later, it will be," Crinán says. "And you are his tanist."

Duncan frowns. "That is no certainty, for the men of the blood might choose another."

"Such visions tell the truth, young king, but the truth has many sides," says Lapwing. "If you wish to make Alba your bride on the stone at Scoine, you must think three times but act only once."

"My son is more given to action than study," says Crinán.

Duncan lifts his shoulders, a horse easing its harness.

"Then he must have a counselor."

"You will be that man?" Duncan says to the unspeaking stones.

"If you will be guided. You as your father has been."

He turns and nods sharply, but his gaze slides past and he avoid my eyes.

Kings are like all men, amenable to the reins if the hand is sure. Those who desire power will give it to gain it.

20

GRUACH

The wort boiled slowly, each bubble rising from the bottom to release a strong clean smell of grain.

I leaned over the copper, let the rich steam flush my face, breathed it deep into my lungs. This was my favorite part of the brewing, a time for slow meditative stirrings. The heavy work was behind and ahead. Behind, the winnowing and the grinding, the mashing and the carrying of water from a clear spring (the well water here having a strong taste of minerals). Ahead, the settling and fermenting and the pouring-off.

Among all the tasks of women, I liked brewing too much to leave it entirely to the farm women and servants. They tended two other kettles in the courtyard. They were mostly silent, plain women coarsened by work, their fair bright children like the children of some other creation.

The fires crackled. Each wooden paddle made soft hollow noises against the cauldron sides, like the distant boom of sea against stone. I struck the paddle hard and the noise was louder but still hollow and strange. Boom, the water rushing into a narrow place. Boom, spouting up through a hole like the breath of the great sea-beasts. There had been such places when Alpia sailed us to the Ring, skerries and sea stacks and holed rocks where the sea shouted.

The wort rolled in its boil, tonguing the copper.

From this little hill community, like any near the sea palisaded and watchful, I could see part of the Loch of Spynie. It reflected the bright skies over Moray, peaceful as if no man needed to stand by a signal-pyre for fear that enemy ships would enter the sea-loch and carve deep into the land. Men cut free of old ties in Norway and Sweden and Daneland sailed for new lands or at least plunder, occasionally urging their ships against Alban shores but increasingly sailing to the far south, to Frank lands, to the cities of the Moors. Travelers boasted over the picked bones of evening meals that the sun stayed all winter in Granada. They said even the fruits were golden in those lands, apples of the sun, and that though the sun parched the soil, the Moors made it green with water channelled from great distances. They said the trees were filled with birds that sang night and day, birds that were red and gold like illustrations risen from a monk's pen. I wondered if these People of the South might be kin to the ones who had settled the far north, or if those voyagers had left entirely in that distant past, their homeland abandoned to newer races.

Here even in mid-summer, with the air warm and sweet with the aroma of melilot and briar, you could not forget the long shadows of winter. The birds were dark, gray and black and brown. They cried and screamed, plundered each other's nests, made war against the smaller or slower. No different from the tribes of people. The youngest of Sigurd's sons, Thorfinn, three winters yet from manhood, had sailed against his elder brothers in Orkney from his portion in Caithness. His forces were doubled by the men his grandfather provided, with Gille-comgan at their head. Malcolm never ceased from his long strategy to exert his will on the north.

A touch at my sleeve shook me from a long stare into the memory of the king and his icy blue eyes.

The boy leaped back, as I must have myself. I smiled and smoothed his rough hair.

"Here it is," he said. A heaping tray of ladyherb rested on the ground, carefully picked over, ready for the cauldrons.

I rolled a piece of the herb between the palms of my hands. Mugwort, some called it. St. John's plant to the monks. Ladyherb, sister to silvery wormwood. I held my open hands out to the boy Ruadan and he sniffed and smiled. He raised his eyes in one of those shy, fleeting glances, like that of an animal tamed from the wild.

Ruadan had eight winters. He was the son of Conamail who had come blinded before the king to report the slaughter in Moray. True to his promise, Gillecomgan had spared the child, also Cornan son of Lorcan the handless. And true to his nature, he then had enslaved the boys. It was customary that those of the blood, if they fell through failure in war or unmet requirement of a bond, should be treated as family rather than chattel. Their holders would see them brought up, and would give them charge of the horses or the valuables of the household. But these boys had instead been awarded to the roughest of people, families barely above slavery themselves. They were thin and dirty and smelled of filthy tasks. They bathed in the sea while they were setting nets, wore rags, went barefoot in all weather. Even so, they walked erect. Their eyes were clear. And when I taught them the histories and genealogies and lore a man should know, during the times I was blessedly left alone, they learned quickly and told no one.

"Run and see that the barrels are clean and ready."

"They are. I saw them."

"Then go to the kitchen and say that I want you to have a wedge of the new cheese, you and Cornan."

"Thank you," Ruadan said, then quick and low and reverently, "my lady," and then he was gone. I watched him run into the hall, his ragged garment flapping, and sighed.

Asa, who was gathering up her kettle's portion of mugwort, looked sharply at me.

"A son of destruction," she said, "and better if he had died with the rest."

The daughter of a settled Dane and wife to another, her son was grown and in Gillecomgan's war-band. I smiled faintly. Had Asa's son cut the throats of Findlaích's people?

Sons of war—why not daughters? We breed boys up to make war, then weep for those men and bury them. Never a time free of war. War from the earliest time, the Old People, the White Folk, and the new-comers in their waves. The brochs and strongholds, stones mortared with blood. The invading Romans, who named their stations up and down the Sinus Vararsis, and marched in their numberless arrays along the seacoast down to Luguballium. The Scotti, leaping from Éireann to follow the great water-threaded valley from the western coast. The Danes, driven out and returning, settling, becoming part of Moray by marriage or by the rot of their bodies under battle-cairns. Everywhere in the land of Moray, piles of stones, the march of the dead who claimed land and were claimed by it.

I took a handful of ladyherb and sifted it into the kettle. The liquid darkened as the herb cooked in, cleansing the ale of impurities, making it bitter and strong. I stirred and the paddle against the metal sounded like a cry from under earth. I recalled Halla, her hips wide as a cow's, sitting back by her loom and speaking of Farulf under earth who did not answer her. Under earth, and earth stuffed your mouth, and death was merely death. The new plant rose from the husk of the seed but I began to doubt the soul did.

There was a legend brought from Éireann and heard among the Cymri in which the bodies of broken warriors, cast into a magical cauldron, lived again, though mute. That was a sign of the violence against the order of the world. Men forcing the powers of health and plenty to the uses of war. Men requiring mothers to birth red-handed warriors.

"I do not care for this plant you use."

Startled, I caught my paddle hard against the swirl and spattered brew out of the kettle.

Asa's face twisted like a root against a rock. She held out her lined palm filled with mugwort. "The creeping herb is better. Your ladyherb, now, it's poison to the herds."

Behind her, Snechta's wife nodded agreement.

"It is stronger," I agreed, "but also will keep the ale better. "

"My mother taught me that the ground-ivy was best," Asa insisted. "'Tis a mint like the water-mints, safe and clean. You can tell by the stems and the purple flowers."

I nodded. The last time I had brewed with Asa's help, the woman had made the same complaint.

"My foster-mother also taught me the plants and their uses, and I do not fear this one," I said. "It wears the moon's light below its leaves."

Asa ran her tongue over a broken tooth, her jaw jutted forward. "All the same, all the same," she said, turning back to her kettle. She grumbled to it and it grumbled back. I stirred my own brew, steeping myself in the steam that now had the harsher note of the herb. I would never convince Asa of anything. There was sour disagreement in every word the woman spoke.

We let the fires die down as the bittering finished its work. I kicked a hotly burning stick away from the ashes. Now the wort must cool and settle in the open air. Yeast skimmed from the top would start the next batch.

It was midday now, the sun standing at its height and shadows short. The women went to their homes and I went into the hall to wait out the slow afternoon. The smell of the brewing clung to my skin, smoky fire and boiled grain, and I did not wash it away. I did not care, and had Gillecomgan been here, would have cared even less. I folded my hands in my damp lap and retreated, remembering Nechtan racing bare-chest-ed against his shadow. I heard people come and go, their feet crashing through the fresh strewings. Gillecomgan's retainers (my keepers) were marked by the weight of their steps, the creak of leather, slither and clank of metal on metal. One of them paused by my chair. I waited for the man (smelled his musk, the sweat of his armpits and crotch) to go on and leave me be.

I opened my eyes. The man was leaning forward in his urgency but had not spoken. "Yes?"

"We need your help," he said.

"Who are you?" I took note of his dress, farmworker in his short jacket and trews, only a knife at his belt.

"Maedoc," he said, inclining a shaggy head turning gray, "of the monastery's people."

"Then you should seek help there."

"None in the monk's house is able to help. But you are the White Lady."

I tensed.

"I am of Findlaích's kin and party, the least of people now," he said. "Some would call you the wife of my enemy. But you are not Gillecomgan's any more than me. You are one of the women of the White Lady and my wife told me that I should say we need you and you will come. My son coughs until he bleeds from his ears and nose."

I got up and walked away from him, looking out the window at the blackened stones and the wisps of smoke from the fires.

"He is all that I have."

People had come to me before, creeping, begging help, afraid to say what it seemed they knew. And often, I had turned them away, in caution of priests, of my husband's spite, but more so, out of fear of my own inadequacy.

"Maedoc," I said softly, "how do you know what I can do, or will do?"

"You heal the world," he said.

It might have been Alpia who spoke. The words were hers. Alpia, far away, unreachable—reaching me now. I turned from the window. Maedoc waited, as simply and surely as before, while I covered my head and from my small kist selected some medicines. I had my fawn-colored mare saddled and he led the way out the gate and down the slope, turning away from the houses that huddled within the protection of the outer walls.

The sun shone in our faces as we followed a track toward the distant swelling of the mountains. Clouds showed far to the west, where the heights faded into blue, but the mountains would wring them out and there would be no rain here. The path ran between a pair of book-stones, the rough image of a Bible cut to mark the limits of the church's lands. There stood the bishop's church, huddled over its treasures of bell and altar, and there the monks' house, while the people's turf-and-wattle huts scattered out on their gardens. A noise of children. Beyond were fields of good loam that thinned and showed gray rock as they neared the hills. The house where we stopped was no better than the others, a farmer's hut, low-slung. Gillecomgan could not empty the province of Findlaích's people, but those he had not turned to his way or killed, he had brought down, alienating their farms and forges to others. This family had found a modest shelter under the church's wing.

I stepped down from the threshold. I could hear mice rustle close overhead. Cords, stained with last winter's dried fruits and salted meats, swung lank and empty.

"His name is Bredan," Maedoc said behind me, and I moved further into the house.

"You are his mother?" though there was no doubt of the woman who sat slumped with weariness, holding the child's hand.

"Fyfa," she answered. "Who thanks you for hearing and coming." I stared at the woman with the ancient name, whose eyes were sea-gray. I wondered what faded truths had come down, mother to daughter to granddaughter, to this woman.

The boy moved under the blanket, half lifted himself and began to cough. His illness said its name as he coughed until his face darkened from lack of air, then breathed in with a harsh whoop.

"At first we thought he had only a cold," Fyfa said. "He sneezed and was warm. He asked for honey to ease his throat. He began to feel better except for the cough."

As though the word summoned the enemy, Bredan sat up and clung to his mother's arm. His eyes were wide and frightened. Then he coughed. He coughed until his body shook with the strain, until his face turned red. At last, he choked out a sticky fluid, then fell back into his pallet. Bredan's hand rested limply on his mother's. Involuntary tremors ran across it and I knew how close he had come to convulsion.

"How many others are sick?" My mind circled a fear that I would try to save the boy, only to have him die in my hands, while the cough spread throughout the community.

"The other people—other children—keep away. He is now the only one sick," said Maedoc. "Two others died and are under earth."

And yet no one had come to me. Nor had I involved myself in their lives to know of the sickness.

"What have you done for him?" I loosened the strings on my bag and brought out a small bottle, carefully stoppered, and herbs folded in squares of linen.

"I asked the monks, but they advised only keeping him warm, day and night by the fire. Their herbalist gave us coltsfoot tea. And prayers," Fifa said, anger crossing her face. "An old woman said that we should wrap a cloth tightly around him to prevent a hernia when he coughed."

"That was good," I said, touching each of the packets, thinking about how few my weapons were against sickness and pain.

Hemlock was the sharpest edge I had. There was a better drug, a purple-flowered bush the Danes called dwale, sleep. It could be found where pale stone made the water sweet, its dark green leaves soaking up the sun in July heat, the bell-shaped flowers drooping. I had none. Instead, I would have to rely on hemlock, dangerous as it was. I opened the bottle and the plant's notorious odor filled the air.

I unfolded a cloth and crushed sweet cicely between my hands, releasing its happy smell to cover the other. "This is hemlock," I said, watching their anguished eyes as I lifted the bottle, "which you well know as poison. If properly given it will calm the cough so your son's chest can heal. This is the juice of the berries, tempered with an extract of the leaves."

I set all that aside, for the moment, and uncovered the boy. As gently as possible, so that he would not be startled into coughing, I exposed his chest and felt the exhausted flutter of his heart.

Surely it would not happen. Even if the White Lady still listened, I'd not recall all the words. Did not, I feared, have the right to ask assistance from the one I had all but abandoned, kneeling with everyone else in the church of Jesus and forgetting the Lady of the Open Sky.

But Maedoc and Fyfa believed.

The father waited, squatting on his heels. The mother slipped her hand from Bredan's and gave him to me.

I lay my head against his chest, let the sound of his breath brush away the webs on my thoughts. Fear and disuse, fragments of other rituals, regrets, regrets. I caught the rhythm of the boy's heart and followed it until I began to feel I could guide it, slow its frantic pace. I placed my hands on the boy's chest, flat on each side of the breastbone that is the keel of life, thumbs and forefingers meeting.

This was the time of growth, the time for Bredan to rise like a sapling. His life was bent by a harsh wind. I saw him as a young rowan-tree. I straightened it, tamped the earth firmly around its roots, and with my body blocked the gale. My hands on the young tree were Alpia's hands. They were sure, strong. I sang to the rowan, a song of quickening and sap-rising, leafing, stretching upward. I sang the sunlight down through the forest to nourish its growth. I sang the return of the moon, teaching the young tree the sway of seasons.

My hands warmed on the thin-barked body. I felt it stand against the wind, its roots holding, and I was filled with peace. This calmness used to come when I immersed myself in joyful, useful work, in planting or making. I had not felt that way very often in recent years.

"The Lady of Green Fields holds you, Bredan, in the lap of life," I chanted. "The Raiser of Flowers makes your bed soft and sweet and you, Bredan, rise refreshed. She who brings the salmon back to the streams calls you, Bredan, back to yourself."

Under my hands, the boy's body eased. My own heart too. My anger, fear of men and their terrible power, faded in the glow of the healing. For a moment, I sat wrapped in stillness.

I measured out the hemlock, drop by drop, stirred it into a small bowl of honey flavored with more of the sweet cicely, and measured the medicine carefully. Bredan accepted it without complaint.

"No more than that," I told Fyfa, watching as the dose took hold and Bredan drowsed. "I have portioned it by his age and size, but every person takes the drug differently. If he is dizzy on standing, or feels sick, then it is too much. Wait, then, and when he needs it give him a dose cut back by a third."

"Will he be like some, weak in the chest for the rest of his life?" asked Maedoc.

"I do not believe so. His coughing will be less and less, and then end, but for a time any sickness will seem like this one returned and he will cough violently. Don't be alarmed—this sickness once it has passed will not come back."

While calming their fears, I set out other materials for the boy's healing. Moss from the high cold moors that would make a thick tea. An infusion of common violet to soothe the cough and ease sleep, when the strong drug was no longer needed. "And you can make a compress of violet leaves and place it on his throat and chest," I said.

There was little to put back in my bag, after leaving a measure of wheat flour and folded packets of herbs for this ailment and that, including one to strengthen Fyfa's blood. Her eyes were dark beneath, and not enough blood showed under her nails. I accepted their quiet thanks and left before the reverence that bent Maedoc's head found words.

I was tired but exhilarated, like a spring stream churning up the stones in its bed, rushing and full. Wanting the feel of the land under my feet, I walked, leading my horse that, without the discipline of a rider, tugged at the reins. The track meandered in the way that walkers had found best, skirting the top of small rises, avoiding the wet of the bottoms. Among the soft grasses, campion held its white petals closed, waiting for dusk, but meadow rue and buttercups offered color and peacock butterflies flashed their bright eyes while they worked the pink flowers of restharrow.

I strayed to one side of the track and the other like the grazing mare. Burnet and dock and allgood could have been added to meals, but not in this place and time, not for the wife of the mormaer to gather. I picked only flowers and herbs meant for healing, savoring the green scent of their broken stems as much as the bee-lure of their blossoms. I could begin to refill those packets newly emptied for Maedoc's family.

An old woman greeted me from her resting place beside the track. Gnarled as a stick herself, she had set down her bundle of sticks under a thorn tree and was letting the sun warm her feet and ankles, knotted by age. "Good day," I returned.

"Bless you and your children," the woman said.

I looked away. "I have no child."

I squatted beside the old woman, beneath stiff branches where young sloes rounded toward blue-black astringency. "Brightness rests on your cheeks and brow," she said. "The light of a new mother shines from you."

"I can say that I have saved a child today, so perhaps that is what you see."

The old woman nodded. Her eyes were set so deeply in wrinkles, under brows springing like badger fur, that it was difficult to tell if they were closed or open, if she was awake or asleep, until she tilted her head and the light caught a bright liquid spark. She touched her bundle of firewood, the bindweed that held it together, then burrowed her hand among the sticks to bring out a fresh, shining apple, red with the harvest that was yet to come.

"Those who eat apples shall live long, they say." She turned the apple in her two hands, suddenly, and it split crosswise in a bloom of apple-scent. The old woman held out the halves and there was the five-pointed star of the Aspects.

"The cycle shows itself in every living thing and we come round-about from birth to death to birth."

I rose and stepped back from the woman whose eyes were dark and clear as a moonless midwinter night.

"Daughter, do you see?"

I could not speak, for awe, but my forlorn heart cried out.

Help me to have strength worthy of you.

Show me when I will be free again.

The cries were not answered. The old woman crutched to her feet, picked up her bundle of sticks, and hobbled away.

༜

GRUACH, AM BROCH, MORAY, 1022

I wrung out a fresh cloth and cleaned myself. The smell of blood was warm, the metallic smelting of my body. From a narrow window I looked down at the sea, lashing and tugging at the rock promontory on which a fortification had stood since the Builders' time. The sea was driven by the moon, and the seasons were, and so was I. No beginning, no returning, ever round.

I began to wash out the cloths that had caught my flow. Poor women of the people used moss, thrusting it into their bodies. They suffered through days of damp and cold and distress with no more comfort than a beast on the moor.

Once I had felt elation at the end of each cycle, a wonder at my body that could sacrifice itself each month and still be whole. The lavishness of the body! Now each month brought sadness. Gillecomgan was gone again, thankfully, yet I remained hostage to his ambition. I was not even left the fiction of my own trusted handmaid—this black-haired girl, like others before, was his, and would yield yet another child for him. He had bought her from a Wendish trader, sending two orphaned Moray boys onto the ship to be taken to the east and made eunuchs. I did not know her story and would not trust my intimacies to her.

I put on a fresh tunic, simple blue and unornamented, and an old silver necklace. The metal was smooth and kind against my skin. Cipia's criticism surfaced, "Silver draws you cold." *So let it be.*

My husband said I refused him a child by magic, repeatedly threatening to bring me before the Culdees for judgment. I wished in my heart that it was so, that I labored with herbs and spells to prevent conception. It was simpler than that. I was barren, as each monthly sign of blood reminded me. My breasts ached in the days before the flow, tender as though they prepared for a child. After, they were slack. I felt myself aging, slowly drying from youth. Sometimes at night I dreamed of death. I fled its many forms, laughing like a child playing catch-me, until turning suddenly back and embracing it.

Four years since I had come to Moray. Had been brought here, a wedded captive. At first, I had battered my heart against the enforced isolation. I was quieter now, kept myself from distressing thought by work, gardening, making. And since the visit to Bredan, sometimes healing, sometimes averting illness or blight. It was best to tend the people in hidden ways, given the hostility of Christ's priests on one hand, and on the other, the remaining worshippers of Lugh and Manannan and all the bloody warring gods of the old land.

Gillecomgan's duties kept him ceaselessly traveling the bounds of the lands he co-ruled. He was a jealous overlord, marking the state of the crops, marking any encroachments. His older brother Cerr, born Malcolm but called after his left-handedness, was elderly and slack and while maintaining the title of King of the North had let Gillecomgan do as he willed. Meanwhile, the Orkneymen were moving further south. I wondered if they had firmed their hold beyond Golspie but received no word. Gillecomgan increased his followers each year. They were almost a king's retinue, and a burden on the people. I was happy to be left behind at times, abandoned like a rough-edged weapon at the edge of the sea, or at the fortress on the River Dee that had been a favorite of Findlaích's, or at abbey guest-houses. I travelled like a queen and a captive, with silent men and their swords to keep me.

I tossed the darkened water from the window. The drops sprayed brightly to the sea. I bundled the damp cloths and went down.

This new girl, she calls herself "wife" and it makes Gillecomgan laugh. The last two such were sent off to raise their children, both daughters, among congregations of nuns in the south. The bishop—once Findlaích's bishop—had warned Gillecomgan: "You must free the slave woman who bears you a child, so state the Penitentials. And now that you have defiled yourself on the body of a captive, you are not to sleep with your lawful wife for a year."

Findlaích's bishop was found floating in the ancient well, a pool of clear, cold water held by squared stone and reached by many stone steps. It had been honored from the time of the Builders, was holy to the Lady for water ceremonies and holy to the Christians for baptism. And Gillecomgan had desecrated it with the murder of the bishop. Or so all believed, though there was no proof of how the bishop's body had come to be there. A battered head might have meant only a fall.

Penitentials or no, it had been many months since Gillecomgan had come to me, and I was thankful for that. Soon, perhaps, when he succeeded in siring a son on some miserable girl, he would have me put aside legally. Divorce was easy enough. Even a nun's imprisonment would mean a kind of peace.

I turned my face up to the slanting sun, this frequent clear sun of the northeast that warmed the land and dried the grain for harvest. I thought back to the rounds the court had made to the realm's western lands where Dál Riata had first come from Éireann and established themselves, recalling the mist and mud and rain. Warmer, yes, but constantly wet. This sun was a blessing. I went out through the rampart of stone and wood, over the wide mouths of ditches meant to catch soldiers, circles of defenses. The Lochlannaig had destroyed the tower many years back, but stones were regathered and the walls again garrisoned. Inside the final rampart, I took a narrow path to the place where women hung their washed privacies. It was protected from the seawind but open to the sun and out of the way of horses. I peeled the pieces of fabric apart and laid them across the branches of the shrubby trees.

A thick-bodied knarr with the lines of one built over the sea rocked at anchor in the bay below. It had come in at the morning tide and Gillecomgan's rechtaire had gone down to assess his fee and see what trade was offered. The captain would be at table tonight and there would be talk, mostly lies, of far places.

Swallows veered overhead, chittering. Their nests were everywhere under the eaves of the stables and in the crevices of the rock. Soon they would be gone. The circles of their flight widened each morning until at last, pulled by the lowering sun, they would break to the south. I imagined myself changed, like in the tales, into a bird small and glossy-feathered, with quick wing beats. Two swallows dipped close and I saw their feet drawn up into the white down of their bellies. They flew up and I watched until they were black specks lost in the bloom of the sun.

I went back through the defenses, watched by my husband's men, and into the hall. A stranger with a traveler's slung bag sat upright, waiting, against the far wall. His face, high-colored from sea winds, seemed to glow in the darkness where he sat.

"Good morning," I said. "You are welcome here."

He stood quickly. His shoulders were broad and his wrists thick, a sturdy young man. One of the knarr's crew, I imagined.

"Good day to my lady," he answered. His accent, yes, was slow and spoke of the borders with Orkney.

I took a footed cup from the shelf and poured him some good ale. I carried it to him, the bowl cradled in my palms, and he wrapped his hand around the cup and nodded thanks. "I will be impolite and ask you plain, are you Gruach also called Daimhin, daughter of Boidh?"

I paused, shocked to hear my private name, my hands still curved from the vessel. *What an odd and urgent visitor!*

"It is usual for the traveler to tell his name to the house," I said, sternly, then smiled to ease him. "But, yes, I am Gruach, daughter of Lonceta and of Boidh. And you sound as if you would be from the northern reaches, Sutherland if not farther?"

"From Sutherland, where the sea brings boats gently to the sands at Golspie," he said. "You know my people. I am Artgus, son of Sythak." I took the young man by the hand and led him close to the open door. Yes, his level brow, and how his ears were set low. He had been a skinny boy when I left Talorc's house.

"Artgus, are you with the boat?"

"I tend the land and mill of my father," he said. "I am merely a passenger on the *Highwina*, out of Westfold."

He undid the leather bag, threw back the flap, and reached inside carefully as though some live creature or sharp edge waited for his hand. He brought out the ivory casket and handed it to me. I sat down on a bench and set it gently in my lap, as if it might shatter.

"My mother is dying." Not dead, she could not be. I would have felt that passing like a winter gale.

"She had a falling," Artgus said. "She cannot use her left hand any longer and her leg is weak on that side."

My face was stiff, numb. I ran my fingertips over the box, the carvings of figures, the loops of vines and animal tails, my fingers sensitive as though scalded. Alpia was dying. Alpia, strong as the rock, was dying. My eyes burned and I knew I was weeping although my face was a lifeless mask.

"Talorc is well," the young man said, filling up the air with his talk. "Ciniod has married a girl from Black Isle. Fode has become a fighter and has never taken a wife."

I saw all their faces, as they were when I left. Ciniod laughing. Talorc with his hands on his hips, talking to a farmer about the measures of grain, the wind whipping his fringe of sandy hair. Fode and Nechtan, wrestling, tumbling in the grass. And Alpia. I saw Alpia on her little stool, her white head bent close over some mending, humming to herself. But the song I heard was the initiation song. "She is lawgiver, peacemaker, the shield of the people. She governs light, renews the seasons, holds the elements in place. She is the Queen of Heaven. She is the Queen of Heaven."

Artgus said, "This boat will put ashore at Golspie before going on to Shetland. It will go out at the first favorable tide and wind, and there is passage for you with my protection."

I wanted—oh, I ached—to be with Alpia and to cradle her head as Alpia had mine when I was fretful and ill. I would make her tea to strengthen her and rub her cold arm with balm.

"I cannot," I said, ashamed.

I was like Gillecomgan's other possessions—valued or not, he would not let them go. He feared that I would flee, shaming him. Therefore, I was guarded. Like an animal, I had been caged away from my family, from my mother Lonceta whom I had never seen in her holy prison, from foster-mother Alpia who had birthed me a second time.

"A woman should be free to attend family, to come and to go as she is needed or desires," he said. "You are no slave, no landsman obligated to his fields." I smiled sadly, hearing Alpia's teachings transferred through Finnchaem and her mother and the whole community. "Come away with me."

My heart beat with shame and hope. I could leave quietly in the night, slipping down to the shore, away from the eyes of my keepers. I would be gone, like the swallows, but would never return. Never return. Never hold myself like insensate iron against Gillecomgan's hand. Alpia would recover with my nursing, and would be able to teach me all the things she had not, the lessons cut short.

I trembled with readiness. *But Nechtan, Nechtan.* My husband's revenge would fall on him. Gillecomgan angbaidh, remorseless kin-slayer, would kill Nechtan to ease his loss, and it would be no clean death. And others clung to me as well, others I was not even willing to admit I helped. The people of Moray, silent as wings, came seeking the White Lady. I employed my small gifts, because that was all I could offer.

I hung my head and accepted the young man's scorn. "I cannot go, but kiss Alpia for me, and tell her that she has all my love and devotion." Silently, *Tell her I was not as strong as she hoped*—but those were not words to send to the dying.

Artgus closed his bag and left without answering.

I sat for a long time with the ivory box in my lap. The bone discs and spindle whorl were already mine, hidden like the priceless treasure they were. What had she sent? Finally, I opened the lid. A crescent of beaten gold and a twig of yew rested together. Yew for the end of the year. Yew for the end of life. Gold she once wore for ceremonies that it would be my duty to continue.

My hand clasped Alpia's, still warm with life. Dark yew against juniper. The round of life. I touched the twig. It was light and dry. "…the Silent Rest, lady of the dark time." Death and life came out of it. The dark moon brooded in the belly of the pregnant sky. I felt a horrible pang swell deep in my stomach, between the blades of my pelvis, and it rose through my body until it pressed past my clenched teeth, a moaning cry. Then, lightness. Where had it come from, this sense of a new space within myself?

Someone was in the hall. Artgus returning? This time I would not say no, I would go over the sea and let everything fall to ruin behind me. Let Nechtan take care of himself. Let him seek a new master far from Gillecomgan's clutches.

There came a sudden pressure, like a noiseless wind.

I slumped to my knees, then went prostrate on the floor.

My daughter.

I pressed myself flat, nuzzled the trodden rushes. I was sharply aware of the scent and taste of fish, old bread, salt mud, urine, spilled wine. Human life.

My daughter.

Now the sound came softly from deep inside me, from the hollow after the pain. The voice seemed to shake the timbers of the hall. This was life, here, my fingers clutching the reeds and dead flowers, the broken, sad things of life. Above me pressed the ancient sky, the deep cold endlessness of the night. I heard myself wail, Who is to be the White Lady when Alpia is gone? Who is it to be?

You are.

I know so little; I have forgotten so much.

"You will remember," Alpia had said, but I did not, did not.

The Mother of All reassured me. *Little by little the words fall away, but devotion continues.* She appeared now, a woman of middle years, ripe and rich with life, her hair streaming gold and brown and red like the harvest. She smiled and offered her hands, raising me to my knees, to my feet. The hall was full of light. I was aware of sunlight at the doors and windows, of the dark forms of people standing outside, but inside the hall was still and full of light. It was peaceful and the golden color of the harvest moon.

Open your hands.

If I could have broken them from the ends of my arms, I would have, the desire was so great to give, to please. I held out my hands, palms cupped like the hip-curves of the moon.

A flame sprang up from each palm. It was steady and clear, like those that had not devoured the grain.

Alpia has crossed.

A shudder went through me. An ache sprouted and set roots at the center of my chest.

You are to be my presence among the people.

Do not be afraid.

21

MACBETH

SUTHERLAND, 1024

In the darkness, the camp of the Albanaig had been a field of lights like the stars, scattered thick or thin. This was only a part of the army gathered to support Thorfinn. Some boasted there would be 10,000 swords behind the Raven Banner—amazement makes two men into twenty, and twenty into a horde.

Now, as day broadened, the camp appeared as a flood between the rivers. Tents stood close together on the best ground, level and dry, and apart from the stony rises. Smoke rose from the fires and was quickly pulled apart by the wind, which popped the banners on their poles and lifted the spread wings of tents. Wind surged always between land and sea, like water from pool to pool. At the edge of the warriors' encampment spread another one, less orderly, seething with the movement of women carrying water for washing or bending over cooking fires, slaves tending horses, dogs wandering, nosing for scraps.

Men walked back and forth, talking, waiting. The movement of men was like the sea that would take them to Orkney.

The Romans had laid out their camps on straight lines, century and cohort setting their tents square along the temporary streets. Macbeth had read of such camps and seen their grids sunk deep in the flesh of Alba. Along with the twin belts of the stone walls they built between sea and sea, and a few bridges, these were the last remaining marks of Roman might. *The irregular outlines of our camp and the black pits of our fires will go more easily back into the ground. The places where we massed will be forgotten as swiftly as our deeds.*

Macbeth smiled to himself. An old man's musings. He did not think the other young men sitting all around, waiting out the time by whetting their edges and oiling their leather gear, considered such things. To his left, Caerel sat on a flat rock, staring into the distance. He was a son of Findlaích's man of the same name who had been known for his six-fingered hands. This son looked much like the father, as Macbeth recalled him, except for the hands. He had thick brown hair and skin as rosy as a woman's. The past winter had made them both seventeen, and men. Caerel polished the bright bindings of his scabbard and the cross-armed hilt of his sword. Even in the early morning, when men wandered naked, their hair uncombed, he wore his braught neatly draped over his mail shirt, with heavy silver at his shoulder and ears. Each day he dressed for the greatest event of his life.

"The fight..."

Macbeth waited.

"Do you think we will take it to the islands?"

"Brusi holds the advantage while he stays home. Only a fool would strike out in search of sword's point, when he can fortify his strong places and wait for the battle to swim over the sea against him."

Caerel nodded slowly. "But maybe he will choose to damage Thorfinn, invade Caithness first and take his wealth."

"Brusi is a milder man than his brother Einar was, or Thorfinn is even at his young age. Unlike Thorfinn, he does not covet his brother's portion," Macbeth said, laughing. "And the bogs of Caithness are in no measure worth the green pastures of Orkney."

Caerel leaned down to straighten a twisted binding at his ankle. He seemed nervous as a girl at marriage. Macbeth did not tell him that the coming battle would be his first great fight as well, past skirmishes being of little more significance than the conflicts of boys on the practice fields.

Macbeth was eager for the test. He would have come even if Malcolm had not named him among the leaders of the host. Black-haired Thorfinn, not yet a man, was nevertheless a leader beyond his years. The Raven Banner that had gone down at Clontarf, pinned to Sigurd's body by the spear that took his life, had been raised in a new form, strengthened by Malcolm's commitment of more men, more wealth. Sigurd's youngest son was now claiming the inheritance of the northern islands as well as Caithness. Macbeth wondered if Malcolm's aid was linked to a lessening of pressure on Sutherland and Ross.

Through the noise of men and beasts came a clear stroke of a harp and then a rolling deep voice singing of glorious battle, "red gold won by blood." By his accent, the singer came from the islands that stretched toward the ancient Dál Riatan homeland. The Alban army had been drawn from throughout the land—many were half Norse, from the Sudrys and the lands beyond the River Nith, men who knew boats. Caerel was more afraid of the sea, Macbeth realized, than of Brusi's boatmen who lay in wait at each passage into his island territories. And not without reason—the passages to Orkney were treacherous, the waters of the Orcadian strait often raging across its skerries and crashing into rocky headlands.

"We could be here many days," he said. "Thorfinn is waiting word from men at Birsay."

The young man smiled at being reassured, then went red with shame to realize that his weakness had been spotted.

"We could go hunting, far enough up river that the game has not all fled or gone to ground," Macbeth continued, drawing away from the subject of boats and sea-voyages. "Is your taste for beast flesh or bird flesh?"

Caerel started to get up, then sat back, his mind shifting. Then he stood again and began to slip off the garments he had chosen for glory or death. Brooch, cloak, armbands, rings. He stripped off his mail shirt and revealed the striking pattern-woven tunic, embroidered by mother or sister with a twisting pattern of red spirals along the hem. He shook out his camp gear, brier-torn and faded, and made himself ready for the hunt. Macbeth threw a braught over his usual plain clothing,

They had not yet located their dogs, equally useful for hunting and war, when the messenger arrived.

The man on the shaggy horse came through the meadows where the long-horned cattle grazed that fed the host. He wore a raven's wing on the side of his nasaled helmet. That badge drew the warriors, made them leave behind songs and banter and gambling.

"Thorfinn Sigurdsson sends me," he said loudly. Cheers. Men made noise with weapons clashing. War was coming. His island horse, so small it was really a pony, shuddered at flies and pulled at the reins, reaching for grass. As the noise ebbed, the messenger called, "Where are your principal men?"

Macbeth stepped forward, joined by the other leaders pushing their way through the clamor.

The messenger took off his helmet and stroked the stiff black feathers of the wing.

"There is no war. Brusi has gone out of the land, fled like a storm-frightened cur to the shelter of Norway. He has taken his son with him. Thorfinn and his closest men are in Birsay now, and he sits unchallenged in the seat of Orkney."

The men shouted, spilling out their anger and need. Macbeth could have added his voice but kept his own frustration in check. A long-faced boatman from Mull was sobbing, from joy or from sorrow, it did not matter. Older men who had come to hear the messenger drifted away, smiling and chaffing each other that there would be no war-geld to warm them in the winter to come. Macbeth and the other leaders would need to master the men's emotions and send them homeward without bloodshed in the camp or casual looting along the way.

They came down from Thing-vollr to cross the Varrar and follow its southern bank as the river widened toward union with the Ness. The army was still a flood, Macbeth thought, but one that was receding, each stream taking back its own water. Men were headed home to consider the grain harvest, forecast the weight of cattle as the year tipped toward winter.

They rode easily in the sun, seven men to rejoin the king. Macbeth had replaced his war-gear with clothing more fit for the war court now halted at Nairn, his best braught fastened with the king's gift-brooch, although he felt the bite of sorrow and anger and pride each time he fastened it, as though it pricked into his soul.

The air was gentle, sweet. Finian had picked a round-eyed flower and plaited its long stem in his hair. "You should have been a fool making bad rhymes," grumbled Rechtabra.

"It was debated among my kinsmen, if I should do that," he answered, "but then, I had beaten them every one in wrestling, and they were ashamed if that were to be made known."

The path followed a stream splashing down to the river. In the pools, char and trout held their places, lined up into the current, while minnows darted and flashed at every shadow.

They rounded a knot of land, hearing the throaty sound of the river ahead but not yet seeing it. The path dipped and turned.

A shout. Finian backed his horse, then urged it forward as more shouts came. Macbeth heard the slither of steel before he saw a blade rise into the sun. He readied his spear, unable yet to see as he rode fourth in line, but then it appeared, a boat drawn up among thick willow on the near bank. Norsemen in their strong mail-shirts were running along the shore toward their escape but Finian, the flower bobbing brightly in his hair, maneuvered his horse between them and the boat.

"Whose men are you?" cried Rechtabra, riding to join him.

The Norsemen, discovered, set their shields before them and formed themselves without discussion into a fighting squad. They made a hard try for their boat, but the mounted Albanaig threw up a spray of mud and water, thrusting their spears down behind the round shields, shouldering the men into a tighter knot. One of the Norse pulled a knife from his belt; his hand snapped and the blade buried itself in the horse's neck just in front of Finian's thigh. He leapt free of his shuddering horse and came up under the knife-man's shield, striking where thigh meets body, and blood spurted high and hot.

"Whose men are you?" Macbeth repeated, as he and the others swung down from their horses and threw off their mantles.

"We are of Westfold," said the tallest, who employed a two-handed axe instead of a sword.

"Brusi's hirelings," Caerel said dismissively.

"No man's hirelings. We fight for the rightful ruler of Orkney."

"If you are Brusi's men, then you should be in Norway, where he has fled, and not skulking on our shores," said Macbeth.

So, they came together. No songs, no drums, no poet's chant. It was a hot, close fight on unchosen ground, a marshy tangle between stream and river. The Norsemen's swords were strong and light and their shields had huge central bosses of bright metal that glittered in the sun. Again and again, they tried to break through to their boat and the swan's path home. One picked up a spear and thrust it hard at Rechtabra, who caught it on his shield, but the point instead of glancing off went deep into the leather and wood and twisted the shield in his grip. He slashed desperately at the spearhead, but iron sheathed it well up the shaft. Alban iron, well forged. Macbeth, grappling with a man on the other side of the stream, watched as the Norseman used his spear-shaft to force down the shield, Rechtabra's broken fingers still entangled in the hand-hold. He swung his sword, and harsh Rechtabra bled.

Macbeth flung his opponent aside and splashed through the stream.

The sword came a second time, and Rechtabra died. His killer broke for the shore but was met by Fergna. Macbeth found himself blocked by the man who first had spoken for the crew. The tall man still carried only his great axe, red sap on its edge. He remembered vividly an axe-man boasting in Malcolm's royal hall at Scoine: "A man who fights with an axe cannot also hold a shield, but then the brave man needs no shield." He looked at the axe and felt the nakedness of his head. His helmet, too hot for riding slowly in the sun, was still tied to the saddle of his wandering horse. His finely made léine was no protection.

"Malcolm does not much estimate Brusi, to send boys to help a boy," the Norseman said, hefting his axe. His eyes glittered under the shadow of his helmet.

"Even a babe is strong enough against a pup who tucks his tail and goes crying to a greater dog's shadow."

His opponent grinned. "Well said, little man."

Macbeth flushed, felt his veins pound with the blood beating up.

The axe swung in a vicious, singing circle. The man was quicker than his bulk promised.

Macbeth deflected with his shield and countered, felt the shudder through his arm where the sword met the Norseman's heavy mail shirt and perhaps found flesh. He pulled away, feinting sideways as the axe swung again.

He wondered briefly about his companions but then the axe whistled past his shoulder and its wind fluttered his hair.

On the back stroke, he avoided the edge but, clubbed by the man's doubled fists on the haft, staggered.

Quickness was defense. Quickness, before the man's sheer size wore him down. He lunged as though to stab awkwardly and then fell back, slicing the inside of the man's elbow. Blood spurted and the hand hung useless from severed tendons.

The man only grunted, hefted his weapon with his good hand, holding it the way a lesser man might prepare to throw a light axe. Macbeth came in again, but his blow hit metal and not flesh. He saw, close in, the heavy muscle of the man's good arm. He saw the runes worked into the axe blade and haft.

The man kicked his knee, sending him down hard.

Macbeth waited for the swing, leaned sideways until his shoulder was pressed deeply into the wet ground, then sprang up and thrust into the unprotected hollow of the armpit.

The axe, released, wobbled through the air and buried in the muck.

His opponent backed away and stood. Blood poured, the artery severed, and he tried to hold his arm close against the flood. Blood dripped still from the opposite elbow. He looked naked without the axe.

"My name is Ottar, the son of Hrafr Five-Cows," he said, his voice beginning strong and then ebbing. "So that my name will be remembered and my end will be told, and cut into stone beside a path."

"I will tell your story, Ottar Hrafrson. Know that I am Macbeth mac Findlaích, son of Moray and fosterling of Malcolm the high king."

The Norseman's eyes seemed to shut, as though he might fall and sleep his final sleep there in the bloodied mire. But Macbeth saw his weight shift, and when Ottar pushed forward, hoping to overwhelm him with a last attack, he was prepared for the gleam of steel that appeared in that bloodied hand.

He set himself to take the man's full weight, letting that rush carry Ottar onto Macbeth's waiting sword that plowed under the lower edge of his mail shirt and deep into his bowels, releasing a sharp stink. The sword jerked from his grip as Ottar fell; Macbeth stumbled and sprawled on his back. He twisted away from a possible renewed attack, but this Norseman was beyond any more fighting.

He rested for a moment on hands and knees, sucking air back into his body. He saw metal among the reeds, the knife that his opponent had palmed. It was broad and curved, quite small, something exotic. Macbeth wiped mud from the ornamented grip. Ottar Hrafrson was dead, the soul that kept the body taut having gone away.

A shout, and he looked toward the river to see the battle, surprisingly, still going on. It seemed he had fought the axeman for a long slow time. Macbeth stood, drawing his breath back, and he watched the strokes that went wide, the man who ran away and the man who pursued. He pushed the Norseman's body over and pulled his sword from the belly. He also found the flat leather sheath that had concealed the curved knife in Ottar's belt, and took that as his own.

Macbeth wiped Ottar's guts from the blade and then ran to the fight.

THE LAICH OF MORAY

Malcolm was not at Nairn. Angry at some failure of hospitality, he had gone on to Forres, leaving the rechtaire to repeat apologies for an error he did not know. Macbeth and his companions—just five now, with Rechtabra and Aed prayed over and a donation made to the monastery to ensure their proper burial—had reached the small fortress only to find the king departed. They ate heartily on the feast that had been prepared, cod and skate, small fish seethed in a broth, cockles, pickled samphire, roasted vegetables. (It was a fast day, yet again.) They lounged by the fire with full stomachs, weary with the ride and the battle that Finian was already working into a song.

"Tell us about the axeman," he urged.

Macbeth shook his head. He felt the black bruise on his side where a spear shaft had been driven. Air bit at the lips of a blade-wound on his leg. But the hot moments of the fight were fading. He remembered the look on Rechtabra's face, set and hard, as he watched his death come for him. That he remembered well.

"If you will not kill the Westfold man for our song, then we will have to," said Caerel.

The others laughed, and Caerel too, easy in his manhood. He had killed one of the Norsemen and had his helmet, sword, and mail, along with a deep spear wound on his thigh, to prove it. The physician had probed the puncture and made a long face; fearing gangrene, he had cauterized it with a great stink of burning flesh.

Macbeth looked out at the bright evening; a golden sky reflected in the waters of the widening firth full with the tide. The light made him restless.

"I am riding on to Forres."

"The day is past, Mac Findlaích. There is time enough to join the king, tomorrow, or the next day when there seems a plenty of hospitality between these walls," said Caerel.

"Perhaps it is our company…"

"No, surely it is a woman of the king's retinue who draws him from his rest."

Finian said nothing, but his glance said that he sensed Macbeth's tumbling emotions. Forres, once his father's hall, now occupied by Cerr backed by his butcher brother.

The chaffing continued, but Macbeth only smiled and continued to the door. There was urgency upon him, a need to move. His companions fell silent, and he saw how they looked at him, what they didn't say. The dangers of traveling alone. A fey spirit must impel him. Caerel and Finian stood with many groans and said they would ride with him, but Macbeth waved them away.

A servant caught him a fresh horse from those loose on the grazing and saddled and bridled it. Spear, sword, shield, a leather bag that held a Gospel, comb, oils, and sparking flint—Macbeth felt himself weighed down with things, including a mail shirt, as he'd not be caught so careless again. The great gate let him out into the evening. There would be light all through the night, between the summer's lingering sun and the full moon.

He rode an old path between the fields and the sea. This was good land, all through the Laich, heavy or light with the presence of sand, but fertile, and amended should that fail with marl carried from an endless pit nearby. The air was warm and sun shone, unlike the mist, fog, and clouds of the west. It was a good place to live, where a ruler might have a light hand on his people and be wealthy enough. White water fell from the sides of the mountains down to the flat, winding through grasslands and grainlands to the sea. The sea's daily movements ran wide here, the water going far out and leaving the shallows drying.

He passed two circular hills that rose high as the trees, burial chambers for the ancient dead. Such mounds were everywhere on the land, and on some of them, offerings of flowers and grain. Old slabs cut with the voiceless symbols of the Picts and overcut with the sign of the Cross. The boat-burials of the Danes and raw new graves in the churchyards that marked the harsh rule of the brothers, Cerr and Gillecomgan. Kin-killers.

The land began to rise above the beach, a plain dropping off sharply. Macbeth angled down to the shore track, galloping his horse on the packed sand. Two men driving an ox hailed him near the stronghold where the Alder-Water fell into the sea, and the accent of his boyhood made him want to stop there. He reined in, hesitated. A seal barked. He loosed the reins and urged his horse forward.

He noted the differing soils as he rode, strong red soil, the black soil that was easier to plow but less fertile, the sandy tracts and marshy ones. All this had been his father's domain, his father's people, yet now that he'd reached his majority, still the Ard Ri Alban enforced his attendance at court while his father's killers ruled here in Moray and led the people of Loairn.

His horse was tired and he let it amble as he reached Tor Rannoch and rode slowly among its high ferns. Along the shore, banks of white sand shimmered that had been raised up by the invading sea in the year he went to fosterage. He stopped at a spring and drank. The mineral tang reminded him of another pool where his father had cupped water in two hands for him to sip. It had a strong taste. The water was bordered by black, hard ground. "Iron," his father had said. "Iron in the stone here, such as makes strong swords and strong men. Drink up." Macbeth remembered. Some things seemed familiar here, yet most remained strange. The small details, the shape of a stone outcrop, how a stream cut parallel to the shore, somehow remained sharp while the whole remained faint, unclear. He had spent little time in Moray since riding away with Conamail to become Malcolm's son.

It was the memory of ravaged Conamail, as much as the more distant memories of his father, that spurred a desire inside that he could not allow to break free. The deep ache in his bruised side might have been from the battle or from looking across the lands that should wear his father's name still. The dog-stoat wore the mormaer's chain entangled with mere ornament, jingling, ruling where his brother would not, or could not. Macbeth felt the weight of leadership without golden circlet or chain, knew what stewardship meant. And he knew he would avenge both his friend and his father. There would come a time.

He smelled blood and smoke.

He faced the Norseman again, but the great man shrank down to become narrow-faced Gillecomgan, and he stood without any weapon because he needed none. He had stolen the king's face and used it for a shield, knowing Macbeth could not strike the king his father, even to avenge his father. Words bound him. Vows. The soft words of the Bible: Turn the other cheek. Vengeance is mine saith the Lord. Seventy times seven.

Macbeth pushed aside the visions, mists brought on by weariness. What had urged him to leave behind good food and soft beds? His horse was wandering with the reins slack. The sky was a soft wash of pink and gold. The moon would change the land to white, before the sun showed itself again across the Northern Sea. He took up the reins.

The first faint stars showed as he crossed the waste lands toward Forres, marked by the blur of smoke above twin hills, a wooded one to the south and what had been his father's fortress on its bald height above the river. The hard heath seemed boundless, a sea, and on it his horse a rocking boat. Seabirds whirled overhead and gorse and heather and reclining berry-plants crested and fell in endless waves. Birds erupted from the tangles, crying over hidden nests. Cut banks showed where turf had been taken, three steps leading down into each cutting to avoid the curse of the saint who had fallen into a peat-cutting and could not climb out.

He saw a person walking, a thin motion on the wide earth. Slowly, as they approached one another, the figure grew and became a slender young woman, walking freely with her blond hair loose on the wind. She carried a large flat basket such as women used for gathering.

"I greet you, son," the woman said.

She was older than he had thought at first, her long hair streaked with gray. Perhaps she was moon-touched, wandering.

"Your greeting is welcome," he said. "Do you live close by here, mother?"

She turned around on her heel, her arms wide.

"Son of this soil, you well know my place."

"How do you know my birth?"

"Macbeth, the Son of Life, you count yourself the son of Findlaích, who is son of the Red One. I remind you that you are the son of Doada, who was daughter of Coblaith, daughter of Ete the Sad."

And he saw her change, her first willowy appearance cramped down by age, and now she was bent and her hair thin, white, straggling. Her eyes remained a sea-washed blue. He remembered tales of the Sidhe and Duncan's fears. The walking-women, the washing-women, the keeners at unseen deaths. Ancient, lost souls, the monk Oswald called them, bred by fallen angels on the daughters of men in the time before the Flood.

Macbeth crossed himself. "May the protection of Jesus the Christ be over me," he said.

"And that of Mary his holy Mother," the woman answered, smiling, growing younger. The basket was a cradle, and in it a newborn baby, and the both of them were surrounded with light like sun in the haze on the sea. All around their light was soft darkness, and a crescent moon gleamed under her feet and stars crowned her head.

He knelt.

She held the broken body of the Savior in her arms.

Aged by grief, she laid him in the ground.

Her Son rose and lived, and stood beside her and she was young again and again and again.

And then there was only her, a simple woman in a farmwife's garb, with the salt wind in her unbound hair. The sun rode up in a new sky. Macbeth felt fear tighten around him as it had not in the battle, not even when the Westfold-man's axe swung whispering by his neck.

"Son of this place," she said. "You will be rewarded for valor with the land where you were born, a part at first, then the whole. Finally, all Alba will be your portion."

He shuddered, as though at crossing his own grave.

"Remember the people who were already in this land when your forefathers came here. When you are king, twice king, remember our meeting. Remember the White Lady."

⁂

FORRES, MORAY, 1024

The walls at Forres were old and thick with moss, and the hall protected by them was old and dark. Dark with smoke, dark with blood.

There is nothing evil about these timbers and stones, Macbeth told himself. It is the knowing. The second King Donald had died here, poisoned, and the annals said that in 900 the kingship passed to his cousin. Then Dubh was killed here by Culen as the struggle for primacy went back and forth between the lines of Alpin, between Atholl and Moray, between north and south, between the twin lineages of Dál Riata and the Picts. The issue had not been not resolved, not these generations later, except in the compromise of alternating the kingship. A compromise now abandoned in Duncan, whose father descended from neither line.

He paused in the doorway, his eyes adjusting to the pools of light and deep shadow, his ears adjusting to the shouting and singing after silence. The hall was filled with Malcolm's retinue and a portion of the returning army. At the center of the throng, Gillecomgain posed in splendor, standing with one hand resting on the back of a high seat. He seemed more the king than the white-haired Ard Ri Alban dozing in the chair. But there was an anxiousness about him. His eyes met Macbeth's and lingered a second longer than was comfortable.

"Where have you wandered? It's come about a full day since you left us!" Caerel leaped from a bench along the near wall, slapped Macbeth on the back, put an arm around his shoulders and walked him toward the king. His voice was thick with drink.

Macbeth was stunned. How had they arrived here before him, when he had left them lounging by the fire?

"We thought you would be here to give us a welcome, but no one had seen you. We began to fear that you had wandered into another band of hirelings," said Finian, who with the others gathered around, asking, insisting.

A day? I have been lost a day, enchanted by that woman?

He remembered the sun rising.

One of the Sidhe, surely, turning the day around, capturing me with her words.

"I found old places that I remembered," he said, haltingly, unable to tell the truth, unwilling to lie. "I turned from the path and rode among the ferns at Tor Rannoch."

"I hope they made a soft place on the ground, then, or you spent a night on cold earth for the sake of sentiment," said Caerel.

"And not a woman?"

He motioned abruptly, no.

"Perhaps it was very large woman, then, the whole land herself," said Finian. Macbeth looked hard at him, but the man babbled on heedlessly. "Were you so besotted that you would not come among us even for the glory of your battle-tale?"

The king lifted his head, roused by the noise.

"I am happy to see you again, son."

"And you, Father," he answered. "You look well."

"You flatter age, always a politic thing to do." The king lifted a hand for wine. Then his brows came down and his eyes gleamed in their shadow. "But they tell me you have had a blooding, a real blooding."

"I honor the death of Ottar, son of Hrafr Five-Cows, a son of West-fold and a mighty axe-man."

"We found a battle even if the Orkneymen would not provide one," cried Caerel. "Let our song be sung."

"These were wild men,
Without loyalty, seeking wealth,
Ten men in a boat of twenty oars,
One of them, Ottar, a man worth three,
A giant to cut down men of the blood
With a giant's axe.

Finian found them skulking, loot

And murder in Moray planning.
The happy son of Cruachan's shadow rode
Fearless among them, barred them
From water and wind
Ever their allies.

Young Macbeth stood bare-headed,
Young tree against Norse steel
And the desperate rush.
He bled the giant like a slaughter-beef.
Red son of Findlaích, king's fosterling
Showed his breeding then.

Four fled before us, but six
Lochlannaig died on Varrar bank,
Their souls Christ-less to wander.
Soft-eyed Aed and Rechtabra,
Their bodies we buried
But their souls are in the Blessed Lands."

The men shouted and cried out at the end of the song, Caerel's clear voice lingering on the last word.

"Your son fought like a warrior of many battles, not only bravely but wisely," said Finian. "Some mistake deliberateness for indecisiveness. And some dare call him the Monk for his learning."

Macbeth gave him another look, wishing he wouldn't blather so from the ale swimming in his belly.

"I say, now, that such a name is not fitting, and call him Ruiadri, the Red One, the ruddy warrior whose skin is stained with the blood of his enemies."

The men shouted again, for approval, but Gillecomgan threw his head back and scowled. Ruiadri was the name of Macbeth's much-honored grandfather—and his own. Macbeth met Gillecomgan's stare and would not look away.

"You have shown yourself sure-handed," Malcolm said, "but more, you are fortunate, and that is a gift not to be earned or taken or found. Your blood-father was once the same."

Once the same. Macbeth took that into his heart like an icy arrow.

The king sat for a moment in thought.

"I would have you with me from hall to hall, the year around, but a son grown must have a place apart from his father, or foster father." Malcolm stood and raised his hand for silence. "A time will come when the derbfine consider you for leadership as your worth is demonstrated, but for your own house as a man and your holding, you shall rule over Findlaích's lands in Ross and Cromarty. These have been held during your minority by your cousins, and now they have agreed to place under your care both hall and loch, wood and stream, field and fallow, fish and cattle, and the people in them."

Macbeth looked only at the king but felt Gillecomgan's glare and knew that if they locked eyes again, there would be no retreating, and Forres would have new blood on its stones.

"Is this not a worthy seat for you?"

Macbeth shook himself out of the grip of anger and sharp memory.

"I am made silent," he said, picking his way among words that threatened to roll underneath him like round rocks in a stream bed, "by a strong recollection of that place."

"Findlaích entertained me with a hunt there," Malcolm said, not seeing how, behind him, Gillecomgan's hand clenched the carvings of the high seat where it had formerly rested with ease. "There is need for a strong arm to defend the boundaries with Sutherland."

"My father was such a man. Strong. And faithful," Macbeth said, stopping himself from saying more.

The king sat down and called for wine, his generosity having driven away the anger that would have flared at the lack of attention to his empty cup.

Macbeth slipped among the crowd and then away.

He crossed the pavement to the chapel. Inside, it was dim as early morning. The shadows were made thicker by the light of a single candle on the altar.

Macbeth went on his knees before the place where God was, then lay flat on the stones. A pain much worse than the pain of wounds twisted him. Why had the king set him a place between dangers, to the north Thorfinn vacillating between ally and enemy, and envious Gillecomgan and his brother in the heart of Moray? Gillecomgan and Cerr ruled by sheer strength and the weight of fear, the men of the blood knowing they must fall in line or find themselves as Findlaích's followers, dead or worse than dead. Was the king hoping, like a farmer encroaching his furrows on a neighbor's fields, to reduce some of the northern power that Gillecomgan had been so readily given and so quickly enlarged? Power against power?

The sweat of anguish came to his brow. *Like Christ's at Gethsemane, praying for release.* Quickly he made amends for so blasphemous a thought. *Lord Jesus and all apostles,* he prayed, *and the saints made in this land, deliver my soul from death.*

He saw the woman, shifting from girl to woman to crone and back to girl. *I have knelt before a demon,* he confessed. *I have been deluded, and have knelt before a demon.*

Oh Lord, deliver me from her prophecies.

22

LAPWING

Soon men will move down the valley. Lapwing saw them in a dream in which a spear rent his body, and the wound bled with the war trumpets of stags in rut. Fighting men come now and before and again. Old armies march bone-on-bone beside the Moray-men, and their unheard war-songs chill the living.

I watch beside this unlit fire.

There is strength in the branches of royal duir and warlike ash. In rock. In nodding reed. There is strength in the great river and the green-headed ducks riding on it and the sedge flies rising from water into air. It prickles the skin like the lash of godfire across the sky. Lapwing feels the thrumming in the land. Bees in the hive. Breath in the body.

Old Fotla's griefs gather, dark water in the footprints of soldiers. I lean on my stick, a lamed man for the gods, and they reward me for my pain. I see through the world as through an outworn garment held up to the light.

War seeks tinder and Alba is dry.

Men come, slow dark streams of men under green trees. Loyalty shifts like a river across the land, finding new ways to the sea.

In Scoine, Malcolm rages as Thorfinn shows him his back and bows to Olaf of Norway. Malcolm cries out, I have two grandsons only, and no longer a third.

Duncan, ensconced in Partick's palace, grows arrogant. Lapwing must curb him like an unruly colt lest he leap too soon and fall broken.

Gillecomgan gathers Moray beneath him. He tells his supporters that the North Kingdom has been reduced, that he must assert its claim if his brother will not. He nourishes their envy on spilled blood. He is a weasel to find it, supple and sharp-toothed. He has thrived with Malcolm's favor but Findláich's heart-blood is on him, Macbeth shadows him, and now his brother's outrage is a curse against him. Still, he persuades the men of Moray to rebellion.

The old boar of Scoine, suspicious of all, will be stung by another spear he did not suspect.

The army comes loudly from the north. It threads the pass of Drumochter, follows the spilling stream to the Tay. It tramps on hay cut and laid down on the slopes above the stream. The army comes softly through the giant trees, follows the wide sweep of the river between the arms of the mountains. It scents the holy water of Bran spilling bright. Gillecomgan's army comes to Dunkeld.

I lean on my staff. The vision unfolds to life.

The men lift their swords and scream war-cries. They run across fields and the gleaners hunker down, and they pass over them. The workers rise and throw off their wrappings, snakes shedding to bright steel and hard leather. Atholl's warriors fall on Gillecomgan's men from behind.

Inside the monastery, monks arm themselves to defend their books. Crinán directs them and his steward leads them to battle with sword and shield.

All this I have foreseen. I am a green alder branch stripped for the gods to whistle through.

Gillecomgan's men do not break and run. They raise torches to the roofs of Dunkeld. Fire and famine, two great warriors.

Lapwing is the warrior now. He lights his fire laid of rowan-twigs, tree of spring's quickening flame, luisiu, beloved of birds.

Smoke rises, below and above.

Fire, fall away from the buildings of Crinán my friend.

The invaders' flames hesitate, do not catch in the wood. My counter-fire rises high and clear. I control fire by fire.

I raise my staff and sing to the great gods. I send the soul of my fire against theirs.

A wind rises from my hill, a wolf-wind, a wet wind, to suck fire from the buildings. Lapwing howls with it.

Let Dunkeld's books remain whole. Let sullen lead keep its hold on window-glass. No fire to destroy, no flame to scar. The defenders see the flames drop by my working and they cheer, push the invaders back.

But the wind falls.

I lay more dry branches on my fire, and green ones, four branches for increase, two for the strength of combat. I summon the wind, return and aid me.

The air is still.

Flames mount again in Dunkeld. Gillecomgan's men run from the burning church with its treasures in their arms. The sun loves gold, the sparking stones.

The bishop holds up his crooked stick. One man pulls the crozier, spinning him around, and another kicks him and he sprawls. Flames are set to his robes. The bishop throws himself into the washing-pool.

Lapwing's fire is dead. He puts his hand to the embers and they are cold, cold.

I smell that Fox of the Christians.

"Colm," I cry, "these your sheep I have worked to protect."

The saint is a cross of fire below the sun.

Columba in his anger wishes his errant flock singed like a ewe's head on the forge for soup. He thinks to return them to the fold from which Crinán is leading them.

I lay down my staff. These lesser gods of the Christ are willful and vindictive, and today the saint prevails.

Let the monastery burn.

I sit by the cold sticks and watch a dream unfold that I did not dream. Flame lights the colored glass of Crinán's church.

23

GRUACH

I held the young moon in my hand.

It was cool and silent, its inner edge glittering sharp.

I stooped at the edge of a field of barley, grain ripened pale like the Lady's mantle that trailed behind as she crossed the night sky; others said it was the abundant milk of a white cow or the flowers that sprang up where beauty placed her feet.

I swung the sickle, and grain sighed to the ground.

I gathered the first cutting and held it close. Ahead of me the field stretched ripe, its flesh streaked with tares. The grain parted around an ancient gray stone, flowed around a patch of moss. A white river. A path of stars. Nourishment of the universe.

I turned to face the waiting harvesters.

"The grain falls to the knife," I chanted. "The season of harvest begins. Each thing in its season, the plowing and manuring, the sowing, the time when flocks go up to the mountains, the making of hay and cutting of peat, the time when berries are ripe. The season of harvest begins. The barley sings in the wind, sings for the knife. Blessings on the harvest, blessings of clear sky and hot sun and nights without blighting damp. Blessings on the strength of arms and backs."

I laid down the first harvest, like a body stretched on its stone. I tucked up my long garment while the women waited beside the men to begin work. I began to cut the grain, not a ritual pass but steady labor. The sickle became dull with stem-dust and the sap of green weeds. Stubble scratched my ankles and insects flew up, struck my face and body, fell.

I worked the length of the quarter-davach plot, from the fallow on one side to the raised ground that marked this sacred field from its neighbor, and back.

"Look," someone said.

Beyond the farthest loop of the stream, along the track that wound between soft hills, came a man riding alone.

I felt a brief, wild surge, like a bird released in my chest. Perhaps he was a messenger carrying word that Gillecomgan, who had marched away to ravage Atholl, has been killed. But I knew, as the rider disappeared behind a rise, that my husband lived. I had received no fire-marker. The man, whoever he was, had a long way to go through the hills to the ford, then must return this side of the river.

I resumed the blessing.

"The grain falls in white age, in the ripeness of its time," I said, calling back the attention of the people. "It falls into the earth and springs again."

I blended words, the chant of the Lady with the prayer of the Church, and twined around them the story of Lugh the Long-Handed that descendants of Éireann loved. I glanced at the worn images of a sea-beast and a mirror cut into the stone in the midst of the grain-field. *Forgive me this.*

I nodded to the youth who stood at the edge of the grove, and he came walking slowly with the eyes of the people on him. Cornan son of Lorcan, thirteen now and growing strong. I had begged him from utter slavery, he and Ruadan, to be my servants and care for my house goods, knowing that the very request might worsen their condition. But Gillecomgan, while he had laughed and thrust his hips in mockery, had granted me the favor.

Cornan's blond hair had been reddened and he was wrapped in a trailing mantle the color of ripe oats. I praised him, and he stood tall like the grain. Then I laid the reaping sickle gently beside his throat and he fell into my arms.

The people groaned.

He was naked and beautiful. I wept for him as I laid him down on a body's length of tilled soil and straightened his limbs. The sun glowed in the nest around his manhood. Then I took the sun away from him, reversing his mantle to its black lining and covering his body with it, concealing him from head to toe.

He lay still, dead as the dead.

And then I invoked his return and he stirred, breathed deeply, curled, knelt, and stood, throwing back the black covering as he lifted his arms and swayed like young grain seeking the sun. The people cheered.

"So we will all of us fall into the earth, and rise again to light."

His body was so lovely, muscles showing clean under clear skin. The harvesters looked at him as though he were indeed a young god.

Cornan ran off into the crowd of farmers and farm women, most of them young, some hardly old but already broken by heavy work and gnarled with rheumatism. They reached to touch his chest, back, shoulders as he passed. For the grain's promise to pass into them. For its flame to light in their bellies the winter long and sustain them.

The harvest was time for the young, as the sowing was for the old. Everything balanced. The young men and women worked beside each other in the sun-bright fields, joking and teasing. They thought as they harvested the grain, *so will I die*, but they never believed it. In the evening, they would sit together, tenderly looking over each other's hands to pull out thorns.

Then the celebration meal after the first day's harvest, the ale and the singing, the lingering light of the sun and the paler moon on the mist that rose from the land. I caught myself envying the girls who would lie back that evening and accept the young men with delight. Accept them and think them the gods of the harvest.

Remember what you are about, I chastised myself, and began again the task of binding the barley into proper sheaves. This grain will bless the next year's sowing, as this season's harvest had been blessed at seedtime with a sprinkling of First Seed. Barley and oats to be cut and sown again, the round of the seasons. I gathered the stalks, twisted another around them, dropped the bundle, moved to the next. The harvesters waited, whispering, but I heard one voice louder than the rest say, "Now that one truly is red-bearded as Lugh himself."

I turned, and saw Nechtan approaching. I finished binding the grain and dusted off my hands. "Welcome," I said, formally as though it were part of the rite, and he seemed to have arrived for that purpose.

Nechtan swung heavily to the ground. Sweat matted his brown hair to black and runnelled through an unkempt beard which he used to keep close-trimmed. He had always been a big man, but had gone soft since I had seen him last—two years, was it, or three? Three harvests taken in? And neither one of us any more free in our movements than the farmers who tended the land. Yet here he was. There was a petulant curve to his lips, now, and for a moment I felt revulsion, followed as quickly by guilt and then the flooding return of love.

"I thank the Lady for her greeting," he said, and I was very much aware, then, of my white gown girdled up for the harvest and the gold crescent at my throat, and my hair loose to my waist and uncovered. I looked down at my feet, bare and dirty in the stubble. I wore the image of mother and Mother, the image of Alpia, and I was ashamed before him. I was not worthy to follow Alpia, remembering her grace and power, thinking of her dying without my hand in hers.

I closed my eyes, breathed deeply.

Do what needs to be done. Finish what needs finishing.

"Begins a journey now as round as the ring of the moon," I chanted. "The soul of the seed is broken from its husk on the threshing-floor, and freed from the flesh in the winnowing basket. Clean and white, it nourishes us. We are earth, to yield grain and desire it. And we are grain, born of earth and returning to earth. We are earth eternal, earth that makes the grain to rise and takes it to its maturity. We are grain that lives and dies and lives again. The grain is cut and falls to earth, is received into the body of that which nourished it, and rises again."

I lifted a harvest cross I'd fashioned from perfect ears.

"Go now to the harvest that has ripened, and blessings go with you!"

I threw the charm among the women and they leaped. A plain girl caught it and cried out in joy for the promise of a child before the next harvest. She would surely find a young man this night.

The reapers moved into the field. One of the women began to sing and the others joined, as they clashed their curved blades together. I shook down my ceremonial gown and found my shoes. I took off the crescent and laid it glittering on the black cloth of the grain god's mantle before folding it.

Alpia would be appalled at the beliefs tangled so, or perhaps amused. She was ever practical, and these fields were far removed from the pure rite of the north.

"I remember when you refused all this," Nechtan said.

"The people need it."

"And you?"

I turned, arms raised as I pulled back my hair and loosely braided it.

"There are things I need that I have learned to live without—family, children, the simple respect between man and woman." The words came harsher than I had expected. I wrapped a scarf over my hair and with that, severed the cord to the immanent world.

"I have been the same," Nechtan said broadly, "but I will not live to another's wishes any longer."

"A man can say as much," I countered, and that harsh tone came without regrets. *I gave myself to bondage to save you*, I thought, *and for what? What have you done all these years, and why come here now?*

"Let's walk," he said, lifting the horse's reins from the thorn branch where he had draped them. We turned back along the track he had come.

"The court was in Strathclyde, Duncan hosting his grandfather and a great following at his royal hall, when word arrived of an attack on Dunkeld. Gillecomgan chose his time, unexpected at harvest, but that has always been his gift."

I said nothing.

"Duncan flew into a rage, spitting like fat meat on the fire, but Malcolm's anger was greater for being quiet. His council gathered around him and his chief men pledged to ride now and kill Gillecomgan for this outrage. But the king said no, they were to prepare fire for fire, destruction for destruction, pursuing Gillecomgan across the mountains and into the sea."

"The group was quickly assembled, the young Macbeth among them with the blood of Moray always hot in him, though it seemed he first served the king in this. He asked for me to join the expedition."

"Malcolm did not speak against that?"

"He watched me preparing my spears, those cold eyes of his never relenting. Perhaps he counted the gray threads among the brown in my hair and thought me well tamed, no longer a concern. Or he might have weighed the chances of my being killed. Or perhaps he thought, because of my friendship with Macbeth, that I too would be bridled and harnessed to pull Atholl's cart. There is never a lone consideration behind any choice Malcolm makes."

Nechtan paused where a little stream crossed the path. I smiled at his concern, but lifted my hems high at the muddy verge and waded across.

"We rode quickly, following the old roads and the way of rivers between the hills until we came down into the valley of the Tay. We smelled the burning from far off. The fields had been set fire, and the homes of the familia, and the abbey itself, its buildings all scorched and roof-fallen. It was desolation, the animals driven off and many of the people killed."

The sound of the horse's hooves behind us was slow and hollow as a mourner's footfalls. "In the ashes of the abbey we found Crinán weeping." Nechtan had begun to walk faster as the tale came, and I lengthened my stride to match. "He was changed, though he had already become strange in recent days, with his son so far away. No longer seeming to be a lord, and never an abbot—I cannot tell what he has become. He shifted in his talk, like a leaf blown on the water, sad and then laughing loudly. The monks were busy repairing their walls and tearing down burned timbers with billhooks and ropes, but he sat by a filthy pool of water, his only companion that limping poet, whose mad rants were blessedly silent for once. They say the bishop was burned to death. I do not know, but I watched the ashes drift from the buildings and float on the water, and it seemed I saw the direction I must take. Macbeth and the rest followed Gillecomgan's track as he rode toward the pass through the Mounth, but I left that night and took the coast way north."

Nechtan paused. When he began again, the chant was out of his voice, the tale ended. "I have watched Malcolm sweep all before him, like a wife plying her broom, gathering this lesser kingdom and that all into a pile. I have tried to ease his suspicions by my lack of ambition, avoiding his restless attention, but I will be sacrificed as well—there must be no danger to Duncan, chosen to claim a greater Alba, this anyone can see. Now there will be war with Gillecomgan and his brother because he has become the great threat, the man who could cut his way to high kingship as Malcolm himself did."

A threat he created himself, where Findlaích had presented little.

"You must know Gillecomgan's plans for this war, that he will draw the forces of the high king into Moray. The war will be as in ancient times, between the King of the North and the men who look back to Dál Riata."

"He confides none of his plans to me," I said, not bothering to add what Nechtan already knew, that my appearances beside my husband occurred rarely and only at occasions of state. I was part of the expected display, like his goshawk and horses, furs and silks stained with his foul sweat.

We had turned from the track along a narrow path. The sound of women singing rose and fell as they stooped and rose together in the field, and it was a slower measure than when they trampled cloth to thicken it. As we returned closer to the harvest we could heard the whisper of the blades against grain. I sat down on a shady bank and Nechtan beside me. The harvest spread out before us like a tapestry, some of the smaller rigs cut, others standing, and the harvesters like a wave that leveled all in its path.

"You have said that Gillecomgan chooses his time," I said, and the weight of counsel made my words come slowly. "He has luck, some would say. Luck in battle, more in his ability to assure friends with an arm across the shoulders and draw them even closer while he readies the knife. There will not be war as you believe."

Nechtan ran a dirty hand through hair that I saw was now in fact streaked with gray. My own hair had darkened from the oat-straw shade of childhood but had not begun to gray. Someday, I would have to keep it in color with steeped bark and herbs, if I chose to do so. If there would be anyone to care that I grew old.

"I have seen no great armies gathering in Moray worthy to meet Malcolm's levies, no great stores of weapons. He is not ready to move. Gillecomgan knows the king well and uses delay and manipulation even as he weakens him," I said. "When his army went into Atholl, it was everywhere told that this was a raid for some trespass of Crinán's. And Gillecomgan is prepared for the punishment due him."

Nechtan laughed and took my hand as he had when I was small and he was my protector. "Remember the raid that brought him all Moray? Findlaích never raised the title of King of the North to challenge the Ard Ri Alban, preferring to call himself mormaer, but Gillecomgan does, despising his brother, calling to himself all the discontented and those who fear the crown will settle forever on one lineage."

"The people do not love him," I replied. "He is a ravening and brutal man. The people will not follow a man they hate, nor will the men of the blood maintain him without Malcolm's heavy hand in the vote."

"He is not loved, true, but neither is Duncan, and your husband has earned a better reputation as war leader."

I did not make any move at the word *husband*. My hand did not tighten against his. I had learned to be ice, be steel, be still as the standing stones on Orkney or those that are frozen eternally in their dance at Calanais.

"Sister," Nechtan said, then took his hand from mine. "I have come here because Gillecomgan will welcome me, a sword against Malcolm, and I will relish the opportunity to raise it."

"Indeed, he will find you a weapon against the king," I said, my voice level. "Your blood and lineage are more powerful than honed metal. He will use you as he once hoped to use me, inheritor of both Dál Riata and the Pictish kingdom. If I were not barren, you would see him in Scoine now, ruling as king even as he proclaims himself the protector of the last of the line of Dubh. This is how women's lives are bartered, as reward or as pretext."

Nechtan gave me a hard look. "You say the last of the line of Dubh. Do you forget me?"

"No, dear brother. Do you think Gillecomgan would have allowed the breath to remain in your body if he had a path to the high seat through a son I bore? You would have been under turf for a long time now."

Nechtan sat staring into his hands. They were hard and scarred as those of a smith, but with the marks of reins and sword-grip and ash-wood. He lifted his head, his eyes showing a mixture of shame and desperation, then looked away.

I thought he had forgotten Gillecomgan the man, my tormentor, his friend's killer, but he had not. He had chosen this as a terrible path, but somehow less terrible than the one that led to certain death. I remembered waking in what seemed my tomb, how I'd dug and clawed for a way out, scraping my fingers on rocks, nuzzling clay and burrowing through soil like a trapped animal. Nechtan was trapped as well—but why now, why did he wait until now? Once I had been given to Gillecomgan like a captive taken in the sack of a city, immured here in Moray, he might have disappeared any time. Other enemies of the king would have taken him in. Malcolm had foes in plenty from Norway to Angle-land.

I looked for wisdom, but everything came apart in my hands.

"Neither Malcolm nor Gillecomgan is worthy of your spilled blood. Perhaps you should return to our old home and swear allegiance to Thorfinn," I offered. "Or go down to Mercia, where Godwine is strong. Over water to Bruges, as many do to find safety. Even a free life among the Wends on their island fortress."

"A hired sword in a foreign land? A beggar at other's tables? A pirate?" His voice was sour, thick. "I am the son of Boidh tanist, son of Kenneth the king, and yes, inheritor of the line of Dubh. Yet I live on Malcolm's grace. I am poorer than one of those men carrying sheaves to the stook, except for the king's sufferance."

Nechtan tore a patch of moss loose and tossed it down the slope toward the field.

"I will never be Ard Ri Alban. It will be for your son to claim, perhaps, not for me or mine. If I had not been so well taught by Alpia, then I would make my claim through the direct male line. I would find men to stand with me, I am sure," he said, the wistfulness gone like smoke. "I would claim the path through Dunollie and not the slaughter of Forteviot. There is no reason that I could not be considered equally with Duncan or any of the blood."

I kept my eyes safely down. Nechtan had idle friends enough, but supporters? That demanded levies of men, grain and cattle from lands he did not rule.

"Malcolm has kept me helpless, without followers of my own—rewarding me with trinkets and ease so long as neither you nor I pressed our claims. And I took his largesse. Who am I to claim the blood of murdered Boidh?" His voice was shaking with anger, and his eyes were bright. I felt less disloyal for my unvoiced criticisms that he now spoke into the open air. I wondered what had pushed him at last from his uneasy perch, always in sight of the execution pool.

A vision came, a grant of memory. Our father, standing quietly at Malcolm's shoulder, noble and handsome, and his face so still.

"Malcolm feels his age, and he feels his sins," Nechtan said. "He has grasped the kingship as Dál Riatans once took this land. He has made the derbfine merely a chorus of assent, even when he leaps beyond tradition to fix the title to his line. The man has not known any limits, but he sees death and he is afraid."

We sat, then, without anything more to say. A thin cry rose from the shaded edge of the field, a baby left swaddled. A woman tied her sheaf, dropped it and ran to give the child her breast. My throat closed against the moan that gathered there. *My son to have the throne? What son was that?* "Bear in fire," I had been promised, or warned, but no child came to me as they did readily to women of the people.

Perhaps he felt my misery, because Nechtan put his arms around me and hugged me.

"I cannot say what welcome you will get from Gillecomgan," I said, "but I would be happy to have you near."

24

MACBETH

THE BLACK ISLE, 1029

Macbeth was at Cromba, taking advantage of fair weather to visit his holdings before winter approached, when three men came riding hot and heavy along the track from Portmahomack.

"What news?" asked his right-hand Bresal, urging his mount forward. The three riders dismounted.

"Cerr the King of the North has died in his own bed, at a ripe age, and without violence. I have seen his body in Kinnedar church and affirm this to be true."

"I know you, Iain of our kin of Loairn, and also your honored uncle Conn of the Narrows," Macbeth said, then regarded the third man, young and with the appearance of a sea-rover. "But you I do not recognize."

"Olaf Magnusson, of the Danish people of Moray."

"Who have joined Cenél Loairn, the People of the Wolf, to pledge our loyalty to you as King of the North," said Iain. They knelt and Macbeth felt an interior shudder, the touch of a cold hand. He closed his eyes. Perhaps they were thinking that he prayed for the soul of the departed king, who had been weak but inoffensive. His death was not unexpected, Malcolm Cerr being no young man, and without the physical power of the Ri Alban whose name he shared. What was unexpected was this decision, when Gillecomgan had more than equal right to the title and the resources to claim it. *You will be rewarded,* Macbeth heard, *with the land where you were born.*

"What of the mormaer?" he heard himself say, as though at a distance. *Gillecomgan would not readily accept this.*

"Men of the derbfine selected you, remembering your father's rule, and aware of your gifts," said Iain.

Macbeth dismounted, went to the men and clasped their hands and embraced them. He looked long into Iain's face. *What gifts do you think I have?* he wondered. *The high king's favor, promising rewards of trade and peace?* How much did they know of his current struggles to fend off both Thorfinn and Gillecomgan?

He glanced at Bresal, who could barely hold back a delighted grin.

"I do not know that I am worthy of your faith, but I will do my all to honor it."

"Then return with us. Preparations are being made to receive you at Rosemarkie."

The making of a king was no simple effort even in times of peace, much less with Gillecomgan's role as war-leader providing him with a ready fighting force. Punished severely the year before for his raid on Dunkeld Abbey, the mormaer had retreated to Buchan and devoted himself to gathering men and rebuilding forts. No one would say that he was preparing rebellion against his brother. But his brother was dead, now, and the derbfine had acted quickly. Gillecomgan would bend the knee to Macbeth or do as all expect and challenge for the title himself.

Macbeth might have preferred Birnie for his investiture, more central to Moray, but Gillecomgan's widening grip on the east made that dangerous. Rosemarkie was not far from his birthplace, the wide golden crescent of its shore making it a popular landing for beach markets. Its cathedral had long been a holy place, dedicated to St. Peter and housing the relics of St. Curadan, protector of innocents. There was, however, no king-making stone at the abbey, nor at Forres, nor indeed anywhere in the realm. When Am Broch was overrun by the Lochlannaig, the stone on which kings had sworn themselves to protection of this land had been lost, thrown from the cliffs into the ocean. This marked the end of a tradition brought out of Éireann and also observed at Scoine, as it had been at Dunadd and Dunollie and other places where kings were made. Oswald and the bishop did not try to hide their satisfaction at its loss. "The king needn't stand on a relic of pagan days," Oswald said. "You can begin a new tradition, putting your hand to the cross on the great stone carved with the symbols of the Pictish kings as well as the holy cross. That will be a fitting symbol of the unification of all the peoples of the north."

There was time for preparation and prayer and confession, as the leaders of clans and families that made up Cenél Loairn were assembled and those who traced their lines back to Pict and Norse as well. In the bishop's chambers, Macbeth felt his soul examined minutely, as though he were a candidate for ecclesiastical office. Although he had not tarnished his soul with carnal sins, at least ones that had not been already absolved, Macbeth knew the weight of bloodshed on his heart. Battles large and small, the deaths of men at his hands, had left him with visible scars and others invisible.

"Do you hold hatred in your heart for any man?"

For a moment, Duncan's face appeared. *But I do not hate Duncan, though I believe he hates me.* Macbeth met the bishop's eyes. "I have a desire for justice against the man who killed my father, yes. That is my right under law. That is my duty as his son."

"Will you pursue this feud?" The bishop's hand covered the pectoral cross that hung at his heart, ancient Roman handiwork with a tiny glass vessel at its center containing a sliver of Peter's cross.

"I will show forbearance, as a Christian king, but I will be vigilant in my rule over Gillecomgan. I do not doubt he will bring war against me. I will not stay my hand when he does."

It was the way the world worked, that the bishop must know.

"We of the church pray that you will conduct your rule as your name suggests, Son of Life," he said. He absolved Macbeth of his sins, affirming that he could take the crown with an untroubled heart and cleared soul, but as Macbeth bowed his head for blessing, he felt far from sanctity.

Time enough, too, in the days before the ceremony for a message to be sent to Scoine and returned. Malcolm gave his support to his grandson as King of the North and ally by land and sea, to be declaimed before the men of the blood at the ceremony—while a second private message, written and sealed for Macbeth to read, was a pledge of men when Gillecomgan made his move.

The day arrived. Macbeth's storehouses and herds provided the makings of a feast. Church services reverberated to the sound of bells and high voices of the oblati. People from all levels of the kinship gathered on the Black Isle, along with their families and a large contingent of Danes settled in his father's time. Still, it was clear this was a smaller gathering than might be expected. Continued pressure from Thorfinn and concern about the mormaer's activities kept many close to their strongholds. Neither Duncan nor any of the underkings except Ech-marcach made the journey.

As the churchmen planned, the investiture began with the assembly around the cross slab in the abbey courtyard. It was taller than a tall man, cut from red sandstone, with the crescents and other designs of the elder kingdom clustered on one side, above a cross, and an equal-armed cross dominating the other. Macbeth placed his right hand on the great cross as his lineage was recited. His vision seemed to swim, but it was just the swirling intricacies of the beasts cut into the side of the stone that he saw in the corner of his eye. He affirmed his right to leadership of his clan and people and pledged to devote his life, blood, and wealth to protecting the northern kingdom from all enemies.

"So let all the peoples, the Pict and the Scot, and newcomers who add their strength, from the western lands to the North Sea, along the Great Glen and in the fertile Laich and mountain fastnesses, let us be one people under the mild rule of a rightful king, and under the cross of Christ," intoned the bishop of Rosemarkie.

The sons of his leading men led the procession into the abbey church, carrying a tall crucifix raised up on a pole and an open Bible and swaying censers, followed by the bishops, and then Macbeth to take his seat in front of the altar. It was a new chair crafted for him with the images of bulls and wolves worked on the side panels and a depiction of David wrestling a lion carved into the tall back. Bishops from across the north celebrated the high Mass with a great many prayers and a long homily on the nature of kingship that Macbeth was certain had been written by Oswald.

He shifted slightly and eased his hip. A high seat was never meant to be comfortable, he realized, remembering his grandfather's weary face as the days went long into the nights. And of course, it was not a comfortable throne as the eastern half of his kingdom was in fact held by Gillecomgan, supposedly as steward and leader of the armies. He had heard the comments as men gathered for this rite.

Findlaích's son, but so young. How many of our kindred can he count to his side and be sure of? Loairn are the people of the wolf. Yes, and wolf packs have but one leader, not two.

Macbeth partook of the Mass. He was crowned in Christ's name with the ancient circlet carried from across the water, fine gold set with garnets and diamonds, to which a large Cairngorm stone had been added a hundred years ago when the Pictish kingdom merged into the Dál Riatans.

As he looked out at the leading men of his kingdom, he thought mostly of his father, buried on the banks of the Ness where he had died. He knew this crown but did not remember his father wearing it, though he did remember the mormaer's chain and bit his tongue to stem the flush of anger, thinking of that insignia around the neck of Gillecomgan angbaidh. Perhaps he'd been too young to see his father acting as king; he had only been beginning to learn about this realm when he'd been sent away.

And no matter how much he tried to put her from his thoughts, he saw the woman, young and old and young again. *You will be rewarded for valor with the land where you were born, a part at first, then the whole. Finally, all Alba will be your portion.*

25

MACBETH

FIFE, 1031

A galloping horse.

Macbeth's head came up and he met the eyes of another man equally dulled by the waiting, sharing the same immediate alertness, how without decision their muscles had tensed and vision sharpened.

A rider strode rapidly into the hall, directly to Malcolm, and spoke only to him, but Macbeth and the others closest by overheard.

"Cnut's ships have passed the marker. There are four, and no watch-fires kindled to show any following, nor movement over land."

Malcolm nodded. "Cellach," he called. The keeper of his arms brought an ancient sword, plain, its grip newly wrapped but the blade like water from ceaseless polishing. It was not a sword for fighting, but one heavy with legend. The scabbard was not for battle, either, with its gold and jewels. The king rose from the high seat and had the sword buckled on. A quilted mantle of heavy red silk, red as the blood of slaves sold to buy it, was settled on his shoulders. He wore the crown ancient when it left the homelands in Éireann.

Malcolm accepted the gold brooch centered on the blind eye of a diamond and would have fastened it himself, but as he tried to guide the point through the loops woven for its passage, his left hand began to tremble.

"The Dark One take it," he cursed, clutching the traitor hand with the other.

Macbeth saw him press the pin with his right hand, holding the cloth with the outer hand braced against his chest to stop the palsy. The lines of his face deepened and his lips drew back over long, yellowed teeth. As the shaking subsided, he finished setting the brooch, only to have another fit move his useless hand against the point. A drop of blood showed in the tender place between his first and second fingers.

"The superstitious would howl, if they saw," he said, glaring at them as he sucked the blood until it stopped. There was something feral in his eyes as he mouthed his own flesh.

Macbeth breathed deeply as they went out into the cool morning air, out of a hall stifling from a roaring fire and shuttered windows. With three kings at his right hand and two bishops on his left, the king advanced ahead of his retinue. Also in Malcolm's party was a brehon, his white head bowed by the weight of the law. The king's praise-poet Aengus carried his ornamented harp proudly and did not wilt under the stares of Crinán's limping poet-seer. An abbess of the blood of Kenneth followed, and a Culdee who wrote from Greek into Gaelic, and other men of art. They settled themselves, coughing and complaining, on the benches of a platform built on the green hill.

The scent of sap and resin from fresh-cut wood, woven willow, wilting plants came up around them. The platform was draped with lengths of fine cloth, purple and yellow, red and blue. Decorations of gold were twined with the pink flowers of burr-rose, red campion, purple cranesbill, and others that Macbeth could not name. Conspicuously missing was elder-flower, which whitened the banks of the streams. It had the title of death and like maythorn was shunned.

The sun shone between clouds lingering from yesterday's rain. Blackheaded gulls drifted on the wind above a field where hay was being cured, swooping down to snatch insects. Young blackbirds, struggling in their first flights, clamored for food from the ground.

A moan and then a roar rose from the crowds further along the river.

"There," said the abbess. Her voice was clear and low.

The first of the boats had come into sight. Though dressed with flags and bright with men in festal clothing, their shapes were dark and high-prowed, lean and wolfish. The Danish ships rode on the sweep of oars, with sails lowered, carried on the tide-swell over the sandbars and among the rocks of the River Tay. They were followed by a straggle on the far bank, people who tracked the boats along the river-path, curious to see the meeting of five kings: Cnut; Malcolm; Duncan, King of Strathclyde; Macbeth, King of the North; and Echmarcach of the Isles.

Macbeth saw the tall young man, blond-haired. Though wrapped in a mantle less ostentatious than those worn by many in his ship, the way he stood with his hand against the mast, surveying the fertile river valley and the hills rising beyond, easily marked him. He had amassed an Empire of the North Sea. Now, though his incursions into Alba had not ended with his hoped-for annexation, he demanded geld and a pact of wary friendship to pull back his troops.

The sun slid behind clouds and emerged, sparkling in the water-drops sliding from raised oars. The boats pushed into the shore. Noble boys waded into the mucky verge, wetting fine shoes to pull the longships against the bank.

Malcolm stood and his poet struck his harp. Surrounded by under-lings and clerics and men of art, he went down to meet Cnut.

It had been an ill-chosen conflict, Malcolm previously having sided with Cnut's opponents. When Cnut moved to punish this alliance, Mac-beth had helped fight the invasion to a standstill, earning his grandfa-ther's respect. Now he saw at close range the Danish king whose men he'd battled. Yes, there was the long, narrow nose given as his mark. What had seemed restraint in his garments from a distance showed itself to be luxury at close hand. An elegant shirt of mail, gilded and adorned with dragons, covered a purple feasting-robe that hung to his feet, and over all, that dark mantle showed itself to be not somber black but another shade of purple so deep that it appeared black. One enor-mous garnet swung on a chain, while another was set into a ring on his forefinger. The golden band of his crown rose into the shapes of jewel-centered flowers. All this glitter, Macbeth knew, was itself gilding over steel. Cnut gleamed with assurance.

He vaulted across the muddy edge and walked the few steps to where Malcolm waited. For a long moment, they held each other by the forearms, then embraced.

"Welcome, my brother," Malcolm said, the interpreter repeating in Anglish and Danish.

"We thank you for such a welcome," came the reply, and the echo in Gaelic.

They spoke loudly, for those who watched and listened.

A skald stepped forward and in rolling verse told the titles of "Cnut Sveinsson, king of Wessex and Essex, the Anglian Lands and the Five Boroughs, Bamburgh and Jorvik and all that depends on them. King of the Danes who holds the sword over Witland and Samland. King of Norway, rightful inheritor of the throne of the Cerdicings, companion of the Emperor Conrad II, and the well-beloved of him who holds the Keys of Peter."

Cnut smiled thoughtfully, the slight hook of his nose deepening, and Macbeth wondered if the last of those titles was not as important to him as all the ones before. Cnut had not missed this opportunity to emphasize his recent pilgrimage to Rome and attendance at the coronation of the Holy Roman Emperor, both of which burnished his luster in places far from the Norse realms.

Malcolm's titles now were sung by his poet, each claim set out by the sound of the harp. Aengus traced the king's lineage like a river from mouth to source—his father Kenneth, second king of that name, back and back, to the great Fergus, and into the mists of Biblical times.

By now the boats had emptied, the retinue arrayed on the shore, their belongings being carried up the slope to the pavilions stretched for Cnut's people.

Crinán's poet limped forward, upon Malcolm's glance at Duncan. "King over the Britons, ruler of Strathclyde, lord of Partick, protector of Govan, rightful lord of Dun Breatánn," he sang, and loudly. "Duncan mac Crínáin, grandson to Malcolm the Great, inheritor of Cenél Gabráin, tanist of all the lands of Alba."

"Know this is a time of joy for my grandson," Malcolm added fondly, his hand resting on Duncan's arm. "Suthen his wife, kinswoman to your friend Siward, has given him a son, my godson and namesake."

"That child will be a fearsome man, then, to blend the blood of your line with that of strong Siward," Cnut said.

Duncan accepted the compliment with a brief nod, but the set of his mouth was just short of a scowl. It was rumored that Siward would soon be earl of Northumbria in place of the fading Eric of Lade, who had himself gained those lands by killing Uhtred. The greater Northumbria grew, the more tenuous the small kingdoms in its environs, including his own, wife or no. Suthen, called the Sharp-tongued, he had taken as wife for the sake of her formidable family—as his brother Maldred had been unluckily matched to Uhtred's daughter.

The introductions continued, a slow savor of titles and ancestries.

Cnut brought his wife forward, holding her hand like any young man with his bride. "Emma," he said simply, "of the Normans."

Her hair had no gray, but fine lines forked from the corners of her eyes, her mouth. She moved with relaxed vigilance. She moved, Macbeth realized, like a warrior. People leaned their heads together; their lips moved behind their hands. This was the woman who had married Cnut after he had killed not only her husband, but one of her sons as well.

He'd heard the stories. That Emma had never suckled her babes, her hard breasts yielding no milk. That she had tested Cnut like a stallion before accepting him. That she had thrown knucklebones to choose which son would be sacrificed and which sent to safety. He believed none of it. He did believe, upon seeing her straight back and large hands and strong gaze, that she had herself drafted the agreement that salvaged her lineage, though Cnut demanded that her sons born to Aethelred would be given second place to any she bore him. Steel matched steel.

Cnut was considered above all to be practical. Macbeth decided that what was called opportunism in a woman was exactly the same virtue, or vice. Emma's choices were limited; she took the best, without apology.

Now a fosterling was presented, a slim, long-faced Pole from the lands where Cnut's mother had been born. There were of course many earls, thanes, and warriors, Danish and English. There were churchmen in black, whom Oswald embraced, and as they stepped aside for the doings of rulers, began a low chatter like rooks.

Malcolm himself introduced "Sea-King Echmarcach, ruler of the Isles, and the prop of my old age and Alba's shield, my second grandson and a powerful warrior, Macbeth, King of the North."

Macbeth met Cnut's piercing blue gaze.

"A prop for old age?" the Dane said lightly, but did not shift his eyes to Malcolm. "When you require a prop, then it is likely I will need one as well."

Laughter. Malcolm smiled broadly. Macbeth nodded and stepped back, aware of the subtle movement of men around him.

Cnut would know, of course, that the title of King of the North did not bring with it a peaceful reign. Upon the death of his cousin Cerr, and with the derbfine's approval and the high king's support, Macbeth had taken control of the north and leadership of Cenél Loairn. Yet Gillecomgan, bypassed, stubbornly held power in the east of Moray as mormaer, a title wrested by force and kin-killing. He was said to be gathering forces again to challenge for the kingship. And Macbeth had inherited from his father a long struggle with Thorfinn over control of Caithness and the timber it yielded. Even now he was planning an expedition by land and sea against Orkney, developments that Cnut must be eying carefully.

Macbeth felt alliances shifting, shaping, and he was at the center of some of them.

And *her*. He remembered her now as he did at night, and in lonely places, even at prayer, the woman who was old and young and eternal. "You will be rewarded for valor with the land where you were born, a part at first, and then the whole," she had whispered to him. He burned with the memory, with the shame of following a demon until he had lost an entire day in her grasp. What he could not know, hardly dared admit to himself, was that he might have lain with her, this White Lady, entranced by her Sidhe charms. During that lost day and night, might he have polluted his immortal soul and perhaps created a demon child?

He pressed his toes hard against the ground, as though pushing the memory away, but it would not go.

"And finally all Alba will be yours," she had said.

The first had come true, and then the second. He looked at Duncan's broad back, laboring up the hill, and refused the third.

The procession turned toward the church to give thanks, and coming down from the monastery with chant and incense and striking of bells were the abbot and his monks. The juniores who attended the great smiled and jostled, their joy increased by festival rules that promised wine, oil, and fat meat for their meal.

The bishops of Kilrymont and Dunkeld, assisted by the priest of Abernethy's church, welcomed the day of peace. "Such wealth is gathered here! Vessels of silver and of gold that the Lord keeps ever filled," said Kilrymont's bishop. He smiled at Cnut and Malcolm, standing side by side, gold and silver. "Noble leaders who abase themselves before the King of All."

The monks sang, the body of Christ was broken and His blood spilled.

The entertainment began with nine matched horses, manes clipped and colored, hooves oiled, drawing battle chariots driven by youths in saffron tunics. Then came nine of the ponies from the islands, pulling delicate gilded chariots of peace driven by girls in white gowns with flowers in their hair. Nine other horses followed, with red wool braided into their manes and tails; they raced, the wool like flames streaming across the eager faces of their riders.

The people across the river cheered and shouted, but for those around the kings, the entertainment was barely noticed. There was too much to watch, too much to interpret in the way Malcolm leaned or how he reacted to Cnut's sudden raucous laughter. *The lesser watch the greater*, Macbeth thought, *and the greater watch each other the most closely of all.*

Macbeth turned instinctively at the scrape of metal on metal—a cleric, bending to scratch a flea-bitten ankle, had tangled his cross with a man's sword belt—and caught Duncan glaring at him. Sometimes the greater watch the lesser, he amended. Macbeth waiting for his foster brother's eyes to gentle, but Duncan only reddened. Beside him, the poet wove signs with his fingers. Macbeth smiled to himself, not believing in the power of such pagan letter-magic to curse.

"Surely you should be gasping for last breath, or at the least spitting blood," Oswald breathed into his ear.

Macbeth turned away from regarding Duncan. "I will take the shield of Christ against such," he said, "as you have taught me."

Oswald, gaunt with repeated fasting, smiled. "Then I did not fail with both my assigned pupils." He glanced toward Duncan, and then down the hill. Macbeth looked, too, drawn by the beauty of the finest youths of Alba, their white bodies like swans against the green, as they competed in wrestling and running matches and contests of accuracy with the spear.

"You have a handsome people, Malcolm," said Cnut. "Your men fight with light armor, as we did in the times before the arrival of the Christ, when we shared drink with the gods."

Some in Cnut's retinue smiled at this and the warriors who surrounded him shifted on their feet, emphasizing the heavy mail they wore. Such armaments had helped win the field over Malcolm's troops.

"It is not that we lack iron, nor smiths to shape it," said Malcolm, his words chosen and his voice level. "But skill and bravery are considered metal among us, and God's protection enough."

Now it was the turn of the Alban men to smile, and Macbeth felt the swell of pride, and the awareness of it as a sin, and was proud despite that.

There was silence between the kings, for a moment, and then Cnut laughed.

"Metal enough!" he repeated.

The athletes finished their contest, and Cnut thanked Malcolm for the diversions. "Let me return your hospitality with this small gift."

A brassy call rang out from downriver. Coming swiftly, the water foaming away from its breast, was a water-beast with a great head and curving tail like those on the ancient stones. Its wide fins splashed. It called again. Mallard and tufted ducks, panicked from their dabbling, flew in squawking alarm.

The Anglish sat silent, holding their faces still, as the beast approached and the people of Alba marveled and some on the far bank retreated in disarray.

"Another!" cried Duncan, half standing, and there was another beast on the river, this one golden instead of silvery, a dragon that beat the water with its wings.

The water-beast slowed and the dragon approached. Fire and smoke burst from its mouth. "What is this," muttered Malcolm.

Another gout of flame, and the water-beast turned slowly, rearing its head. The people across the river shrieked in fear and fled as it seemed to move toward them.

The creatures touched, and suddenly they released a cloud of doves, fluttering above the river. By some marvelous control, or simply good omen, the birds gathered into a single flock and flew directly over the kings on the platform toward the hills beyond.

The beasts shed their wrappings and became a pair of small boats laden with gifts. Everyone was talking at once. Duncan, his face dark with anger at being fooled, loudly questioned how these boats had arrived unnoticed. Many looked at Cnut with a new wariness, but the young king grinned with delight at his successful surprise. "So may our peoples, so often enemies, be always met in peace," he said.

Malcolm nodded. "Peace thrives on full stomachs," he said.

A sulfurous cloud drifted across the ground from the dragon's fire. Where it came against a low hill and was torn apart in the breeze, suddenly five men appeared in white tunics. This new wonder drove the old one from people's eyes.

The men paced forward, one at the front, three abreast, one following. They raised their arms, marked with swirling designs in ochre and blue. The same colors patterned their legs and circled their eyes. They moved slowly, as though all the age of the land moved on their shoulders. When they began to chant, their voices were hollow and deep.

They knelt, touched earth. Stones rose from the soil, appearing through the grass to form a low circle.

Clerics and layfolk began to cross themselves to protect their souls.

The crippled poet, Macbeth noticed, made no sign but turned his staff rapidly in his hands.

The ancient priests began a new chant, dropping into single file and walking toward the royal hall. Their right hands dipped to the earth and lifted like those of sowers planting seed, and where they had touched, flat stones appeared to mark the path. Then they spiraled away, back to where the first stones had been raised on the brow of a small hill, passed through that circle and into the ground.

Even Cnut took a moment to recover from the solemnity of the rite.

Malcolm rose, spread his arms wide. "Come, our path has been made and the table is spread." It was his turn to smile, though it was a wintry one. The promise of food lifted the shadows from all faces. As the great followed their kings, most avoided the stones, keeping their feet to the familiar grass.

Macbeth did not know how they had magicked the stones, but he had seen the staircase that went into the back of the hill, and the fitted blocks of turf covering the entrance. He doubted there was anything evil, nor anything holy, in these stones he stepped on.

"Such great knobs of rock," Cnut remarked that evening. "Coming into the river, where salt mixed with fresh, there was a great balk of stone."

"The river changes," Malcolm said. "Boatmen say that the Tay is a cat that litters rocks and eats those litters."

"So that land there," and Cnut gestured toward the island and the Standers, blots on the darkening water, "which seems eternally island, has been at one time perhaps a part of the far shore. And another, part of this?" Macbeth set down his cup. Only moments before, the great kings had been affably discussing some disputed borderland as they sat side by side, each on his high seat.

"Does the island choose its place, or is it the river that by its strength decides?" Malcolm said blandly. "The question is not the fate of the island, but whether the river can be trusted not to eat into the shore and take more for its own."

Cnut chewed a bit of beef reflectively. "The river is powerful and will win in the end," he said, "but the earth has its own strength and endures."

The banquet proceeded with toasts and professed admiration, and nothing was said, and everything was said. Macbeth watched Cnut. The

marks of a true king, so Oswald had taught him, were fortitude, humility, constancy, bravery, generosity. But policy mouthed in one ear and
then another in a different ear kept a king in power, while the honed
sword-edge of his supporters likewise must be maintained if the king
is to remain king. Even Charlemagne and Alexander, whose stories had
been exemplars bound into books of instruction, even those model
kings had told politic lies.

Cnut had come to accept Malcolm's friendship, a gloss for submission after Alba's green lands had been invaded as far as this same
river. Malcolm received him as a brother, with under kings present to
represent firm support and evidence of alliances both north and west
through his grandsons. It was a visible reminder that Cnut could not
expect to turn Malcolm's people against him. Cnut on his part received
reassurance that Alba would not help his foes in Scandinavia.

Neither one of them had to mention Bernicia, or Lothian, or
Durham, or the names of the fortifications and villages that had been
burned on each side of the uneasy southern borders for many years.

Malcolm called for his best wine, carried gently from over the sea,
thick and dark, to fill their golden goblets.

"A pledge," he said, his battlefield voice rolling over the noise of the
banquet. "We will drink together and we will swear together."

The kings lifted their goblets and drank deep, looking at each other over the shining rims. There was near silence, and when they had
downed the wine, a roar of approval sounded all along the tables. The
bishops came forward now, holding a great Testament between them,
and the kings placed their hands on its worked ivory cover, Cnut's covering Malcolm's. They swore peace and friendship, again, but it was
Cnut's voice that was strong and prayerful on the names of the Trinity
that would bind their actions.

The pact, like a betrothal, was sealed with gifts—from the Anglish,
purple cloth embroidered and over-embroidered in gold, jewelled metal
work, and lace; from the mountains of Alba, a cloak of glossy sable,
an ancient torc of gold, and a pair of goshawks, their hoods closely set
with the garnets that both Angles and Danes so loved. Malcolm formally submitted his southern territories to Cnut, who graciously awarded
them back. Not in evidence was the gold that bought this peace.

The king's poet struck his harp and began to sing praises of the
peacemaking.

"He has no right," Macbeth heard the crippled poet complain to Duncan. "That man is a mere mouther of verses, not one of the filid, not Lapwing who keeps the nation like a child against his breast."

Malcolm's head nodded forward, heavy with wine. Beside him, Cnut lifted the sable cloak and draped it around the shoulders of silent, watchful Emma.

"Mere bard, paid in drink. No sight, no sight." Lapwing leaned to Crinán's son. "The Purple Wind brought these strangers, as it brings rain and chill and fog. Turn our faces lest we wither." They were close as young lovers, and Macbeth felt a growing unease. The crippled poet urged Duncan, his eyes narrowed in argument, his hands rising and falling like sea-birds over a swell of small fish. Once Macbeth heard the name of Siward, and later, "Both blond kings sit in this house." Duncan glared at Cnut, glorious and golden, and at Malcolm, seemingly half asleep in his high seat.

If they had not grown up into different men, Macbeth could have risen, gone to where Duncan slumped with his ear drinking in the poet's words, pulled him to his feet and told him bluntly as brother to brother that the man was dangerous. If they had not turned away from each other, Macbeth could have walked with him out into the clean air and asked his advice on matters of Moray. But Duncan was envious and petty, thinking every gift, every smile from the Ard Ri Alban— and every obligation—diminished what he would surely inherit. When Duncan became high king, then Duncan would weigh him only as an element to maintain his power, and not as brother.

The king had passed through his earlier drowsiness and now was flushed and loud, shaping some battle on the air for Cnut's understanding. Macbeth watched his grandfather, who soon would assist him to regain what had been rashly awarded to Gillecomgan, as he worked to claw the shifting borders of the kingdom into one realm for Duncan's waiting hand.

He did not love him any less for this.

Macbeth looked down from the royal chambers. The stars had swung toward morning. The only ones awake in the hall below were the men at the doors, and the honor guards who, swords drawn, watched at each corner of the high seat of Alba. He leaned on the rail, ragged with alertness over long hours.

He turned around to where Malcolm and Cnut conferred by the small light of a squat yellow candle. With ceremony done, they could meet over their cups like other men, except they had people to bend like grass before their will. When the crowns were on their heads, they were not men but forces, like high tides or wind or the tremors that sometimes shook the earth. For a moment, he was awed to see them, huddled against the darkness, more like grandfather and grandson than great rivals. But kings. Kings ruling over kings.

Lives pass quickly, he thought. *Like grass, growing tall, cut down, dead. But together they shape greatness, like water on stone.*

Macbeth moved back toward them. The upper chamber was filled to one side with Malcolm's chosen few, to the other with Cnut's bodyguard and a bed overflowing with furs and silks where Emma appeared to nap. She was Cnut's adviser in all things, it was said. He paused, oddly entranced. Then he realized that he, too, was being watched. A girl lay, bright-eyed and listening, undoubtedly to inform Emma of the men's discussions should she nod. She lifted herself from her covers and revealed her rosy young breasts. He was stirred, and with that way of women, her downcast eyes showed that she knew that she had enticed him. The girl cupped her hands under her breasts. Suddenly, she was the woman on the moor. Macbeth turned quickly away and went to stand with the other witness behind Malcolm.

"But Thorfinn," Malcolm repeated, speaking a blend of Norse, English, and Gaelic, now that the ceremonies were past. They would have no interpreters for this meeting.

Cnut stretched his arms, his large hands interlocked. "He is your grandson."

"Aye." Malcolm seemed to brush that aside. "I gave him a place to stand when he was a fatherless child, and as soon as he is grown he swears himself to Norway. A contrary, faithless man."

"But now that I am Norway, remember, he is my man." Cnut sucked in his cheeks; with his thin nose and the deep shadows cast by the flame, it made his face a death's head.

"You will find that Thorfinn remains no man's man."

"You need my ships," Cnut said, the banquet hall's metaphors abandoned. "If I allow you to leash Thorfinn, what do I gain?"

Macbeth saw how Cnut's blue eyes glittered, so much like Malcolm's, cold with calculation.

"An independent Orkney is trouble for you as well as me. He treads deep into Sutherland, demands tribute of the merchants who make their way down both coasts. And he will cause you trouble in Norway, when he grows great enough. You can count how many sword hands would be pledged to him already, for he is close and you are far away."

There was a nod of assent from the Danish thane who, with a priest, stood behind Cnut to offer advice and witness. "If we chastise him," the young king drawled, "together, you and I—and this young king who stands at your shoulder—then it would be a warning to others."

Malcolm chuckled. "What we say can be heard by listening ears far away."

"It is easier to lead a horse," Cnut observed, "than to drive an ox."

Malcolm did not answer. A shaking fit had taken his hand again. Cnut did not pretend to ignore the palsy, and Malcolm did not attempt to disguise it. He met the Anglish king's direct gaze, but Macbeth could see in the cords that showed at his neck and wrist that he restrained a mammoth rage. At weakness, at age, at this kingdom-rich youth who waited so gracefully for the fit to pass.

"So—should Thorfinn be replaced?" Malcolm asked. "He has removed all but one of his brothers, and that one is sick. I have no designs, understand, on Orkney and Shetland. I wish only for peace in the north, and the sea-lanes open."

Cnut sucked in his cheeks again.

"Put a man of your choice in Birsay," Malcolm continued. "Choose one of a loyal house in Norway. You will have the tribute that has been withheld, and our people will not be pressed by his incursions."

"I think Thorfinn can be managed. So far as Sutherland, that is more a concern of the King of the North, is it not?" Cnut said casually. "I will not enter that dispute, any more than that you would intervene in Northumbria."

Macbeth thought, *Duncan should be here,* yet his cousin had drunk himself into a stupor and could not be roused for these late discussions.

"But even with Orkney controlled, that will not ensure peace for Moray," Cnut added.

"There will be an accounting in Moray," Malcolm said grimly.

Cnut looked past him to Macbeth, who thought, *He believes my grandfather does this for me. This is only for Duncan, to solidify the realm he waits to rule.*

He admired Cnut, an enemy who had fought so well and bargained so skillfully with the formidable old warrior. Of course, he was strong, with Angle-land and Daneland and Norway at his back, able to win battles on the lowlands. But such strength ebbed as it broke against the mountain walls of Alba. The Romans knew that and built walls to hide behind. And he himself had seen how the bones of Ecgfrith's army lit the marshes near Dunnichen.

Cnut would slice off and devour Alba piece by piece, if he thought he could. But Macbeth did not expect that as long as Malcolm breathed. He feared the time when the old man died. He had no son, sometimes becoming tearful when he recalled the lost child. Choosing then among his daughters' sons, he had settled on Duncan. That did not promise calm rule. Crinán's people were not part of the king-lines, and Duncan himself, reckless and erratic, would quickly seek to prove himself as battle-leader and satisfy his followers with looted treasure. He trusted this Dane, this rover become an emperor, more than he did the foster brother whose bed and board he had shared from childhood.

"There is no security in our succession," Malcolm said abruptly, as if he overheard Macbeth's thoughts. "The choice falls here or falls there, as old bloodlines are asserted, as popularity or strength of arms decides. We would be better off if son naturally succeeded father. None of this election by a squabbling, politicking council, one man as good as another and the high seat to the strongest."

Macbeth thought of how Malcolm had risen through blood and cousin-right. He remembered Oswald's comments, "From the death of Kenneth mac Alpin until this day, no king had succeeded his father on the high seat of Alba," and how he, a child then, had responded with his father's words—that it was better to choose a strong leader than to place a fool or a child on the high seat because of paternity alone.

A rat struggled in the ceiling overhead, lost its footing and fell. For a moment, it lay stunned. Malcolm snatched it up. He clenched his fist around it, no trace of palsy in his right hand. The rat squealed and clawed.

"The superstitious make much of rats," he observed. "If they gnaw, then death is near. If they multiply and invade the barns and halls, then disaster and war are at hand."

He squeezed. Several small cracks, bones breaking, and the rat ceased struggling. Malcolm tossed it aside.

"But it is no more than a rat, for all of that talk."

26

GRUACH

MORAY, 1032

The moon set into the last clear band of sky before clouds covered the whole. With it went all my hopes.

When the weather had closed in and we'd settled in a Buchan hall for the festal season, Gillecomgan raged endlessly that Malcolm and the derbfine had done him out of the kingship of Moray, leaving him with "the rump of the mormaership." He issued bitter threats again Macbeth "the usurper." During the season of long nights and much feasting, he was a brooding presence at table, intemperate with supporters, brutal to servants. It was not surprising that he had found my bed twice during that time, taking his anger out on my body.

The surprise came later, when my season failed to arrive. Now, as I put away the cloths that were meant to have caught my flow, I pondered how, and when, I should tell him.

The end of January came cold and clear, old snow frozen to ice, the tracks like flint, the trees groaning when night gave way to brilliant sun. Gillecomgan took advantage of the open weather to woo supporters in Marr. Left behind to fill my days with the round of household management, I told no one but longed for a confidant. Since Cipia's betrayal, I'd maintained a remoteness from women. Certainly, the wives of my husband's people were not to be trusted. I thought of my foster mother, over and over, guiding her own daughter through pregnancy, bringing wisdom and care to all the nearby women.

Then I remembered the little glass bottle of hemlock that Alpia had entrusted to me, the one I'd used to save Bredan from whooping cough. Bredan's mother, Fyfa—she lived close by, had no love for Gillecomgan, and retained some memory of the White Goddess and the old ways.

"Cornan," I called. He had been carrying in wood for the fire, but brushed off the bark and dirt as he came quickly. "I need to travel to the monastery. Will you accompany me?"

I gathered some remedies into a small bag, and in the larder found a joint of smoked pork and a cake sweetened with honey that went into a larger sack. When the lad brought my horse close to the door, I draped myself with a fur-lined mantle and looked to be sure he was well wrapped from the cold, much as I did from day to day without raising Gillecomgan's wrath. The wind was behind us, a blessing that would not be repeated on the return trip.

Cornan led the horse carefully, glancing back at me often, choosing our path around frozen pools and frost-rutted tracks. I remembered Alpia guiding her own horse, but things were done differently here, I'd learned.

It was not far from the hall to the small house on the monastery's lands. Fyfa opened the door with a smile of welcome that did not dispel the wariness that showed in her stiff posture.

"My lady," she said, her eyes cast down.

"I hope you have a good fire, Fyfa, as Cornan would surely like to warm himself." I felt the cold blast find its way under all my garments. "As would I."

She welcomed us in, visitors filling up the space scarcely big enough for Maedoc, Bredan, and a baby swaddled in its cradle. Bredan, I was happy to see, was looking hale and growing rapidly toward his father's build. I could see her eyes searching scanty shelves, wondering what would be acceptable for hospitality. The winter months were not kind to the people, even those who served the church.

"I've come to ask for help."

She glanced at me and the wariness was back in her eyes. Those sea-gray eyes.

"And I've brought something for you." Cornan opened the sack and lifted out the cake and meat. She glanced at her husband, and his avid face told me no more than I already suspected.

"Would ale warm you?" she asked. "I have that, or blackberry leaves steeped."

So we made a little celebration together of the cake, like a family, happy in sharing a sweet thing. The meat disappeared into the larder and would plump out many meals that likely would have been only kale and root vegetables and oats.

"The monks tell us the Lord will provide, but I see it is the Lady," said Maedoc, wiping crumbs from his lips. "Thank you."

"You have given me the pleasure of warm company in the midst of winter."

"We can give little else," said Fyfa. "We are only farmers now, though there is some benefit to that—my men are less likely to be killed by the sword unless battle comes here on a Northmen's ship."

"Our needs are simple," added Maedoc, softening his wife's plain speech.

"What did you want of me?" Fyfa asked at last.

I nodded toward the bed-spaces, away from the men huddled by the hearth fire. We settled there but at first I could talk only of weather and the gossip brought by travelers. I was unsettled by Fyfa's steady regard, her waiting posture.

"I am pregnant," I blurted out.

"I should offer you congratulations, my lady."

"But you know Gillecomgan."

She nodded.

I unburdened myself, yet felt no less sick at heart. I remembered Derelei's pride in her blooming pregnancy, the strong kick of the child against my hand spread across her belly. And then her birth-struggle, without Alpia's aid, the sobbing husband telling us the baby's first cry was also its last and that Derelei had ebbed away with the little body in her arms, bleeding to death before we arrived.

"I keep hoping that I will lose the child," I admitted, "but there has been no trace of blood. It means to stay."

"And you won't visit the juniper-tree?"

I shook my head at the suggestion I might induce a miscarriage. "I cannot bring myself to end it, even though it is Gillecomgan's."

The men laughed, a blend of the child's treble with Maedoc's deep voice. Perhaps their lives were uncomplicated, work and duty to those who demanded their allegiance, a straight line that women so often had to bend themselves under and around. Our battles were no less bloody, even if limited to the narrow field of the bedchamber.

"What is it you fear?" she asked. "The birthing, or what comes after?"

"If the child is a boy, and it achieves its first year..."

"Then he will claim his heir and have you put away."

"Or strangled in my bed." I tried to brush that away with a bitter laugh, though we both knew it was all too possible.

"And so you have not yet told him."

"He's been off intriguing against King Macbeth in hopes of raising his station. His men have learned to call him the King of the North."

Fyfa looked toward her men, perhaps thinking of her earlier boast. "Gillecomgan will have that crown, if this young king is not more wary. Findlaích knew the nature of his nephew but that did not save him."

27

MACBETH

MORAY, 1032

The man who'd spoken in Macbeth's ear brought no unexpected news. "Gillecomgan has moved in force from the east, seizing your royal hall at Forres and declaring himself King of the North. He rallies men to his side with pleasing words, saying he will liberate Moray from Alba's overlordship."

Macbeth had been preparing for this, showing patience and restraint while meeting his cousin's provocations, meanwhile rebuilding damaged forts and gathering intelligence. Malcolm had promised his support, but on this side of the Mounth, Macbeth knew he must solidify his reign one handclasp, one man, one family at a time.

Gillecomgan had been well supported earlier in his reign as mormaer, out of mingled Moray pride and fear. He was a strong man in war and those who sided with him were rewarded as he led raids north and south to bring back wealth. Then he had begun to exert his power without regard for custom or mercy. When his brother died, he had expected the derbfine would choose him; now he'd try to wrest away the kingship he thought he deserved.

Macbeth shifted in the saddle. He had his own war-band from Ross and Cromarty, men provided by Malcolm, and he had sent word to trusted kin. Few warriors remained who had stood with Findlaích. But word came back, there would be men to join the army. And now they moved, with stealth, against Gillecomgan.

They rode past mounds of earth and stone, some of them old circles with their stones tilting or sunken level with the sod, some of them the barrows of warriors whose names were fading or forgotten. On one, a rough triangle of stones that might mark a giant's tomb could not report who lay beneath. Macbeth thought that good men often had no stone to tell their end, no song or book. They died and were laid down, for good and for bad, until all were summoned at the end of days.

The sky was bright though the sun had dipped behind the mountains. Shadows spread long and blue, irregular as the treetops on the slopes above the floodlands. Leather creaked and metal fittings clashed, steel on steel or the softer notes of bronze. The men joked and sometimes sang. After the march on narrow tracks through forests dank with gleaming moss, after storms and chilly nights, this respite was welcome.

"The sun does shine here in Moray," said one of the Atholl men in grudging admiration.

Macbeth glanced back at the mounted men, their helmets gleaming and their mail and the tips of their spears, and behind them, the mass of walking warriors and young men, not yet seasoned fighters, who supported the army by carrying additional spears into battle. Were they enough? Perhaps. Back in the shadows were shaggy horses laden with bedding and weapons and food, a few cattle driven along by the rod, and slaves who cooked and washed and served.

It had been a difficult march from the borders of Atholl, tracing river valleys and mountain passes. Waterfalls leaped from the hillsides to the river, and in their foam the white-breasted dippers scudded and bobbed, breathing water instead of air. They had forded the Spey without incident, but lost a man and two horses where a hillside path crumbled. Now the mountains stepped back and the river flowed softly in curves through a level meadow, the grass tall and richly green. Regular floods kept trees from growing here, kept the ground soft and springy and fertile.

A palisade surrounded the house and byre and kitchen-garden of a solitary farmstead. The house was low and black, ancient wood, old thatch, a long huddle for people and animals against harsh weather. A man and a youth with only the shadow of a mustache came from the house. They approached the wooden wall, stood there and did not move.

Macbeth's right-hand, Bresal, rode forward. "Whose house is this?"

The man, lean and weather-worn as his farm, answered slowly, "As you are many and we are few, I answer, Sluadach of the kindred of Forcus the Long."

Bresal smiled at the obvious irony, the farmer behind his fence had a name that boasted One Who Has an Army, facing an army in fact. But Sluadach did not smile. His eyes seemed to retreat deeper into their hollows.

"The hand of justice has been set against the rebel Gillecomgan, to restore order. Does this house honor King Macbeth and his right over mormaer and toiseach?"

"I am a poor man," he said, "who tends his land and pays what is due. When the great say, go, or come, then I go, or come."

All the time, he looked not at Bresal nor at Macbeth, but at the animals milling behind the army, cattle taken from high grazings.

Macbeth urged his horse forward. "Who is your protector?" he asked.

"Cano mac Cathub, whose hall is at the Gray Cliff."

"Then I tell you, Sluadach, that you will be made whole for what is needed for our cause, for each boll of oats, then two in compensation. For each cow, a cow with a calf beside her. That is my pledge, Macbeth son of Findláich, a man of Moray, by God's will King of the North."

The farmer's eyes gleamed at the names and his square chin lifted. He said nothing. An old caution rested on him, of a man who has seen many armies. He opened the gate and stood back as servants carried out sacks of grain. As they disappeared to the baggage train, Sluadach remained by his fence.

"You are small in number."

"But we become greater as we go," Macbeth answered. "All who have been harmed by Gillecomgan are eager to see the honor of mormaer lifted from his shoulders."

"I have been injured," the farmer said. "He killed one of my sons, and his brother declared there would be no restitution."

"So a debt must be settled."

Sluadach nodded and held up one finger—a moment. He ducked into the house and returned with a short sword in a thin scabbard.

"I will help Gillecomgan find his brother, in hell." He moved to join the ranks of foot soldiers.

Macbeth thought of him as the army moved forward. These people were like the land itself, unmovable, waiting out the rage of storms, reemerging after floods. As the saying went, when the great contend, the children starve. He weighed that, and their fear of the men at their door or Gillecomgan, against shared kinship or lingering affection for his father or the frail air of his own name and new title. Already those had been enough to open the gates of a fortress where those who remembered his father had lifted the bar by night, and it had been short, harsh work to quell the rest. They had sheltered warm and dry, well fed on Gillecomgan's wine and bread and pike pulled from the loch that had formed when a roaring stream built up a wall of stones and dammed itself. His men stepped forward well, and the horses carried their necks high. They had rest, and he had hope.

Sluadach, now. If Gillecomgan had come riding up, demanding his loyalty, he might have acceded as readily. Lesser men knelt to the great—so it had ever been. How many of the kindred of Loairn would choose Findlaích's son over Gillecomgan? How many war leaders would change their allegiance, and how many of their lesser kindred, like Sluadach, would march behind him?

๛

FORTEVIOT, EARLIER IN 1032

The fire had spit at wet wood. Thick with damp, the smoke had sagged and lingered under the roof, curled against the walls. Malcolm's eyes were closed, his head resting against gilded carvings.

"You can read their scratchings," he said. "Do they do this right? Monks are like women, soft and fearful, not to be trusted."

Macbeth leaned close to read the documents the king had spread across his lap. The light of torch and candle showed careful script, the names that receded from Malcolm's back through time, to the Peace King, to the warriors who took Éireann from the giants, to Adam.

"They have labored diligently."

"Tying up threads that were never joined," the king said wryly. "It does not matter. Once it was enough to have a poet who could sing your genealogy, but this writing is something that will not be forgotten. So we keep these nattering monks beside us."

He leaned forward, his eyes intense despite the cloud that age was casting over them. "This makes truth," he said, stabbing a finger at the vellum. "These marks."

A man stirred, coughed, rolled, pulled the braught up over his shoulders and exposed his hairy legs. Otherwise, all was silent. The banquet celebrating the army's departure for Moray had ended very late, after much drink and boasting. Only the king's bed lay empty. Macbeth's own bedding was bundled and ready for a horse's back come first light, as he was.

"That is why I allowed you to be stained with ink, even at the threat of your manhood," Malcolm said. "Because you were taught by a monk, you understand them. You will be a good adviser to Duncan."

Macbeth nodded. The king seldom slept, as though age had stolen that capacity. He talked restlessly to whomever was awake or could be wakened, night after night.

"Your foster-brother might be tricked. Monasteries bring documents to claim land. Ambassadors come showing letters and treaties. But you, you understand this." He dismissed the genealogy with a wave of his bony hand, pushing it to the floor as being of no matter. He settled back in his seat, closed his eyes.

Macbeth was restless too. He stared at the close lines of uncial letters running down into shadow until his eyes burned. Each line a man who was the son of another man, brother, father, all part of a wider kindred.

"You will support me in this war against Gillecomgan, a man who was for long your favorite," he said into the silence. "There is something I must know."

Malcolm did not open his eyes, but tension in his shoulders said that he did not sleep.

"I have never asked, though often I have heard whispers. In respect for you as Ri Alban and love for you as grandfather and fosterer, I have not asked, but now I will, because I may not return from this endeavor. It is said that you ordered my father killed."

Silence.

Finally, the king spoke.

"There are places—you have ridden past them, times enough—where a smooth green meadow seems to stretch." His dry lips moved for a moment, but no words. "A child would run out and be swallowed up. A man chooses the long path around the bog. Dangerous ground." Malcolm sat up straight. "Better not to venture there."

"Sometimes that is exactly where a man must venture."

"You are no child. You see how this world lays." The king's hands rested together between his thighs, as though the golden bands were shackles, the jewels simply weight of stone to sink him. "Moray has always been a place of conflict, from the time we of Dál Riata found our way there among the Picts, and lately made worse with the Norse and Danes. Moray is far beyond the mountains, and it remembers when it was the jewel of Fortiu and a king sat on Craig Phadrig and ruled all from the Mouth of the Ness."

He met Macbeth's waiting eyes.

"Moray is dear to me as a lifelong friend, sharer of bed and board. People can tell lies about such a one, because friends can fall away, and the betrayal is all the more painful. Gillecomgan is of your father's kindred, yours too of course. He said——and others said——that Findlaích had become proud, that he took too much on himself. That he claimed, if quietly, that he was more than king beyond the Mounth. All this I heard, and I watched as well. I spent much time visiting Moray, as you will remember. When finally your father refused me in a small matter, then punishment was due."

"So Gillecomgan was sent to kill him."

"To punish him! To reduce his army and break his walls, drive off his cattle. To make him remember that he had pledged himself as a supporter." Malcolm's voice was passionate, but he lifted his hands again and let them fall back, and again Macbeth was reminded of fetters and chains. "You have begun to learn, in ruling men and lands of your own, that the proud and unruly must be brought down before harsher measures are needed."

Macbeth felt the liquid quaking of the ground under his feet, but spoke. "And so my father was butchered, and his good men blinded and their hands hacked off. Men who had fought the Lochlannaig beside you, who had bled to protect Alba as much as their own land."

"Not that!" Malcolm challenged. "That was not my wish." He pulled at his beard. "But once Findlaích was dead and the nephews had consolidated power, then the support of Moray was still needed. It seemed wise to let them keep what Gillecomgan had conquered."

"Lest he turn his army around and march on Scoine."

The king stood and began to pace the small area bounded by his seat, the sleeping men. His soft shoes whispered.

"Alba was at its strongest in the past, when it had one king from the western islands to the North Sea and south to the Roman walls. The Norsemen have hurt us, aye, both east and west. The Danes have not taken our heartlands. We have beaten back the Angles and the Orkneymen."

Macbeth thought of the men dead from adventures into Northumbria. He remembered the Danes now tilling the soil in Moray. They had given their voice to his kingship, yet their presence was a compromise. It was called a compromise and not a loss.

"We are not torn apart from the inside or pierced to the vitals by invasion," Malcolm said. "Look south and see where British lands have been carved and bartered, Angles, Danes, Saxons each with their claim. And Éireann—there, each man with a herd of cattle and two horses is a king."

Macbeth knew that this was the truth. A truth. But another truth was standing like a shadow behind Malcolm's words, and that was his desire that Duncan would rule after him and bring Strathclyde into a greater Alba. The line of Fergus would become the only royal line, with the Pictish descent cast aside and the line of Dubh extinguished and the ancient rights of Loairn forgotten.

The whispers came. If Duncan was to rule, then other claimants had to be put down. Boidh. Findlaích. Now Gillecomgan. The strongest and most able of the contenders to the high seat, who could have relied on the support of Moray and of those whom Malcolm had pushed aside. And the whispers reminded him, you are a claimant as well, or could be. Born of Moray, reared in Atholl. Son to both. *Where does my heart lie?*

Malcolm came and put his hands on Macbeth's shoulders. "You are my son. I know that you will not betray me. Make Moray yours, control all the north as your father did—none will speak against you. And listen to an old man who has been much wronged. Be careful in your advisers, be cautious where you place your trust."

His hands gripped tightly, old and palsied, but on some days still strong enough to raise a sword. Surely God strengthened this king into his old age, as it was written. Macbeth felt a welling of respect and fear and confused affection for his grandfather, his father, this formidable old warrior. He sighed.

"I will purge rebellion from Moray, if it is in my power to do so, and will restore the alliance between my northern kingdom and Alba." He knelt to accept his grandfather's blessing. As hands touched his head, he felt Malcolm's fingers begin to tremble against his skull. The king sat down, cradling the errant hand, and seemed at last ready to rest. The tension slackened from his face, his lips parted, and as he slid into sleep, he seemed to truly be an old man.

Macbeth left him and went down. A soft brightness filled the hall, lighting the embroideries of old battles, shining on the curves of the glassware, lingering in the carvings and ornaments. He stepped among the sleepers and out into the long gray light before the day. A horse nickered on the grazing, then threw up its head and ran. Now he felt as cool and light as the air. It was better to leave the doubts and envies of the court behind and seek his own northern lands—a life spent facing outward enemies and not inward. His hot desire to kill Gillecomgan had tempered, but he had become stronger for that quenching. He had been forged into a deadly weapon against his enemy.

ॐ

Moray, 1032

He felt something touch his knee, and looked down to see Oswald sag, exhausted, to the earth. "A horse," Macbeth called, stopping the march.

"I am weak, weak." Oswald hung his head, gray hair sprouting stiff from a tonsure not made recently. "The saints of God did not need to ride."

"The saints of God did not go to war," he answered, though that was not true. Still, Oswald did not object. Macbeth took the reins of the bay horse, his own second mount, and led it close to a lichened stone. Oswald would not let himself be helped when his humility was on him.

The monk clambered from ground to stone and into the saddle. The bay whickered at the ungainly burden. Once up, Oswald straightened and took the reins.

"I would walk beside you," he said. "That was to be my offering for our success." Tears ran from the corners of his eyes. The army moved forward; Oswald allowed them to pass so that he might join the column at a humbler spot. Macbeth dismissed his spiritual plight from thought.

He counted back the days. He wondered about the weather along the coast while they had been deep inland, if the boats had assembled as promised, if that small body of men would be able to put out from Cromarty on the agreed date and make their way to Findhorn. That feint was meant to draw some of Gillecomgan's forces away from For-res, as well as his attention. But would they make the sea-passage and arrive at the time they had set? Macbeth did not trust boats.

He recalled how the fortification and royal hall of Forres stood, on the slopes overlooking the Findhorn River. It would be a long and dif-ficult siege, as its walls had been expanded to provide more protection for its community of metalworkers and farmers, the fortress hardened to face the threats from the seas. The tall pillar of Sven's defeat by Pic-tish forces many decades ago was a reminder of how quickly such danger could arrive. Macbeth closed his eyes and waited until the memory came clear. Sun glimmered off wide water, and his father was standing on the walls of Forres. The image was faceless, as it was always. A small man but wide-shouldered, black against the brightness. Only the longing in his heart assured him that this was Findlaích.

His blood spilled, given like the Christ's. He wondered if Oswald would think that blasphemy, decided not. As above, so below. Blood manured this land of Moray, nourished the grass and trees, the oats and barley, cattle and men.

He had seen the broad lands of Lothian where soil nourished crops without balks of stone, without incursions of peat or sand. The plow could take a straight course in such ground. That land supported many people, many animals; that was an easy place to love. This land of Moray was changeable—cold and harsh in the mountains, fertile in the valleys and the wide lands along the sea. Blessed with sun and bitten by frost. Rich with crystals and silver and timber, leaping with fish in swift streams and lochs without bottom. Macbeth knew that he himself desired this land above all other, though he was barely coming to know it.

They rode into the soft lingering twilight. Stars were showing when they approached the smooth bare hill topped with a single ancient slab, upright against the deep blue sky. This was the place they were to make an army: the men he'd brought and those who would break their pledges to the mormaer to honor the ones they'd make to him as king. This was the place and the night, the eve of the Feast of St. Hippolytus.

There was no talk, no laughter as they approached the meeting place.

"Smoke," Bresal said quietly, and Macbeth nodded. He had scented the fires as well, though they could not be seen.

A ringing call, and an answer—the horses knew their own, a stallion challenging another. Or perhaps they greeted the day set aside for the martyr dragged to death by horses.

They rode around the lower side of the hill, the stone slab above them seeming to turn its face like the marker of a sun-dial. Light reflected on the trunks of the trees, moving light of flames. The white trunks of young birches gleamed. The path opened at the foot of the hill, and there were fires cut into the bank, and the faces of men around them, waiting.

In the quiet, a tawny owl called, a wavering hoo-ooh, and a spark snapped from a stick and arced into darkness.

Aidan rode forward, carrying the standard. Between the two armies, he untied the cords that bound heavy silk to the wood and shook the banner free. Emblems worked in gold thread flashed in the firelight—the wolf signifying the cénel's name, and two smaller bulls of ancient Pictland.

The standing men drew their swords and beat them against their shields. It was a noise like the sea rushing against stones. Their horses forgot weariness, lifted their feet and greeted the sound of battle.

"I am Macbeth mac Findlaích mac Ruaidri, a son of this soil," he said as he rode forward. The din increased, and he shouted, "King of the North, inheritor of both the blood of Loairn and the blood of the Picts. I come seeking Findlaích's true men."

The last restraint was gone. The waiting men poured forward, surrounding his horse, and more came, those in the firelight only a tithe of those gathered back in the trees. Macbeth grinned with surprise and joy to find so many waiting here in the dark. A grizzled man took hold of his saddle. "I was with your father against the Danes," he said.

"My son fights for me," said a man whose right arm ended at the wrist. "He is my sword-arm now, and yours, to lift this curse from our land."

Men grown old in the fight, muscles ropy and hands knotted into burls, stood beside young warriors in their prime, and tears ran down their faces. Macbeth gripped their hands, spoke to them on one side and the other, greeting men he knew and many more whose lineage was familiar but not their faces—faces looking up with firelight deepening their shadows.

He touched his heels to his horse's belly, gently moving forward until he was alone on the slope of the hill. His banner was carried up and wedged into a tumble of stones, so that it rose and rippled in the breeze.

"I had not dared to hope that so many would be here," he said, aware of the tremor in his voice, unashamed that it was there. "My kinsmen."

"Aye." The word ran through the throng. "Aye."

"This land has groaned under a bloody-handed murderer. The king has heard your outcry and sends his army to join mine, to join you, to free Moray and restore order in the land."

The name of the king was shouted by the men of Atholl, but the echo from the local men was weak; he knew their support was for Findlaích's son, for Moray and not for that distant king.

"To mark our purpose, the cross of the Lord Jesus Christ will be made on this hill and we will give thanks for the victory to come," Macbeth said, raising his sword to gleam redly in the firelight. Another great shout rang from the mountainsides.

Men lit torches from the fires and illuminated the stone at the top of the hill. The slab had been incised with the thin, curling symbols of the ancient dwellers in the land, crescents and sea-beasts. The carver unwrapped his chisel from its oiled leather, put edge to stone and set the hammer to it. Macbeth shuddered involuntarily. The sound of metal on stone was a complaint, and as the upright of the cross began to take shape and obliterate the old marks, he remembered the woman on the moor. *Remember the White Lady.* Again, he was bound for Forres. He crossed himself against that demon.

Sparks flew. The stoneworker cut a simple cross into the red sandstone, channels meeting at a circle like the central boss of a shield.

Now Oswald and the priest came forward, their hands wet from cleansing in a spring at the foot of the hill, and they lifted their hands in prayer.

"On this day that precedes the Feast of St. Hippolytus, soldier and martyr, we recall also St. Lawrence, martyr, who brought him into the fullness of faith. Let the light so come into our land," intoned the priest, "and pray their blessings on our host, to drive out the night of evil on this land and bring the Sun of Righteousness to dawn here."

Macbeth, head bowed, thought that a dead soldier was a poor advocate for their army. As the priest droned on, he thought of faces that were not among the waiting host—Conamail, who had found a friend later that evil day who was willing to free him from his ruined body, and Baetán and Andrew the Open-Handed and slew-footed Dubelane. All of them dead.

"The Lord made Joshua the victor over armies as many as the sands of the seacoast. The Lord doubled the might of David against the Philistines," Oswald said. "The Lord of Hosts strengthens those who fight in his name." Oswald lifted his open palms in a blessing. "Let us wear the whole armor of God. Let us wield the sharp spear of truth and the sword of righteousness. Let us vow to be brothers to each other, to lift the shield above our friend and to beat down the arm of the enemy. Let us follow Christ even to red martyrdom, for the end time comes upon us and the Lord calls his army for the battle that is to come."

❧

So thick was the fog that rolled down from the summits that Macbeth could·hear grumbling close by but not see the man. Macbeth shook his head and water flew from it, where it had beaded on every hair like dew on grass. He flexed chilled fingers and took a fresh grip on wet reins.

They had passed between the Gray Mountains and one called Green, but there was no color here but gray—the faces of the men, their horses, the mossy stones that came suddenly out of the swathing mist. The path was slick, its turns invisible. The army went at a child's pace. Macbeth blessed the fog, nonetheless, because it concealed their descent into the low hills. From there it would be a matter of speed and luck, skirting the rock-strewn shores of Loch Moigh—he recalled the island pinched in the middle, and the smaller one beside it. Then through the birches along the Findhorn River to the dangerous crossing of the Naked Land, where rocks stood bare from the worthless soil and morasses waited for the unwary. The natives of Moray knew the paths and could lead them with speed now that they had swelled the ranks of the small army. Along the way, walled farmsteads and abbeys and small hillforts stood, each toughened by the years of invasion from across the ocean. Their path took account of which ones were considered friendly, according to the Moray men. Scouts would be returning with better word about Gillecomgan's readiness. If word remained true, and Gillecomgan was settled into ancient Forres, this would be a bloody taking.

"Would it not have been easier to go over Corrairach into the Great Glen and approach along that river to the coast?" Oswald asked. He had urged that route before. Macbeth thought that passing the fortress where his father died was poor strategy as well as bad omen. And no path would be easy.

The pace became quicker; the fog seemed less, or perhaps it was only because the mountains drew back.

Shouting, ahead. "Come up, come up!" called one; it seemed a familiar voice, but the mist made everything both close and distant, known and not. "There!" another voice, muffled. "Whose men are you? Whose men?" And then a strangled cry.

They moved forward faster, not so fast as to overrun whatever had happened, wary of the rocks around them and the unseen ahead. A man stumbled out of the mist—a scout, holding his shattered arm.

"Two score men, at the least," he panted. "Gillecomgan has laid an ambush."

Macbeth opened his fisted hand.

A little way ahead, a stranger lay with his leg cut nearly through above the knee. Blood still pumped although the arcing stream marked on the leaves showed how the force was ebbing. He was white as the exposed bone.

"How many?" Macbeth demanded. He swung down and knelt beside him, took a hard grip on his shoulder and shook him. "How many, where?"

The blood pulsed lower; the man's breathing became thin as a whisper through a dry reed. He was not yet dead, but he was beyond the reach of the living.

Macbeth looked up to see the Atholl warriors clustered around, waiting on his word, while the men of Moray were gone ahead into the fog. He pushed the limp body aside and stood. "Go! They cannot be allowed to warn Gillecomgan."

The sounds of fresh battle came from down the slope, but still the southern men hung back, uncertain in the fog and the unknown terrain. Macbeth remounted, grabbed a spear, and spurred toward the fight. Behind him, he heard swords unsheathed as the men followed.

The path snaked through stones as big as a man. Ferns just as tall showered down water. A turn of the path and he was upon the battle. Men fought in the close quarters of a forest clearing, and it was hard to know who were friends and which were strangers who'd had lain in wait. This was no place for jeweled banners and brave challenges. This was a slaughtering-pen. The fog softened and enlarged forms. Blood was dark, not bright, and smells were thick in the cold, saturated air, blood and bile and the spilled soil of the bowel.

A warrior wearing a helmet with a long nasal guard pulled his sword from the red swamp of a man's belly and ran at him from the right. He swung and Macbeth took the blow on the shaft of his spear, which exploded at the force and sent splinters like fairy-darts everywhere. The horse cried alarm as one of the splinters drove into its neck. Macbeth reined back hard, turning the horse between himself and the next stroke.

He felt the horse slip on the wet ground and slide down on its haunches, hard, just as the blade bit near its tail. It screamed and struggled, pushed itself up and slid again. Macbeth felt it falling left and he threw himself to the right, clear of the crushing weight. The horse kicked and a hoof crashed into his side. He gasped for breath, dizzy, knowing the enemy was close, all around, rising to find his nearest foe.

The man had himself fallen, going down in the steaming slick of horse's blood. Now he came on, a broad sword held at an angle to drive in and down. Half dazed, Macbeth countered the thrust. He met blow with blow, all on defense. The man smiled, seeing a beaten foe in his backing stance. The warrior's iron helmet gleamed like running water, soft as skin in the eerie light. Macbeth raised his sword and brought it slantwise at the base of the helmet and the man's neck, cleaving away part of the jaw with a shock of steel on metal and bone. The warrior's hands stiffened and his half-lifted sword wheeled to the earth.

Panting and holding his side against the pain of each breath, Macbeth retrieved his sword. He saw it was slightly bent, set it into a crack in a stone and straightened it, hoping the temper was good enough. As he strained against the metal, he looked into the forest and saw, like a spirit sent in warning, Nechtan mac Boidh.

The fog roiled around him and for a moment Macbeth thought he was indeed a ghost, not yet entirely parted from the body. His hair was untrimmed and he wore a ragged beard like a hermit. But his shield was held firmly and his sword, and gold flashed at his wrists and throat. Then a black-haired man came up beside him and they turned and disappeared among the boulders.

He stood, momentarily caught between pain and shock and anger. Nechtan had disappeared on the earlier campaign, and Macbeth had thought then, *He is gone*, taking his chance to go over sea. When a report had him instead with Gillecomgan, leader of his forces raiding and burning deep into Atholl, then Malcolm had declared him cimbid, his life forfeit and no blood-guilt for the taking.

Macbeth found a spear on the ground, the dead man's, perhaps— Norse work like his helmet and cape of ring-mail. He went into the forest, seeking Nechtan among the jumble of rocks and fallen trees. Moving shadows, a man fleeing, another following. He went after them. The first man turned to fight and Macbeth recognized him, the youth whose sword-arm had been pledged by his maimed father. He was winded, panicked. The pursuer closed.

Macbeth drove the spear into the attacker's side, into the place between the ribs and the rise of the pelvis. The man fell forward and rolled with agony as Macbeth pulled the spear away, and the vitals followed. It was the youth who made the killing blow, however, driving his blade into the man's unguarded throat. Death came with the hot release of bladder and bowels. The young man stared at Macbeth as though he did not know who he was, and ran off.

Macbeth heard the fight drifting away behind him. Men's calls, the harsh notes of steel on steel and steel on stone. He was well away from his men, leaving them leaderless, but the battle had them now, blood urged them. He felt the sword heavy in his hand, the blade foul with dried blood, bracken, flesh-grease. He had lost his shield under the fallen horse, and as he searched for a replacement, Nechtan walked out of the fog.

The spear he carried was dark with fresh blood, the only color, it seemed, in the whole world. He was winded, like Macbeth, worn out in the fight that seemed too close and yet without boundaries. His hair curled wetly on his neck.

Macbeth tightened his fingers on the slippery sword-grip, twisted his heel down into soft earth to firm his footing. Nechtan laughed and tilted his spear toward him.

"You are at a disadvantage."

Macbeth circled left.

"A man of importance should not allow himself beyond the help of his supporters, to be taken by any wandering man with the wit to keep a spear."

"Will you not close with me?" Macbeth taunted.

"I remember your embrace, old friend."

"Friend, then, how are you here?"

"How are you here," Nechtan echoed, "so far from Scoine's warm fireside?"

"Boidh's blood must curdle in your veins, that you run to Gille-comgan's whistle."

"Boidh's blood knows that butcher in the south too well," Nechtan grated. "Boidh's blood in me cries vengeance."

The rage was there, but under control. Macbeth knew he could not bait him into an unwise move.

They stood, then, each knowing the other would not fight.

"I thought you wise, that you had left Alba," Macbeth said. "There is no place for you here."

"Is there for you? With Duncan grown so great?" Nechtan mocked.

"I am vowed to him before God and kin, and I do not seek that high seat. But the question remains, why have you allied yourself with Gillecomgan angbaidh?"

"You speak harshly of your own cousin, and so well do the bidding of your father's true murderer."

Macbeth felt the heat rising in him. "For the sake of our friendship, that you must also hold dear as I still stand—for that I offer you my protection when Gillecomgan is dead."

Nechtan shook his head. "No, I do not find such protection reassuring. Not when you rule by Malcolm's allowance."

"Abandon this course."

"Are you not son to Alba's father?" Nechtan's voice was sad. He stepped backward and the mist folded around him. He stopped at the very edge of sight.

"My sister Daimhin—Gruach—know that she is no wife to Gillecomgan but a hostage and pregnant," he called. "She carries his child without joy. For the sake of the friendship, the brotherhood, we once shared, then spare her." There was a muted gleam, perhaps from a bracelet as Nechtan raised his hand, perhaps from a lifted sword. And Nechtan was gone.

Macbeth stood alone among the trees. He was strongly aware now, as his flesh cooled from the struggle, of broken ribs stabbing his side, a deep slash on his upper arm. He turned toward the sound of voices. As he walked, searching for and finding a shield, he thought of Nechtan's wild, forsaken eyes, and again recalled the woman on the heath—her proud chin, her unchanging eyes the color of the ocean.

He came upon three men carrying a fourth. Slowly, the army reassembled. Two men dead and two badly wounded among them, against six casualties of the enemy. Twenty men or so had encountered as many of their scouts here. Hardly an army to face his army, intended only to ambush them and raise the alarm. Instead, they had been equally surprised in the fog of Monadhliath. Had they been betrayed? Had the boatmen gone too early, or failed, or been captured?

Off the path, beneath a rowan with its berries ripening, Oswald and the priest were sending off the souls of the dead. Nearby, the physician had made a hot fire and was preparing his wound-bindings and cautery. Macbeth sat down to wait his turn. A tight wrapping would pull the broken ribs together and allow him to fight. A new breeze came up through the funnel of the pass, and it smelled of the sea. The fog was moving, pulling apart.

"Look!"

Fire flared on a hilltop. Warning. That flame would leap hill to hill, to where Gillecomgan waited. Bresal stood beside him, pressing his palm to a black stab-wound, and his face showed the dismay that Macbeth felt.

"There is no more time for stealth," he said, watching the path open and the sun bright on the farmlands below.

28

GRUACH

The pain struck through me like a knife, plunged deep, pulled upward to gut an enemy.

I did not cry out—the men would hear, and know that Gillecomgan had been the author of this pain as well as all the earlier ones. I would not allow that but panted, unashamed, to cut the birth-pangs. One of the serving women gripped my hand. They had built a nest in a corner of this miserable place, screened and pillowed away from the men who had no time to be concerned with a birthing. *Battle with battle*, I thought. *The baby fights its way from my womb.*

I could hear the shouts of the men, taunts and boasts from the walls, others thrown back from the army massed at the edge of the forest. They had been cursing each other since daybreak, and it was now dusk.

Another pain. They were coming closer together.

Thank you, Mother of Life, for the thirteen moons ago springing of this seed, that it might come to birth in the midst of bloodshed.

I was no longer angry, or frightened. My body had settled around the struggle in my womb and my mind was freed. I was light with laughter at the movements of the divine, shaking human lives like bones in a cup and throwing them across the floor. The White Lady and her son the Savior pondered the patterns that they threw.

Look, here, this army cramped into a fortress on an inadequate hill, a hump of sand with a ditch and a timber wall that would scarcely keep cattle. When the fire-signal came from the mountains, warning of Macbeth's army, we had been inside strong walls. And Gillecomgan had laughed and ordered a move. Horses were saddled, treasures and comforts piled onto pack animals or left behind. I was lifted into a cart, though the midwife protested that I was now at the point of childbirth and should not be moved. And where had we gone in such a mad rush? Not to an island stronghold or a seacoast fortress. He had chosen this modest hillfort that could scarcely house his retinue and the army of fifty or so men that Gillecomgan considered enough to meet Macbeth's forces.

Another pain. I waited it out, tracing the strangeness of this situation.

"The king in the south backs this stripling," Gillecomgan had ranted. "A monk in all but the tonsure. His father was a better man, and no match for me. I am the King of the North! All of Cenél Loairn will rise against him and I will crush him like a cockle shell underfoot. I'll send his head to Scoine so that dotard Malcolm can prepare for the same treatment."

Gillecomgan, who had become accustomed to wearing much armor like the Norse and Danes, left mail and helms lying like bones in the abandoned hall. He said there was no need, that the place of his triumph had been chosen and assured. He could put down this invasion naked. He kept only his sword, shield, chosen spears, and the mormaer's chain draped over a leather jerkin. Some whispered that he had been touched by the Sidhe and was being drawn toward his death, but I saw only the final flowering of his long-nurtured arrogance. He believed that Macbeth's army would not arrive in strength, having been bloodied by the ambush and by loyal followers along his route. Even the sea had obeyed him, rising in a gale and throwing the boats of a small naval force against the rocks, drowning them as defenders watched from the headlands.

Pain caught me unprepared and this time I could not hold in my scream. My wildcat howl was caught up in the wolfish baying of the men on the walls.

The battle had begun.

I settled back into the bedding, suddenly cold and still. I felt like a birthing hind beset by hounds. Before the crazed shift to this place, I had marked the signs, how the baby rode low. Phantom pains had moved through me, unproductive but warning. The crisis when it came arrived too quickly, the pain swelling. My body was thrusting forth this child.

I waited for the next pain, met it, rode it across without a sound. Hide boat riding a handspan of water over black jagged rocks.

Someone touched the drooping cloth that darkened the corner. The old woman put her head out and spoke with a man.

"Cover yourself," she said.

The cloth was lifted aside. Young Cornan stood there, his eyes wide, cheeks flushed.

"My lady," he said, "we are given safe passage. King Macbeth has sworn upon the holy bones of Columba that he will give safe passage to women, and all men who will return their allegiance to him and the Ri Alban."

"Gillecomgan will not let us go," I said, turning inward again, to the workings of my body.

"He will."

The son of Conamail was there too. Such tall men they had become.

"Macbeth has pulled his army back," Cornan said, shaking his head as though that was a great error.

Ruadan's strong hands burrowed under my shoulders, and Cornan lifted my thighs.

"My ivory box," I gasped. "I must have it."

The old woman found a blanket and draped it over me, and set the carved box between the fullness of my breasts and the descended swell of my pregnancy. I put my two hands across it, clutching it close, feeling the subtle vibration as the sealskin bag of bone discs slid to one corner.

Ruadan was talking. "...Gillecomgan," I heard, and the name was sour metal on his tongue, in my mind. "...on the walls shouting defiance. He dared Macbeth to throw the lance that would make him truly King of the North."

"There would have been a hundred in the air, if I led the army," muttered Cornan.

"He has taken his men far back, into the woods," Ruadan said.

They carried me slowly through the hall, into the open yard. A few serving women were crowded like sheep at the gate, but no men. One of the women turned her head and I caught my breath.

"Are you in pain?" asked Ruadan.

I smiled at that, he not understanding the waves that passed through me. "No." It was only that the woman appeared to be Lonceta. And that one with the hunched back, like Alpia. Their faces and hair and the way they lifted their hands, all familiar from better places and times. A flash of white light seemed to cross the group, but it was nothing, only a parting in the clouds.

They pushed open the gate a crack and we went through. Some of the women glanced up at the men who stood on catwalks behind the walls. Others pushed forward, heads down, in a panic to escape. I did not look up, not wanting to catch Gillecomgan's mad eye. He might call us back, as he had insisted we travel here, and then set me beside him in the battle, raise our newborn child as a shield and catch the eventual steel in its soft body.

Macbeth's army was a thin line of grim men, silent as trees in the forest edge.

We crossed a great silence between the fortress and those men. One woman broke and ran. Then two others.

I heard a cry, felt a jolt as though Cornan had slipped. Then his hands were gone and I fell hard across his legs and yelped at the impact, the pain crashing into another contraction like waves competing at a river mouth.

The blood. For a moment I thought it came from me, from a dead child, but it bubbled from Cornan's mouth and body, spreading across us both. I looked wildly around—treachery from Macbeth? The women were gone, having been absorbed into that motionless line. Ruadan knelt beside his friend and cradled his head. He pulled up his garment and the point of an arrow showed just off center of his chest, the corners of the wound pulsing blood. Cornan roused and tried to speak, but his life whistled from his lungs and his lips foamed with blood.

Ruadan laid his friend's body down and scooped me up. My soft old garment was heavy with blood and sweat, my own as well as Cornan's, and the sea-scent of my water, and all I could think of was a shepherd coddling a sickly new lamb, carrying it wet and trembling to safety.

Ruadan was crying, his eyes so full that he surely could not see. He struggled to carry me toward the woods. I opened my eyes again to see that thin line had become a mass of men.

An army was emerging from deeper in the forest, the line at the edge of the trees just the edge of a wide blade. It moved forward, split like a stream around a rock, passing around us. I craned my neck and saw that Gillecomgan's men were attempting a break-out, using the distraction of the women's flight. The king's men ran past us, shields up and spears high. I could see the gate suddenly pulled shut by the defenders, trapping the ones who had ventured out. For a moment, they stood confused, then ran from the advancing host toward the river. I was racked by pain then, or the pain was a gift that turned my face away from the vengeance taken on that handful of Gillecomgan's followers.

And there, Macbeth himself. He wore black like a monk of the south, or colors so near to black as made no difference. The only light reflected from mail, from shield and sword and dagger hilt. His hair and beard were ruddy. He opened his mouth and shouted an order, motioning with his sword, and the men obeyed him and turned like a great wheel of birds in the sky. For a moment, his glance fell on me, a spark of dispassionate interest before his focus returned to the battle, but in that moment I burned.

The second wave of the army came around us. I saw their faces, some set and emotionless, others flushed and bright-eyed as lovers. Once the men had passed, we made our way through the forest on a track to the nearest shelter. The old woman had rejoined us and a sturdy young woman had replaced Cornan to help carry me. Ruadan wept silently—I saw the tears streaming when he turned. The other women who had made their escape were waiting in the woods, afraid of the army, of the horrors at their back, of the horrors that might lie ahead. They seemed to be reassured by Ruadan's presence. *Sheep to the shepherd, this weaponless man who would not harm them.*

The path turned and the trees thinned to pasture, to tended fields. The farmstead buildings were dark. The people had fled driving their animals before them as contending armies closed on this place.

I heard a soft exclamation. Ruadan stopped, and I opened my eyes to see that the underside of the low-hanging clouds were reddened by fire.

"The hall is burning," he said fervently. "I pray to any god who will listen that Gillecomgan is roasting in it."

Women's voices rose to a wail, the forsaken sound of wind among ancient boulders. I heard one sobbing and another laughing hysterically. I felt nothing, not joy, not hatred, not even relief. I felt only the gathering of the child toward its entrance in the world and I added my own wails.

The old woman pulled Ruadan from his absorbed stare at the fire's glow, prodded him toward the farm. "Not the house," she muttered. "Fire breeds fire."

Ruadan carried me instead to a stone granary where the threshing floor was clean and swept. He laid me down there and disappeared. It was cold, cheerless, but quiet. Some of the other women had followed us and the old woman ordered one to find water, another to strike a light. She pulled away my sopping garment, spread her own thin mantle under me and took one from another woman to shield my laboring form. There was no stool for me to birth upon, no soft swaddling to accept my child.

"There was a king once in Éireann," the old woman crooned, half talking, half singing. "Cobthach was his name, an under-king, and he was never satisfied with the fortresses he had built."

A spark and a sputter of light. One of the women searching in the near-blackness had put her hand on a tallow lamp, and beside it, flint and steel. Shadows leaped against the wall like men fighting.

"Palisades would not suffice, nor timber-laced walls of stone for which slaves broke their hands and his people groaned at the cost in grain and stock. And each fortress as it was built, was abandoned, and the men of art who put their skill to design it were killed or driven off, empty-handed."

The old woman hummed and worked, massaging my thighs and stomach so that the flesh would ease and let the child come.

"There was in Éireann a man of art called Labraid, who knew the ways of metal, and he was feasted by petty kings for his knowledge and gifted handsomely by great kings as well. And he passed freely among all people, for this was an age when learning was honored and the laws were kept. So Cobthach, discontented as he was with all his works, summoned Labraid and ordered him to build a strong hall such as no army could tear down, stone by stone, and no wind damage nor flood overtake. For this he promised Labraid wonderful gifts, but the worker knew this king and his ways."

I felt the pains come one upon the other, and my back ached and my hips were on fire with the passage of the child. My throat tightened, as though to prevent my stomach from expelling whatever it might contain.

"An iron house was built by Labraid," the old woman chanted. "The walls and the floors and the doors were made of iron, and the roof was covered with iron sheets. The fortress walls were of stone covered over with hammered iron. Cobthach looked at his iron house, gleaming in the sun, and he thought it a strong place where not fire nor arrow, gath nor gale, could thrust. So when the high king was passing through his lands, Cobthach barred the door and would not let him in, and said that he did not know this king to have an iron house such as his."

I cried out. The old woman stroked my stomach and massaged my private parts. "Bear down, now," she urged. "The blood shows the way for the child. It will be soon."

Then she continued her story. "Iron first knows earth, but then knows fire. Labraid had forged the iron with fire, and heated it with fire to cast it into doors and roof and walls, softened it with fire to be hammered and shaped. Iron remembers fire and the iron house was no different. And Labraid, who had been paid not a tithe of what had been promised and then been roughly shown the path out of Cobthach's realm, knew this. Push, child, now push."

I clenched my body. Smelled urine and feces, my body releasing control of itself, as though I died in the birthing. Perhaps I would.

"Cobthach held a feast and thirty kings he invited to it, to make alliance with them and to become high king over all. And as they were drinking and eating, and their bold songs echoed, fire was set against the iron house, and the doors were barred from the outside. So, thirty kings plus one roasted inside the iron fortress that could not be destroyed by wind or by force. The child comes, now, work and do not cry, for soon you will have joy."

I clenched my hands against the floor and pushed, until it seemed my body would turn itself inside out.

"It is a sad thing when men die for the arrogance of their leaders," the old woman said, and the rocking of her voice was soothing. If the words were meant to sting, they had no effect here—I knew the men who had cleaved to Gillecomgan's side because like all rulers he provided them with food and drink and a chance at plunder, but others because he provided them with license to follow their worst impulses. My brother, at least, was not in that doomed assembly.

The fire seemed to have come inside the granary, it was so warm now. I clutched the old woman's hand and I held the Lady in my thoughts. White and cool. Distant, so distant. I wanted to tell the Lady about this man, this Macbeth who seemed like the fiery Thor of cow-hipped Halla's tales, and how I had burned at the sight of him with memory and desire, shame and fear. Of course she would know. But Alpia was dead. They were one, my mother and the Goddess, and yet not.

Please let Nechtan not meet him, I prayed, because with the war-spirit on him, Macbeth would surely kill him.

The old woman said, "The head is crowning."

Bear in fire, bear in fire, in fire.

And I thought that the Lady had abandoned me again, but here she was, the old woman's wrinkled hand that I had torn with my nails became smooth and cool and strong like the touch of the earth itself.

"I am here, always. How can you abandon what is of your spirit?" I was reminded. "Now push, the baby is here."

There was a last rending pain, then space, and emptiness like the forgotten spiral of a stone house. I heard a weak cry.

"It is a male child."

Gillecomgan has his son, I thought, and looked at the raw red baby, slick with its passage, the squinting face and tapered head, and I did not love him.

The women continued their work to tie the cord and wash him with water brought from the well. I seemed to regain my senses even more sharply. Cold, harsh smells of earth and minerals and blood. The pressure of the old woman's hands on my stomach, urging out the afterbirth. The roar of a fire feeding on the tallow of men. Women's feet whispering on the floor. The strange silence of their absent voices.

"Bring me my child," I commanded.

But no one responded.

"Bring him now."

At last the old woman carried the baby, roughly cleaned and wrapped, and wordlessly set him at my breast. I saw scarlet birthmarks that licked from fingertips to elbow of both arms. The child lay, feebly moving, the severed end of the cord red below the knot. His skin was covered with a fine dark down and a scurf of white, and the birthmarks blazed.

"Let us quickly christen the babe," one of the women said, "lest it come unnamed before God."

I set the baby to my breast and covered us from their sight.

MACBETH, MORAY, 1032

The air was still heavy with the scent of burning, sharper now as rain began to fall that would eventually wash it from the air.

Macbeth welcomed the drizzling rain on his face. It eased the ache in his heart. He had lost men, and for them he grieved, but the horror of Gillecomgan's retainers trapped and burning was not the clean fight he had anticipated. The screams haunted him. When they had breached the inner wall and dispatched a handful of defenders, they found the fire already raging, and the hall's doors still barred from inside.

He stank of smoke and blood and sin, and did not mind if the cold rain soaked him clear through.

He followed a path that came down from the forest into the fields and the farmstead. The place appeared prosperous, the buildings tidy, but then the bareness became evident. No one moved in the fields. The smell of cattle, but no sound. A thin trail of smoke rose from the house and layered itself on the wet air. He reined his horse left, keeping close to the path to avoid crops had that not been harvested, though they were much trampled by the armies. Black scorch showed like the swipe of the devil's hand across the one end of the field. Set by his men or Gillecomgan's? Or merely by an ember carried aloft? It mattered not to the farmer. Macbeth kept any sighing to himself. He had no reason for sighs, Oswald would say as he rode beside him. He would pray for the souls of the Christians, but there was no guilt in this battle. He did as a rightful king should, offering terms, and after that no quarter was to be given. He had removed a rebellious subject and kin-killer, a threat to the peace of his kingdom and also to Alba. Any regrets would be womanish.

After the battle, the men had danced, wild with their lives, and made songs. Macbeth had not been able to sing with them, though he had reason to celebrate. His father avenged, his honor satisfied, his kingdom restored. Instead, he felt choked. The finding of Gillecomgan's body had brought relief and reassurance, for until he saw his cousin's corpse, there was the suspicion that he had made his own escape and left his retainers to die. One foot was charred to the bone where his body had lain in the fire. The smoke-blackened chain still rested around his neck.

The Moray men urged him to claim it. "We who have been bloodied to destroy the tyrant wish you to accept the mormaership, like your father," said one who held the double-linked chain out to him.

"There must be a proper council," he demurred.

"Until that time—the people of Moray need to know they are not prey to anyone with a sword. They need to see a leader." He placed it around Macbeth's neck, the weight of that ancient silver, a reminder of all his responsibilities.

"See to the proper burials of our men first," he ordered. "Then the others."

"And Gillecomgan?"

"Take his head, as proof of his death." *Was that what it took to become a king in fact, that I could say those words without emotion?*

Macbeth turned his thoughts to the pregnant woman carried from the battle by a pair of slaves. One had been killed by a cowardly bow-shot from the walls. The other had gotten her to safety, then returned with salvaged weapons. He had been among those who forced the gate.

"A man without a name," he had said when he was brought before Macbeth. He was tall and strong but his hands were soft—a house servant, then. His shorn head remained properly bent, but he had changed his servant's garb for some warrior's fine linen tunic, slashed and bloodied. Though once again weaponless, he did not hold himself like a slave.

"You are of this place?"

"I was a slave in the household of Gruach, wife to Gillecomgan angbaidh. Before I lost my name, I was Ruadan mac Conamail," and he raised his face to the light.

"Conamail?" He could not believe it, would believe nothing else when the youth showed his father in his peaked hairline and a mouth made for smiling. Macbeth embraced him as a brother, each of them heedless of the wounds they'd suffered. He ordered clothing and weapons appropriate to his restored place and took the one silver band he wore from his wrist and set it on Ruadan's. He questioned him about his life, how he came there.

"Gillecomgan gave us, Cornan and I, to the lowest people, to be abused and made even lower than they were. That was how he honored the promise he made to our fathers. But the lady, the woman I carried from the battlefield, she was our savior," Ruadan said, his voice full of emotion. "She was married to Gillecomgan, but truly, she was no better than a slave herself. At great risk, she asked for us—not for our freedom, which he would never have given, but that we would be her household servants, and thus have some shred of honor."

It was beyond comprehension. Gillecomgan had brought about this battle, then had dragged his own wife, on the point of childbearing, into such jeopardy. He had seen the woman's face, briefly, distorted by labor pains, but had not stopped to consider that she might be the wife of his enemy and Nechtan's sister.

"Where is Gillecomgan's wife, widow, now?"

"She would have you call her Boidh's daughter. She was shamefully treated. Cruelly treated." Ruadan had been caught again between smiles and tears, his old life and his new, as he had stood there with his hand gripping the gift-silver on his arm. "We carried her through the woods to a farm. She was in the granary, birthing her child, when I left her."

Macbeth paused outside the farm buildings. So, she gave birth there, in the midst of a wild battle night, brought to childbed in a rude shelter.

"There is honor to giving birth in a barn," Oswald said.

"Indeed." Macbeth smiled to see how well Oswald tracked his thoughts.

He dismounted as a man came from the house to greet him. "A woman was brought here, a pregnant woman," he said, looking again toward the granary. "Has she survived the labor, and her child?"

"She and her babe rest inside the house. My wife tends her." The man's voice was soft, suppliant.

Macbeth left the others outside and went in, wiping the rain from his face and hands. The house was bare, the owners having quickly returned to protect their property but not feeling secure enough to unearth their wealth or return their livestock. He saw movement outside the open window, the wife carrying a jar toward the stone surround of the well. A soft bed had been made near the fire and the woman was sleeping there, the baby in the hollow of her arm. With her face relaxed, she was familiar again and he remembered her beside Gillecomgan, and even years earlier, when she had been one of the older girls in the court, pitied for her orphaning but of little concern to a boy. He had recalled her face as much older—perhaps it had been the pain of her life with Gillecomgan that had aged her—but here she appeared young and almost untroubled.

He stepped closer. Her hair was loose and uncovered, like an unmarried girl's, and her face pale. There was a lingering scent of blood. It was different from the smell of battle.

"I would rise," she said, her eyes still closed, startling him. "But there is the baby, and I am quite weak."

She opened her eyes and they were blue-green as the sea, but there were shadows behind them and he remembered Ruadan's words. Treated shamefully.

"I do not wish to disturb you, but I thought you might need a physician."

"That is kind, but I have had women. Surely your physician has wounds to tend, and you have much else to occupy your thoughts. My king." Her eyes lingered on the chain and he wondered what she was thinking. She did not ask about her husband's fate.

He almost told her of meeting Nechtan but did not, and then wondered at his own reluctance. "If you are well, then," he said.

She inclined her head, smiled slightly. The baby woke, made a thin animal kind of cry, and its head trembled.

"And the child?"

"It is a boy," she said flatly.

"I will take the child for a little while."

Panic came into her eyes and she struggled to get up. He realized what she must see, this rough fighter, reeking of death, an ugly wound seeping on his head. Demanding her child like some Moloch hungry for more sacrifice.

"For baptism," he explained quickly. "I have a monk, a priest, who will baptize your child."

The baby cried outright and she put it to her heavy breast. Now Macbeth saw the red stains on the baby's hands, like flames. Marked by the events of its birth-night. He opened the door and spoke with Oswald. The monk remained outside—a woman was unclean after childbirth—but gazed at the mother and child as though they were an altar-image of Mary and Jesus. He held up his hands in blessing and she stared at him but did not seem to welcome his prayer.

The baby immediately tired of suckling and released the nipple, dropping away to sleep. Milk dribbled at the edge of its budlike mouth and leaked from her abandoned breast. Macbeth could not look away, realized that his staring was causing her discomfort. *The child of my enemy,* he thought. *If I were a tomcat, I'd tear it apart.* Perhaps that was what Gruach pondered as he stood watching.

"Of course this is not usual," Macbeth began, awkwardly. "But this fight is not finished, and the child's—condition."

A hint of a smile came to her lips.

"You have godparents chosen?" Though if there were, Gillecomgan's death would have cancelled that obligation.

"No, none," she said, and again came that odd, private smile. He wondered if she were sane.

"Circumstances demand this child be baptized," he said, and no more, had no need to. "The man and woman of this farm, will they suffice to bring the child into the arms of Heaven? They are honest people."

"They have been good to me," she said. She would not be allowed in a church for many days, so could not have expected to take part in a hurried baptism. But there was something else, some undercurrent.

She swaddled the baby with care and laid him in his hands, then covered herself and turned her head away from the crackling fire as though she could not bear to see flame.

Macbeth did not disturb her further. He went out with the child uneasily resting in his arms. He had never had cause to hold a new baby. This one seemed particularly sickly and frail. *This is the son of my enemy*, he thought again, but the words were meaningless. Gillecomgan's name sifted into sand and blew away. The boy's little fists, red as though freshly scalded, shook. A helpless child, and a kinsman.

The wife came and took the child and he saw how she carried it easily, pulling her own mantle over the baby's face to shield it from the rain.

An oratory built by a solitary monk seeking freedom from the press of his brethren stood on a green knoll not far away. They walked along the edges of the fields, where rough walls had been stacked from stones cast out of the soil. Oswald first, then the godparents, then Macbeth. The oratory was barely large enough for them to fit inside. Gaps showed in the back wall and the roof, and bird droppings and broken seeds littered the altar. It had been some time since the monk offered his prayers here. Still, it was consecrated space. Oswald cleared the debris from the altar and covered it with a white cloth. The farmer had carried a bowl of clean water, and Oswald had the necessities of baptism.

The woman unwrapped the child and bathed him in the chilly water, her fingers unable to avoid touching and retouching the odd birthmarks. Then, wrapping him back up, she held him while Oswald intoned: "Let the fire by which God has marked this child remind us all that the wrath of God awaits the unfaithful. In the end time that approaches, we will walk unmarked through fire and blood, the faithful in Christ borne up by his angels, to enter his Eternal Kingdom."

Outside the holy place, Oswald blessed the child and put a few grains of salt in his mouth. "The salt of wisdom," he said. "I am the Alpha and the Omega, the beginning and the end. To the thirsty I will give water without price from the fountain of the water of life. He who conquers shall have this heritage, and I will be his God and he shall be my son. So says the Lamb of God, the King of Kings."

Macbeth's thoughts dwelled on that text, which of all the verses in his book and his memory, Oswald would choose. It was a sign, he realized. He who conquers…and he shall be my son.

He heard the godparents give their names, Lulach and Ranvaig. Oswald repeated them. He took the baby back inside, baptized him, and signed him with the name he was to bear, Lulach. Ranvaig dried him and took a piece of new lambswool cloth from inside her gown, wrapped Lulach in it, and held him for Oswald to complete the anointing. Macbeth stood apart while they professed Christian faith for the child in front of the tiny altar. This was irregular, this abandoned chapel, these people scarcely fit godparents for a child who would need protectors and allies as he grew. But to go unbaptized, such a frail being, here in lands ungoverned and with armies on the loose—that was not possible.

Lulach rested passively in the woman's arms. He had not cried during the handling and baptism, even when cold water chilled his head. Truly, it seemed that he might die before seeing his first month. It was best the rite had been completed quickly.

When it was over, Macbeth took the child to Gruach and laid him in her arms. "His name is Lulach. A good name."

29

GRUACH

Moray, 1032

I knelt at the door to the church and offered a lighted candle. The priest came out to bless me with holy water and admit me to the sanctuary.

The church was small, dark, and narrow, and it smelled of burned candles and old cloth, with no warm live scent of breath and bodies. *Like a breached tomb*, I thought, *dug open by animals*. Unglassed openings between the timbers of the walls, no wider than my spread hand, admitted shafts of morning sun that burned on the stone floor. The far end was dim, only a single flame to illuminate the precious things on the altar—a silver crucifix stark as a naked sword, a hanging bowl, and an enameled chalice, its colors clanging harshly against the soft shades of stone and worn wood and silver.

I knelt and the women settled behind me. The altar seemed far away, even in such a little church, glimmering like those retold visions of the Blest Lands. Sanctissimus, where the relics resided, where layfolk were not allowed. I folded my hands because it was expected; the women watched me pray, but as the ritual unfolded, in my heart the prayer went north.

"Praise to the One from whom life springs, who brings forth the Son of Light to brighten the world." I shaped each petition in my mind. "Praise to the Lady, guardian of sky and sea and all living things under and in them. Praise to the renewer of cycles and the rest of souls. Praise and honor to you, Maiden bringer of flowers, to the honest heart and the open eye. Praise and thanks to the Mother of the world, the fruitful woman of spindle and loom, whose ruddy hand rests on every fruit. Praise and respect to the Wise One, who knows secrets, who enfolds mystery in the blue-black of the night sky. Honor I give to you, in all your shapes the One Eternal, White Lady, and to your Son of Light who interposes his body against the power of death.

"For deliverance, I praise you. For the child born, I praise you." I waited for the image of Lulach's face to come, for the reality of his small body, but I could see only his tiny hands, red as embers, clutching the white of my breast.

"For deliverance, I thank you. For my enemy removed, a harsh burden, I thank you."

This time the image came and I accepted it without wishing it, the image of fire—not the soft reflection on the belly of the clouds but thick smoke, heat, the flare as smolder caught in timber and flames licked high. I gagged on the sickening odor of human flesh burning. I tasted cinders on my tongue and accepted the price of my freedom.

"For deliverance, I honor you. For the safety of my brother, taken out of the teeth of war, I honor you." The messenger had found his way to the farmhouse and said, Nechtan lives, but no more. Nothing of where he was. I had a memory of my brother's hand resting loosely on his knee. Nothing more.

I waited in silence but the women behind me whispered and I was caught up, hearing their soft prayers to saints and the Virgin.

Cleansed according to the church, I gave thanks for my safe delivery and the new life, then stood and twisted the bracelet from my arm, an offering of heavy gold. It was the last vestige of my life as Gillecomgan's wife, the adornment I had worn at the evening meal as the king's army approached and Gillecomgan sang violently of ancient battles. I lifted the bracelet toward the altar, that I might be received back among the people. Such a fear of the things of women, of the blood that brought all life to the world, the red earth out of which all emerged!

I could feel my body returning to its own form, shrinking back around the house it had made. What was foul about that? What made blood from between my legs unclean, while blood from a slash across the guts was clean? I laid down my offering to the tortured god, hanging on his tree, more like the oak-king of the pagans, stretched on his tau and murdered at midsummer by tanist holly, than the clean renewal of the Son of Light, dying and reborn willingly as the grain that symbolized him. There was too much shame in this church.

There would be no shame in the night when I offered Lulach to the Lady's care, when I was free to take him out to open air and the clear face of the moon. Still, going out of the church I felt renewed, perhaps only for leaving behind that weight of gold. I could not leave other memories behind, however.

The smell of fire was still in the air, and the timbers of the hall showed—blackened, broken fingers—through the breached walls of the fortress on its inadequate hillock.

Lulach had been baptized, I had learned, not in this church but in a disused oratory closest to the farmhouse. All agreed the child would not thrive, so thought it best to name him quickly so that he gained a place in the courts of God. Still, he lived and sucked. That broken place was not sufficient to my churching, though it meant some difficulty in reaching this other. They had readied me and led me, like a cow to be sold, along careful ways, making certain I did not cross a horse-path because of the belief that, unclean, I would cross the luck of a man in his way to war or the sea. Such care, now, for the rites and rules, when Lulach on his body showed the violence of his making and his entrance into the world.

They chattered like birds, forgetting that I was even among them now, dandling the baby and letting me drop back, heavy with my widowhood, heavy with the milk in my breasts. I was made safe, now. One looked back over her shoulder—the farmer's wife, a Dane, her face pinched but her heart kind. I waved her on. My breasts, veined and full as a freshened cow's, ached with the milk that came so heavily. It was an embarrassment, this wealth I created, an overabundance, enough for two infants, or three. I folded my scarf across my chest to cover the leakage.

The way was dry and hard, the mud gone. Barefoot tracks and irregular shoe-prints were overlain with marks made by the harder shoes of soldiers. I put my foot in one print and then the next, felt the man's too-long stride. He had been running. I saw where those footprints stopped, turned aside, and I turned aside as well. My heels went deep into the soft turf, wet from a spring. And here another set of tracks, coming from the path ahead, and then the footprints meshed.

I smelled him before I found him, the remains of a man curled like an animal in the shelter of a blowdown. Curled around the wound that had killed him. The carrion beetles and rove beetles, red and black like their work, had labored at the mountain of flesh. I knew the carcass by the bald head and the buckle on a belt sagging into the flesh. One of Gillecomgan's close companions.

I watched the flesh-eaters at work. With ravens and kites and hooded crows, and animals on the ground, these insects already had reduced a muscular body to bones poking through drying skin. Where had he been? Hiding, perhaps, one of the few who survived the breakout, or one who escaped during the final assault. I could not remember him having a wife or a woman, though I assumed he used slaves and captives as such men did. Nor did I recall any amount of wealth, so surely, he had not come back after that. He was a fighter and a brawler, a man who could have disappeared into any other sword-band once he had gotten away from this defeat.

I left him, a dead man without burial, abandoned in disrespect to be devoured and to rot. His sword and shield were gone, but the man who had killed him had disdained his ornaments—the bronze buckle, the silver in his ears. Crows might carry away the ear-ornaments soon, as the flesh withered.

I stood and brushed grass and sticks from my worn garment, borrowed from the farmer's wife. Perhaps I should have taken the silver. I had nothing now, no family I could call upon, no wealth but what I myself produced for the nourishment of the child I did not want. No place left to go but the church, and I thought of Lonceta in her cell and shuddered.

I walked more quickly, my breasts aching full. Near the corner of the woods, I met a man-at-arms coming from the farmhouse. Immediately I knew why he was there, realized that I had been expecting this messenger for many days and had been disappointed that he did not arrive. I waited, standing with my hands folded like the nun I might have to become, but with my head up.

"You are Gruach, widow of Gillecomgan?" He sounded doubtful.

"I am the daughter of Boidh and Lonceta. But yes, that too."

"King Macbeth has asked that you come to him."

And to what purpose, I wondered. The prophecy had worked its way once, but I did not believe the second part. What I did believe was that I would be put away at some island monastery, to create no problems. *And Lulach?* "I thought he had gone with his army."

"My lady," he began, shifting nervously at this interrogation. "Some of his leading men have gone to assume control of fortifications, but he remains."

"Then I must not delay him more." The man walked past me, back the way I had come, and he turned once to be sure I still followed.

The encampment had been moved once already as the fields were stripped of forage. Everywhere the grass was beaten down or grazed to flatness around clumps of thistle and gorse. The land was naked as the grain-bins of the farms all around. An army ate its way across the land, regardless of whether it was a defender or invader who tramped its soil. Now the army was shrunken, the places left from tents and fires showing its former reach. What was left was a retinue, no army, and that was on the verge of departing as well. A group of warriors stood in the sun. They barely looked up as I went by, a country woman, milk from my breasts showing through the cloth. I refused the shame that other women knew, seeing men at their ease, talking, balancing the weight of their swords on one hip with a hand on the opposite one.

The King of the North was not among them. I saw him past the camp, sitting under a tree away from the dust and noise. One knee was caught in his hands as he leaned back to see something overhead. He was watching a red squirrel leap from branch to branch. It was trying to work its way into a bird nest to steal the nestlings, its ear-tufts twitching and bushy tail shivering as it maneuvered. *The great man looks like a common herdsman*, though I was careful to keep such thoughts from my face.

The man said, "I have brought her."

Macbeth sat up straight—he must have been aware of us approaching, could not have been so absorbed—so was this genuine or feigning? I did not trust the surface to reveal the depths. When he stood, assurance settled on his shoulders like the chain of Moray.

I had planned, for when this moment came, to be aloof and cautious in my statements. Distant as a rock stack out in the sea, no longer in connection to the land. But he said nothing for a long time, simply looked at me with the same interest he had shown in the red squirrel. He—considered me. I could not settle the uneasy swirl of fear, hope, denial, suspicion.

"I go to Forres soon," he said, each word chosen, "to begin the work of restoring this land."

Malcolm, I thought, *remember that Malcolm has supported him*. I crossed my arms to better conceal my leaking breasts. I must not forget that, while he had freed me from Gillecomgan's grip, he was also the foster-son and ally of my father's killer.

"…an odd thing, to be in this place. I was sent away from Moray as a young boy and return as a man, but not as I expected. My family has been shattered. I do not have the support of many relatives. Father and mother gone, no brothers, no sisters. Many of my cousins are dead or at enmity with me. Most of my father's people who did not choose Gillecomgan were killed by him or driven to destitution or exile." He looked closely at me. "And this has been the way also with you."

"Gin fine, gin tír, gin inille," I agreed, unable to hide the bitterness. "Without family, land, or wealth."

"I have gained power and wealth beyond my expectation, and must use them with care. I had a son's right to vengeance and a king's duty to his people—still, I carry a great burden of sin from this war."

"One act brings many consequences," I said. "Revenge. Power. Wealth. A little blood let out to bring all these things."

"A little blood," he repeated, shaking his head. "You have every right to consider me an enemy. Through my actions, you are a widow. You should hate the mention of my name, and I should fear the day your son grows to manhood. But I have found a true man here, Ruadan, son of a true friend, Conamail. He has told me how Gillecomgan tormented you, affirming what was widely rumored."

He paused and looked down at his hands, and seemed to shift again, not a farmer now or a red-haired warrior or a leader of men, but a book-bound cleric in his plain garments. "It is with this understanding that I offer to take you as wife, and to accept your son as my own child—if that is agreeable to you."

I heard the sober words as if they were echoes of a pledge made long before. I looked far back among the trees, where a spreading patch of ground-elder lifted white flowers on hollow, grooved stems.

"Will you wed me, Gruach?"

I hung my head like a chastised servant, afraid of what my face might reveal. "I would bring you no allies, only ancient troubles. There are better matches for a young king who is so favored in his lineage."

Macbeth waited. My hand trembled and I hid it in the pit of my other arm. I feared this working-out of vision, the implacability of promise. And his cool management of this situation, far too much like his grandfather.

"There should be no objection from either kin or church," he said.

"Kin and king," I snapped back. "The Ard Ri Alban will demand his say in my disposition, now that I'm widowed. And why would he accept such a marriage, the danger to his plans presented by a union of the royal lines of Alba and Moray?"

"Malcolm will for my success surely grant me this."

"I am a spoil of war, then."

"This is a Christian action, and no poor alliance," he countered, "daughter of Boidh, granddaughter of Kenneth the king, with the royal women of Pictland in your line."

I laughed. "Do not follow that path or it will lead you to the same narrow empire as theirs. Ask my brother, if he can be found."

"I have been friends with Nechtan, and I have met him at sword's point. Very recently." I could not help myself—I looked up and my eyes locked with his. "We have both lost fathers and can set their deaths at the feet of the Ard Ri Alban. My foster-father, yes. My grandfather. Your uncle. So I ask you again, as man to woman, without concern for name or people between us, if you will stand beside me."

Fire showed in him, the flush in his cheeks and spark in his eyes. Honesty crackled in him like lightning. I could not look away now. The lover I had seen long ago as a flame consumed a girl's silly charm stood before me, stiff-backed in the way of a man who, having made a difficult decision, is then balked in the moving forward of that choice.

Wind from the east, from the great sea, tossed the trees and carried the scent of pine, blowing away the smoke and death that had hung over this place. It lifted his hair and caught mine from its covering, sifting it across my sight like a veil.

"I will be wife to you," I said. "But in the coming year, when the proper interval has been observed."

Macbeth seemed startled by my surrender. In that, I felt a kind of victory.

30

LAPWING

CIRCINN, 1032

Swords.

Month of swords, tinne, tinne, tinne is your name. Sacred holly lifts its points against the oak and the king's blood flows.

Cuileann, cuileann, cuileann, among the chief of trees. Lapwing salutes you, bloody tree.

Edges glitter in Lapwing's thoughts. King's blood.

Distraction or message? Wait, wait. Like water settle to clarity. Let none of these watchers disturb. Mind like water in a tarn, high in the mountains, no shadow falls, no ripple.

Columba's stone lies under water, under sand and mud, under bones. Bones of men, bones of fishes. Finger-ends of trees fallen.

Once, Lapwing remembers, he told Crinán that he did not know this stone, but that knowledge had been concealed until his full flowering. Now golden bells announce Lapwing, bells for the coming of the ollave, highest of poets.

This stone. Not greenstones like those called by Columba's name, no pebble scattered by flood. By this stone the saint had healed a king and made his people bow to dead Jesus. By this stone one of the wise, Broichan, also was healed.

Broichan knew. Lapwing knows. This is no mere pebble that Columba took up from the ground. He spirited it from out of the circles of the wise, a truestone, when he fled Éireann. Now it rests in the belly of this pond. I recite the lore, "Where it rolled from Brude's hand in battle at Asreth."

"Like Nazareth," Crinán echoes, for the nodding of his hangers-on to say, see, his mind is all on God.

Crinán will have this stone, this power. He rocks from foot to foot, urgent as a child.

He works for his son but also for himself, fearing the turn of the year as the sheep-church marks years. This next year is one thousand from their god's death, so surely at last the Christ must return, and they tremble.

See how the peacemaker's garment rests on his bloodletter's back. Crinán now will have himself called abbas, now that his abbey has been scorched, but his kin call him princeps still. See the fine weave of the cowl he affects. His body slumps from muscle to fat.

Stone, stone, stone.

Lapwing sees you glimmer, truestone, heart in flesh. The monks' chronicles say it was a white stone, after their lambs and their doves, but you are yellow crystal flashed with red, king's blood in golden body. This is the time of your rising, this the season of your star red-gold in the southern sky, golden boat of the harvest.

Stars set and sun rises. Morning breeze riffles water, sets the branches moving. Lapwing reads the letters their shadows make.

A fox waits on the far shore. It watches the grass then goes leaping after the mouse, three bounds, stiff legs punching down, and the red fox raises its muzzle empty. That is no good sign.

"Go, go."

Crinán pauses.

"All of you, leave me. Even you, Crinán."

And Crinán follows the soft sound of golden bells on their branch. Now in Lapwing's retinue a boy carries the emblem of an ollave. Reckoned chief among the wise, sevenfold in wisdom, highest of poets, Lapwing might have as many attend him as a king, but his time comes, it comes.

The gods return. This Lapwing has seen.

The rightful gods return, the ones we brought with us over water from Éireann. Lugh and Manannan, Oghma and Don and the wide-handed Dagda reclaim their own. The sheep-church waits on dead Jesus to return but the cold that shakes their bones is holy breath of the gods of water and war and the rich land.

One time before, believers fought for their gods. We of Éireann and of the Norselands marching right and left, to drive out the sheep-church. The time was wrong and failure fated.

Now an ollave leads, with tonguing bells before him, and a king will follow. Now the time comes.

Lapwing serves Crinán, Crinán serves Duncan, and Duncan will serve Lapwing to maintain his high seat when he comes to rule over Alba.

The pond trembles with the power it holds.

In the shallows, water-soldier spreads its sword-shaped leaves and white flowers. Water-soldier grows in still pools beside battlefields, to heal the wounds of iron. In these leaves, King Brude's blood flows.

Swords. Teeth of the great, bite to blood.

The breeze stills. Water stills.

Lapwing's hands wait, knowledge written on them, power in them like light.

Lapwing sees the stone in a cradle of mud. Round as the sun sunk deep in winter. His hands shape a path for the stone to rise through water.

The stone rocks, lifts, settles back.

Lapwing raises his hands again; Lapwing calls on the strength of Lugh Long-Handed.

Stone lifts, holds in the water like a bubble.

Some other strength is here, countering. Lapwing sends his thoughts about. Bickering rooks. She-willow.

Ah, the fox.

The fox trots onto the water, dark eyes wise and sarcastic. His paws are delicate, barely pressing the surface, but his shadow is great, the shadow of a man.

Lapwing salutes you, Colm of the Church.

The fox sits on his haunches on the blue field of the pond, above the place where the stone rests.

Lapwing puts his force against the stone, but instead of rising, it burrows deeper into the mud.

Yours and it seems you will keep it, then.

The fox opens his mouth and laughs.

Lapwing knows your name and your house, Columba son of kings. Your father was great-great-grandson to Niall of the Nine Hostages. Why did you choose the sheep-church?

The fox sits, prick-eared.

I know your name and who taught you, instructed by Gemman the bard, befriender of the filid. You had the gift of vision, present and future always twinned before your eyes. Why did you follow a dead god from another soil?

The fox lifts one black foot and sets it down. The stone drives deep, through water, past silt and branches, past bones, diving into the mother rock under the world. Behind the fox, now, a fiery sword.

Lapwing lets fall his hands. The gods do not wish this truestone raised.

Crinán is there, his face red and brows like cliffs. "Where is the stone? Why have you turned away?"

Lapwing holds his tongue.

Crinán puts a heavy hand on the ollave's shoulder, pulls him backward. Lapwing stumbles. Pain, pain, pain. Bullfoot clenches and leg trembles with holy pain. "I demand to know what you are doing!"

Lapwing finds his balance, raises his open hands.

Crinán's face goes white, then mottled. Fear and rage struggle. He knows an ollave's ire could break the bones within him, peel soft flesh like a rotten apple.

But Lapwing pauses, Lapwing waits. He has need of this foolish man for a little while.

"Know this, your St. Columba himself was here, and laid his hand on his stone."

"I saw nothing."

"The Fox stood on the water above his stone, and would not allow it to rise. If you have complaint, then it is with the very saint of your church."

Crinán seems to shrink. Crinán falls to his knees and the fine bleached wool of his garment soaks up the darkness in the soil. "I did not see him," he sobs into his hands. "A sign. The saint whose relics sanctify Dunkeld and I was not permitted to see him."

Lapwing turns away.

Swords. Fiery swords. And the blood of kings spilled.

ACKNOWLEDGMENTS

This book developed over three decades of reading, writing, and reflecting. So many writers helped during that time that it's impossible to name them all, or even remember, but among the most faithful readers and listeners have been Kevin Rippin, Grace Marcus, Al Sirois, Marjorie Hudson, Teresa Frohock, Shymala Dason, David Halperin, Fred and Susan Chappell, Kandace Brill Lombart, Timothy Russell, Sarah Lindsay, John Thomas York, Elaine Neil Orr—and so, so many others who have heard me go on and on about all things Scotland and Macbeth. Thank you all.

The first inklings of this book appeared at a Brockport Summer Writers Workshop, with Nancy Kress and Lisa Goldstein as the workshop leaders. That was in 1989…two years later, I received a National Endowment for the Arts fellowship and spent part of that year doing research that would inform the novel. In pre-internet days, that meant seeking out books for interlibrary loan and receiving wonderful packets of documents including an eighteenth-century edition of a survey of Moray!

When I felt the pressing need to see the places I was writing about, I spent a month in 2014 solo hiking across and around Scotland. Many people offered insight and encouragement along the way, including other walkers on the Great Glen Way, the woman at The Post in Burghead, a ferryman who pointed out Fingal's Dogstone, fellow wayfarer Dennis Douglas, wonderful B&B hosts, train riders and bus passengers. Thank you to Walk Highlands for invaluable route information, to museums large and small including ones in Thurso and Elgin and Glasgow that brought me up close with Pictish, Norse, and early Scottish cultural artifacts.

I returned in 2023 for another circuit, Edinburgh to Perth to Kinross, Abernethy, Aberdeen and Royal Deeside and St. Andrew's, Black Isle including Groam House Museum, Glasgow with its stunning monuments at Govan Old Church, with side trips to Glencoe and Arran. I spent many delightful hours in the National Library of Scotland and am the proud owner of a very cool library card!

While I drew heavily on the work of historians past and present, the records of this period are limited, fragmentary, and not always in agreement. Any errors or infelicities that may have appeared as I've developed characters and connected events are entirely my own. Among the scholars whose work has been essential are Benjamin Hudson, Gordon Noble and Nicholas Evans, James Fraser, Edward J. Cowan and Lizanne Henderson, Dauvit Broun, Peter Berresford Ellis, G.W.S. Barrow, A.J. Hartley and David Hewson, H.R. Ellis Davidson, Robert Macfarlane, R.J. Stewart, Mary Condren, Isabel Henderson, Anthony Jackson, Robert Lacey and Danny Danziger, and Robert Graves.

Grants from the National Endowment for the Arts, West Virginia Commission on the Arts, and the North Carolina Arts Council have assisted in this writing, as well as residencies at the Weymouth Center for the Arts and Humanities.

Countless thanks to editor and publisher extraordinaire Jaynie Royal, for her faith in this story.

Finally, fond if hazy memories of a traveling theatrical troupe that presented *Macbeth* at an auditorium in western New York sometime in the 1960s. My father, also a Shakespeare fan, took me to see my first staged play, and this child was enchanted. I remain so to this day.

Author's Note

Gaelic is a beautiful and supple language, but pronunciation can be daunting. Because the historical figures are best known by their Shakespearean names, I have chosen to use Macbeth, Malcolm, and Duncan rather than the original spellings, and have employed Gaelic, Pictish, and Norse as well as Anglicized versions for other characters and places, as seemed to best serve the reader.

Among online sites that might be useful is the "Learn Gaelic" site, https://learnGaelic.scot/sounds/ and this compact guide by The Cambridge University Hillwalking Club - https://cuhwc.org.uk/resources/the-unofficial-guide-to-pronouncing-Gaelic/

In the early medieval period, Irish and Scottish Gaelic already had embarked upon their diverging journeys from Middle Irish. Numerous regional dialects existed both then and now; we view names and phrases from a thousand years ago through modern lenses.

DISCUSSION QUESTIONS

1. Why do you think the author decided to begin *Upon the Corner of the Moon* with the childhoods of the main characters?

2. Scotland is the setting for many historical novels and films. In what ways does this book meet your expectations—or completely change your understanding?

3. In this time and place, it was routine for noble children to be sent to another, usually more powerful, family for fostering. What would be the advantages? What does this do to a child's idea of family and sense of belonging?

4. Do you think Gruach's fostering prepares her for eventual life at court?

5. There's an ongoing theme of language, of written text versus memory, and what is held to be true. In what ways do words have power in this story?

6. If you know the play, then you quickly recognize some names, but the characters and their motivations are quite different. How did that feel as you read? Did you hear Shakespeare as well?

7. History is based on who wrote the stories, and which stories survive. The Picts were described as naked, tattooed barbarians by the Romans who could not conquer them. How much can we rely on historical accounts? Do we see such denigration of enemies repeated through the centuries?

8. Kinship and family were and are central to the Scottish people—how is this both a source of unity and the cause of violence?

9. How are Macbeth's family loyalties tested?

10. In this time period, Scotland was known as Alba—a multiethnic society of Picts, Scots, Norse, Danes, British, and Angles. In what ways does Malcolm II try to unite the kingdom? Are they productive or counterproductive?

11. Gruach is raised in an ancient tradition where women shape power both spiritual and secular. What are her strategies when she's thrust into a patriarchal society?

12. At the beginning of the second millennium, Alba was thinly settled and had neither cities nor coinage. How does the economy work?

13. Gruach's forced marriage to Gillecomgan has left her scarred physically and mentally. How does that affect her view of life and her meeting with the man who had been the focus of her childish romantic visions?

14. Columba's conversion of King Brude and the Picts began the integration of that earlier British population with the Gaelic-speaking Scots. The Picts did not die out, yet they disappeared from history. What do you think happened?

15. Lapwing is quite the strange character, a believer in the older gods brought from Éireann. What is his role in the story?

16. Alba was geographically at the edge of Europe. How is it also part of a wider society? What other nations have an impact on this remote place?

17. Given Macbeth's education by a monk and Gruach's by a devotee of the Goddess, what do you anticipate for their marriage in the second book?

18. Part II of this story will follow Macbeth's rise and reign, with Gruach by his side. What kinds of challenges do you think they might face?

THE LAST HIGHLAND KING

Book Two of Alba

Coming Fall 2027